SOLITARY REFINEMENT

SOLITARY REFINEMENT

A story of reconciling, redemption, and second chances

ANNE MARIE ROSADO

Solitary Refinement
A story of reconciling, redemption, and second chances
By Anne Marie Rosado

First Edition Copyright © 2025 by Anne Marie Rosado

Published by
Munn Avenue Press
300 Main Street, Ste 21
Madison, NJ 07940
MunnAvenuePress.com

For permission requests, contact MunnAvenuePress.com

Hardcover: 978-1-960299-85-7
Paperback: 978-1-960299-84-0

Printed in the United States of America

To my family who benevolently accepts my eccentricities. You are my unwavering source of love, motivation, and comedy relief.

To my dear friend who offers encouragement in the form of uplifting affirmations and celebratory pancakes. Too bad you don't read.

To the Eeyores who are the speed bumps of life. Your persistent pessimism may slow me down but will never stop me.

Lastly, my deepest gratitude to the terminally entitled; for without them there would be no stories to tell.

Prologue

Angela stands in the arched doorway looking toward the darkened street, an undulating veil of fog lightly obscures her view. With arms crossed, she holds tightly to her elbows, subconsciously consoling herself as she sways side to side. A gentle breeze catches the hem of her robe causing it to dance around her ankles as if impish fairies were swinging on the delicate fabric. If there were a chill in the air, she wouldn't notice. She couldn't possibly feel any colder inside, or any more alone.

Not knowing what else to do, Angela rises at the same time each day and waits at the top landing of the main entry. She tries to recall when common sense had abandoned her. When did she decide to put on this show, with repetitive behavior that does little more than deprive her of sleep? She can't remember a time when she wasn't trying to impress someone. Or a time when she wasn't constantly feeding unquenchable egos. She'd become just as dependent on them, her self-worth resting on their approval, an unspoken reciprocal agreement.

Surveying her neighborhood, she considers the sinewy upright posts illuminating stately homes. The haloed glow of decorative lampposts and dusk-to-dawn ambient lighting punctuate the inert darkness. If she stares at them long enough, the posts seem to morph into an army of angels, sentinels guarding the streets. She sniffs at the thought, finding the symbolism absurd. After all, there's nothing angelic about this place.

By design, life in Bryn Mawr is symmetrical and orderly, and the cul-de-sac manors are no exception. The homes stand proportionately together yet separated by just enough distance to be private. They resemble a legion of teenage girls showing off their lissome figures while whispering unpardonably juicy gossip.

Like their occupants, the homes are mischievous and flirtatious, desperate to maintain their youthful glow while trying to outclass one another. These towering bastions with immoveable brick and stone arches, aristocratic Roman columns, and sculpted statues make Angela think of decorative marble chess sets; weighted pieces evenly spaced on a carved wooden board, stoically watching over neatly manicured grounds.

How many people played chess these days, she did not know. Perhaps many chess sets served only as untouchable, static displays, giving the impression of heightened intellect or refined amusement. Long ago, Angela's grandfather had tried to teach her to play chess, but she found the game excruciatingly slow. For her grandfather's sake, she played as well as she could while her mind danced, preoccupied with more interesting subjects.

Desperate to find something to fill her time, her eyes settle on the curves of her driveway. She studies the periphery where concrete edges meet thick turf as it twists down the knoll to the looming gate below. At the end of each winding drive are massive iron gates with monogrammed insets, aesthetically appealing but also well-built. These steely defenders open wide for their occupants and then electronically grind to a close, indicating that the owners are unapproachable. They serve their purpose well, making one pause before entering. No solicitor would put forth the effort. No one would drop by to say *Hello* or enter a neighbor's private domain without an engraved invitation. An imaginary hand prohibits entrance—*Halt! Who goes there?*

Outwardly, the homes are well-appointed, projecting an air of blithe contentedness. Inside, lies another story entirely. The prophetic swansong of common decency has taken flight; bumptious decoys of one-upmanship have replaced a warm regard for others.

These mighty fortresses shelter the affluent, segregating isolationists from the outside world. Sentenced to a life of solitary refinement, residents lock themselves behind electronic gates and reinforced doors interspersed with codes, alarms, and cameras. Those who call this neighborhood home are suspicious of strangers and go to great lengths to keep people away. They remain guarded, distancing themselves from other neighbors as well, as if something would be taken from them if they dared open up to anyone. The dour expressions and distrustful scowls make Angela think of wealthy old pinchpennies who constantly inspect the contents of their pocketbook just to make sure no one is stealing from them.

She has driven past neighborhoods where people gather on sidewalks, driveways, or lawns to chat, and wonders what it might be like to live in a place where people have a sense of community. People who genuinely show care and concern for one another. If someone stumbles and falls, you pick them up. If they go on vacation, you water their plants, feed their pets, and keep a watchful eye on their house. If they're ill, you bring them meals, mow their lawn, or hold their hand. Angela has never seen this type of kindness here and concludes that she never will.

The citizens of Bryn Mawr have an obvious love/hate relationship with one another. They're antisocial socialites, reserved and withdrawn unless attending functions closely scrutinized by the public eye. While home, the iron curtain goes up and animosity comes out. Conversely, these same people mingle with one another at the country club, daggers placed in a velvet-lined box and locked away during a collaborative truce. Showy pearlescent smiles appear, brought out for special occasions and laissez-faire evenings filled with harmonious hobnobbing.

Afterward, the hypocrites disperse, returning to their unaltered exiled state—a textbook example of unhealthy interpersonal behavior.

Angelarosa Katerina Magdalena Morgan was born into wealth, though her family was never pretentious like this congregation of the idle rich. Many of them hold high positions in the white-collar world or manage their fortunes through family foundations. When she was younger, she loathed this type and all they stood for. The generations of trust fund babies who will never know how to do a damn thing for themselves.

Her husband, Robert, was the one who insisted that they live here, inserting themselves into high society. Angela made every effort to be accepted, sacrificing her beliefs to please those around her. At Robert's urging, she shortened her name. She forfeited her family legacy as well, using only her married name to accommodate the abstruse in this homogenous region, those who refused to even *try* pronouncing her given name.

Not long ago, Angela's social calendar overflowed with events. She was invited to the finest parties, where the Who's Who of Bryn Mawr took center stage. She complained that she never had that alone time needed to relax and recuperate. Now she has nothing but time. Empty days with time to wonder what life would have been like had she never met Robert, had she never moved to Bryn Mawr. What would be different had she not been transplanted to a residential compound that lacks humanity?

Angela never understood how people here functioned as a cohesive unit; the mysterious rubric that others seemed to know, but she did not. She could not interpret the language of this secret society with their unspoken gestures of raised brows, censorious stares, and derisive smirks. Armed with the knowledge that she was only accepted because she came from old money, Angela decided her life would be less difficult if she were received as a member of the café society, than not. After all, she's seen how they tear outsiders apart, and given the choice, she preferred being predator rather than prey.

So Angela changed her name, her appearance, and her personality to please her husband and suit others. She became a product of her environment and adopted their ostentatious ways. A conceited convert, she was now one of *them*. But they could make her life a living hell if they ever found out her secret, and she's doing her best to ensure that doesn't happen.

Angela's home was her one true sanctuary. A dependable calm swept over her whenever she entered its intricately scrolled iron gates. She took pride in her home and entertained often. After all, this was the gathering place, the setting of many benefits and private parties, always humming with activity. But that was before her life had taken such a dramatic turn.

Instead of pride, what she now feels is resentment, jealousy, and distrust—for one particular woman. An intensifying anger festers inside of her, squeezing tightly with its poisonous grip. Sharon Bartelson had been her best friend and closest confidante until Angela ran out of money. Friendships take years to build and very little effort to destroy, especially when the relationship rests entirely on a caste system. No longer on equal footing, Angela has been bumped down several rungs into a subservient position and there's nothing that can change this.

As much as she tries, she can't remember being truly happy, or a time when she wasn't performing some ridiculous enactment of her former life. It's as if she's a small animal, trapped in a cage with no escape, running back and forth, back and forth, until the mind gives way to insanity and the body dissolves into itself.

Angela thinks about this every morning as she sits in the dark and waits. It's one of many niggling thoughts that when combined with other worries, picks away at her brain, keeping her awake. After sufficiently replaying the what-ifs and regrets that come with sleep deprivation, she shakes off the sadness and rises to her feet. Then she steps onto the flagstone portico, where she apprehensively glances left, then right, searching for any movement in the immediate vicinity.

It's time.

Tiptoeing to the end of the driveway on slippered feet, she makes her deposit and returns to her post, sitting down heavily on the stone entry steps. Were there others in her neighborhood that would be up pacing the floors at this hour? Besides sharing a zip code, did anyone here share the same worries as she? Or are they all obliviously content, with full bellies and full bank accounts, only suffering from incurable apathy? This gives her something else to contemplate while she waits with her knees bent to her chest to stave off the foreboding feeling that has taken up residence in her gut.

Startled by automatic sprinklers as they pop up in unison through-out the subdivision, Angela ascertains that her neighbors must use the same company to turn the water on in the spring and winterize the system in the fall. They must have their irrigation systems synchronized to come on at the same time, which she finds both humorous and disturbing. Hers is the only one that does not activate, the lawn turned to an ugly carpet of brown . Perennials and shrubs slump wilting, defeated. They beg for water, but she cannot help them, because she cannot even help herself.

She's received stacks of letters steeped in legal jargon, reminding her that she must keep her property in acceptable condition—*or else!* Now, she's a fugitive, an enemy of the people because she can't afford to water her yard. Lulled by the pulsating hiss of sprinklers, she hears the susurrant throbbing of water as it slaps against a tree. In the distance, parched plants and delicate annuals breathe a sigh of relief, bolstering them as the days begin to warm and summer approaches.

Angela uncurls her hands from around her knees and looks around. Reliably, her neighbors begin stirring, soft lights giving off honeyed glows from a bedroom or bathroom window. Lights randomly pop on, then off, as people move inaudibly through their homes.

Sitting in the pre-dawn darkness each day, she has unintentionally learned the routines of her immediate neighbors. She likes this part of the morning best, as it makes her feel not so alone; imagining them as they wake, stretching, readying for whatever plans they may have. Angela likes to believe that all people are innocent when they first wake up, not yet having committed the sins of the day. It's hard to dislike even the vilest individual in the early morning, a new day unfolding, ripe with possibility, and a promise that anything can happen. A choice can be made to be good—or not.

As they slowly come to life, she imagines her slumberous neighbors instinctively shuffling to the kitchen or en suite kitchenette where a steaming hot cup of coffee awaits. The ultimate reward just for getting out of bed. She has a built-in coffee bar in the master suite, long deserted and empty of its full-bodied morning tinctures. She tries not to think too much about this, because she would give anything for a cup of coffee and wishes she could catch the scent of whatever may be brewing in neighboring homes. The visceral aroma of a hot caffeinated beverage just might give her reason to live.

There are lights and movement across the street, refocusing her attention from her growling stomach. Dr. Rayhill Burton departs each morning at exactly five-thirty, bound for a renowned medical research center where he's the department chair of gene therapy research. Affectionately known as Dr. B, he coexists with his intolerable wife, Nikki, in a stone castle complete with turrets, secret passageways, and a small kitchen better suited for an Airstream trailer than a grand estate. Built by Dr. Burton and his first wife, Clarice, their atypical castle home is an anomalous curiosity.

As strange as his home may be, Dr. Burton has always been cordial to Angela. His wife, on the other hand, is another sort and forbids her husband to mingle with anyone outside her urbane circle of friends. In her glory days, Nikki was a supermodel and centerfold. Now, she lives vicariously through others, surrounding herself with young beauties. The aging fashion guru with her own clothing line and emaciated adolescent groupies rarely leaves her home.

Angela has always wondered how these two polar opposites merged as a couple. She settles on one scenario and giggles at the image of a brain standing at the altar, marrying a colossal set of knockers. She shakes her head as she tries to remove the strange image brought forth by her overactive imagination. Thankfully, she need only wait several minutes as her focus turns to another neighborhood oddity.

Darcy Danforth, overzealous skeletal jogger, and ill-reputed scandalmonger, rounds the corner, barely covered in spandex and sweatbands—no matter the temperature. Besides outdistancing other runners, she excels in conversational endurance. Her ability to extract the minutest detail from neighbors is notorious. Angela crouches lower in her position to avoid detection, watching as Darcy moves smoothly along her preplanned course. She runs past, smiling and waving into the air, no doubt involuntary motions from her pageant days.

Redford Nester is up and about as well, though it's hard to imagine how. A single medical malpractice lawyer with a penchant for prostitutes, gambling, and uncharacteristically, a morning routine of filling half a dozen bird feeders. Red's nocturnal lifestyle also contributes to a heightened sense of night vision, allowing him clear navigation through darkened grounds. While continuing his pre-dawn tasks, he pauses, cocking his head up and around, a wolf catching the scent of his prey. Somehow, he always knows she's there. He stares in Angela's direction as she sits in the shadows, pending cue for her daily performance.

Daybreak comes with glorious sunrise vistas and a six-a.m. promise that newspapers will be accurately thrown to the edge of each winding driveway, silently awaiting retrieval for a cursory morning read. Many have made the switch to the e-edition, but Angela had opted for both. Even though she no longer knows what's going on in the world, she likes the unaltered routine of retrieving the paper. This gives her a brief measure of stability while sending a beacon of false assurance that nothing has changed.

She waits and watches. When she sees a set of headlights slicing through the darkness and hears the smack of folded newsprint hitting driveways, she knows it's time. Tightening the belt of her silken robe, she straightens herself and gracefully meanders down the walkway to claim the morning paper with her head held high, as she's done each morning for the past twenty years. She reverses her steps and with a relieved breath of exhalation, places the paper just inside the front door next to the bulky Saturday edition, still tightly encased in its colorless plastic wrapper.

For months, she's perfected her routine of depositing the Monday through Saturday *Wall Street Journal* at the end of her driveway each morning at four a.m. Several hours from first light, yet still early enough to avoid running into her immediate neighbors, or her delivery person, who she'd only seen driving past in profile. She convinced herself that her daily routine would continue. Nothing would look out of place, no one would ask questions. But the life she'd known is over. Now all that's left is a rapidly dissipating air of superiority as she sits alone in the dark, clinging to deceit.

Chapter One

"Listen, Sharon, I need your full cooperation, otherwise, I won't divulge a thing. If I can't trust you, you may kiss your ass and your future 6 percent goodbye."

"Well from where I'm standing, you look like a woman at the end of her tether. You need to offload this place before you lose it."

"I won't sell right now, no matter what you *think* you know about the situation. I've got some ideas of my own..."

"What ideas?" Sharon leans in with rapt attention, hoping to eliminate any doubt that she'll remain my devoted best friend.

"I'm not telling *you*. I need to maintain anonymity. I may want a pocket listing in the future, but no gaudy yard sign, no open houses, and no interior photographs. I can't risk having anyone find out about my circumstances. The minute you post online photos of my empty home, I'll have every ingrate within a hundred miles driving by for a little sneak-a-peek. Not to mention the neighbors. They're the worst of the lot! I've seen them hungrily line up during an open house or auction in this unspoiled colony of über-snobs, salivating over the prospect of critiquing a neighbor's taste in furnishings, or sharing delightful tidbits of their financial demise."

"I know you won't sell this minute," she echoed, "but someday you'll sell and people will be lining up to buy an estate from a celebrated author. I have an Asian couple who've already inquired..."

"What have you been telling people, Shar?!"

"Don't get your thong in a knot, Ang. I haven't said a word. I simply mean that foreigners are all over the real estate market right now. They're buying up America!"

Sharon showed up unannounced this morning with a glut of paperwork spilling from her Gucci messenger bag. I rue the day that I gave that woman full access to my home. Besides keys to the front door, she has codes for the gated entry and security system. I can't afford to have my home monitored anymore, but I continue arming the alarms in case of intrusion. At least there will be the clamoring urgency of sirens, calling out to no one in particular.

I'm acutely aware that today's intruder won't harm me, but that could change at any time. Shar has come to collect on our recently arranged agreement to color and trim my hair in exchange for editorial services. I can no longer pay the entrance fee at the pricey salon where I was formerly a client in good standing. However, according to the reliable gossip pool, Mr. P thinks I've gone elsewhere and that I've been cheating on him with a rival hairdresser.

Hovering over an ornate copper sink in the master bath, I'm heavily cloaked in plastic while feebly dripping with colorant. If Mr. P could see me now, he would pale with the revelation, then stiffen and faint dead away.

For her monthly coiffeur assignment, Sharon has donned heavy elbow-length rubber gloves and a plastic shower cap while standing elegantly swathed from the neck down in a floral rain poncho. Adding a scientific quality to her appearance, she complements the ensemble with a pair of designer ski goggles.

"You look like an idiot," I tell her.

"You look pathetic," she counters. "Your version of a brunette is slightly less conspicuous than the darkly stained goatee of a Saudi prince."

Similarly, Shar can't chance anyone finding out about her steady stream of sweetheart deals. She's driven by quantity over quality, pushing sales through as if she's trying to win a ham. And now, with my help, she inserts deceptive diatribes into her real estate listings, duping inexperienced homebuyers into making impulsive purchases. Yet I believe she got the better end of the deal. The only thing that I'm trying to conceal is gray hair and lack of funds. Sharon Bartelson has more scandals to cover up than a career politician.

As Shar hastily rinses my hair, she informs me that her work here is done. "Clean up your own mess," she states matter-of-factly. Though I know she's referring to the bathroom that's now splattered with dark pigment, I can't help thinking that she means much more.

According to Sharon, I made my bed, and now I can lie in it. No matter how poorly Robert treated me, she encouraged me to stay with him. "Stand by your man," she said. "Nothing good will ever come of you leaving Robert. He's so damn good looking and who wouldn't want that hunka-hunka burnin' love as arm candy?"

As always, I recklessly followed her tainted advice, staying in a marriage long past the expiration date and losing everything in the process.

I didn't know a soul when we moved to Bryn Mawr and had little time to establish and foster lasting relationships. Sharon Bartelson was the selling agent when we bought this home and sought out a relationship before the ink on the contract even dried. She would never have befriended me had I not been a new writer from old money, and she, a gluttonous neophyte urgently in need of new clients. Robert was always just out of reach when it came to meaningful conversation, and I found myself desperately needing a gal pal to confide in.

Early in our friendship, we used to laugh at the most outlandish things. True uproarious laughter at nothing in particular. Just a cleansing belly laugh that naturally washed away stress and brought us closer together. I never had a close friend growing up and only transient friends in college. But I found a dedicated comradery with Sharon, and we became fast friends.

We shared our diet secrets and struggles, then would go completely off the wagon with a large bag of greasy chips and a tub of gas station dip. We would go see cheesy chick flicks and come out of the theater complete wrecks from all the crying. We chatted daily about this and that. We innocently compared our husbands' quirks and bad habits and shared our darkest secrets and dreams for the future.

I craved the friendship of this woman, but over time, the toxicity of this one-sided relationship became evident. I was used by Shar to impress prospective clients and demonstrative business associates. There was never any real substance to our friendship and that reality has always been a gnawing datum; a dense layer of disloyalty resting just beneath the surface that I foolishly chose to ignore.

It seems that my insecurities led me down the path with Little Red Hen. Sharon, whose intentions are half-baked; someone who will always help me eat the bread but will never help in the laborious preparation. According to the score in this unbalanced relationship, she owes me. Turning to leave, Sharon mentions that she'll need to have her listings complete by this evening.

"Please pay attention to detail and elaborate on the descriptions that I've been kind enough to jot down. You're quite proficient when it comes to unearthing the character and charm of each home and show-casing the qualities..."

"What *qualities*, Shar? I write fiction, when translated, means lying! I lie for a living and you require my assistance selecting new adjectives to replace your stagnant repartee."

"Well, you don't have to get snarky about it, Angela! For years, I've done just fine without your editing or your commentaries on a business you know absolutely nothing about. I'm doing you a favor. Obviously, I'm the top producer of an international real estate corporation and you're a..."

"A what Sharon? A desperate, lonely woman living in an empty home that she can scarcely afford, pretending to be something she's not? A woman with a second-rate hairstyle made even more inferior by a do-it-yourself hair color kit? Well, fuck you Sharon *and* the horse you rode in on! Just leave your filthy stacks of duplicity, and I'll email them when I'm finished."

"Well, be curt with me if you must, but I brought you a tall café mocha with extra crème. It's in the microwave."

On that note, Shar stuck her nose high into the air, pivoted on her kitten heels, and during her hasty departure, somehow left deep marks on my Brazilian wood floors.

As exasperating as Sharon can be, at least she brought me a barista coffee, a luxury that I now only have when she's around. I make a beeline for the microwave, heat my caffeinated prize, and for a few pleasurable moments, forget about my troubles.

Chapter Two

Each night, I rewind and replay my past. Reaching as far back as college, I search for answers to an unanswerable question. I'd reluctantly tagged along during an end of finals celebration when the call came. If I'd done just one thing differently, would it have stopped an unspeakable tragedy? Would my parents still be alive? It was during my senior year at university that the world stopped spinning and time stood still. As an only child, I navigated the fallout of this tragic accident, feeling directionless and alone.

When I had no one else to turn to, I could always rely on Uncle Sal. Salvatore Natale was not only my parents' attorney, but also a loyal friend. Sal had been old since I was a little girl, and I always thought he looked more like Santa Claus than Santa himself. Even though we weren't related by blood, Sal was the backbone of my family and a guiding light in any storm. He promised that he'd always be there for me, and Sal was never one to break a promise.

Robert Morgan arrived on the scene during my parents' probate hearing. Sal recommended Robert as someone who could liquidate estates quickly, no questions asked. He encouraged me to let Robert chaperone me through the process of cataloging and pricing valuables. I knew that the sooner my parents' estate was settled, the sooner I could begin the healing process. Grief-stricken, I complied without protest.

As executor of my parents' will, Sal guided me through the probate procedures. Putting one foot in front of the other, I completed each task in staggered repetition. After spending a proper amount of time grieving, I still couldn't manage to restart my life. Occasionally, I heard my father's voice in my head saying, *Get up and dust yourself off! Pull up your bootstraps and move on!* That was easier said than done.

Finally, I returned to the only constant I knew. Academia. I applied to graduate school and retreated to university, immersing myself in my studies. But this was not enough to occupy my mind or mend a broken heart. The weight of profound isolation pressed down on my vulnerable insides, a coagulating loss accumulating in my soul.

The occasional call or text from Robert had become a welcome distraction from my regimented schedule. It didn't hurt that he was strikingly handsome with wavy black hair, expressive blue eyes, and an acerbic wit that I found quixotic. He called with questions regarding the estate, always using the excuse that he couldn't reach Sal.

As comfortable as Robert was in his own skin, I became the opposite. My parents' death left me depressed, anxious, and insecure. My weakened insides caused me to be easily swayed, and I became increasingly reliant on Robert. I knew this was no time to start a relationship, but he was seductive, dangerous, and available. I'd dated casually in high school and college but had never been in a serious relationship. Treading in uncharted waters, I couldn't stop thinking about this man, who I was falling in love with.

Robert gave me a sense of adventure and belonging that I'd never felt before. It was comforting to be held by someone, and his consoling quickly led to other intimacies. I was as giving with my lovemaking as my money, and Robert eagerly consumed both, taking advantage of my generous nature. Being older and more experienced, he kept in just enough contact that I wouldn't become interested in anyone else. He would disappear for weeks and reemerge with much ceremony, bringing me expensive gifts poached from estate sales. Ferreting out properties around the country, he was the official receiver of mass accumulations of a person's life, and without hesitation, he used those items to his advantage.

Robert was wild and unpredictable, and the temptation of this man became too much to resist. After a short six-month courtship, on bended knee, Robert presented me with an engagement ring. A glittering, four-carat, pear-cut diamond that he said belonged to his dear departed grandmother. It surely once belonged to someone's grandmother, but not Robert's. Poor naive Angela. So touched by the gesture, and with tears in my eyes, I accepted his proposal.

Sal was not happy with the news and urged me to have Robert sign a prenup to protect my assets. When I broached the subject with Robert, he was outraged and suggested that maybe we should just call the whole thing off. I couldn't bear being alone again, so I tore up the documents and persuaded him to marry me that day. He whisked me off to Vegas for a quickie marriage and an even quicker honeymoon in the bowels of a gambling den on the strip.

With my new husband by my side, I felt like I was part of a family again. Robert settled comfortably into married life as well, and his induction into the world of high finance had him spending money hand over fist. He bankrolled indiscriminate ventures with unsavory characters, merging old money with newfound wealth. Besides estate sales, it was unclear exactly what type of business Robert was in. Whenever I asked, his answers were cryptic or he avoided the conversation altogether.

"If you can't trust your own husband, Ang, who can you trust?" he'd say, smiling charismatically.

Sal warned me that I would eventually run out of money if Robert didn't slow down his spending habits. To protect my assets, Sal urged me to put money in private holdings in my name only. Offended at the thought that Robert was anything less than brilliant, I'd insisted that he had my best interest in mind. Not one to be distrustful or to keep secrets, especially from my husband, I shared Sal's plan. Robert gave me an ultimatum: *Him or me.* In my mind, there was only one thing to do. I immediately cut ties with Sal.

As the novelty of being newlyweds wore off, Robert became restless and easily agitated. He was not satisfied with spending time alone with me and preferred large parties where he could show off his wife and his fortune—anywhere he didn't have to engage in serious conversation. I'd not seen this side of my husband before. He became a braggart and I never knew what would come flying out of his mouth—or when. He was manipulative and controlling, and insisted on making all financial decisions.

I'd been perfectly happy living in our small city loft, content with the idea of setting up housekeeping with Robert; a mated pair, building a nest together and starting a family. Our whirlwind romance never gave way to serious discussions about the future, but I'd assumed that he felt the same when it came to having children. Robert didn't have any people that I knew of, and I wanted to change that with a houseful of Morgans. Our children would be close and would never feel alone, as I sometimes did growing up.

On our first anniversary, Robert surprised me by purchasing a manor home in the suburbs of Bryn Mawr. This was neither the home nor the lifestyle that I would have chosen, but Robert reminded me that we would be moving up, in more ways than one. "You'd better learn to keep up appearances and familiarize yourself with country club life," he said. "You want your man to be happy, don't you?"

I couldn't have cared less about an exclusive address. What I really longed for was a family. And so, it began. The life of my dreams. I learned I was pregnant before the movers packed the first box and miscarried before I'd begun decorating our new home. Robert's reaction to both the joyful and heartbreaking news was the same. Distant and unemotional.

The months ahead were filled with lonely visits to the best fertility doctors, all experts in their field. Robert wanted no part of this nonsense and made excuses whenever he was asked to go with me to appointments. When I had exhausted all avenues, I asked my physician if there would be another. With downcast eyes, he reverently patted my hand and shook his head *no*.

I was experienced with personal tragedy, but this added heartbreak was more than I could bear. Robert and I were living together but estranged, only speaking when necessary. Sometimes, all it takes to harden a heart is a single tipping of the scales, and my future hung askew at an unsteady angle. Without bothering anyone, I politely imploded, spinning myself into an impenetrable cocoon.

Robert moved out over a year ago. Although practiced in the fabrication department, I'm having difficulty crafting new explanations for his long absence. First, I'd tell people that he's away on business, followed by his acceptance of a new position abroad. The thought then conjures up a detailed image in my mind and I burst forth with manic laughter, followed by prolonged weeping. He's taken a new position on a broad all right.

I head straight to Robert's closet. Eyeing an expensive silk shirt, I rip it off the hanger and blow my nose heartily into the fabric. "Bastard!" I scream between sobs. Realizing I could sell his forgotten items for a little extra cash, I abruptly stop and begin the arduous task of blotting snot off the sleeves.

Chapter Three

Since running out of money, I've also run out of friends. I've alienated everyone I know and lack a social life. My cable has been cut off, and all forms of digital entertainment have been canceled. I've sold or traded the televisions and most of the electronics; though I still have my laptop, cell phone, and basic internet connection. With no distractions, I've run out of excuses to become Sharon's literary bitch for the evening.

It's hard to imagine how a woman with a string of degrees and extensive knowledge of the real estate industry can't figure out how to email files, post them to cloud storage, or save them to a thumb drive. "Don't want to leave any evidence," she said when pressed on the subject. It will take less time to do Sharon's dirty work than to figure out what she means by her imperceptive comments. Overwhelmed by what my life has become, I grab the overstuffed messenger bag and climb the winding staircase to my office for some good, old-fashioned real estate double-dealing.

I've spent many years spinning lies from my cozy upstairs retreat, and if ever there were a need for feng shui, the office space is paramount. I could not be productive in a cramped studio whose only window faces a narrow bricked-over alleyway. Enclosed spaces are for losers and lunatics, and I am neither. Having been abandoned, I sit down heavily at my desk. An emotional castaway, left with nothing but a failed marriage and a false life. In my newfound exiled state, I wax and wane in a listing sea of loveless existence with nary a lifeboat in sight.

Oh my, I'm dramatic! I jot this down, as I may be able to use it someday in a piece of crap novella: Pain for sale at $5.99 a pop or $1.99 for e-book download. That thought always makes me feel a little better.

As bleak as things seem, at least I have a lovely vantage point to write. If I can hold onto my home, I'll remain on familiar ground while I figure out what to do. From my office, I have a view of the grounds and infinity pool. And until I quit irrigating, the yard popped with color. Perennials in my favorite hues of deep purples and fuchsia blanketed the gardens, complimented by carpets of delicate white blossoms. The contents of a dozen urns once overflowed with trailing annuals in the same shades. Now long dead, they look depressing, like giant dried-up bridal bouquets.

I try to focus on the positive. The trees haven't suffered from neglect, and I'm grateful for their steadfast resolve to stay alive. The malleable whoosh of the Japanese willows energizes me, and the commanding respectability of rows of Italian Cypress make an interminable effort to protect me from the outside world.

I need to remember to pawn more jewelry to pay Juan, my devoted gardener. Under the circumstances, he's doing what he can to help, but plants can't live on air alone. Articulate, and more fluent than I with the English language, Juan remained quiet for years, feigning the ability to understand when pressed on matters of my personal life. I would talk and Juan would listen, remaining respectfully silent.

But all that changed a year ago. Upon Robert's exodus, Juan served as my trusted confidant when there was no one else to listen. Sweet and understanding, he was the first person I told when I became a statistic. Juan listened intently as I went on about my circumstances, giving details of Robert's many infidelities. He brought me tissues when I wept and nodded silent approvals when I poured out my heart regarding my intended course of action.

When Juan felt that I had neatly purged my sorrows, he bent forward, gently took my hand, and stated matter-of-factly, "Your husband
was an asshole who never fully appreciated what he had. Unequivocally,
his loss will be your gain."

I stood dumbstruck as Juan retreated to the front courtyard to
assist me in maintaining my home, partnering in the upkeep of this
important facade. And we never spoke of Robert again.

Settling in my leather-tufted chair, I begin thumbing through
stacks of papers. There must be forty new listings, which means I'll
really have to get creative aggrandizing Shar's half-truths. Sharon out-
lists her colleagues two to one, simply because she can unload even the
worst properties in a short amount of time. Even so, she must acquire
supplementary listings to offset her ham-fisted, bridge-burning tactics.
She's also included an oversized business card as if I don't know how to
reach her. I look closely at the card and wonder just how old the picture
is, given the big hair, shoulder pads, and obvious digital enhancement.
I've questioned her many times regarding a necessary update.

"Why mess with perfection?" she said the last time I asked.

I've always found Sharon's professional photo to be a tad intimidating. Her head is tilted slightly to the left and her chin juts up as if
she's been challenged to a duel. She stares wide-eyed into the camera,
baring a full set of teeth. Not smiling in an attractive manner, mind
you. She looks as if she'll leap from the page and rip your throat out.
Well, if you're in the market for an aggressive, ball-buster of an agent, I
guess she's your man!

Unfortunately, Sharon's dull descriptions and flavorless parsing
make many homes sound alike with the same stale slogans. She needs
help selling the unsellable, and listings need to be tightly written. Even
so, the Multiple Listing Service has strict word and character restrictions and there's only so much I can do.

Sharon's assistant, Amanda, tried to write copy for her listings with uncomplicated fill-in-the-blank software, like Mad Libs for realtors. But Amanda's writing skills were even more limited than her vocabulary and the outcome was horrendous. I feel sorry for the girl for having to endure Shar's daily rants, but she stays and puts up with the abuse. God only knows why.

The last time Amanda took a crack at writing listing descriptions, Sharon came unglued, sending the copy through the shredder and shouting at Amanda, calling her a dull-witted, no-talent simpleton. Shar then produced a hundred-dollar bill, cruelly pushed it into Amanda's palm, and said, "Here, you idiot! Go to the toy store and buy yourself a Speak and Spell!"

And sadly, she did.

Having been demoted, Amanda is now relegated to the mundane tasks of picking up Sharon's dry cleaning, delivering her car for detailing, retrieving her lunch, and acting as her personal shopper. However, after reading Amanda's loquacious babble, misspelled words, and sentences that end in mid-thought or fall sharply into a void, I can see why Sharon is frustrated. People are selling their pricey homes and the listings appear written by a third grader. After rewriting the first ten listings, I wanted to ring Amanda's neck myself. Some noteworthy jargon included:

> *Surround yourself in peach and quiet! 5 acres in Lincolnshire Estates. This 4 bedroom & 4 bath home & attached 4 car garage is just what your looking for. Close to everthing w/loads of room for the kiddies & elbow room! Fine crapsman details!*

I should stop reading, but I can't seem to look away. Much like perusing the voyeuristic information that people post on social media, or the idiotic comments that you shouldn't read, but do anyway. I wince at the way Amanda has murdered the English language. Taking a deep breath, I dig in and complete the unpleasant task of rewriting.

The first home looks stately, yet also appears sad, as if something tragic has happened and no one's talking about it. It's like your creepy Uncle Albert. Everybody has a creepy Uncle Albert in the family but won't admit it. He's the shirttail uncle who drools a little with an objectionable kiss on the mouth, or an inappropriate hug during family gatherings. Something more grotesque may have occurred, but no one wants to know the awful truth.

Homes often bear the same consequence. It's easier to ignore that although things appear immaculate on the surface, inside lies an unspeakable history drenched in enigmas. Sharon has scrawled something across the bottom of the page, and yup, here it is!

> *Remember this house? Vacant for eleven years—scene of that messy DeCarlo divorce that ended in murder/ suicide?*

Perfect, my favorite subjects. Divorce, murder, and suicide. My job as Shar's personal essayist has begun.

> *Come home to this private eight-bedroom luxury abode, nestled amongst a thickly wooded two-acre lot at the end of a quiet cul-de-sac. Romantic master bedroom. Six en suite bedrooms, his and hers offices, third-floor library with hand-carved spiral staircase, and gourmet chef's kitchen. This unique paradigm of opulence boasts two substantial great rooms for intimate soirees or a glorious setting for elegant galas. Make this your family gathering place.*
>
> *Imagine banqueting in the richly paneled formal dining room. Decorous banter fills the air, as victuals are passed among kindred souls. One's mind can almost evoke imagery of a sweet Norman Rockwell scene of*

yesteryear, envisioning spirited conversations and delightful tittle-tattle.

Séance anyone?

The lower level boasts a 10,000-bottle wine cellar, indoor putting green, and cerulean lap pool with artistic capiz shell surround. New carpet throughout! Move-in ready. Former owners have relocated.

I asked Sharon about the legalities surrounding the disclosure of stigmatized properties. "You mean Ghoul Disclosures?" she said. "Ha! Who has time for that nonsense? I attended a real estate seminar once, and an appraiser specializing in diminution in value said that a well-publicized murder substantially lowers the selling price. But what buyers don't know won't hurt them, or more importantly, *me!*"

She also told me that every state is different and most have no disclosure laws in place or the law is vague at best. It bothers me that she can be so flippant!

I send her a text asking the same tired question.

> How can u live w/ yourself? Can't u share info w/ clients? Murder, death, illicit activity? Poltergeist?

Sharon must have a series of automatic text messages at her disposal because no one can text—or think—that fast. I receive an instantaneous reply.

> Memories fade. People forget. Ignorant newbies arrive. WTF! MYOB! Get 2 work!

Sharon is a real living doll. She's also the one who'll be named in a lawsuit when something more than buyer's remorse occurs. I smile with satisfaction at the thought.

Here's another treasure that's been on and off the market for years. Everyone knows it has termites, dry rot, and a terminal case of fugliness that even an extensive makeover from the most discriminating designer can't overcome. But then, world-renown interior decorators don't have the resources that Sharon Bartelson has. Shar has a certified team of specialists at her disposal from the state penitentiary's early release program. And they are quite adept at making things happen! What this foursome lacks in formal carpentry skills, they compensate for in speed. I surmise they might also break a kneecap or two if instructed to do so by their buxom boss lady.

Several years ago, Shar and her husband, Bart, purchased a 6,000-square-foot mini-manse in my neighborhood formerly owned by an orthopedic surgeon. It was in foreclosure due to a medical malpractice suit, but also because the woman that the surgeon chose to perform late-night operations with was not his wife.

After the divorce and foreclosure, this early American white elephant was unsuccessfully bank auctioned a half dozen times. Then the Bartelsons stepped in to save the day. Because Bart has a standing Sunday tee time with the lienholder, they bought the place for what was owed to the bank; a promissory note of a wink and a nod. They took possession immediately and busily went to work with a so-called "total remodel" which took Shar's handy quartet a mere six weeks to transform. The sign went up before the paint dried and the neighbors gushed at the renovation, calling the Bartelsons heroes for shoring up their property value and saving the neighborhood. Fortunately, I was not privy to the copious amount of bloated discourse that went into selling that dilapidated monstrosity!

People prattled on over the rich hues of paint colors and spectacularly staged furnishings. They *ooohed* and *ahhed* over the antique-inspired fixtures and faucets that I happened to know were purchased at a plumbing supplies' scratch and dent sale. They burbled and cooed over the embellishments and baubles that Shar found at a country flea market, costing her next to nothing.

During weekly open houses, prospective buyers as well as lookie-loos praised her for the expeditious way the home was transformed, naïvely mistaking painted cabinets, Pergo floors, and marble veneers as a contemporary work of genius. Despite having been duped by the famous Sharon Bartelson, realtor extraordinaire, I surmise that this counterfeit masterpiece will be quickly purchased for ten times what they paid for it. Well, if someone is that foolish, I suppose it's justified. After all, who would admit to such an expensive blunder?

"Hello everyone. Let me introduce myself. My name is Stupid."

The next house is your classic upper middle-class hovel and may prove to be a challenge. It's in an aging neighborhood, in a ramshackle part of the city where violent crime is an everyday occurrence. It has good bones, opulent appointments, and a lovely yard, but may still be a hard sell. I'm all about marketing distressed properties with embellished imagery, but this is ridiculous.

> *Fabulous find in sought-after neighborhood. If you like feeling secure and isolated, this home is for you!*

There's an alarm system, security cameras, and bars on the windows, so it may be difficult to leave.

> *Well-equipped chef's kitchen.*

Perhaps for Chef Boyardee.

> *Manicured grounds to die for.*

You will literally die if you step into your yard.

> *Conveniently located close to shopping and pharmacy.*

Crack house next door.

> *Friendly neighbors with many opportunities to partake in communal gatherings.*

Crack whore next door.

> *May need some redecorating. Bring your ideas!*

...and your .357 Magnum and a baseball bat for which to whomp thugs and gangbangers upside the head.

Call for a showing today and make this your dream come true!

More like your worst nightmare.

I've seen this listing firsthand. I accompanied Sharon to check on her crew as they tried to cheaply resurrect the kitchen. She'd stopped by early one Saturday morning, asking if I'd like to go for a ride into the Old Town district. I thought we might go to the spice shop that I like and perhaps grab a bite to eat afterward. That's not what happened. Shar needed to check on several properties and wanted a warm body to act as her human shield.

The home was probably spectacular a hundred years ago. Then, like many large cities, reputable citizens moved out when crime moved in. I tried to picture what this home must have been like in the days when butler pantries were still in use, and working-class families gathered at the dining room table using their best posture at exactly five p.m.

How was your day, Papa? Please pass the potatoes... May I have another helping of green beans, Mama?

I casually looked around the spacious kitchen, asking the contractors if the cast iron stove was original to the home.

"Well, well, well... Lookie here," they said. "We gots ourselves a regular Betty Cracker."

I shot Sharon a fish-eyed glare and asked why she even brought me along. She shrugged.

"I know, Shar. You're scared. Well, I'm the one you should be scared of right now. Let's *go.*"

Next is an assortment of photos with nothing more than a notation: *Make up something good!*

Seriously? What I conclude from the provided evidence is that the home has long been vacant, on the market for years, and the owner doesn't want to put any money into the property. Even the most obtuse individual knows that it's all about first impressions. I hold up a blurred photograph, squinting at the details of this decrepit property.

A once lovely portico now overtaken by rambling ivy, cries out for attention. Ah yes, one of the oldest tricks of concealment. The abundance of verdure allows for a notable impact of old-world charm, yet what lies beneath is old-world plaster, deviously cracking and peeling. Rats and snails also have a proclivity to ivy, making it a double bonus for the budding naturalist. Noting the deep mounds of dried vegetation, the deciduous trees have lost their leaves many times over, transforming the lawn into a spreading compost pile. What can I say about this fleapit?

> *Nature calling! Come home to an enchanting bungalow exuding effortless charm. If you are a knowledgeable environmentalist, this home is for you! Only a savvy preservationist with a green thumb could fully appreciate what this homegrown address has to offer.*

There are no photos of the home's interior, which I conclude might only be accessed by way of a machete-wielding landscaper. In anticipation of my literary quandary, Shar has scribbled almost illegibly on a coffee-stained Post-it: *Homeowner refuses to pay for yard maintenance.*

No kidding. I fail to see the purpose of elaborating further without using the words plague and pestilence.

Next!

As broken down as the last property was, the subsequent photograph appears to be plucked right out of *Architectural Digest*. For an unoccupied home, the interior photos look like an impeccable showplace. Impeccable typically equates to disguise, especially since all furnishings are included. It's an attention-grabbing Italianate-style villa with a golf course view and authentic Tuscan appointments throughout. It appears that the owners simply walked away.

A story lies hidden somewhere among the muck and mire. I put it aside to explore further this evening. Exploring typically equates to creeping, and one only needs an internet connection and address to get to the bottom of a blemished property. Fortunately, I still have a router and Wi-Fi, and I'll give up food and air before I'll ever give up my connection to the outside world.

Next is your classic split-level nightmare. It's an octagonal sphere and appears to be a combination upscale yurt and an interplanetary observatory. Probably a VRBO vision of glamping gone wrong. I attempt to dream up a fresh perspective for this property, yet nothing comes to mind. I stare at the photos until my eyes cross and my tummy begins to churn from the haphazard construction. All I can manage is the following:

> *Step up to your flight of fancy, as you tread lightly on your own Stairway to Heaven!*

You'll need to pace yourself, folks, because there are steps leading to steps...

> *Telescopic views for novice stargazers or avid astrophysicists. An unequaled property that is not for the faint of heart.*

You should have an EKG and a doctor's note before taking the strenuous hour-long tour.

> *Give up that costly gym membership in exchange for in-home isometrics!*

You won't be capable of exerting any more energy than what it takes to traverse staircases leading to every room in the house.

In addition to a multitude of stairways, the rooms are either sunken or raised. For those who don't require symmetry, the kitchen was constructed with sharply disproportionate angles and edges. Appliances are either too high or too low and one may require celestial navigation to plot a course through living spaces.

The four guest bedrooms have raised platforms, with each platform housing twin mattresses. These innovative sleeping chambers are close to the ceiling and only accessible by ladders. Who were the architects? Monkeys?

I assume prospective buyers will be funambulists or rodeo clowns, certainly someone physically flexible and mentally adaptable to dwell in such an unconventional design. I'm going out on a limb here, but I'll assume that this home isn't ADA compliant.

The following listing makes my neighborhood look like a ghetto. Shar's notations, or "aide-mémoire" as she calls them, flaunting her rudimentary high school French, reminds me to mention that this is the first time on the market for this little crème de la crème.

Bartelson Development Corporation generally adheres to the rule of only duping small businesses and medical practices out of millions with their shoddy commercial properties. But Bart made an exception, deciding to dabble in residential development for about five minutes. He begins projects arbitrarily and with great fanfare using a simple blueprint consisting of his favorite ingredients: impetuousness and recklessness. His ambitions were fueled by nothing more than an intense desire to turn a quick profit. Unfortunately, Bart is not adept at finishing anything that he's started. Yet the planning commission, hungrily looking for expansion, has never denied a proposed project by Bartelson Development. A practice that's blatantly obvious by the excess of unfinished structures and abandoned projects.

Bart's minions are quick to clear-cut trees, rendering the property useless for anything but his bogus plans. They strip the land of any remaining life, leaving barren ground to fissure and flood. Once blanketed by dense woodland, private older homes now sit splayed open, exposing them to the harshness of weather and the prying eyes of others. Previously sheltered wildlife flee their once quiet habitat, frantically relocating offspring while struggling to survive.

Throughout the county, gigantic signage advertising a new industrial park or shopping center appears. As far as the eye can see, vast wastelands of leveled terrain and immobilized heavy equipment dot the landscape. The ground pounded and pulverized to a fine dust, could only be the work of the ignoble Bart Bartelson. His projects are abandoned shortly after the cash flow is depleted, leaving uncompleted eyesores and a trail of individuals who'd like to see him dead.

Built on speculation, Bart's residential encore combined the inadequate marriage of stupidity and money. Desperate for investors, he met his new best friends while gambling on the riverfront, other dime store millionaires eager to pool and flaunt their liquid assets. This connubial pairing resulted in the birth of a 12,000-square-foot mansion built on filled-in swampland. The property was inexpensive, but property tends to be cheap when it sits below the water table. It was the last parcel nestled in the affluent gated community of Villa del Sol, or as it should have been named, Villa del Agua.

The development boasts a private lake, an award-winning eighteen-hole golf course, and an elite country club. It wasn't a buildable parcel, but the city turned a blind eye and let Bart loose to obliterate some poor soul's dream. To say that he's a deceitful individual who plays by his own rules is an understatement. But the man has tenacity, his only virtuous quality.

The puffery continues, as I persist with an economical version of the truth.

> *Life aquatic! Elitism can be yours for only $12.5 million. Gorgeous selective country club living where sophistication is a lifestyle. Relax knowing that you will one-up even your closest friends with the exclusivity of this fabulous address. Don't miss the opportunity to*

purchase this gem that sits on the last remaining five-acre parcel in Villa del Sol, complete with water view. Amenities galore, abundant wildlife, and a private lower-level wing for maid or mother-in-law quarters.

One good rain and the mother-in-law is history.

Because of the asking price, there will be no open house. Showings will be permitted for pre-approved, serious buyers only. Cognizant of the Bartelson's past dealings, the little water problem will not be included in the seller's disclosure.

I save everything and close my laptop, giving my mind and fingers a rest. I wonder how Bart and Shar sleep at night. I also wonder if they completely skipped over the ethics portion of the real estate course.

Chapter Four

Sharon is a merciless social climber willing to claw her way to the top. Known for her obsessive drive, she's determined to maintain her position as the top real estate producer in the bi-state area. You can't drive for a mile in any direction without seeing her mug plastered upon illuminated electronic billboards or tackily splayed across city buses. Having been born without scruples, conscience, or heart, she's well suited for the bottom rung of the real estate industry, letting nothing get in the way of a sale.

When she lags in existing home sales, she purchases distressed properties in expectation of a quick flip. Sharon and Bart can cosmetically transform a derelict property in less than a month and market it to unsuspecting buyers. Bargain hunters, wowed by the glitz of staged furnishings, rented houseplants, and a fresh coat of paint are easy targets. Clients are awestruck by the address, yet pay no attention to substance or quality, unaware of concealed defects.

After many years in the real estate industry, Sharon continues to give a convincing performance. She escorts prospective buyers to properties via a leased black Mercedes S 550 sedan, the official pace car of impostors. Poised confidently, she stands predictably garbed in full combat regalia: a luxurious, low-cut chemise revealing an older but well-preserved décolleté, the condensed version of a little black skirt, and come-fuck-me stilettos sure to equal any worn by high-priced escorts.

Spreading her arms wide with a flourish, Sharon enthuses over curb appeal, overstating the privileges of living in such an exclusive locale. Her heels snap smartly around expansive stone walkways, leading to extravagantly landscaped patios and garish poolside cabanas. When the gullible few begin to linger, she sashays into the conversation, where they become enraptured by her flowing perfunctory dissertations. She then ushers them back inside where they are graced with yet more of her grandiose bullshit.

"Call me Shar," she tells clients, as she segues into her chummy mode.

Sharon's approach to home sales is unorthodox at best, leaving one flummoxed by her ability to win over prospective buyers. Clients should find her hardline approach and rough diction insulting. To the contrary. Her satirical wit and ample breasts charm the men, and many women find her irresistible as well. She needs only a hint of encouragement to fuel her sales act, and then, *It's Showtime!*

No one puts on an open house like Shar. In preparation, she spends an obscene amount of money on fresh flower arrangements, carefully smattering them about the home. She reminds everyone that this is a tax deduction. A deduction that quickly makes its way to her foyer. She also caters the events with lavish hors d'oeuvres and finger sandwiches and pops the cork of overpriced bubbly to anyone willing to make an offer on the spot. She repeats this phrase to her fellow realtors who customarily purchase slice-and-bake cookies for their open houses: "Dear ones, the elementary school aroma of mediocre baked goods is so passé..."

As anticipated, these staged events also attract opportunists looking for a free meal, yet she finds a way to exploit them as well. Shar will have them doing favors for her or vice versa. The things this woman will do to hook a potential client would rival anything the pornographic mind could fantasize.

As extroverted as Sharon is, her husband is quite the opposite. Bartholomew Bartelson is a weasel of a man with eyes that avert during conversation. However, I have caught him staring at my breasts when he speaks as if he's having a private conversation with them.

Bart embodies all the attributes of an archetypical scumbag, preying on the upper crust while making no attempt to hide it. Once a deep-pocket developer, the only thing he now holds in his pocket are politicians seeking solutions to faltering economic growth. He plays musical chairs on various committees, sharing authoritative kerfuffle with cradle-to-gravers. By allowing Bart to partake in the drumming machine of city government, the *I'll scratch your back if you'll scratch mine* philosophy is alive and well. And Bart scarfs up whatever table scraps he's fed.

Bart Bartelson was not always a mainstay in the Bryn Mawr community. He was born Barney Chuck in a shanty river town thirty miles to the south and fifty years in the past. There was always confusion over whether Chuck was his first name or his last. Nevertheless, this oddly incompatible name did not deter him, for at the ripe old age of fifteen, he left home and changed his name and his identity.

Barney Chuck, nka Bart Bartelson, is a true innovator and has the skills to continue reinventing himself. The man can spin a good yarn, making his underhanded ways seem quite convincing. That, combined with a pioneering spirit, temporarily increased his net worth. The zoning board and planning commission gave him an open-ended license to steal, as Bart took from the rich and gave to himself. But the bottomless well of capital investments has since dried up, and people are starting to pay attention to how their money is being spent.

Bart only pays his contractors, sub-contractors, and attorneys when they threaten him with bodily harm. It's no longer advantageous to file lawsuits, as countless cases are pending against him. As long as the practice of cronyism exists, and as long as the courts remain backlogged, cases against Bartelson Development will continue into infinity.

Mistreating commercial builders or your attorney may get you into legal trouble. But cross the less-than-benevolent residential contractors and you'll find your carcass comingled with concrete and dumped into the East River.

One night, Sharon called me, frantically asking for my help. "Bart's been roughed up and left in a golf cart behind the country club! And I found a note pinned to his bloodied shirt that said, 'Pay me, shithead!'"

Everyone, including Sharon, is surprised to find Bart living and breathing each day. But someday, his luck will run out.

I'm aware of the Bartelson's shady backroom deals, and I'm prepared to recite their illicit transgressions to the authorities should it become necessary. This is why Sharon agreed to protect my secret. As long as we each possess scandalous information on one another, we're sure to remain devoted best friends. And in our case, *only* friends, as no one else will have us.

Winning my trust and adoration had always been a preoccupation for Sharon. Now, she's fixated less on me and more on my estate, which promises to be a tidy tithe toward her dwindling bank accounts and deteriorating reputation.

Chapter Five

Robert rode high on my fame and my money. My inheritance, as well as earnings from book sales, film rights, and speaking engagements, bought this house and accompanying lifestyle. It also purchased a scenic ski-in/ski-out chalet in Vale and a small, but cozy beach cottage in Maui. Besides our principal residence, included in our real estate portfolio were houses smattered across the globe; homes purchased on impulse when traveling to remarkable places that we'd promised to visit again, but never did. These were eventually turned into rental properties, trashed by entitled American tourists or vandalized by the locals.

I should have paid more attention to the many calls that Robert refused to answer in my presence. The unknown numbers on caller ID and the overseas calls to our private line in the middle of the night shook me out of a dead sleep, women speaking broken English, asking for "Bobert." The old Angela was a trusting enabler, oblivious to the fact that my husband used these faraway locales to facilitate his little trysts.

Early in our relationship, I stupidly assumed we were both enterprising people, working toward the same goals. I became obsessed with furthering my career and thought that Robert was doing the same. He was never home but accused me of being a workaholic; though he didn't complain, as he benefited from my achievements. Unfortunately, his ambitions were self-serving, with the predicted target settling somewhere in his crotch.

At least Robert always knew my whereabouts. I never knew what kind of business he was conducting or with whom he was entangled. One minute he claimed to be in the import/export business, and the next he was a big game hunter, arranging chartered safaris for Southern billionaires. Once, while attending a fundraiser, he mentioned in casual conversation that he was a real estate tycoon. From a silver engraved case in his breast pocket, he produced authentic-looking business cards and passed them all around. I almost choked trying to swallow his lies during the frosty silence that ensued.

When questioned about his cagey business dealings, he became irate and condescending. "It's complicated, Ang. You're too stupid to understand the nitty-gritty of the business world. Besides, if you ask too many questions, you might not like the answer."

Our lives became a vicious cycle of embittered spats. The house was mercifully spacious and we devolved to separate bedrooms, retreating to our own insulated worlds. We adapted to the taciturn schedules of ghostlike roommates, occasionally passing in the halls. This arrangement felt more like being single than being married and the more distant Robert became, the more I replaced love and affection with work. Eventually, he ceased coming home at all, which restored serenity and temporarily left me feeling at ease.

I tried putting a positive spin on the situation. I was now free to be myself, unchained from his volatile outbursts and amoral lifestyle. I could breathe. Emotionally- absent Robert was no longer punctuating my days with intermittent appearances and antagonistic bickering, ceaselessly placing blame on *me*. Robert's arguments always began with some evocative justification: *If only...* "If only you were better looking, had bigger boobs, were more supportive, or available when I need you, this would never have happened..."

The fleeting sensation of good riddance quickly evaporated, when without warning, Robert drained bank accounts and sold off investments, leaving me with our primary residence and a small offer of monthly maintenance. This measly disbursement doesn't even begin to cover the cost of interest on the second and third mortgages that he took out on the equity. Nor does it adequately cover my lawyer's exorbitant fees. I was a fool to let him manage our funds, and a bigger fool for believing he could be anything more than what he is. Robert is your conventional salesman, a predictable wheeler-dealer, a fickle negotiator who's always looking out for number one. He's a vile man who insists that his juvenile concubine call him Big Daddy.

The last time I had any communication with him was several months ago at the urging of my attorney. We were encouraged to work out an amicable agreement on the house, which he quickly walked away from. This was no surprise as he leveraged every bit of equity, and the house, as well as me, was no longer of any use to him.

He spent our money on strip clubs. He entertained exotic dancers and took lavish trips to hunt trophy animals on every continent, sending them off to the taxidermist to be prepared for his murder room. I should have known that anyone callous enough to kill a majestic elephant simply to have the legs made into end tables was beyond redemption.

Our last stab at mannerly conversation turned ugly as he said the one thing he knew would hurt the most. "Well, at least there aren't children involved, right Ang?"

"Oh, but there is a child involved, Robert. What's her name, again? Precious Cox?"

I am well past being pissed off. What I'd really like is revenge. Nevertheless, if I summon enough hateful voodoo and visualize Robert's torturous demise, I'll suffer the ill effects of immediate karma. This is the way it's always been. Some wait for years to be repaid for evil thoughts. My wait is never long and I'll be paid back swiftly and painfully.

I don't attend church, and I'm not a very good Christian, but I pray that a higher power will someday deliver Robert his just reward. And I'd surely like to bear witness to the event! I'd walk up to the ticket counter with my limitless platinum card or a sack of newly minted gold coins.

"I'll take the best seat in the house," I'd say to the ticket agent.

"You must be the ex-wife," she'd say. "We've been expecting you. Enjoy the show!"

I continue to give myself an unconvincing pep talk to let Robert's hateful comments roll off. I also called my attorney and left a brief, but clear message: "No amicable agreement reached. Make it hurt."

I used to find the rich and powerful repulsive. People who feel a sense of entitlement because of where they live, what they drive, and how much they have. The pretentious upper crust who are constantly vying for a position at the popular table; those who have no problem walking over others to make themselves look good. I suppose that by way of osmosis, I became one of them. Here I am living among the privileged, whose shit, apparently does not stink.

As much as I detest these people and all they stand for, I don't want to lose my home. Like fish introduced to more generous aquariums, they grow to the size of their accommodations. It becomes impossible to move them to smaller lodgings where they will flounder and fail to thrive. I know how they feel. I've grown accustomed to living here and it would be hard to downsize to a smaller aquarium. I'm not ready to give up and I will not go down without a fight! And that's precisely what I intend to do. *Fight.*

After embellishing the last surge of listings, I begin to wonder how I'll market my home when the time comes. What can I possibly say to promote this inglorious sanctuary and endorse a shell of a home that does little more than hide a small, damaged life, and the accompanying embarrassment of misfortune?

> *An enchanting estate once owned by a divorced, childless author of questionable moral values. Fantabulous master suite used for fitful sleeping and little else...*

When I start feeling sorry for myself, I stare out the windows and wait for movement in the neighborhood. I love to observe people in their natural habitat, so when the hard-bitten pleatherette twins plod along during their evening prowl, I straighten in my seat to examine their odd behavior.

Mr. and Mrs. Horace Clap must spend every waking moment in their tanning beds or braising by the pool in the hot sun. They're not just tanned. Their hides are taxidermy tanned—suitable for mounting, which I find ironic. Their wrinkled skin and craggy complexions lead one to believe that these two are prehistoric, but for all we know, they could be in their thirties. Horace and Eunice Clap are towering, mannequin-esque creatures yoked together by disturbing traits and depraved pastimes. Even though I'm used to their lurking presence during their twice-daily constitutionals, I shudder when I see them. There's something about these two that just isn't right, and I have an overwhelming urge to shower and scrub myself with muriatic acid and a wire brush.

Besides never managing a smile and their involvement with the not-so-secret swingers set, I can't put my finger on it. As if that's not enough to digest! I try willing myself not to think about it, yet the needle on the creep indicator advances off the chart, making the hair on my arms rise in repulsion.

Their mannerisms are rigid as they skulk down the street, gesticulating at each home on their calculated route. I wish I could hear what they're saying as they stop in front of my gate to pluck something from the sidewalk. Inspiration strikes and I reach over and hit the intercom button for a little technological eavesdropping that would make the

NSA proud.

"Do you think her yard man is capable of pulling a weed?" says Eunice Clap, frowning at the stalk of flaccid greenery dangling from her hand. "How long do you think it's been growing out of this crack?"

I'm sure Eunice has seen her share of oddities growing out of cracks. I cover my mouth with my hand, stifling a mischievous giggle.

"What does she do all day but sit on her derriere and type? Any fool can write gobbledygook. I wouldn't read one of her namby-pamby novels if you paid me," states Horace pragmatically as he glances up toward my home, shaking his head in disgust.

"And where is that husband of hers? Hmmm? Has he tired of her odd reclusiveness as well?" Eunice chimes in.

I turn off the intercom and quickly conclude that these two aren't just out randomly exercising. They're training for the Asshole Olympics.

I refuse to become flustered over my insolent neighbors and damn it, I'm tired of writing mind-numbing real estate listings for a cutthroat narcissist. Slowly beginning to fade, I lean back in my chair and start rubbing my temples to ease an approaching headache, the poor woman's method of stress relief. A hot bath would be heavenly, but my water heater is on the fritz and the hot water only lasts for a few minutes. Because of this, my sporadic shower sessions have been reduced to two minutes or less. I've begun turning off the water while lathering because time is of the essence! And because water costs money. Rinsing off in a cold shower is certainly a paralyzing eye-opener, so one cannot help but hurry through.

On the upside, this forced frugality also lowers my power and water bills. I've been playing Russian roulette with the bills lately, calling my creditors each month begging for an extension. I'm learning that begging takes a lot of time and boy, do they make you work for it! The phone calls alone can be daunting, and you must pay close attention, hitting the right prompts at just the right time. If you make a mistake, you must begin the process all over again. That only exacerbates an already tense situation, which leaves one no choice but to let fly with a selection of four-letter words.

I don't qualify for financial aid, and I believe that the criteria for assistance are homelessness, joblessness, and abject poverty. Knowing this, I make the calls anyway, hoping to reduce or defer payments.

If you are calling for a business, press or say one. If you are calling for a residence, press or say two. If you would like to hear a breakdown of your bill, press, or say three. If you'd like to make a payment, press, or say six. If you would like to hear in exhaustive detail, our privacy policy, press or say four. If any of these options do not meet your requirements, say other.

"Other!"

Okay, got it. Let's try to help you.

If you are calling to schedule a new service, press or say seven. If you are calling for an existing account, please enter your account number followed by the pound sign, your address, followed by the pound sign, and the last four digits of your social security number, followed by the pound sign.

Thank you. If you need to speak with a representative, press or say zero, or say representative.

"Representative!"

Okay. Got it. Please hold. Your call is important to us. You are caller number 543.

As I continue to wait for a live person, the line comes to life. Excitement turns to disappointment when I realize it's only a recording. The silence, intermittently disrupted by a scratchy mechanical voice with spasmodic affirmations, reminds me that I'm still important.

Most of the large utility and credit companies have outsourced their customer service departments. "You live *where?*" they would say suspiciously while homing in on a satellite view of my address.

I think about customer service employees living in impoverished countries who speak to terminally dissatisfied Americans each day. How their society is so poor that they cram many generations into one or two rooms. People who regularly endure food shortages, unsanitary living conditions, and interruptions to the power grid. I don't think they'd be as accommodating knowing that a single woman rattling around in a posh estate is asking for extra time because her credit cards are maxed out.

I don't know how many times I can ask for an extension or beg to make installments, but I do know that my finances must improve significantly or I'll soon be left in the dark. Over the past few months, the power and phone companies have been understanding and have worked with me, arranging to spread out payments. They've also waived all late fees. But I feel like a malingering skiver, not paying my bills, and staying just one step ahead of the collectors. All this running and hiding, negotiating, and begging is tiring!

I'm not the only one who's ever been through this. Although I try to have empathy, I don't have it in me right now. I feel like the last person on earth, isolated and alone. I've considered filing for bankruptcy, but I still need money to live on. With what little I have left, I've put myself on a tight budget, inserting my credits and debts on a worksheet, and then calculating the data. The result: I'm overdrawn and in the red with no definitive solution.

I'm also finding that being poor is stressful as the finer points of living in destitution are still new to me. I wonder if they offer a non-credit course at the local community college: Poverty 101. I'd sign up tomorrow if it were free.

But I don't want to think about any of this right now. I need a restorative session from my past life. Closing my eyes, I dream of a lavender and rose pedal steam bath, a deep-tissue massage, and a Swedish diamond-infused facial.

Sharon once flew me across the country to an exclusive New York spa on my birthday, insisting that I relax and pamper myself. Since she was treating, I'd decided to go for broke with the White Caviar illuminating facial—a bargain at $1,200. I chose this after poo-pooing the bizarre bird poop facial, which the estheticians swore would make me look ten years younger. It may be an avant-garde beauty regime for Japanese geishas and the beautiful people, but it's not for me. If I wanted bird shit on my face, I'd go to the city park and look skyward.

As it turns out, that little birthday excursion cost me over $15,000. Several weeks later, Shar presented me with a bill for reimbursement of airfare, hotel, meals, and spa treatments.

"You didn't think I was going to pay for this, did you Ang?" Throwing her head back, she howled with laughter. "I was purely your facilitator and guide!"

"There's nothing pure about you," I said, handing her a check for my expenses.

What I could do with that wasted $15,000 now!

The ringtone of my cell phone shakes me out of a boredom-induced stupor. I flinch at the theme song of the Wicked Witch of the West. Sharon reminds me of Miss Gulch and I hear a cackling voice in my head, *"I'll get you my pretty... And your little dog, Whatshisname too!"*

I barely have a chance to say hello before the interrogation begins.

"Ang, are you finished with my listings? I really need to post them tonight. I have an all-inclusive trip to the Bahamas riding on a sales contest. The team of LeeLee Breckenridge and Sissy Parsons are following a close second right now and I refuse to relinquish any contest to that gruesome twosome."

"I'm still revising, but I'll have them finished and emailed in a few hours. It isn't easy to polish a turd, you know."

"Neither is dyeing your unmanageable mane. Snap to it, sister! Chop-chop! Bart and I have raping and pillaging to do and you're holding up the show!"

With that, Shar rudely disconnects the call and I sit stunned, wondering how we ever became friends. I also wonder how this woman manages to charm people into buying homes that they can scarcely afford and will eventually regret living in. Anyone can bleach her teeth and plump up a chest, but there's something about the allure of this bitchy coquette that even I don't understand. I lean my head on folded hands and gaze out the window into oblivion at my dead-end life.

As curvaceous as Sharon's figure may be, her antithesis, Darcy Danforth, is jogging around the cul-de-sac. Something is out of whack, as she normally runs in the early morning. She appears nimble and lithe as her feet glide effortlessly along the pathway. How could she not be light on her feet? She weighs about fifteen pounds and I don't think she even perspires.

For today's talent competition, Darcy is multitasking: Fishin' with one eye and huntin' with the other, examining each home and yard for breaches in the covenants and restrictions. She continues to run and wave, while occasionally glancing at the fitness monitor on her left arm. The heartless bitch is probably checking for a pulse.

Darcy Danforth isn't your average busybody, but a cold, calculating schemer. To amuse myself, I devise alliterations as she goes bouncing down the street—she's the Machiavelli of Maliciousness. The Svengali of Spitefulness. The Antagonist of Anarchy. She delights in starting rumors, which creates mobocracies, eventually resulting in total anarchy. Darcy Danforth is irrefutably, a shit-stirrer extraordinaire and the crowned head of the Bryn Mawr Homeowners Association.

Privately, Darcy is spurned by all. But publicly, no one will stand up to her. The neighbors are afraid of having their good names marred by her brand of revenge, which can best be described as dyslogistic draconian.

Like Bart Bartelson, Darcy also came from backwoods rural stock, spawned from a gene pool no deeper than a puddle in a pothole. Darleen

Jean Grubwell was an only child who quickly grew into the privileged lifestyle that her parents created. Daddy was a small-town lawyer who worked his way up to senior partner at a reputable downtown law firm. Garth Grubwell passed his unprincipled practices and obsessive competitiveness down to Daddy's little girl.

Darcy's mother hailed from royalty. Back in the day, Mrs. Grubwell was a former Miss Rural America and Miss Milkweed and was runner-up in a Marilyn Monroe lookalike contest. I suppose that was her life accomplishment, as I can visualize just one line on her résumé: *Betsy Louise Markham-Grubwell, Beauty Queen.*

From what I understand, Darcy spent her childhood in the pageant circuit as well, forced by her mom and sponsored by her dad. Her parents couldn't wait to see how their daughter would grow and change, as all children eventually will. So, they changed her appearance for her, beginning with plastic surgery on her protuberant schnozzle at age twelve. But once that addictive can of worms is opened, there's no turning back.

I don't believe that evil is born into most people. I believe for many, it's created. I'm no expert, and I don't have children, but looking into Darcy's past, the apple didn't fall far from the tree. Darcy grew up completely unrestrained and was taught that she should never take no for an answer. She was overindulged by pandering parents who sent her to charm school and entered her in beauty pageants, bowing to her every whim. She grew to expect the same treatment from the many men who came into, and just as quickly retreated, from her life.

Word on the street is that Darcy's first suitor didn't make it out of the relationship unscathed. Darcy and Blake were traditional high school sweethearts at the private academy where they both attended. She, the predictable blonde cheerleader with breasts just as perky as her fake persona. And he, the strapping football standout who made first string and all-state his freshman year.

Darcy naturally assumed that they'd make a life together after college and spent hours writing elaborate summaries of what their future would be like. When the Internet came along, Darcy switched to a more public platform, chronicling their lives via social media. She reported each date, each event, and each intimate detail, complete with pictures that will live for eternity.

In their junior year of college, she surprised Blake during spring break at Notre Dame, arriving at his off-campus apartment. However, it was she who was surprised as Blake was not alone. He'd told Darcy that he wouldn't be able to accompany her to the Cayman Islands for spring break because he was under the weather and not well enough to travel. In response, Darcy abandoned her vacation plans to paradise, changed her airline tickets, and darted off to comfort her handsome boyfriend, whom she hadn't seen in months.

Darcy became enraged, screeching ruthless prolixities. She then physically attacked the other woman, who was more surprised than anyone over the arrival of one emotionally unstable Darleen Grubwell. Unable to quietly accept the breakup, Darcy launched into a tirade, erratically destroying Blake's apartment, and gouging his face with a set of impeccably manicured talons. It was fear of such a reaction that Blake didn't break up with her sooner. He'd hoped that she would find another object of affection while she was away at university. After all, Darcy's life goal was to earn her MRS degree with someone who could afford to maintain her extravagant lifestyle.

Darcy was eventually arrested and charged with trespassing, destroying property, and assault with intent to do bodily harm. Because no weapon was involved during the unprovoked attack, she was charged with several misdemeanors and released into the custody of her father. A hefty surety was also exacted and a stern warning was given to her legal counsel/father that guaranteed her return for arraignment. But in the end, Daddy had her criminal record expunged and paid Blake a tidy stipend never to speak of this unfortunate incident again.

Since universities tend to frown on violent behavior by scorned lovers, Darcy was asked not to return. So she moved back to her parents' home and earned a degree in fashion merchandizing from the local university. While there, she met the man of her dreams, one Richard Danforth II. A quiet fellow, who I surmise would also love to be free of his captor but dare not leave her for fear he would meet a fate far worse than young Blake.

The Danforths have two children, now teens. By way of nature or nurture, they are equally as unstable as their indifferent matriarch. During their formative years, Darcy frequently employed the use of burner phones after many country club hangovers, sending her youngsters to the golf course to play. *Mommy's had too many cocktails. Call me ONLY in an emergency!*

Samantha is the oldest, and towers over her younger brother. Her given name sounds lighthearted and by very definition means listener. It does not mean nonstop nattering. Samantha Danforth is the product of permissiveness, always demanding to be the focal jewel in the crown. I suppose she was a child whose parents gave her a standing ovation for crapping in her toddler potty or properly articulating the word, *"Mine!"*

Despite her leviathan size, Samantha's mother is constantly trying to starve her into a vision of withered loveliness—size zero, an unreasonable and harmful objective that will no doubt result in counseling, rehab, or worse. Darcy also insists on dressing Samantha in provocative attire, and orders daily applications of heavy makeup, thus making the poor girl appear ready for a career in the oldest profession. Sam's favorite saying is "Totes adorbs!" which is about as eloquent as Godzilla enunciating, "OMG."

Darcy's male protégée, Richard Danforth III, needs no introduction. His name says it all. The first time I met the little shit, he was wearing a starched white shirt, pleated slacks, and a sweater draped over his shoulders, tied loosely at the neck. Upon formal introductions, Richard III crossed his arms, stuck out his tongue, and screeched in his shrill little boy voice, "My mom is the president of the Homeowners Association!" From that day forward, I avoided engaging in even the most mundane of conversations with the Danforth family.

Besides being disrespectful and mean, I couldn't quite figure out the Danforth boy. The kid is socially stunted and abnormally uninhibited. And he's a holy terror! Other children tend to find kids like Richie a bit scary as well. There's something about him that's just *off*. He would probably mount the family dog, or if not that, may try to drown it in the swimming pool. I wouldn't turn my back on the young man because if I had to venture a guess, I'd say the little bastard doesn't have a conscience.

Their mother has greatly contributed to the anguish of her small, dystopian family. I've seen Darcy pit Richie against Samantha, standing back with a validated smirk as the siblings engage in verbally devastating melees. I don't have kids, but even I know psychological abuse when I see it, and that's just messed up!

Unfortunately, Darcy's acrimonious splendor is not limited to next of kin. As our association president, she chooses neighborhood favorites, depending on one's inclination to participate in planned social functions, and who might be a willing informant. Her faves get the royal treatment, ignoring infractions to the CC&Rs. Instead, she'll go after some poor soul displaying an American flag without prior written approval, or make sure one's ambient lighting is up to code.

Chapter Six

I've wasted time trying to figure out my neighbors' deviant behavior when I should be writing. I look down at my laptop, a glowing blank screen of nothingness. Any confidence in my writing ability has been deflated like a three-day-old balloon.

I've never experienced writer's block. I'd always thought of it as a lazy, made-up excuse for those who didn't want to work, mocking anyone who used this sorry defense. Now, here I am, self-satirized by my own inadequacies. I'm running out of time and don't know where to start!

It's like my recurring New Year's Eve dream. It's almost midnight and I have no one to kiss. A decision must be made to either run away or grab a stranger, planting a long kiss on unfamiliar lips. I'd suffer embarrassment for the rest of my life, and in the process, contract strep or mono or hepatitis. Or a less invasive, but still serious ailment: cooties.

There's no set rule to the writing process and each has their method. I tried storyboarding and outlining, cutting pictures from magazines and newspapers, hoping to spark the creative muse. But I didn't need the added noise or steps, which eventually led to the same place. The words are already in my head, just waiting to be typed out. A never-ending well of ideas. Or so I thought. Writer's block is real. I thought I was immune, but I've caught the deadly disease and there's no known cure.

There must be something that will spark my imagination, but I haven't found the catalyst that will help me become unstuck. I open the file cabinets and go through the alphabetized documents. There, merrily parked in the annals of my drawers are the Bryn Mawr Country Club Estates HOA documents, filed under "J" for joke. For grins and giggles, I've saved every newsletter. They always make for a good laugh.

I begin thumbing through old publications, but nothing seems interesting enough.

Rifling through the inbox on my desk, I unearth the most recent bi-annual newsletter. It's been living there for several months, inter-mingled with other nuisance mail. There's nothing that our HOA has to say that I'm remotely interested in, but I need a diversion from these insipid real estate listings. I may be able to harvest some material for the manuscript I'm working on, and what better place to start than in one's own backyard?

I head down to the wine cellar, searching for liquid comfort to help me wade through the shallowness of this inane circular. Over the past year, I've either imbibed or bartered with our extensive wine collection, leaving a lone box of rosé that was given as a gag gift years ago. This cheap concoction couldn't possibly improve with age! Hopefully, it will give me a buzz, taking the edge off another lonely evening at home. I climb back up the stairs to my office with a box of wine and a large plastic cup from 7-Eleven.

"Bottoms up," I say, as I begin reading the thickly collated bulletin and the amended version of the CC&Rs.

Our rogue board of directors has maintained a solid oligarchy for years; self-appointed keepers of the Holy Grail on neighborly conduct. Those who can't think for themselves must follow a written doctrine on how to be good neighbors. The newsletters contain directives consisting of regulations and confusing mumbo jumbo. Leading by intimidation, they flaunt their authority by frightening people into submission. But it's all smoke and mirrors, distracting from the fact that they're powerless and ineffective.

Photos of our HOA board line the top of the newsletter, with name and designating title. I consider the person in each photo, looking for a trace of mutuality. Nothing. All I see are a bunch of glassy-eyed totalitarians with bad haircuts. There's something peculiar about people who aspire to be in command of a homeowners association. In Darcy's case, she's motivated by an unhealthy fascination with the lives of others. Like grade-schoolers who sit in the front row of the classroom with their hand permanently raised, so too, are there adults who ingratiate themselves with toady behavior. With supplicating hands held high, *"Oooh, pick me! Pick me!"*

I laugh at neighbors who cozy up to the HOA board. They lobby the nominating committee with baked goods from popular artisan bakeries, sought-after theater tickets, or spa certificates, simply to have their name placed on an upcoming ballot. I wonder if, as preschoolers, they were never chosen as Cubby Captain or a member of the Potty Police. This would certainly explain why seemingly intelligent adults desire to tyrannically dictate the lives of their neighbors. Once, just to mess with them, I nominated myself. I was crushed when I didn't receive a response.

What catches my eye is the curlicue font that Darcy's virtual assistant used to spell out *newsletter*. I bite my lower lip, amused that people can be so unreasonably demanding, yet use puerile fonts and clumsy wording. It's difficult to take them seriously. Even so, I appreciate the guidance. Unable to think for ourselves, we'd be lost without this helpful instruction manual on the proper protocol of being acceptable neighbors. There are indispensable tutorials on how to protect your home from burglars by leaving lights on all night and locking your doors. Also useful is keeping a nine-iron bedside to surprise unwanted intruders with a swing that wouldn't do on the golf course, let alone the bedroom, during a late-night break-in.

Scanning the financial reports splayed across spreadsheets, I skim through to the bottom line. It seems that we have a surplus of money. In the spirit of all things governmental, and by the power vested in the country club community, let's not place it in an emergency fund. Let's spend it! There were many ideas on how to squander the excess funds. As Darcy's opinion is the only one that matters, she decrees that a neighborhood party is in order, complete with clowns, live entertainment, pony rides, bounce houses, and catered barbeque from a local smokehouse. At least they won't have to order out for the clowns!

My view on planned neighborhood events is the same as class reunions. If I haven't kept in contact with you; if I haven't sought you out and maintained a social relationship, then I most likely don't want to be coerced into mingling with you. *Ever.*

I read on...

The landscaping committee strongly suggests that we begin coordinating our yard services. Lawns shall be mowed in a festive checkerboard pattern on Saturday mornings. As well, out of respect for other neighbors, thou shalt not mow before noon or on Sundays. *No exceptions!* The announcement, underscored in caps, emphasizes the magnitude of the challenge. This year's shrubbery theme is shrubs gone wild! I begin to perspire. How will I keep a straight face when I ask Juan to sculpt a convincing topless dancer out of desolate, thorny undergrowth and a pair of rusty pruning shears?

The newly appointed garbage committee mandates that garbage receptacles CANNOT be placed streetside before five a.m. on pickup day. As well, recyclables shall be placed in color-coordinated containers and all materials shall be positioned in said containers in alphabetical order. "Please inform the help," was an added reminder.

I've been sneaking wine bottles into Mrs. Kemper's recycling bin for years, making my neighboring octogenarian look like a lush. Mrs. Kemper has never smiled nor returned a wave, and I've taken to ignoring her, as most neighbors do. The old battleax has a sprawling split-level home decorated in passé combinations of stark white and ashen gray; complete with an ungodly number of crystal chandeliers and enough iron scrollwork to make her live-in housekeeper go mad.

I happen to know that she grossly underpays her housekeeper, Mary Ann Munch. Mary Ann benignly looks away while I deposit my empties, the bottles clink together toasting a subtle revenge. I presume that Mary Ann bequeaths the old woman a few of her own surprises as well, her upturned mouth, inconspicuously giving consent.

The pages containing the quarterly report of fines and demerits always make for a good read. I quickly examine the list for my surname, defiantly highlighted in bold print. The misdeeds are numerous. Even my unattractive dog, Snaggletooth, was issued a citation for relieving himself in my front yard. The infraction? Illegal dumping. A handwritten note appears next to my name with a valuable suggestion: *Angela, try training little "What's-his-name" to poo-poo in the back of your property. Thnx!*

Darcy cannot manage to spell out *thanks*. She could also send this monstrous report electronically but has transposed my email address every time. Though knowing her, she will ask for it again and again. Once, during the HOA directory update, I carefully explained that if she simply types my name, then @ followed by the provider.net, everyone will be happy and many trees will be saved. Darcy did exactly as she was instructed: *myname@provider.net.*

As I read on, I stare mindlessly at the outside world, struggling to understand the illogical accusations. While pondering the fact that this isn't a planned retirement community where this type of nonsense is expected, Priscilla Pennybone and her registered pug, Patricia, stroll by, promenading through the neighborhood wearing matching designer hoodies and rhinestone tiaras. Pris is doing the walking while Patricia rides proudly in her Louis Vuitton stroller, her feet only touching the ground when lifted from her perch to poo-poo on someone's lawn.

According to the amended CC&Rs, if the dog is a small breed, purchased for an incalculable amount of money and the neighbor is popular, they do not have to pick up after their pooch. Besides, everyone knows that miniature breeds leave behind waste that is small, odorless, and sensibly formed; therefore, the requirement for cleaning up after diminutive dogs has been waived.

For those of us with sizable mutts, the HOA can request that we submit a DNA swab for testing within thirty days of receiving notice. If a ne'er-do-well fails to pick up after their canine companion, the poo will be confiscated and sent to an independent lab for testing. This will officially determine who the offender is, and the owner will be promptly fined. The canine in question will be placed on doggie probation for a period of six months and shall not be allowed to socialize with others.

I'm not sure if this is scientifically possible or if it's just another formulated threat to control people. I pensively consider how I might surreptitiously deposit a human turd on the lawn of our treasured HOA president. She would surely lose consciousness after receiving the analysis report from the lab. Sometimes, I surprise myself. Disgusting, shocking, and ingenious—all rolled into one.

For those who crankily covet thy sacred suburban green space, there is the prickly subject of lawns. During the last HOA meeting, Darcy's husband, Richard Charles Danforth II, stood in front of his fellow neighbors and had a full-blown estrogen attack. He was close to tears and sniveled about how hard he works on his lawn and how much he pays his greenkeepers to keep it pristine. He also contributes by strapping on his Saturday morning kneepads, lying on the sidewalk, and trimming the edges of his lawn with a pair of scissors. The impassioned sacrifices that he makes for the betterment of humankind stirs something within me. I begin convulsing in hysterical fits of laughter.

Richard number two is a real hoot!

Besides his lawn dilemma, he continued to whine that it is our duty to keep dogs from urinating on his lawn during walks. I innocently raised my hand and offered a supportive suggestion. "Should I catheterize my dog or simply diaper him? Would that be helpful?" I said while Richard glared at me, clearly overcome with emotion.

During my tenure here in Bryn Mawr, I've learned the fundamentals of keeping companion animals. Properly naming your pet is crucial if you want acceptance into the upscale canine community. A sampling of respectable names may include Sir William III of Normandy, Muffy Vandersnoot, Webster (Unabridged), or Precious. Extra points are awarded if your dog sports two hyphenated last names. And should you happen to live on golf course frontage, it's mandatory to name your priceless pooch using clever golf terminology such as Bogey, Birdie, Ace, or Bunker.

My drooling mutt of unspecified lineage, Snaggletooth, proudly sports his threadbare T-shirt, which boldly states the sorry truth: "What Happens on the Sidewalk, Stays on the Sidewalk." He's outlasted several owners and three presidents and exasperated countless veterinarians. He's now a wanted man after being issued numerous warrant-worthy demerits by our illustrious HOA.

Sadly, I believe I've stifled his creativity and stunted his status in the doggie community by saddling him with the moniker Snaggletooth. I dream of filing a name change on beaglezoom.com, followed by the purchase of a trendy studded collar, and Sons of Bitches leather jacket. I believe this courageous move would give him a new purpose, sending his social status and self-esteem soaring. In a perfect world, my reinvented dream dog, 3-Under-Par, would be booked solidly through the end of the year with doggie play dates.

When a lavishly embellished supplement spills from the newsletter, I curiously scoop it up from the floor. It's a colorful eye-catching insert sprayed with fine glitter. As I hold it up, the glitter rains onto my lap like fairy dust, and I want to beat the hell out of whoever thought this was a good idea. Perhaps this is a magical inhalant, meant to send people into a euphorically submissive state.

"Welcome to Stepford..." I say sardonically while rubbing glitter from my eyes.

Adding to the bravado of the season, the just of this annoying insert is to announce the annual holiday lighting contest. Some may be struggling, even in our magnificently well-resourced little hamlet. Still, nothing says frugality in hard times like adding hundreds of dollars to your power bill to out-illumine your neighbors. Despite the minor unpleasantness of a lasting economic downturn, the neighborhood pretense must go on!

The victors of last year's contest went to none other than Biff and Babs Bloomfield for their dazzling light and sound display, which emanated joie de vivre in our neighborhood and was visible on Google Earth. The winners were selected by their status at the country club, willingness to participate in all extracurricular activities, and their number of followers on social media. Never mind the piles of dog doo that besiege the sidewalks around their lovely home. Disregard the accumulation of playground equipment, inflatable toys, patio furniture, and outsized garden statues that overwhelm their property. Notwithstanding, the home itself is palatial, and the display is showy beyond compare. *We have a winner!*

Unsure if glitter is recyclable, and not wanting to commit an environmental faux pas, I pitch the sparkly supplement straight into the trash. I continue reading the rest of the newsletter while swilling cheap wine, which I'm finding is suitably paired with consuming mass quantities of bullshit.

Aha! I knew it! Rumors of clandestine activity have been confirmed. It seems that via secret ballot in an undisclosed location, the board has elected a Special Ops branch of the HOA. By filling a much-needed niche, they've officially deputized individuals as street captains. During the last meeting, when this idea was still in the embryonic stages, I'd asked what purpose a street captain serves. I was met with stares of disbelief and indignant huffs of outrage. Why, street captains, I was told, are to keep people informed of upcoming events, tattle on people when they need to be tattled on, and keep peace and tranquility in our lovely, unspoiled neighborhood.

For practical purposes, one street captain is designated for each street and has about as much authority as the UN. Longer streets may require more than one street captain. Say, those with seven homes instead of six. I fear that finding enough highly qualified, intrusive individuals to staff the streets must be a logistics nightmare! Though, I've been told ad nauseam, that this position is a *thankless job.*

To properly identify neighbors of authority, street captains have been authorized by the HOA to wear embroidered shirts and caps. Since street captain-wear is not readily available, they must be custom-made for our subdivision, the cost subsidized by raising our yearly dues. This attire is not considered inessential luxury items but needed accoutrements that are critical to our way of life. *Well, duh. Even I understand the concept of necessities!*

The rules regarding the new chain of command are clear: If you know of any good gossip or scandalous dealings, contact your street captain. Should your neighbor have a fallen branch in their yard, report them forthwith! They will in turn contact the board of directors and discuss whether the offender should be shunned or excluded from future neighborhood events.

Finally, by order of the HOA secretary and newsletter publication committee, we are given the following directive: *"Talk to your neighbors—it's fun!"*

And lucrative.

When one writes fiction, one must do a great deal of people-watching, harvesting behavioral quirks for character development. The acts I've witnessed from my elevated office are indefensible, and I intend to turn the tables on their intemperate ways. What was once considered leisurely walks through the neighborhood are now thorough Gestapo-quality marches initiated by team leaders as they enthusiastically search for violators of the covenants. Some walk the beat daily, zealously flushing out the villains among us. The out-of-control patrol unfailingly gives terse warnings and verbal citations peppered with public chants of humiliation. I've watched their little game for years and even I can't make this stuff up! If you consistently draw attention to yourselves by being overbearing prudes, then you're deserving of the fallout.

I enter the date and set a reminder on my laptop calendar to attend the next HOA meeting where I shall ask the following question: *Why does our community require weighty tomes of instructions to be good neighbors?* I also vow to drink an excessive amount of complimentary cocktails and linger as a one-woman heckler.

Chapter Seven

It's five a.m., and I am roused from blissful slumber by a familiar squawking sound emanating from my phone. Who else but Sharon, chattering insipid verbosities about an upcoming open house with a non-compliant client?

"This better be an emergency. Do you even care that you woke me up?"

"Listen, Ang, nobody sleeps anymore, so what makes you think you're special? I have real problems here and I need an ear to bend!"

"What is it this time?" I ask, bleary-eyed. "Lack of staged furnishings or failure to remove refrigerator magnets?"

"None of the above and much worse than even you can imagine. It's Buffy Van Zandt."

All one must do is mention the name Buffy Van Zandt and you will see even the most tolerant people scatter like spilled ball bearings. Buffy lives in my neighborhood and although I have learned her routine, it remains difficult to avoid her. I've tried walking the dog at different times throughout the day and evening when I'm sure she won't be out. Yet at any time between dawn and midnight, she magically appears clad completely in black spandex, deploying her refined power-walking technique.

When she's not toddling around on foot, she's dressed to the nines, driving aimlessly around the neighborhood, critically assessing our homes. Buffy opines endlessly on any subject and prattles on about the ghastly decline of property values. However, because she wears one of those tasteless cellular earpieces, one can never tell if she's talking to herself or ruining another poor soul's day.

Buffy's power-waddling amuses me, so I always employ a wave or upbeat *Hello!* when passing her on the street. She inevitably points to her trusty earpiece and glares in my direction, letting me know that I have interrupted a private conversation; a conversation that can be heard blocks away, but private, nonetheless. She then rambles off in another direction, erratically swatting at a stray gnat or fly while theatrically bloviating into the air.

Buffy embraces the don't-speak-unless-spoken-to mindset. Despite this, she will spontaneously divert from her planned route and cross the street to ambush me.

"What kind of dog is *that*? Curious little beast isn't he?" she says, staring down at Snags as if she's just seen him for the first time. During the ill-timed occasions when I've been caught in her web of gibberish, I want to wrap my hands around her neck and choke her. I conclude that I would be handsomely rewarded by way of plaque or prize for ridding the world of such an annoyance; yet the action would no doubt lead to incarceration. I'm on the verge of insolvency and may be homeless soon, but I don't intend for my next move to be the county jail. I've grown far too fond of my present amenities to let that happen.

Lying somewhere between wakefulness and sleep, Sharon purges her frustration. She's taken on Buffy as a client and must now endure her wrath.

"Have you seen her house? *Don't tell anybody I said this,*" she whispers. It looks like Liberace and Zsa Zsa Gabor gave birth to a decorator who threw up 6,000 square feet of garishness. For Christ's sake! We don't live in Vegas! How in the hell am I supposed to market that eyesore?"

I rub my eyes impatiently. "You boast that you can sell anything, so what do you want from me, Shar?"

"What I want, is for you to talk to Mrs. Van Zandt and explain that she needs to spend a little less time socializing at the club and more time following my suggestions on how to clean up that pigsty of hers."

"Isn't that what you pay your real estate coach for? Let him talk you through your bilious marketing quandaries. You've told me that I'm not a professional and couldn't possibly understand the complexity of the housing market."

Sharon hired a real estate coach to the tune of $2,000 a month for a half-hour consultation per week. She insisted that a professional coach would help boost her gross commission by providing her with invaluable information. So far, she's studied the lost art of standing erect while speaking on the phone, a proven method of sounding more confident. She once learned, as she put it, "How to Twitter," something she used to think was a dance routine. I suspect that a 280-character X post from Sharon would be cringeworthy, leaving clients confused by her disjointed compositions.

"My coach is helping me reach my monthly goals by increasing sales," she said. "Plus, I've learned more about social media and marketing than I ever cared to. Now, if I can only find someone competent enough to execute these neoteric suggestions."

"Did your coach also mention that you should try taking on a more modest persona? Or enroll in a self-improvement course? Maybe start by checking yourself into rehab and cease dressing like a skank?"

All I hear on the other end of the line is the weighted in-and-out breathing of a spoiled child pouting, demanding attention. As always, this has become a battle of the wills. If I wait it out, I'll never get any sleep.

For some reason, Sharon believes that her problems are also my problems. To hasten my return to a horizontal position, I quickly agree to the distasteful deed, though I have no intention of persuading Buffy to comply with Sharon's demands. My intended goal of avoiding the narcissistic old bag would be in vain. Sharon ends the conversation in her usual manner, with no closing salutation but rather a coarse "har-rumph" and disconnect. I go back to bed with the comforting thought that some other crisis will replace this one, knowing that the ever-selfish Sharon Bartelson will never remember having this conversation.

As soon as my head hits the pillow, I'm out, though not for long. Some schmuck is incessantly ringing the buzzer at the front gate.

Good grief, people! I have a boxed wine hangover and no reason to get up. I want to be depressed without interruption!

I reach over and log onto the bedside screen to view the front security footage. It's Darcy Danforth, and she's not giving up easily. Darcy has perfected her stalking skills, and for months, has been asking for updates for the HOA directory. All the neighbors, except one outlier, cooperatively fill out this yearly questionnaire.

Angela Morgan. The lone holdout. The one who prefers to remain anonymous. The one who wonders how such highly educated, successful lemmings made it this far without following one another off a cliff. Still, they disclose all personal information without question, then suffer nervous breakdowns when they realize that their information has been compromised.

I've tried explaining that disclosing delicate information is not smart—or safe. Yet I'm met with vacant expressions and told that the directory is only shared with other neighbors. I'm sorry, I don't know all my neighbors. I don't want other homeowners to have the number to my private line, cell number, and email addresses. Additionally, they immodestly ask for pet's names and ages, children's names and ages, and a variety of other private data. Truthfully, those privy to this com-prehensive directory are other neighbors, the HOA, the Bryn Mawr Country Club, Darcy's virtual assistant, and anyone else who requests a copy. I bet the creepy guy in the ice cream truck even has a directory!

I've told Darcy that I don't want my name nor my personal information listed, yet she persists as if I've never said a thing. I reach over to the intercom, press the button, and pretending I don't know who it is, give a cheerful, "Good Morning!"

"Oooh. Oooh. Hi there, Angela... I'm so glad I caught you at home!"

"Where the hell did you think you'd catch me?" I mumble under my breath.

Hearing her gasp confirmed that Darcy's audible range was far superior than I had imagined.

"Well, I'm sorry to be a bother but I did try to call. I must have transposed some digits because that last number you gave me doesn't work."

"For goodness' sake," I say sarcastically. "What number have you been calling?"

I hear paper rustling and stick my tongue out malevolently while watching Darcy on the security camera fumble through her leather planner. Everyone in the world has gone digital—except this one.

"...oh, here it is. I have 867-5309. The recording says it's a non-working number."

I hear Tommy Tutone belting out "Jenny" in my head. I imagine that in another time, a young Darcy was listed pruriently on many bathroom wall directories: *For a good time, call...*

"I'm so sorry Darcy. Silly me! I must have inadvertently given you my friend Joan Jett's cell number—it's one digit off from mine. The last digit of my number is 10."

I see her scribbling in her notebook.

"Joan? Joan Jett? Does she belong to the club? Do I know her?"

Knowing that Darcy would now obsess over the fact that I may be acquainted with someone that she's not, affords me the opportunity to interrupt.

"My cell's ringing. Must run! *Toodles!*"

By the time Darcy's virtual assistant types and publishes the new directory, I will have bought another year free from her questioning. I can't wait to see their faces when they realize that someone in the neighborhood has an eleven-digit phone number, and subsequently hiring a statistical analyst to determine how this is possible. *Fabulous!*

Throughout the afternoon, I receive three separate visits from women on the HOA social committee, repeatedly pushing the intercom button on the gate until I answer. They all ask the same thing: "Are you coming to the neighborhood social next month?" and "Will you bring a covered dish?" The answer to both questions is a resounding *No,* yet experience dictates that they won't give up easily.

A few years ago on Halloween, I dressed up as a Stepford Wife and met children at the door with a covered Corningware dish full of candy. Still, they don't understand that I'm making fun of them. Besides using the word *No,* I'm at a loss for creative ways to say that I'll never participate in their self-indulgent little soirees. I'm also at a loss on ways to demonstrate the fact that they're worthless individuals and I'd like to be left alone. I close and lock the gate and turn off my phone, the modern-day version of a cease-fire. If I had a moat, I'd fill it with water and release crocodiles for added assurance that I'll no longer receive uninvited guests.

I can see them now—the women of Bryn Mawr Country Club, passing out flyers featuring one of their own. An in-depth biographic history, complete with a glamorous professional headshot.

> *Have you seen this woman? Her name is Marisol. Mar-i-sol. Rhymes with parasol. Missing since she asked Angela Morgan to bring a covered dish. Last seen attempting to cross the moat at the Morgan residence. Please call with any information! Generous reward for*

*her safe return. BMCC Ma Jong Club is desperate to
locate her!*

I don't care to explain that even if I wanted to partake in their ridiculous event, I wouldn't have anything to put in a covered dish. I was subsisting on tomato sandwiches for a month until I ran out of tomatoes. And mayo. And bread. I've never had so many canker sores in my life! But it saw me through until I began stealing weekly staples. Before my Costco membership expired, I was eating samples for dinner. I'd promise the little ladies that I would purchase whatever product they were peddling, though I never did. I'd wander from station to station wolfing down samples and then look around for something to wash it down. On the days when they weren't handing out juices or coconut water, I'd hit the drinking fountain by the restrooms, hoping that my immune system would adequately protect me from whatever microorganisms lurked on the spout.

Some of the sample ladies would give me the fisheye during my evening hunger rampages, but only one hardboiled old broad questioned my motives.

"Hard times or tapeworm?" she asked drolly.

"Tapeworm," I said while shoving another sample cup of cheesy doodles in my mouth.

Even Snags is hungry. I give him a pat on the head and tell him he's a good boy. He looks up expectantly, employing his familiar begging technique which has taken years to perfect. He furls his brows, softens his eyes, and sits up, his front paws bent downward. He waits a reasonable amount of time and when that doesn't work, he closes his eyes and dramatically falls backward onto the floor, stiffly raising all four paws into the air. I give him credit for putting forth the effort, but I can't change the fact that there are no more daily treats to be dispensed. I'm sure he's wondering why he's being deprived of his doggie delicacies;

why his finely honed performances are no longer producing the desired effect.

They occasionally get bags of open or expired pet food at the food pantry where I volunteer one day a week. I've been sneaking small bags of dog food into my tote bag and feeding Snags this deficient fare for months. It's without nutrients and barely life-sustaining, but it's filling. Mostly Old Ray, or something comparable to eating cardboard or dirt, which I've seen Snags consume with regularity.

Kneeling on the floor, I give my faithful friend ear rubs assuring him that things will get better. He replies by emitting soft grunts, a sign that he is for now, blissfully content. One day, I hope to be able to give him those over-processed, chemically enhanced treats that he adores. The treats look like meat but are closer in molecular structure to plastic packaging than animal protein.

I hoof up the wide-reaching stairs to my office, knowing that Snags no longer has the strength nor the desire to tag along; though I can feel his puppy dog eyes following me. When I'm out of sight, he'll eventually pick a space and begin turning in circles before plopping down somewhere on the cold floor. Snags has a nice memory foam bed with cooling gel inserts but prefers the act of martyrdom, his tired bones hitting the hardwood with a thud.

Before continuing my writing assignment, I open the windows, letting in the calming effects of nature. The arched French windows frame a lovely morning, an image worthy of hanging in any upmarket gallery. The deep blue skies, radiant sunlight, and emerald green landscape are awash with color. A welcoming day that promises to be neither too hot nor too cold. It's days like this that can make you forget your problems, if only for a while.

I close my eyes, grateful for the warm sun on my face. Besides the added benefit of vitamin D, there's something about sunshine that lifts your spirits. Flocks of birds interject melodic affirmation, as they flit about rejoicing in song over this perfect day. If I wasn't worried about shattering glass or making Snags howl, I'd sing along with my feathered friends in exulted bliss.

As I slowly open my eyes, I see Phyllis Mallet backing out of her driveway. I've heard that her husband, Paul, is ailing. I've only caught sight of him from afar, a male caretaker pushing him around the court-yard in a wheelchair. Still, I see Phyllis coming and going at the same time each day without her husband. Out at nine, home by four.

She must be volunteering with some charity.

Phyllis doesn't speak to me often, but when she does, she brashly reveals too much information and is completely without filters. The first time we had a lengthy conversation was many years ago, the week they moved in. I'd taken over some freshly baked blueberry muffins and introduced myself. Phyllis returned the neighborly gesture by offering exhausting details of their personal lives.

"I married an old ca-ca. That's why you'll never see kids or pets over here. Wouldn't let me have 'em. And can you just imagine what a tight-wad he is? Paul is a shrink. Just opened a new practice here, the reason for the relo.

I'm his one-person office manager, accountant, cook, housekeeper, and slave. You'll only see one car over here because we only *have* one car. Dr. Paul says it's all we need since we go everywhere together or not at all. That fogyish windbag has me drive him around like his chauffeur and treats me like something stuck to the bottom of his geriatric loafers. But I'll wait it out—he's thirty years my senior..."

I tried to get a word in to excuse myself, my mind racing as I searched for reasons to bolt. But I was no match for Phyllis as her indelicate jabbering continued.

"Until we opened the psychiatry practice, I didn't know there were so many nutjobs around here. But let me tell you—it's profitable! Dr. Paul is already booked solid with appointments. We're going to make a mint off the hoity-toity wackadoodles of Bryn Mawr!"

I'd been taken captive. My tormentor's weapon—her mouth. I nodded and smiled, slowly walking backward while planning my getaway. Thank heavens I had the good sense to put the muffins in a disposable container that didn't require returning. I subtly thanked Phyllis for the visit, scurrying back across the street as she waved an arm yelling, "But you haven't told me anything about yourself!"

I wouldn't want Dr. Paul to be my psychiatrist, because it seems, it takes crazy to know crazy. I also have a feeling that patient confidentiality is a foreign concept with those two. But what truly surprised me was the thirty-year age difference. I didn't see that one coming, estimating Phyllis to be nearly as ripened as the good doctor. It must have been the short, tightly permed hair, elastic-waist polyester pants, and sensible, orthopedic shoes that Phyllis was sporting. Or the Pall Mall menthol cigarette hanging precariously from the side of her mouth as she puffed away, the butt stained with orangey-red lipstick. Perhaps it was merely the look in her cloudy eyes that screamed, *I just won at Canasta!* Instead, *I'm a prickly, chain-smoking, potty-mouth bigot who looks and acts decades older than I am!*

Whatever her story, that was the last time I reached out to a new neighbor and the last time I shared my muffins with anyone.

Chapter Eight

I get down to business and begin pecking away at another stack of Sharon's listings. The way people are selling off property, I'd say there was a mass exodus of wealth going on. Vacation homes aren't selling and many have ended up on the auction block, gobbled up by super lotto winners or overseas investors. A few, it seems, still have liquid assets; those who chose not to keep re-financing, using their primary residence as an ATM.

Who am I to talk? I've been known to juggle meager funds in a desperate bid to hold onto this place. Though, in comparison, many of the high-ticket addresses on the market today make my home look like an outhouse. The taxes alone must be a tremendous burden, not to mention the maintenance costs. Besides, one can only gloss over veneer so many times. Too many facelifts make these monstrosities look like they're trying too hard, causing them to lose their original appeal. Fleshy lips and a taut face on top of a wrinkly body is not a good look— even for a mansion.

However vulgar the super-rich may seem, I'm intrigued by one property in particular. Its architectural drawing is washed in pastel shades and appears to be a lavish hotel or castle in the country—like an enchanting nineteenth-century illustration from a children's story-book. Looking closely at the image, I imagine stepping onto the page.

I then read the included features sheet. It's not a hotel, but a private home. I wonder who might require a 22,000-square-foot residence. Included in the sale are six measly 3,000-square-foot cottages along with indoor and outdoor pools, an equestrian facility, basketball and tennis courts, and an underground shooting range. All are situated on a paltry 1,100 acres. *This isn't a primary residence, it's a time-share!*

There's only one line inscribed across the bottom of the drawing: *Prescott Estate.*

I decided that I'd like a closer peek at this one and will investigate further. Surely there must be something deliciously scandalous involved, and I could certainly use some fresh material for the novel that I'm supposed to be working on. A novel without a plot or characters. A blank screen without a beginning, middle, or end. I then called Sharon and asked if I might accompany her to whatever dirty deed she had in store for the homeowner.

"You're not using my clients as a character study, Ang! Go sit in a mall and people-watch or loiter in some dank coffee shop like other affected writers. Sorry honey hoo-ha, but the answer is *No!*"

I believe that A. A. Milne said it best: "If one is to be called a liar, one may as well make an effort to deserve the name."

Sharon doesn't hold the exclusive rights to lying, and I'm afraid she's grossly underestimated what I'm capable of when the curiosity gene kicks in. Possessing exemplary acting abilities from years of comingling with fictitious characters, I fling open my closet doors to search for my best realtor attire.

The field trip is on.

As I exit the interstate bound for a secluded country manor from an illustrated watercolor print, I see an array of red and blue flashing lights in my rearview mirror. An emergency vehicle is rapidly bearing down on me and I quickly pull over to let them pass.

When I realize that I'm the emergency, my heart inexplicably sinks into my stomach. A state trooper has pulled in behind my car and panic sets in. I'm sure that Sharon has found out what I'm up to and has sent law enforcement to intercept my devious plan. As the trooper walks to the driver's window I think of an excuse for whatever accusation will come. Obediently, I put my window down.

"Good morning, ma'am. Please turn off the ignition. License, registration, and proof of insurance, please."

I'm involuntarily shaking and stammering as I turn off the ignition and reach into the glovebox. "Yessir."

The officer is wearing one of those wide-brimmed trooper hats that scare the living daylights out of me. I find police uniforms in general to be attractive, but that hat. It adds an overshadowing flair to the mix, confirming that one is in deep doo-doo. I suppose that when uniforms were designed, top mob bosses were consulted from prison cells. They cut a deal to reduce their sentences if they assisted in the design process, coming up with crisp official uniforms and this intimidating Mountie hat.

"Come up with something scary," they told the convicts.

I picture a roomful of police officers expectantly waiting for the new uniform line to be revealed. Just before the muscle-bound men and women launch down the runway in uniforms weighted down with insignias, duty belts, and other crime-fighting gear, the top designer begins yelling at his assistant, Bugsy.

"Yoose gots it all wrong! Somethin' is missin'!"

"Hows abouts a big hat, boss?" Bugsy suggests cautiously.

The officer examines my license and looks me over several times. "Be right back," he says.

When he discovers what I've done, that'll be it. I was unable to renew my tags because of all the unpaid parking fines. When Sharon mentioned that the idiots at DMV couldn't get their shit together and inadvertently sent her two renewal stickers, I offered to straighten out that little matter for her. It was an opportunity to buy some time.

I also hocked the last piece of artwork that was worth anything to pay for a year's worth of car and homeowner's insurance. But the year went by quickly. My insurance expires at the end of the month and I have no idea how I'll pay for the next installment. For now, the auto insurance will have to wait. My property taxes must be satisfied or I'll lose the house.

That's it. I'm going to jail! I've seen this before on *Cops*. The officer will run my driver's license and plates and besides current offenses, will find something so secretive and perverse that even I didn't know about. I'll be asked to step out of the vehicle as he calls for cover. When a female officer arrives, she'll pat me down, searching for weapons and drugs. She will shake her head in the negative, then step to the side, waiting to assist if I become uncompliant. The arresting officer will then have me turn around while reciting my *Miranda* rights, tightly locking cold handcuffs around my delicate wrists.

As they lead me to the squad car by my elbows, passing cars will slow to gape at the spectacle, wondering what crime this well-dressed, affluent woman could be capable of. He will place his hand on the top of my head in the practiced manner of protecting my noggin from hitting the top of the door opening. Then I'll sit in the back of the cruiser, looking out longingly at the free world as they call to have my car towed away.

Before long, the officer is back at my open window.

"Do you know why I pulled you over?" he asks.

I can see my reflection in his sunglasses, my guilty face staring back at me.

"I... I... I'm not sure."

"You were speeding. Do you have any idea how fast you were going?"

"I... I... I don't know."

He bends down, looks around the inside of my car, and cocking his head to the side, nods at the dashboard.

"Well, someone who drives a car like this with a precision instrument panel *should* know how fast they're going. What's the rush, Slick?"

Why stop lying now?

"I'm going to meet a client. I wanted to make a good impression, but I was running late."

"Well, you're really going to be late now. You also have a turn signal going out and a load of unpaid parking fines."

I can feel the heat rising in my face.

"But I've never been in trouble with the law! I've tried to live my life well. My husband left me for the featured attraction at a strip club! He drained our bank accounts and left me with nothing. I'm doing the best I can! Am I a criminal for spying on Sharon's client? Is that a sin? So, now I'm going to jail and I have no one to blame but myself and I won't have anyone to contact for my one phone call and who's going to take care of my dog, and..."

The officer holds up his hand as if directing traffic.

"You're not going to jail. Besides parking tickets, you have a squeaky-clean record. It sounds as if you've gotten stuck on one of life's speedbumps—as we all will at one time or another. I'm writing you up for expired tags, which you'll need to take care of immediately. Pay your parking fines like a respectable citizen. I'm not even going to ask how the tag from a different vehicle managed to affix itself onto your plate. And get that right turn signal fixed as well. It's a good idea to let people know what your intentions are."

The officer hands me a written warning and gives me back my license, registration, and insurance card. He then bids me a good day and hastily walks back to his cruiser shaking his head, no doubt glad to be free of my blathering nonsense.

I'm so relieved that this officer is a real person, and I have a new-found respect for what law enforcement must endure every day. Like never knowing what they're in for when approaching a vehicle—a hard-ened criminal with nefarious intent, or a babbling idiot like me. At least they have protocol in place to deal with some degenerate or escaped convict. But there would be infinitely more paperwork to explain why he tased me.

"She wouldn't *shut up!*" he'd tell investigators.

"Case closed," they'd tell him while nodding their heads with tacit understanding.

Pulling onto the winding cobblestone road far from civilization, I enter a huge scrolled iron gate with an ornamental arched sign above: *Hidden Acres.* I drive for several miles before catching a glimpse of an imposing French château befitting royalty. Massive stones have been stacked and locked together, creating a masterpiece that will likely remain standing for centuries. The picture doesn't do this place justice.

I've lived in this community for years and had no idea that this place existed. I'm surprised that I can easily meander upon private property and effortlessly interlope onto a sequestered compound. Someone went to great expense to ensure that no one visited often, yet I can't believe how easy it was to gain access. Then I see the plethora of security cam-eras on the home, driveway, trees, and outbuildings, following my every move. They have most likely already recorded the make and model of my car, taken stills of my license plate, and performed retinal eye scans as I gaped out the windshield at the gorgeous grounds.

I straighten in my seat and put on my best fake realtor face. Emulating Shar, I have on an indecent amount of lip liner and gloss and have penciled in my eyebrows to arch in a perpetually surprised fashion. I exit my vehicle and confidently begin smartening my disguise and smoothing my suit skirt when I hear a man yelling in the distance.

I look in the direction of the commotion and see what appears to be a cross between Popeye and Willie Nelson, kicking dirt high in the air and cussing up a storm. I'm studying the man intently, capturing and storing peculiarities and quirks to memory, incorporating them into future characters.

The man doesn't seem to notice me, though whenever I glance in his direction, he stops whatever he's doing. I look away and sure enough, the madness resumes. With a rake in his gnarled hands, the man repeatedly strikes something on the ground in a combative fashion. I try to imagine what's causing him so much distress but the thought is interrupted by a deeply soothing voice.

"When you're finished primping and analyzing Wilson over there," jutting his chin upward, pointing in the direction of the crazed man, "perhaps I can entice you to come inside. Or would you prefer watching the irrational actions of a mean-spirited eccentric?"

"Oh, I believe I'd like to come inside. Sorry for the intrusion, I'm ..."

"You are Ms. Bartelson, correct?"

Uh, oh.

"That's correct! But, how did you know?"

"We don't get many visitors out this way. Well, none actually. I've already e-signed all the documents, and according to your assistant, you would not need to make a personal visit. Be that as it may, I'm glad you're here. I'm Randolph Prescott, though you already know that."

Randolph Prescott? You've got to be kidding! I must have accidentally wandered onto the set of a soap opera!

Oh, boy. I'm beginning to regret my impulsiveness. I should have studied real estate phraseology! What do I say during an unrehearsed meeting with a homeowner? I vigorously shake his hand like a seasoned politician running for reelection.

"Pleased to finally meet you, Mr. Prescott. I'm not accustomed to just dropping by unannounced, but your listing so intrigued me. I wanted to get started on preparations while capturing the true persona of the property."

The true persona of the property? I sound so amateurish! I need to think about what Sharon might do in such an awkward situation. Then, remembering what she's capable of, and not willing to have casual sex with a total stranger, I decide to continue with my own ad hoc narrative.

"Your home is lovely," I tell him.

"It's my great-uncle's home. But thank you. May I get you anything? A cup of tea? Coffee perhaps?" queries my considerate host.

With an estate this size, I wonder where the servants are. Who is answering doors and pushing around carts with warm scones and midday tea?

"No thank you. I don't want to take up too much of your time, especially since I've already intruded."

"Our attorneys typically handle all transactions as I find the invasion of privacy combined with the negotiating process to be boorishly offensive. Uncle Wilson refers to lawyers and realtors as land sharks, and it would only upset him more to know they are involved with this process. Though I must say, in this instance, it's a refreshing change to deal with someone in the real estate industry with such obvious decorum. Judging by your reputation, I'd expected someone quite different."

I was beginning to wonder if Mr. Randolph Prescott knew that I was a fraud. Surely, he'd seen Sharon's outdated photos throughout the city and could see that I looked nothing like her. I was also concerned that he may recognize me. Though, after meeting him, I'm quite sure that he has no idea who I am. He's certainly not the type who would read my lurid creations.

"I'm here just long enough to negotiate the sale of my uncle's estate. He doesn't want to sell, but I'm afraid we must. He's never been much for conversation, but I believe he may be dementing. Sad, really. The old chap has lived an extraordinary life."

Randolph Prescott is certainly easy on the eyes and the added lilt of a deep British accent makes him even more charming.

"Would you like to start with a tour of the grounds? Or do you prefer starting with the home itself?"

A tour? I had no idea it would be this easy.

He probably wants to lure me into a secret passageway so he can murder me, leaving my body underground to quietly desiccate. It's conceivable that he will enlist Wilson to assist in a burial deep in the woods. Wild animals will timidly pace over my shallow grave, curious of the smell emanating from disturbed earth. Randolph Prescott appears harmless, but Wilson looks like he's quite capable and perhaps experienced in concealment of the dearly departed.

"You choose," I sigh softly, benumbed to the fact that I'm probably a goner.

"Well, we're already inside, so let's begin here, shall we?"

The interior sightseeing expedition required more time to complete than I anticipated. After five hours, we'd not even toured all of the main residence, let alone the cottages and the grounds. The larger guest homes on the outskirts of the property house caretakers, housekeeping staff, and equestrian trainers. I'm reminded that an added stipulation to the sale is that all employees retain custodial status of their jobs and living arrangements.

I thought this would just be a sneaky preview into the lives of strangers. Something naughty. Something sinful and licentious. Done and over with. But I'm not even close to finding anything scandalous to write about, and we agree to resume the tour in the morning. I find the company as fascinating as the home itself and I'm looking forward to more of Mr. Prescott's witty anecdotes. I'd also like to learn Wilson's backstory. Perhaps there will be something of significance there.

I noticed Sharon has called numerous times. Not wanting to seem unprofessional or uninterested by continually checking my phone, I turn it off. If Shar knew what I was doing, she'd snatch me baldheaded. And that would just be the appetizer. Being murdered here might not necessarily be a bad thing, because at least it would be quick. Sharon's punishment will be painful and everlasting.

When I arrive home, Shar's car is in the driveway. She had let herself in and was waiting for me in the kitchen. I take a deep breath, hold my head high, and march inward, unaware of what I may be walking into.

"Well...look what the cat dragged in..." says Sharon snarkily. "Where have you been dressed like that? Good Lord! Are you looking for a *job*?"

"I had a lunch date," I say guiltily.

"A date. In a suit?

Sharon is laughing hysterically. She sounds like a hyena or a braying donkey. Even Snags, the crudest dog in the world, is staring at her through thickly outlined beagle eyes as if she's the biggest jackass he's ever seen. I nonchalantly slip off my heels, uncomfortably aware that my feet are not accustomed to such torture. I stare blandly at my friend, waiting for the laughing to cease and my pinched toes to unfurl.

"You may think you know everything about me, but you don't. And there are some things that are absolutely none of your concern," I state contrarily.

Poised for action, Sharon has begun her skillful interrogation technique. She has the ability to raise one eyebrow, which has always intimidated the hell out of me. Knowing this, she uses it to coerce me into telling her everything.

"Put the eyebrow away, Sharon. It's not working this time."

"I only want to know who he is. Did you take my advice and find yourself a sugar daddy?"

I become incredulous at the thought and involuntarily snort.

"Are you kidding me? At my age, exactly how old would a sugar daddy have to be? Well, Shar, thanks for stopping by. Always a pleasure to be criticized by a wholesome, upstanding individual. Now, may I see you to the door and call you a cab?"

"A cab? No! You know I have my car..."

"I meant CAB, you crazy ass bitch."

"I've been calling and texting you all day. I just want an explanation as to where you've been, that's all. You know you're supposed to be reworking my listings. Here's the scoop: unless you can perform magic and revive your career, you're a nobody right now. We have a deal. And in my case, time is money!"

I stare without flinching at one of the most self-centered individuals I've ever met. I take a deep cleansing breath and dogmatically pronounce, "Why bother with an eloquent explanation when a simple *fuck you* will do?" And with that, I slam the door in Sharon Bartelson's startled face.

Chapter Nine

The initial viewing of the Prescott Estate was only a starter. There's a rich history here and it's impossible to see everything in a couple of days. Undoubtedly, there is much more to this house than four walls and a floor and more to the inhabitants than an aged oddball and his fine-looking nephew.

Over the course of the following week, I'd met with Randolph Prescott many times to go over the property. Our talks were multifaceted as we candidly discussed the human condition. I learned that he'd just arrived from the UK, having recently accepted the appointment of conservatorship for his great-uncle Wilson. The sprawling country estate is to be sold, and Wilson, not being of sound mind nor body, will be moved to more manageable accommodations.

Randolph and I strolled through the estate sharing stories, most of which were unrelated to marketing this property. I wish I were writing historical fiction, for this family is a boon of information! Even though the Prescott men are not titled aristocracy, they are perhaps, landed gentry from a privileged class. Uncle Wilson is Randolph's only surviving relative and is the black sheep of the family, finding more in common with the unpretentious Cornish people than his peers of the realm.

Today, as we wander through the estate, each room stretches into the next as if extending a silent invitation. We regard the unusual appointments assembled in this residential museum, ceilings soaring thirty feet above our heads. The ceilings stand out prominently as works of art with hammered copper stiacciato reliefs bordering the perimeter; the rooms are crammed with ancient relics and antique novelties as far as the eye can see. Old World meets new, uniting artifacts and personal treasures from faraway lands.

"Packed to the gunwales..." says Randolph, acceptingly.

We walk the length of a wide hallway and turn several corners until we come upon a long, narrow room at the end. A chapel. I feel as though I'm intruding as we step into this consecrated space. My eyes scan the plaster walls, every inch covered in apostolic frescoes, the quality equaling any in the Sistine Chapel.

Feeling the sanctity of this private sanctuary, we slowly make our way to the altar. Rows of glowing candles reflect light as it dances across gilded statuettes. Randolph stops suddenly as if an imaginary line is drawn across the aisle. He does not advance to the altar but genuflects and bows his head. Out of respect, I do the same, remaining by his side between rows of pews draped in black bunting.

When we rise, I see two single red roses and two framed photos centered on the altar. From this distance, I can't make out the people in the photos, so my eyes lift upward to a flawless marble statue of Jesus framed by a backlit wall of stained glass. Jesus presides over the shrine that spans the length of the altar, His arms spread in sad resignation, a single glass tear trailing from His eye.

I know that I'm unworthy and shouldn't be here, especially after entering this private domain on false pretenses. I don't know what to do, so I stand motionless, clasp my hands, and bow my head in silent prayer. When Randolph turns to leave, I docilely follow.

I have many conflicting feelings, but mostly I feel honored to be permitted in this hallowed space. There is a certain sadness here, but also a feeling of great love. For a moment, I feel the pull of surrender and struggle against the emotion.

Oh, no you don't. I'm in control here!

It's been years since I've stepped foot in a church. I wouldn't know where to go or even how to pray anymore. I was surprised when the expected lightning bolt didn't thunder down into my lying self. Plus, as hungry as I've been lately, I do know that I wouldn't bother with the Catholic Church and their stupid communion wafers. *Cheapskates!* I would side with the Protestants for both the spiritual union and the leavened bread. *Give us this day, our daily bread...* No one mentioned thin wafers!

The Prescott Estate looks like a mini-Chatsworth, complete with gravity-fed fountains and extensive gardens. I wonder if Wilson borrowed some of the concepts from the grand castle when building this home.

Randolph offered snippets of information along the way. "To retain his wealth, Wilson sold off properties and renounced his British citizenship. As high as income and property tax is here in the States, Great Britain is worse, taxing every spigot, chimney, and pebble in one's driveway."

As housekeepers mill about in the background, I watch as they capably dust and vacuum, plumping pillows and fussing over the minutiae of placement. I can only imagine how tedious the task can be, moving and dusting every inch of every room and every intricate object. By the time they reach the end of the house, it's time to start all over again. Clean, clean, clean, repeat.

I wonder if the housekeeping staff ever breaks things, and if so, with all these bits and bobs, would anyone even know? Do they tell someone or discreetly sneak it into the trash bin?

Oops! Oh, well. Sir Wilson will never miss this old woolly mammoth tooth...

Besides the phenomenal architecture, it's difficult to concentrate on any one thing. My eyes wander to each oddity during a tour that has left me surprisingly speechless. There's a collection of hundreds of masterfully carved fertility masks from the former Belgian Congo and the largest private military arms collection that I've ever seen. Groupings of heartwarming photographs over a hundred years old depict Aboriginal people in their native land, each photo with a story to tell.

In contrast to the sepia-toned portraits in this room, the walls of an adjoining parlor are whimsically decorated with framed butterfly montages of every size, shape, and color. As one hallway unfolds into another, every inch of wall space is smattered with pastiches of artwork by the masters. Matisse, Rembrandt, Degas, Monet.

"Your uncle certainly has an extensive variety of replicas," I exclaim prematurely.

"Oh that," states Randall wryly, "Yes, some are close facsimiles, and others are originals. It takes a trained eye to tell the difference."

I am dumbfounded by Mr. Prescott's nonchalant attitude as if everyone could afford to hang works of fine art among flea market finds. I begin examining each curiosity with reverence.

Mysteriously, with all this space, Wilson spends most of his time confined to a small bedroom on the uppermost level, outdoors tending to a flock of free-range chickens, or raking one stubborn leaf that has left him no choice but a declaration of war. Occasionally, Wilson wordlessly follows us through the house, peering around corners from a distance to see what we're doing. Just as quietly he slips away, only to reappear later in the day. Seemingly aware of my thoughts, Randolph places a hand on my shoulder which instantly puts me at ease.

"Uncle Wilson is not a danger. He simply does not associate well with people."

This, it seems, is a quintessential understatement.

"When I was a young lad, I remember hearing stories of my great-uncle. He was quite the jovial chap, so full of life and always mingling with large groups of people. The life of the party, he was."

"So, what happened? If I'm not being too intrusive…"

"Wilson went to war and came home completely unscathed. Unfortunately, his wife and child did not. They died in a car accident on the way to welcome him home. He's never been the same since."

"Jesus…" I mutter softly. "That's tragic."

"Wilson threw himself into his work. He did very well for himself as you can see. He also used to be quite the accomplished horseman but has lost interest in that as well. He never remarried and came to the States to live out his life as a recluse here on this land. Slowing down was not an option, as it leaves one time to think about the past. And for Uncle Wilson, the past is just too painful a reminder."

We conclude our meeting with a meaningful handshake and I leave feeling humiliated for having deceived this man and his uncle. I will tell Randolph the truth tomorrow when we meet to continue the tour. I owe him that much.

When I enter my home, I notice a glaring variance between the Prescott Estate and the Morgan shack: proper lighting. To save on electricity, I use several jar candles to illuminate whatever room I'm in, carrying them with me throughout the house. I efficiently extinguish each one at bedtime and wonder if I'm actually saving money by doing this. Perfumed candles generally make me nauseous, but that's what I have. I've squirreled away boxes of these putrid-smelling candles; rejected hostess gifts or event swag bags, shoved to the back of closets never to be seen, or smelled, again.

Or so I'd hoped.

I light a blue three-wick candle called Ocean Breeze and immediately feel seasick. It has a label showing a sandy beach and seashells, but it smells nothing like the ocean. *False advertising!* If anything, it reeks of chum from an old fishing vessel. With time, the smell may dissipate or I'll get used to it. Unfortunately, that doesn't happen.

To conserve energy, I've also turned off the breaker for the outdoor accent lights, which formerly illuminated the house like the New York skyline. If anyone asks why my home is so dark, I'll tell them the truth: I'm having electrical issues.

Yeah, I'm having electrical issues. I can't pay my power bill!

As I go about the humdrum task of meal preparation with my appetite-reducing candle in tow, I lean back on the kitchen counter waiting for the small pan of water to come to a boil. My grandmother used to say, *a watched pot never boils,* an axiom that I never really understood until I was older.

Have patience, give it time...

As all I seem to have is time, I will not stare at the pan on the cooktop and will act surprised when the water finally comes to a rolling boil. I retrieve the box of mac and cheese and turn it over to read the ingredients. This is a bad idea. There's absolutely no nutritional value in starch and powdered cheese. I thought it was a complete meal, but I see that the instructions call for milk and butter, neither of which I have. There are options for substitution, but when I open the fridge, there is only a half jar of sweet gherkins and a can of diet soda.

Water it is!

Still waiting for the water to boil, I sort through the cans in my otherwise bare kitchen pantry—meal planning for the week. This should see me through until next Wednesday when I return to the food pantry. I justify stealing donations by only taking what they have the most of: cans of chili beans, tuna, over-processed vegetables, and boxes of mac and cheese.

After I added the elbow macaroni to the boiling water, I reduced the heat and set the timer. I've never seen such minuscule pasta! As I stir, a rising starchy steam releases from the bubbles. I begin to fantasize about all the kinds of pasta; how each is delectably paired with a creamy sauce.

This carton of macaroni does not swell up like the pasta that I'm accustomed to, and I doubt it will taste the same. The timer goes off, but the macaroni is still hard, and there is nothing al dente about this. Yes, it should be firm to the bite, but I don't want to lose a tooth! I increase the heat just a touch and continue to stir.

While I wait, I say aloud all the pasta that I can remember: *tortellini, pipette rigate, casarecce, fusilli, penne, fettuccine, lasagna, campanelle, rigatoni, gemelli, linguine, orecchiette, ravioli, cavatapi, vermicelli, manicotti, gigli, cavatelli, spaghetti...*

The extra cooking did nothing to improve the texture of the macaroni, so I drained half the water and poured the pasta back into the pan with the powdered cheese. Making a last-minute decision to splurge, I open a can of creamed corn, to add a certain sweetness to an otherwise bland meal. I feel the need to name this newly discovered dish. I dub thee *Mac crème de la crème de la corn.*

I wish I had some fresh veggies to turn this into a well-balanced meal. What I wouldn't give for an artichoke or any vegetable wrapped in bacon. Or asparagus with hollandaise. I'd even settle for roasted corn on the cob!

In the summer months, people unload their leftover zucchini, tomatoes, and bug-infested corn at the food pantry. I'm sure they hope that someone can use it, though much of it sits untouched, or is jettisoned into a compost pile or dumpster. And since most folks lock their cars these days, there is little room for inventive ways to unburden oneself of unwanted produce.

Even though fresh produce is a luxury item, most clients at the food pantry still bypass it for the expediency of a box or can, seeking meals that are fast and easy. The Hamburger Helper is always the first to go, but apparently, one must also have hamburger to make it a meal. I've never tried this dish, because I don't have any hamburger or the required box of helper.

I can see why people just want uncomplicated food. When I think about how depressing it is to eat alone, mealtime becomes just another mechanical function to sustain life. When I wasn't spending every cent maintaining this house, I still had money for nourishing meals. Now, I have only this white albatross hanging from my neck, my penance for not paying attention to what was going on.

I take my plate to the foyer and sit down on the stairs to eat. My dinner partner is velcroed to my leg concentrating with all his might, willing food to fall to the floor. I briefly succumb to his persuasive soliciting and give him a bite of mac and cheese from my fork. I figure that sharing utensils with His Royal Nastiness is better than losing a finger.

I wonder what fripperies the Prescott men are enjoying this evening. I bet they aren't sitting on the stairs, hunched over a paper plate full of gruel. Are they lingering over a palatable meal that is not boxed macaroni and cheese? Is their dutiful cook, Felecia, serving them after-dinner aperitifs on a silver tray? Is there someone who turns down their bedding in the evening, leaving mouth-watering chocolate mints on their pillows?

Oh, no. Why did I have to think about chocolate?

Chocolate.

I need chocolate.

I need chocolate, now!

The thing is, once the thought of chocolate is planted in a woman's mind, it fuses itself with every thought and every molecule of her being until the craving is satisfied. Months ago, during a hormonal uprising, my stomach was held hostage by my ovaries as they demanded a chocolate fix. I caved to their demands and ransacked the house, gorging on anything sweet. I'd already wolfed down the semi-sweet morsels and even the unsweetened bars of baking chocolate and chocolate sprinkles. Then, in a moment of embarrassing desperation, I ate a box of chocolate cake mix—with a serving spoon. I could have mixed it with water, but there wasn't time! As I coughed my way through the entire box,

I wondered why there wasn't a warning on the package: *Please do not consume dry mix. If you're stupid enough to do so, please don't inhale. You will choke and die.*

Even though I've looked many times, I turn the knob on the pantry door and gingerly turn on the light, peering inside. If there is chocolate in there, I don't want to scare it away. There's nothing in plain view but empty shelf space and a small quantity of canned goods. There could be a stray candy bar, an old piece of Halloween candy, or even a concealed thin mint just waiting to be found. I stand on the tips of my toes to reach the high shelves while running my hands back and forth. When I pull my hand back, I am bathed in dust and crumbs.

I shake the dust from my hair and grab my purse, frenetically emptying the contents onto the counter. I decided that even if it isn't chocolate, and even if the wrapper is missing and the candy is caked with lint, I shall eat it anyway.

Nothing.

I look in my car, go through every cabinet, every closet and drawer, panic-stricken, knowing that I should have rationed the chocolate. But everyone knows that if you have a vagina, rationing chocolate is an impossible and unreasonable probability. Having worn myself out on the chocolate campaign, I ultimately give up and head upstairs with my foul-smelling candle. I blow it out and climb into bed.

I'm pretty sure that I'm getting ready to start my period, given the cramps, fatigue, and irrational cravings. The random crying is always a dead giveaway. When I still had medical insurance, my doctor told me that I should be done with this nonsense soon. He placed me neatly into a category, calling me peri-menopausal, and then asked if I'd like a prescription for anti-depressants. Then he and his man-parts sent me on my way with a load of drugs and a pamphlet explaining all about changes to the female anatomy.

When I had a comfortable income, I never considered how much more it cost to be a woman. The overinflated price of feminine hygiene products is just not right. When you have indoor plumbing, there's just more to maintain. Baby girl is born, wears diapers, then plugs and pads, and eventually is back to diapers. Really, we girls are high maintenance without even trying.

Before becoming a poor hermit, I used to perform peacock-quality preening rituals each night before bed. I removed makeup and gently washed my face, then commenced slathering myself in the finest skin care products: wrinkle removers, firming night creams, eye creams, lip balms, neck and décolleté creams, hand creams, balms, body lotions, ointments, salves, emulsions, all supposedly guaranteed to make you look years younger.

After the moisturizing routine, I would brush my hair, touch up my nails, pluck and trim, primp and powder, and voilà! Ready to choose from any number of salacious negligees and risqué lingerie. A process that took approximately two hours.

Now, getting ready for bed takes much less time and effort. I pull my hair into a high ponytail and scrub my face with a washcloth using a small bar of hotel soap that makes my skin desiccated and puckered like dried egg whites. Then I grab what's left of my exclusive Staybridge Suites collection and slather my face with body lotion. I run a toothbrush over my teeth, throw on an old T-shirt, and if I'm feeling super special, a clean pair of panties. Then I leap into bed and pray for sleep.

As easy as my new routine is, tonight has become a *fuck-it-all* night. I climb into bed with an unwashed face and my clothes on, curl into a tight ball, and fall asleep quickly.

I'm reclining on a teak beach chair at a tropical seaside resort, sipping a fruity alcoholic beverage with chunks of fresh pineapple speared on tiny neon umbrellas atop a frosted glass. I can feel the brightness of the sun baking down on my perfectly tanned body as I lay in scanty white bikini bottoms—no top. My butt and thighs are extraordinarily firm and my breasts are standing at attention, which makes me suspect. *This must be a dream.*

I hear an annoying buzzing, like a mosquito oscillating close to my ear. I keep swatting at my head, but the buzzing continues. Realizing that the sound is my phone and the pest is likely Sharon, I drowsily reach over, pull my cell from the nightstand drawer, and power it down completely. If I didn't turn off my phone and put it in the charging drawer at night, I'd never get any sleep. Sharon has no concept of time, and I wonder if Vampiress of the Night ever sleeps, noting the times of her scalding voice messages and texts, persecuting me for not answering immediately.

Sharon has become enraged that she no longer influences me. I'm tired of her monitoring my every move and telling me how to live my life. As I've begun to pull away from this top-heavy broad with the sketchy background and pushy attitude, I begin to feel better. Except the more I ignore Shar, the angrier she becomes. This time, I'm the one who's pissed off. Not only did she wake me, but she's ruined an enjoyable fantasy as well.

I close my eyes and flip to my back. Then to my side, stomach, side, and back again, trying to continue my semi-nude beach dream. *Nothing.* I try re-lighting the Ocean Breeze candle but that only makes me queasy. Not only was I unable to continue my dream, I was unable to dream at all. It took forever to fall back asleep and I feel like I've slept with my eyes open. They feel gritty, as if someone kicked sand in them; undoubtedly the psychosomatic side effect of beach dreaming.

I kick off the covers and sit up, swinging my legs over the side of the bed. My hair hangs knotted in front of my face as I push off the bed and stand, wondering how I'll make it through the day.

Chapter Ten

I'm meeting Randolph again this morning, so I hope that lack of sleep and sand-filled eyes have not left telltale signs of dark circles and puffiness. I reach up and lightly knead the area around my eyes with my fingertips, checking for inflammation. With my luck, this is also the day when a monstrous zit or fast-growing wart appears on the end of my nose; the kind of prominent nodule that you try for hours to eradicate, but everything you do only makes it worse. And larger. And angrier. And more conspicuous.

I continue my sightless examination, running my fingers across every inch of my face and neck with relief. Nothing. No puffy eyes, pimples, or gangrenous abscesses. Bolstered by the fact that this will be a goiter-free day, I feel victorious and shuffle to the end of the bed to retrieve my robe.

I power up my phone and check for messages with the exuberance of a teenage girl waiting for her boyfriend to call. I scroll through dozens of snappish messages from Sharon. I don't bother reading any of them because they're always the same. They all begin with, "I want..."

My heart swells when I see that Randolph sent a text with explicit instructions to dress down for the conclusion of today's tour, which I surmise will be outdoors. I asked Randolph to not call my (Sharon's) office but to exclusively use my cell for all future communication. I'm both thrilled and frightened. I'm so far into this lie with no easy way out.

It wasn't difficult to find something old and casual from my now limited wardrobe. I choose a worn pair of form-flattering jeans, a signature black turtleneck (*signature, as that's all I have that's clean!*), and a russet tweed jacket with suede elbow patches. I pull on my only pair of high boots and look in the mirror. I appear to be preparing for a fox hunt through the lush English countryside. I hope that the outdoor tour won't require more than one day because Randolph Prescott may be seeing me in a repeat of today's attire.

The day couldn't be more perfect, an invigorating chill fills the air as clear skies escort rays of bright sunlight through the tree-lined canopies. I've always been in a hurry to get from point A to B, driving as if I'm pushing other cars out of the way. I can't recall a time when I've taken a leisurely drive anywhere, or paid attention to the changing seasons.

For an early weekday morning, this twisting backroad is eerily deserted, empty of morning commuters who prefer a faster, more direct route to work. Cruising with intent toward Hidden Acres, I slow to watch a skein of geese circle, then land heavily on a large lake, their arrival generating a wake that has roused a paddling of ducks as they bob and sway in the water. I pull over onto the dirt shoulder, turn off the ignition, and walk across the road to get a closer look. I'm certain that Randolph will understand when I tell him why I'm late.

I climb to the top of a rocky ledge to get a better view. Balancing on my newly conquered hillock, I hold up a hand, shielding my eyes from brilliant sunshine reflecting off the water. My eyes then drift down and across the shoreline, settling on a protected cove where gangly groups of birds sport feathered comb-overs. My mother would have pointed and exclaimed, "Look! A sedge of cranes!" I feel as though she's here with me as the graceful, long-legged cranes take calculated steps, feeding at the water's edge, the splash landing of their corpulent comrades barely garnering attention.

I observe colorful hordes of segregated waterfowl on the adjacent shore and stream, basking in the sun. I feel as though I've gone to another part of the country entirely, for I never knew we had such prolific wildlife in the area. I also feel as though I've had my head buried in my small world. What exactly have I wasted my time doing? Along with the rest of the herd, I'm always looking down texting, scrolling social media; computers, phones, and navigation systems telling me what to do, where to go, and how to get there. Now I'm looking up and around, a newborn blinking in the bright light.

Scanning the shore, I spot some freshwater fowl that I've never seen before. Included in this surprise assemblage is a flock of birds with gorgeous iridescent cinnamon heads. My mother would know what they are. I stand very still, my eyes rolling upward, waiting for her voice to pop into my head and tell me. When she doesn't answer, I continue studying the captivating fowl. Their bodies appear to be wearing black business suits of feathers, rafting through the reedy lakeside in unison, and they're all speaking at once. I imagine they're late for a board meeting where they will review corporate policies, yielding the floor to elders whose judicious wisdom will send them to their feet, clapping enthusiastically with tiny wings. I'll have to ask Randolph what they are as I've never seen such an unusual species.

My dear mother was the birder of the family and a passionate environmentalist. She was an observer of nature and I wish I'd paid more attention when she eagerly attempted to share her love and knowledge of wildlife. In my teen years, I dismissed her excitement as a silly pastime brought about by boredom—or age. I was more interested in my clothes, hair, and makeup than the great outdoors. If she could see me now, struggling to pull myself together, she would say with motherly sarcasm, "Well now, Angela dear, look at you! All that attention to your hair and clothes really paid off, huh?"

Maybe we spend the first part of life being self-centered. Maybe it's that humans are incapable of taking an interest in anything or anyone until we come into our own. Maybe we must lose things to find things. Maybe only then are we able to weed out the superfluous noise and really listen to that inner voice, realizing what's truly important.

Regretfully, I've somehow lost my true self during this shit-storm called life. The old me would have been ashamed to admit this, but I suddenly find looking at birds to be an uplifting, almost spiritual experience. I allow myself to surrender to mindfulness, wondering if this may be the beginning of a transformative rebirth, looking at the world with a fresh set of eyes. I feel relaxed, without the help of Xanax or Prozac, or copious amounts of alcohol, all of which I've run out of.

Feeling refreshed from my unplanned nature walk, I pull up to Hidden Acres and park. Randolph meets me in the driveway and in a magnanimous gesture, opens my car door. As I exit my vehicle, we both begin to chuckle. We are comically wearing similar outfits, right down to the hues and fabric.

"We're Twinkies!" I say as Randolph shoots me a perplexed look.

"It's an American idiotism for twins," I explain.

"Well then, Twinkie, shall we?"

I feel like a dog, straining at the leash, excitedly pulling my handler along as we motor about the property in a side-by-side, stopping at each building along the way.

The ride is punishing as we bounce along service roads, a grass peninsula growing between worn dirt tracks. I think that a sports bra would have been a better choice because the lacy number I have on just isn't doing its job.

"My apologies for the jostling ride!" he says. "This buggy is a real boneshaker!"

The tour takes us through cavernous stables and barns, each offering top-rate lodging for Wilson's equine family. We continue unhurried strolls through elaborate five-star compartments where expectant mares are pampered and groomed, their swollen bellies causing them to shift uncomfortably from one hoof to another. Each mare has a skilled attendant, ever ready to assist with labor and delivery.

"The maternity ward," Randolph clarifies as if there was any doubt.

"Pregnant mares and pregnant women scare me," he shares for no apparent reason. "Wilson is the one who should be giving this portion of the tour. It is he who has made this facility so grand."

We continue through the maternity ward and onward to the foaling rooms, where new arrivals totter close to mom on wobbly legs. The shine of the foals' dark coats resembles the smooth Breyer horses that I played with as a child. Lining them up on the window ledge in my bedroom, I'd pretended they were real horses. Though plastic and unbending, they were real to me. Each had a name and each was special. My favorite was Misty. I wish I still had her, but at least I still have the book, *Misty of Chincoteague*, one remembrance from my childhood that I'm glad I held onto.

I'd spend hours inventing adventures for Misty and me, as we galloped through the countryside, riding bareback through mountains and streams. The entirety of my horsemanship skills, all rolled into a child's imagination.

"Do you ride?" Randolph asks as if reading my mind.

"I'd always wanted to, but sadly, I do not."

"That's a shame," he says. "Perhaps we can change that. It's never too late to learn."

The utility vehicle jerks to a start and we're off to the male-dominated building far from the mares and foals. "Gentlemen's quarters," says Randolph coyly.

A heavy musk envelops the air as we pass by stalls of muscular stallions that nicker and snort, pawing at the paddocks in testosterone-induced frustration.

The equestrian managers join the tour and interact with Randolph in a comfortable raillery. He is sociable and generous and speaks to them as his contemporaries, asking with genuine concern how they're doing, and listening intently as they speak. Randolph exposes his calm, unhurried demeanor, as the personnel light up with excitement and delight in sharing the genesis of the compound. I nod and feign interest in the particulars of this impressive equestrian facility, though I concede not to know a thing about horses.

Randolph's playful elocution is mesmerizing and I could listen to the charismatic sound of his voice all day. His proper English is poetic and I dare say that the good chap might even make the intonation of *fuck off* sound articulate. I catch myself smiling at nothing in particular and realize that I must look like an adolescent girl staring dreamily at a photo of her first crush.

We conclude the tour through vast storage facilities and finally visit the climate-controlled garage which is larger than my home. The floors are natural white stone, polished to a mirrored shine. I'm trying unsuccessfully to quell my excitement.

"This is not what I expected! Do you know what you have here? Oh, of course you do!"

There are dozens of classic automobiles, collector's editions, and models that have never been driven. My eyes dart dizzyingly from one to another. A regiment of goosebumps have appeared on my arms in clustered formation, as a tingling sensation lattices up and down my spine. *This collection would even make Jay Leno pop a boner!*

Each vehicle, painstakingly cared for, reminds me of a hospital nursery with babies carefully swaddled and arranged in a sterile lineup. My sloppy attempt to contain myself fails as I jump up and down with excitement, pointing and giggling.

"A white Rolls Royce Phantom Coupe, Bugatti, Lamborghini, Porsche 918 Spyder, and a first-gen Tesla Roadster 2.5 Sport! Wait. Is that a 1964 Aston Martin DB5 4.2-Litre Sports Saloon?" I sputter.

"Yup. The same one James Bond drove in *Goldfinger*."

"You mean the same model?" I say disbelievingly.

"I mean the same *car*," says Randolph proudly.

"Oh. My. God." I am floating across the floor in a zombie-like trance, arms extended as I conspicuously levitate to the next intended target.

"A Koenigsegg Agera...S?" Hesitating for a moment, my eyes settle directly on the gold leaf inlays, *Hundra*. I turn to look at Randolph, my mouth opened wide in stunned euphoria.

"Well, I am impressed. The lady knows her cars!"

"My father was a car buff," I say wistfully. "When I was growing up, he took me to all the shows, auctions, and private sales. He taught me everything I know about the history of automobiles and my interest has remained. We even crossed the pond several times in search of the ever-elusive rare find. But this collection is...exceptional. My father would have loved this."

When he asks the following, I wonder if Randolph has grown suspicious of my behavior or the time that I've invested here the past few days.

"I'm afraid I've been monopolizing your time, Ms. Bartelson. Do you always give your clients such personal attention?"

That would be a no.

"Well, I try to give my clients the attention they deserve," I say with misguided confidence.

Having completed the grand tour, Randolph and I part company. I agree to contact him with any updates and wave goodbye from my open sunroof as I drive back to my real life.

What am I doing? I have no idea where this is headed, but I believe I've landed squarely between a rock and a hard place. I still haven't told Randolph the truth. How could I? I'm a liar pretending to be a liar! But doesn't everyone lie in the business world? As H. G. Wells sagaciously said, "Advertising is legalized lying." If that's true, then Sharon Bartelson epitomizes this concept. And because her lies are greater than mine, I'll surely be exonerated.

Sharon was recently asked to host an hour-long Saturday morning real estate show on a local radio station. She replied with a boisterous, *Yes!* How she ever got that gig is beyond me. Still, opportunity just lands in her lap and without question, she drinks greedily from the fountain of good fortune.

I have no appetite for her tall tales and only listened to the show one time. The agony of listening to Sharon's nasal butchery of the English language was brutal. Her grating voice fray and droning rhetoric were painful, causing me to be embarrassed for her. Ordinarily, I find banal radio and television commercials irritating, but in this instance, they were a welcome break and infinitely better than the program itself.

"I give my customers the same service no matter who they are...," she droned.

Liar!

"I give the same service to all my customers whether their price point is fifty thousand or fifty million," says the only person I know who can turn one-syllable words into two.

Liar, liar, pants on fire!

"I'm ready to answer any, and all of your real estate questions," she stated undauntedly. She also made erotic noises, making the show sound more like a call to a sex chat line than a professional real estate broadcast. Sharon would be better suited whispering in a sultry voice, "Hi there...my name is Sharona Marona. Tell me what you're wearing, caller..."

I hope that Randolph doesn't listen to talk radio, because he will quickly realize that I'm not Sharon Bartelson; though I can't imagine anyone willingly listening to her show. If they really wanted to punish Guantanamo detainees, they would broadcast her real estate program on loudspeakers throughout the prison. Conceivably, her listening audience may very well be death-row inmates and comatose patients, in which case, it could be a long wait for a caller.

The rationale for my lies is that Randolph Prescott will never know my identity, nor will Sharon find out that I was pretending to be her. The strange woman who toured the Prescott property will puzzle everyone, but no one was hurt in the process. No property was damaged. Nothing was stolen. They will all have a good laugh and go on about their business. The Prescott property will be on the market and the Prescott men will return to their native country without giving it another thought.

Sharon sent their office photographer to capture the Prescott property with a sole shot of the estate's exterior. It was then converted to a computer-generated watercolor, which she swore was hand-painted. She also mentioned that there's no need for her to make a personal appearance. "I don't do country," she said. "But I did hire a videographer. The package comes with aspiring actors and stage props. How great is that!"

It's a sad reality that people lack vision and cannot on their own imagine living in a home without actors showing them how to chop onions in a well-equipped kitchen. Splayed out on the Internet, are lavish video presentations, appearing more like over-the-top movie trailers than residential real estate advertising. Sharon texted a link and asked that I watch some of the promos. "You might be able to copy some of the wording," she explained.

"And what about plagiarism?" I questioned with concern, already knowing what her answer would be.

"Aww...look at perfect little Angela, disconnected from us commoners with your unsullied reputation. Well, this is the real world, pal! Everything is put out there to be used. So, *use it!*"

Begrudgingly, I followed the provided links, watching several marketing trailers. Famous decorators place staged furnishings among theatrical lighting and props, highlighting the main features of the home. It appears as if no one has ever walked on a floor, used a bathroom, or slept in a bed.

The actors are plastic replicas of real people with fake personas to match. Certainly, no one you would want to live next door to; but the men are handsome, the women voluptuous, perhaps porn stars supplementing their incomes. Male actors are squeezed into slim-cut business suits, with a generous helping of high-end loafers, hold the socks. And the women, well, their personalities are spilling out in all directions.

Thus far, my favorite performer is a woman dressed in a skintight mini-skirt whose legs appear as if they're immovably bound together with duct tape. A revealing white blouse with a plunging neckline to her belly button, dares her to move in any direction without losing a nipple. She's wearing a sensational pair of Guiseppe Zanottis with elevated scalpel-sharp heels. The model, positioned inflexibly in a capacious two-story foyer, gestures with outspread arms, indicating an impressive sweeping staircase. The forced smile on her face is telling. I imagine she achingly wishes she could ascend to the master bedroom and forage through her closet for a roomy pair of sweats and fuzzy slippers—if only she could move her legs.

The outdoor scenes show vulgarly equipped men with bulges that leave little to the imagination. The women wear skimpy bikinis, their augmented breasts stretching already threadbare fabric to unreasonable limits. In one vignette, a gathering of thespian homeowners recline poolside. Slathered in body oil, they watch a CGI fireworks display in the background—clearly enough pyrotechnics to take out a small city.

In another production, children star as squatters in their very own McMansion. Their co-stars are famous athletes, playing with them on a full-scale basketball court, professional tennis court, and extreme home gyms on wooded lots. One darling diva zip-lines through a spacious backyard. She's modeling full outdoor rig-out, compliments of Needless Markup for Kids. Where are their parents, I wonder? Probably working three jobs to give the little darlings their own YMCA.

I find these unrealistic mockups of home life to be laughable and wonder who's dumb enough to bite. According to statistics, many people. These high-end choreographed homes sell faster and fetch 15 to 30 percent more than the orthodox method of real estate promotion.

I force myself to watch one more clip just to see if they get better. They don't. Sharon will try to replicate these online samplings on the cheap and suck me into her evil plan. I turn down the volume on my laptop to spare my ears from the tinny background music. The display is asinine. Still, I can't stop watching. Taken from drone footage high above a secluded hilltop property, the camera homes in on a red Lamborghini Diablo winding up the hillside driveway. The sun is shining as a man exits his vehicle with a glint of effervescence emanating from his bleached pearly whites. His perfectly styled hair is unmovable, even though the wind whips around him at forty knots.

As the man enters his Italianate Tuscan villa, he's met by a scantily clad siren summoning him to the kitchen, where he will predictably rip off her clothes and have sex on the counters and floor. To give the happy couple some privacy, the camera pans around the room and down the hall taking us on a virtual tour; though I can't get past the thought of what those two are doing in the kitchen. All I can think of is Clorox wipes, gallons of hand sanitizer, and the need to scrub the kitchen clean.

When it comes to purchasing a home, I don't like to be lied to. I want to be told of the leaky faucets and uneven floors. I want to know what I'm getting into, so don't sugarcoat the ol' homestead's foibles and faults. I become suspicious when things seem too perfect. I want to know which window sticks and how awful the neighbors really are. Show me the lord of the manor in true form: strolling through a dirty house clad only in boxers or not-so-tighty-whities, enthusiastically scratching the family jewels. Show me the lady of the house in her natural element: cooking in a grease-laden kitchen while indifferently picking yesterday's salad out of her teeth.

Though I've only known him for a short time, Randolph would never agree to a phony-baloney production. I believe he drew the line at photographs, and even that came with an added confidentiality agreement from their attorneys. All personal items, valuables, and family portraitures will first be removed or Photoshopped out of the pictures. Whatever mendacious act my degenerate friend has planned, I need to stop her.

Chapter Eleven

When I return home, I smell it before I see it. Snaggletooth has left a mess by the kitchen door and stands staring bald-faced in my direction. If he could speak, he would say, "You've been gone too long, *bitch*."

He has a doggy door, but not always the smarts necessary to use it. I launch him into the courtyard and yell an obviously belated command, "Go potty!"

Sometimes I wonder what goes through that dog's mind. Since Robert was never home, I longed for some form of companionship. Initially, I'd wanted a puppy, but valued my furniture and fingers, and didn't have the patience to go through training. I discussed the possibility of adding a four-legged family member with Robert, but he viewed pets the same way he viewed children—as a nuisance. The way he pronounced nuisance always made me suspect that Robert wasn't as well educated as he claimed to be. I used to find his pronunciation of the word "new-aw-sawnce" adorable. Now, I find it pitiful.

Since Robert was aloof, barely managing to make an appearance at home, I felt the decision was mine alone. I pressed onward, determined to find the perfect mongrel. I never considered buying a dog, no matter how much money we had. There are so many throwaway dogs in need but going to the local shelters proved to be a long, emotional process. My heart would melt as I walked by the cages—rows of inmates with pleading eyes and wagging tails. The panicked barking of some who jumped and clawed at the cages left me unnerved. Others curled deep into a corner trembling nervously, looking up with cheerless eyes and a last-chance plea, "*Choose me...choose me...*" Finding it difficult to choose just one, I always left guilt-ridden and empty-handed.

I'd all but given up on finding a match when I saw him. Snaggletooth was the featured hard-luck case on the morning news. In a moment of weakness, I adopted him. He was certainly not pick-of-the-litter and had already been adopted and returned several times. I wonder if someone at the Humane Society won a ham for finally offloading this slow-moving dud. I'm sure that when I drove away with Snags, the volunteers were high-fiving one another, wondering if this day would ever come.

Snaggletooth, formerly known as Lucky, is a stubborn beagle/basset hound mix who has inherited the worst tendencies of both breeds. He has a distinct overbite putting his canines on constant display. His upper lip curls under, repelled by the way his teeth protrude, giving way to the appearance of a perpetual snarl. He is larger than he should be and just plain galumphy.

In his younger days, he was a runner and was hit by a car—twice. He's had his tail amputated, has arthritis, an inoperable brain tumor, and a plethora of other afflictions that require daily doses of expensive medication. Snags is remarkably cunning and tremendously food-driven and will devour gourmet or garbage, it doesn't matter which. He moves languidly at a sloth-like pace, unless he smells food, at which time he's entering the last stretch of the Indy 500 or sliding into home plate during the World Series.

I've cut my budget to the bare bones and have sacrificed many accoutrements to keep Snaggletooth alive. He repays my benevolent deeds by shitting on the floor. It's not his fault that he's old and infirm, I remind myself; though I believe much of what he does is vindictive. Even so, I feel sorry for him and decide to head out for a walkabout. If nothing else, the poor old guy deserves an unhurried stroll.

As we round the first corner, a large car is moving slowly toward us. The woman is shaking her fist and screaming. I can't understand what she's saying because the windows are up. What I do understand is that she's accelerating and heading straight for my dog. I grab Snags and leap out of harm's way. He lies listlessly in my arms, unaware of the fact that he's been spared certain doom—again. Now parked on the sidewalk is a white Cadillac sedan housing a shriveled Yoda-esque creature who's yelling at me to put a leash on my dog.

"He's wearing a collar and he's under my control!" I say in a sing-song voice, pointing to his neck.

She continues shrieking an unintelligible garble of words in an Eastern Bloc accent. "That dog must have a leash! Is law! You break law, you go to jail! You no even live in this neighborhood! Your dog, he poop on my lawn! You know who I am? You go to jail, lady! I call police!"

Yes, I know who you are. You're Wilhelmina Smith, an irrational old woman whose husband was a former judge who left you financially well off. You think that because you were married to a magistrate who served on the bench for five minutes during the Roosevelt administration, you're beyond reproach.

Willa has become the self-appointed, yet still unofficial warden of the neighborhood. I imagine that neighbors will continue to ignore her uncontrolled rants until she runs over someone in her American car with the handwritten "Stalin for President" bumper sticker.

I simply walk away, knowing that one cannot have an intelligent conversation with a person who is, undeniably, batshit crazy. Odds are good that she'll give herself an aneurysm during this angry outburst; though she continues yelping and yodeling unfamiliar phrases while slowly backing her car down the street to follow me.

I look over my shoulder and wave her away. "I'd love to visit, but I'm busy, and I see you have a crazy train to catch! Don't let me keep you!" I yell sweetly.

I hold tightly onto Snaggletooth and jog off in another direction, his eyes bulging anxiously as excess folds of bagle skin flap over my arms.

Crisis averted, though it won't be the last we see of good ol' Willa. That old hag will never die, though by all appearances it seems that she's already been embalmed. Smart. Timesaver. I like that about her.

As I round the corner to my gated estate, our mail carrier, Mrs. Lasley, pulls to the curb with her arm out. She hands me a stack of mail rubber-banded together—mostly bills, which I hesitantly take from her. I'm sure she suspects that something is awry because she's seen my mail go through a metamorphic change. From happy, thoughtful correspondence to an inundation of bills marked "Urgent" or "Final notice!"

Although I receive most of my bills electronically, I've been ignoring them. When you ignore the electronic version and don't respond to calls, they move on to a different approach. Nothing gets your attention like a red-letter mailing demanding payment. Now the whole world can see that I'm in arrears with my bills.

I walk up the driveway with Snags by my side and pause, leafing through the stack of mail. There are insufficient funds notices from several banks. I never open them because I don't want to know how bad it really is. But I need to know. However, if I don't open them, it won't be real, and I can honestly say that I wasn't properly notified. I hold each one up to the sun. I may be able to see through the envelope for a preview without opening it. Of course, I can't see a thing because the banks use those damn indecipherable privacy envelopes! I advance to Plan B, artfully lifting the celluloid cover on the address window, peering in with a probing eye.

Mrs. Lasley sits in her mail truck pretending to sort mail for the next few houses on her route, but I can feel her watching me. The mail has ceased altogether for Robert and there's a dwindling supply of catalogs and periodicals as well. Thick manila envelopes from lawyers have taken the place of uplifting parcels. I try not to look distressed by today's offering because it's not the fault of the messenger.

Mrs. Lasley has a pained expression on her face and is motioning for me to come back. She must have forgotten to give me something or she knows more about me than I thought. I walk back down the driveway with a smile mortared to my deadbeat face.

I don't even know Mrs. Lasley's first name, but I've always liked her. Besides delivering mail through sleet and snow and gloom of night, there's also the unwritten code of mail carrier secrecy. The confidentiality of Mrs. Lasley, Mail Lady, is more secure than HIPAA. She's a jovial woman who limits conversation to weather-related topics and never asks personal questions. Though today, she looks sullen.

She hesitates a moment then leans out the open window, asking if I've heard about poor Mr. Barkley. "Heart attack. Passed away suddenly. Funeral is tomorrow. Well, have a good rest of your day..."

As she drives away in her sputtering, aged mail truck, I feel a horrible pang of guilt for not keeping in closer contact with Mr. and Mrs. Barkley. After all, they've always been respectable human beings and terrific neighbors, which is more than I can say about the rest of this lot. I feel grief pressing down as I escort Snags inside the house, fill his water bowl, and walk up the street.

I knock softly on Mrs. Barkley's front door and when no one answers, I ring the bell. There's no quiet way to ring a doorbell and this one is especially obnoxious. I wince at the disrespectful modulating tone, immediately feeling shame for whatever disruption I've caused. The heavy wooden door opens wide and there stands Mrs. Barkley, newly widowed and newly lost, blinking back tears. For a moment, I wasn't sure that she recognized me, then realized that her expression was solely one of raw grief.

"Oh Betty, I'm so very sorry for your loss. I had no idea..."

"It was in the paper," she says.

I didn't want to tell her that the only papers I've read lately are two *Wall Street Journals* from a year ago and an even older trial copy of the *Bryn Mawr Daily Register*. Having reread the same hoary newspapers, I've memorized the obituaries of notable people that appeared in one Saturday/Sunday WSJ and nothing beyond. How do I tell Betty that I have no idea what's going on in the world? I've been caught up in my tangled web of drama, and never once thought about what others may be going through. More so, I'm angry that other neighbors, in their constant quest to spread gossip, didn't have the decency to tell me about Mr. Barkley's passing.

I step forward and gently pull Betty Barkley into my arms. She stands shuddering, her small bony shoulders heaving up and down as she sobbed. I never knew she was so tiny until I looked down at the top of her white cotton head resting delicately on my breastbone. She's as light as a dove and I imagine her as such, flitting about, then landing nimbly on a thinly tapered branch.

I feel idiotic, searching for the right words. "What can I do for you?" I ask.

Betty regains her composure, running her dainty hands down a perfectly pleated wool skirt, then shyly dots both eyes with an embroidered handkerchief. Many strands of pearls envelop her neckline and weighty matching earrings overpower her lolling lobes. Standing regally erect, she looks searchingly into my eyes.

"Oh, dear one, Jackson thought the world of you. Would you consider coming to his memorial service tomorrow?"

"I'll be there," I say without hesitation. "I wouldn't miss it for anything."

The memorial service is lovely and Mr. Jackson Barkley's sendoff is as tasteful and genuine as the man himself. By the outpouring of sorrow, he was loved by all. But why don't we find out how amazing a life was lived until they're no longer with us? The stellar careers, the adoring children and grandchildren that have been raised with unconditional love. The acts of kindness and humility and small successes that evolved into lifelong realizations. An individual who was not famous; just a simple person who quietly and without pageantry stopped to help, saved a life, paid the tuition, opened a door, mentored a child, took in a stranger, or held a hand. These are all things that matter in the end.

There are hundreds of people at the service. Family, friends, colleagues, acquaintances, and neighbors. Anyone wishing to speak was given the opportunity and was not rushed through, as some pious religions tend to do—a two-minute allotment for this, three minutes for that. Each person told the story of a humble man who selflessly served others.

Mr. Barkley's memorial service made me reflect on my pitiable existence. What have I done with my life? What difference have I made in the lives of others? Who would miss me when I'm gone? Not one person. Just an old dog standing at an empty bowl, waiting to be fed. "Where the hell is she?" he would bay.

After the service, I stand in a long receiving line to offer my condolences to Betty Barkley, who looks as if she's aged twenty years in twenty-four hours. As I reach the front of the line, she extends her frail arms, giving me a firm hug while speaking softly into my ear. "Please stay for the luncheon, Angela. Please say you will. Jackson would have wanted you to."

As uncomfortable as this will be, it's not about me. I make my way into the capacious fellowship hall and step into the buffet line. Long tables, set end-to-end, house a superfluity of silver chafing dishes and platters. Several people give me the chin-up or chin-down greeting, neither of which I have ever been able to decipher. Whatever issues we've had, this isn't the time to play into such pettiness. Plus, this is the first decent meal that I've had in some time and the carefully planned epicurean feast looks scrumptious.

After unashamedly filling my plate, I see some neighbors from my street sitting at a large round table in the back, echoing with sociable conversation. I walk over to say hello and ask if I may join them. From the horrified expressions on the faces of General (ret) and Mrs. Ronald Grilla, I conclude that I'm not welcome. They quickly remove napkins from their laps, synchronically blotting the sides of their mouths. Both Mr. and Mrs. go into protective mode and practically throw their bodies over the empty seats, sputtering, "We're saving these for the Maxwells, the Danforths, and the Benways."

One thought churned through my mind at their ludicrous remark: *This is not the damn country club!* I turn to walk away but decide to make these two just a wee bit uncomfortable by sitting at the empty table next to them.

"I trust this little piece of real estate won't encroach upon you," I chirp, sitting down at the adjacent table.

The Grillas refuse to make eye contact as I exchange niceties with passersby, commenting on many stories about Mr. Barkley. "A life well lived!" I chime in loudly, hoping that the good General catches the dissimilarities between being welcoming, as Mr. Barkley was, and being an elitist asshole.

Jackson Barkley would rise from freshly turned earth if he could see how these two are behaving at his funeral luncheon. The significance of why we're gathered in the first place is lost on the idiocy of establishing a popular table; a table where the Grillas continue to dine alone as their highbrow cronies are a no-show.

Chapter Twelve

Feeling indebted to Randolph Prescott, I've spent an inordinate amount of time writing descriptive jargon for Hidden Acres. For deceiving such a hospitable gentleman, I believe he should have nothing less than the magnum opus of real estate listings. Of course, I'm full of crap, but it sounds good and as a wordsmith, I secretly hope to impress him. Before beginning, I check my cell for messages. I laugh at Sharon's voicemail which is analogously smattered with equine references.

"Ang, I'm chomping at the bit! I need the listing for the Prescott Estate—NOW! Quit horsing around and call me!"

Yeah, like I'm going to call that old gray mare, who indubitably, ain't what she used to be.

Braiding my fingers together, I extend my arms into a full stretch. I feel like I'm about to perform at Carnegie Hall as I position my hands over the keyboard, waiting for my cue to begin.

> *Camelot awaits! Feel like royalty in your own handsomely appointed French Château designed by distinguished architect, Devereux DeBaliviere.*
>
> *Layers of stress peel away as you meander down the winding drive, the quieting sensation welcoming you to paradise. Secluded, gated grounds separate this once-in-a-lifetime country estate from the rest of the world.*

Only forty minutes from the city center, this 1,100-acre equestrian property is a rare find.

Of significance, the flourishing equine facility includes 100 climate-controlled mahogany stalls, a foaling center, hay/feed storage buildings, private stud quarters, two tack buildings, an indoor riding arena, veterinary exam/operating rooms, and separate laundry facilities. The vast pastureland is fenced, cross-fenced, and immaculately maintained.

The far-reaching riding trails parallel a major waterway, allowing unhurried jaunts through the peripheral wilds while enjoying the resplendent viewing of flora and fauna. Meander over covered bridges, evoking the simpler times of yesteryear. Stop for a picnic or take a swim in the salubrious deep green waters of Emerald Pools, a spring-fed limestone quarry in the middle of your very own utopia. As well, a protected game preserve offers daily viewing of wildlife in their natural habitat.

The lush grounds and gardens have been meticulously planned and remotely preserved by renowned horticultural architect, Dame Penelope Howells. The grounds include four greenhouses, walking trails, yew hedges, lavender fields, garden statuaries, and glorious blooming vegetation, sure to take your breath away. A rainwater collection system, private reserve water tower, and state-of-the-art computerized irrigation system allow for accurately metered watering for each plant species. The punctiliously cataloged flora from the private botanical gardens will leave you speechless.

The seventy-acre lake, spring-fed ponds, wetlands, and water rights from year-round Clearwater Creek guarantee that water will always be available for livestock, nomadic waterfowl, and irrigation.

The remoteness of this residential parkland meshes nicely with modern conveniences. The château, along with all the other buildings, is integrated with smart home technology, complex state-of-the-art conveniences featuring security cameras, hardwired/wireless communication, entertainment systems, and technological amenities too numerous to list.

Included are a helipad, underground shooting range, wine cellar, two infinity pools, and cabanas with full outdoor kitchens for effortless entertaining. Take your breakfast or morning tea in the lovely east-facing conservatory, exuding natural light that glistens through exquisite European imported windows. Perchance you may wish to sit in quiet repose in the richly paneled library or in front of one of the many hand-carved limestone fireplaces.

Fifteen private residences for caretakers, equine attendants, groundskeepers, farriers, trainers, security personnel, and housekeeping staff are discriminatingly positioned on a dedicated 100 acres and act as its own fully functioning community.

The vast collection of antique furnishings and art collections is negotiable. Private viewing for serious, pre-qualified buyers. Price upon request.

After sending Sharon the listing, I lean back in my chair, wondering how I might return to Hidden Acres. A good story is like crack for fiction writers, and Mr. Prescott's storytelling abilities are beguiling. I've become addicted to the rich history of his family, waiting intently for the next chapter to begin.

But I'm in constant danger of Randolph finding out that I'm a fraud. It feels as though I'm on an elevator that's plunging downward, the bottom dropping out of my stomach. I see the blunt reality of how one lie turns into another and another until there's no coming back. Full of self-loathing, I mull over the possible scenarios when I sheepishly admit what I've done.

When I'm conflicted, I often play a little game with myself called, *What's the Worst Thing That Can Happen?* Death is always at the top of the list. But in this instance, there are so many legal and moral repercussions, that it makes me weak-kneed just thinking about it.

My parents were perfect in every way. What they must think of me and the miserable path I've taken. I was not raised to be a liar, but here I am—a reflection of my professional life. I'm sure they're looking down from the heavens in disgust, mournfully shaking their heads.

My folks came from wealthy, well-heeled ancestors, and were first-generation Americans who didn't have to work. They *wanted* to work—they were in fact driven by the idea of service before self. Before I was born, they proudly served our country in the military. Yet when I arrived on the scene, they forfeited their military careers for the stability of one home in one location.

They never relied on the family trust. Instead, they segued into successful private-sector careers. My parents did everything together. They even died together. They were well respected by their friends and colleagues, apparent by the hundreds of people present during their funeral. They were from a hearty stock who never crumbled when faced with hardship.

I gulp back tears when I think of the disappointment I've caused my long-deceased family and how I've besmirched their good name. I married the wrong man and allowed him to take advantage of me. I lost everything my parents and grandparents worked for. I've let them down, and I don't see a way to climb out of the deep hole that I've dug myself into.

Looking skyward from the trenches, I see a sliver of light. If there's light, there's hope. Just as I'm about to encounter some solid inspiration, my cell phone buzzes me back to reality. It's Sharon, gushing over the listing.

"How did you know so much about the Prescott Estate? I only gave you an artist's rendering and a brief informational sheet."

"I write fiction, Shar..."

"Well, I know *that!* But how could you be so accurate without even seeing the property?"

"I'm just that good, Mrs. Bartelson."

I immediately change the subject.

"The house across the street is finished. What was supposed to be a quick flip turned out to be a flop. It took over a year to complete. The rehabbers held a tactless unveiling for the neighbors to introduce us to the made-over version of what can only be called Shabby Shit. I didn't attend, but I watched people who normally don't step outside their comfort zone beat feet to the open house. They pretended that they were just out for a breath of fresh air, but they were not fooling anyone. I guess it gives the poor little lambs a new topic for the lively gossip mill. I don't know if it's an agented property. Do you intend to pursue the listing?"

"I wouldn't touch that atrocity if they tripled my commission! Do you know what went on there? Bad juju! You can't erase bad juju with a completely gutted redo and new appointments. Those poor animals! It makes me sick just thinking about it. I can't believe the neighbors didn't know what was going on."

"Oh, they all knew. The neighbors, the HOA, and the city officials. They sent letters to the owner and put an official notice on the door condemning the property and called it good. Neither the city nor the HOA, nor the Humane Society ever followed up. No one wants to get involved, and people naturally turn a blind eye to distasteful situations. It's easier to pick on people for lesser offenses than to open one's eyes to the dark side of humanity.

Plenty of complaining went on, but no one asked what happened to the surviving animals because they didn't want to know; though I'm sure that they'll each write a big fat tax-deductible check to some benevolent animal fund, given of the purest form of guilt."

Sharon becomes too quiet. I must have hit a nerve. She's probably already cleansed her soul and memory with a donation. I interrupt the awkward silence.

"Well let me tell you, I've had a bird's eye view during the renovation and it's been unremarkable. They've used Walmart fixtures in a Neiman neighborhood. That's all I can say, and the smell is unbearable. They will never be able to get rid of that smell. Snaggletooth still puts his ears back and cowers when he walks by..."

"Spare me the details! Smell isn't the only thing working against them. This was highly publicized and you'd have to have lived in a cave not to know the specifics. Every realtor in the bi-state area will be practicing ignorance and avoidance when they put that one on the market. They should have razed the structure and sold the lot, though who would buy a ghastly pet cemetery in a residential neighborhood?"

"I can't think of anyone..." I lament.

"Well, I'm not touching that stigmatized property, even if this state doesn't require disclosure. I might not be the brightest bulb in the box, but by God, I'm not stupid! Oh well, as the Latinos say, Caveat emptor!"

"That would be Latin," I say though it goes sailing completely over Sharon's head. As much as I'd like to address one of her many incomprehensible statements, there are matters of more importance to attend to.

"Listen Shar, gotta run. Linda's calling."

Linda has been my agent for over twenty years and is no longer the young apprentice I once manipulated. She has the upper hand and knows every trick of author avoidance. I've been ignoring her emails, voicemails, and texts. I answer the call like a receptionist in some nondescript office.

"Good afternoon! Angela Morgan speaking. How may I help you?"

"Remember me?" she questions dryly.

"Well, Linda Cooper, how the heck are you?"

"Please Angela, don't patronize me. It's unbecoming. Why haven't you returned my calls?"

"You know, the divorce. I'm still in a fragile state..."

"It's been a year. Are you still grieving for a relationship that died ages ago or are you looking for sympathy? Either way, you're not finding it with me. I'm the star of failed relationships, and I'm seriously considering that I may be playing on the wrong team."

"Now you think you're gay because you can't find the right guy?"

"Listen, Angela, that's not why I called. This is strictly business. I want to know how the book is coming. I'm getting pressure from all sides right now and it's an uncomfortable situation. We have a contract and I need to see some progress. Besides excuses, what do you have for me?"

"I'm feeling pressure myself right now and have a bit of the block going on. You know tabula-rasa-phobia and all that rigmarole. I can send you the pages that I have, but it doesn't seem to be going in the direction that I was shooting for."

"And what direction might that be? Finished or started?"

"Well, I'll pretend that didn't hurt. Please, just give me a little more time, Linda. And just so you know, I have plenty of gay friends, and you're not one of them."

"I'm not your friend?" she asks ruefully.

"You're not gay. Plus, do you really want me to start calling you Lesbolinda?"

"I'll give you another month to produce something tangible to send to the publishers. We have a long history here, Angela. I don't want it to end on a sour note."

I sit back in my chair and stare blankly into my future. I've spent so much time concocting imaginary lives that I never took the time to envision the direction of my own life. I abhor most of my characters and no longer enjoy writing degrading erotica or being looked upon as a starry-eyed romanticist. Many successfully write in multiple genres, but I'm struggling to discover a new niche. Writers seem to have jumped on the vampire bandwagon or the dystopian biopunk bored housewife genre, or crossed over to completely dark subject matter, writing anything that the publishers ask for. I want to earn an income, but I also want to have self-respect at the end of the day.

Now I understand why Robert found my writing so fascinating and why he ravenously devoured my novels, overtly praising the storylines. Of course, I made it easy for him to cheat! He used my narratives to fulfill his sick sexual fantasies.

Well, I'm tired of satisfying the dreams of others! I lean far over the sink in my office bathroom and look closely into the mirror. Fine lines frame my eyes and mouth and worry lines squiggle across my forehead. The woman in the mirror has stopped practicing the most basic grooming techniques, and I don't like what I see. I seem to have adopted the lazy mantra of "No makeup, no hairbrush, no shower, no problem." At least my new colorist did her job sufficiently and no one is the wiser.

Chapter Thirteen

I feel trapped and out of time. As if I'm stuck in a corn maze or other such silly pastime. As a child, I was often the last one invited to parties or excluded altogether. After all, who would want to invite an introvert, let alone a girl who wasn't a joiner.

I picture a classmate's mother standing over her daughter as she printed names on the envelopes of party invitations. The mother would examine the stack of small white envelopes and ask, "What about Angelarosa?" Her daughter would shake her head, but the mother would insist that it wouldn't be fair to exclude just one person from her class. Their mothers forced them to invite me and mine forced me to go. I was an outcast and often peed my pants as I spent too much time daydreaming and waiting too long to use the bathroom.

Having started school a year early, I was younger, smaller, slower, and uninvolved. I didn't comprehend the need for organized play and preferred adult conversation to wasteful, immature gatherings. I hated birthday parties and especially musical chairs. When the music stops, everyone scrambles to get a chair and the one left standing is eliminated and banished from the game. It's cruel to have fewer chairs than there are people. *What sadistic son of a bitch invented that game, anyway!*

I never realized how much that little amusement damaged me until I purchased my formal dining room set. It is the behemoth of all dining room furniture and was absurdly expensive. The wood is elegantly carved and intensely welcoming and the seating is overstuffed, the way I'd hoped my guests felt after partaking in the dinner parties I've thrown over the years. The intricate Italian marquetry of my rosewood dining table is stunning and there's ample seating for twelve. With it, came several leaves and a dozen extra chairs that I've squirreled away—just in case. Besides my desk and a lone mattress, my dining room remains intact. I'll starve before I ever sell that elemental amenity. And as long as I have breath left in me, no one will ever be left without a chair in my home.

Writing came easy for me. It's a solitary profession after all. There's only one person to depend on and only one person to blame when things go wrong. However, at present, I do not welcome the solitude. I wish there was someone to lean on, someone to catch me when I fall. Someone to spoon and fork around with.

I walk to my lonely bedroom which I once thought was the ideal love nest. The decorator who designed it was dynamic and conversed with an exaggerated flair. She was no slouch in the creative department, easily capturing the feel of the room with a series of classic pencil sketches that left me in awe of her talent. We spent hours poring over fabric swatches and trims and I recall her petitionary delight in sharing what she loves.

"Touch it!" she'd say. "Close your eyes and run the fabric down your cheek and really *feel* it. Sense the lightness of the tassel trim as it drops between your fingers and takes on another shape altogether. *Feel* the texture of the tapestry and imagine the inviting sumptuousness of it all..."

She was able to create style, sophistication, and comfort—all that I'd dreamed of. Now, my well-designed bedroom has been stripped of its furnishings, leaving just the mattress, a somber king-size reminder that I'm sleeping alone. To the right of the bed sits one small night-stand with an integrated charging station. Since I have no more lamps, the nightstand serves as a surface to place my candle. *A pioneer woman hitting the hay after a long day on the prairie.*

I ease under the sheets with the ridiculously high thread count and curl up tightly into a fetal position, seeking comfort. Well, that maneuver doesn't work. It makes my lumbar ache and gives me a charley horse! I quickly flip onto my back, kick off the covers, and massage my right calf until the pinching pain subsides.

What do babies do to self-soothe when they feel insecure? I can't believe I'm doing this, but I hold up my right thumb with the chipped pink polish and plant it firmly in my mouth. Just as quickly, I pull out the salty appendage. *Thumb-sucking is certainly overrated!*

As a last resort, I reach for my pillow, which I call Eduardo. Wrapping my arms around him in a tight embrace, I kiss him. It's an unreciprocated kiss because Eduardo is a pillow. Unfortunately, I still don't feel soothed or pacified or mollified, or whatever the hell I was trying to accomplish by this lunacy.

"Get lost, loser!" I scream, chucking Ed across the room into the wall.

It's indeed easier to make life-altering decisions when it doesn't involve deadlines. As well, all the experts say that it's easier to become romantically involved when you're in a relationship. It's also easier to make money when you already have money. *If that's the case, I'm screwed on all counts.*

Sharon is the only one who knows how dire my situation really is, and she's using it to her advantage. Everyone, including my agent, has no idea of my financial woes or the exhaustion caused by keeping up appearances. Besides Shar and Linda, the collection agencies are the only people who call anymore. I continue to be punished for Robert's debt. Most agencies, clamoring for money, won't even acknowledge the divorce unless I provide documentation. It amazes me that debt collectors can be the lowest life forms yet callously scold me for my economic downfall.

I don't work well in panic mode, so I resolve to try a new approach. I need to be clearheaded and find my inner hippie—stat! My knees creak and pop as I sit cross-legged on the floor. Closing my eyes, I take in a lungful of air through my mouth and release it slowly through my nostrils. Breathe...breathe...breathe.... An improvised 30-second meditation is all I can tolerate of this shit! Time is wasting and I decree that my mind is officially cleansed.

Back on my feet and on to the next phase: Cleaning the house. Working in a clean house should allow the creative juices to flow. After letting my housekeeper go over a year ago, the place is a wreck. I grab an empty spray bottle and fill it with white vinegar and water. My only ammunition is this homemade mixture and an armload of Robert's forgotten socks and undershirts. I turn knobs and kick doors open like the sheriff making a grand entrance into the town saloon. I then switch on the lights to survey the damage—as if sneaking up on filth will scare it away. If only!

There's not a lot of surface dust because there's not a lot of surfaces left; though the bathrooms are nasty! Anyone who thinks that they've made it to the big leagues by having six full bathrooms and two half-baths is a nincompoop. Letting a bathroom go for long without cleaning is the worst! The rusty stains in the sinks and showers, the sour smell emanating from stagnant brown water in the toilets, and bidets that haven't sprayed an ass clean in years, are enough to make a person gag. All in all, bathrooms that sit unused for long periods don't fare well, and even the act of a cleansing flush only makes me think of my water bill.

Spiders have taken up residence in darkened corners of commodious sinks and showers. I bend down to examine one long-legged spider. "What have you been eating?" I ask. Her translucent body tells me she hasn't caught anything lately as she hangs onto her web that crisscrosses haphazardly across the sink. She looks as desperate as I feel and I can't bear to tear down her home. I back out of the room, turn off the lights, and leave her to the lonely pursuit of survival.

The rest of the house isn't any better. It's dingy, dank, and cheerless. The lamps are gone and the only illumination is overhead spotlights that draw attention to deserted spaces. Many bulbs have burned out, which seems apropos. A pall of sadness casts shadows over bare walls and floors as I quietly survey the ruins of my life. The house is bare. I've sold most of my furnishings on consignment, because let's face it, pennies on the dollar are better than nothing. I keep the shades closed to elude curious interlopers, though I don't know how anyone could see in without a set of high-powered binoculars.

One thing that I've always liked about this house is its positioning. As the sun comes up on the east side diffusing through the trees, the living areas are bathed in natural light. And as the sun sets at the end of each day, my west-facing bedroom brings a certain forgiveness, a promise to try to do better tomorrow.

Even though my home sits on a hillside, I can't take the chance of anyone skulking around and peering in the windows. I've told neighbors that I'm redecorating, though some have questioned this. There's been a plethora of furnishings going out but nothing new coming in. I'm sure there's a statistician in our midst, tallying the incoming and outgoing results of my furnishings. "Have you seen...? Can you believe...? I wonder what she's up to?" I would never dream of invading the privacy of others, but here, being impolite is standard practice.

The dispiriting dullness of a dark house underscores my misery. What's needed is a little mood-enhancing daylight! I grab a remote control and point it toward the wall of windows overlooking the courtyard. The mechanical shades move laboriously upward, stopping halfway. The batteries may have run out, or like me, have just given up. We should have invested more in this creature comfort, opting for a solar or hardwired system. I can think of only one thing left in this house with working batteries, and I'm not giving *that* up for anything.

When I look through the half-open blinds, I see a scene from the apocalypse. The swimming pool, polluted with debris and left for months without attention, is flaunting a robust algae bloom. With cupped hands, I press my face against dirty windows and assess the situation. It's hard to imagine that there's water underneath the gloppy flotsam. It looks more like a moss-covered forest floor than an open-air pool. I imagine hiking across the spongy substance, backpacking through giant redwoods with power bars and bottled water.

I step outside for a closer look. Walking around the pool several times, I try to think of something that can be done to clean the polluted water. I've tried ignoring it, but now that the shades are stuck open, I'll be forced to look at this calamitous crater each time I pass by the windows. I could turn my head the other way, but I know that it's there, worsening every day.

The pool used to be the focal point of the backyard; a pictorial setting crowded with one-dimensional guests and trifling conversation. Knowing I would never again have visitors, I sold the thirty-two-piece set of patio furniture. I also cannibalized the alfresco kitchen, removing appliances, barbeque grill, and pizza oven, selling off anything that wasn't nailed down. And while the pool was still clear, I was bathing in it. This, I rationalized, was a cost-conscious way to save money.

Since discontinuing the pool service, it was only a matter of time before the pool became completely unusable. Whatever they were doing to keep it clean, I was sure that I could do the same by using products that I already had lying around the house. I find some surplus chlorine in the pool house and dump it into the pool along with several jugs of bleach from the laundry room.

Think, think, think... There must be something else I can add.

I enter the house, wild-eyed and radical, like looters after a natural disaster. Pulling open cabinets and drawers, I brutally grab whatever I can carry. Remembering that we'd switched to saltwater years ago, I take a grinder of Mediterranean sea salt for good measure. Adding a handful of colorful dishwasher pods to the medley of household items leaves me feeling hopeful. I throw everything into the pool and walk around the perimeter, a witch stirring her cauldron with a long-handled skimmer.

Turning to walk away, I trip over the sea salt. I consider the grinding apparatus and struggle unsuccessfully to remove the top. Reverting to brute strength, I throw it to the ground and stomp on it until it cracks open, leaving salt crystals scattered at my feet. I reach down, take a pinch of salt, and throw it over my shoulder for good luck. Lobbing what's left of the grinder into the pool, I watch it bubble and gurgle through the debris as it sinks to the bottom. The remains of the day.

After several hours of armed combat with the pool, I despairingly return to the confines of my asylum and turn in early. I'll check on the pool tomorrow. By then, I hope to see some positive results.

The pool is all I thought about while trying to sleep, dreaming that it was restored to a sparkling clear blue. I knelt beside it and could see my reflection on its smooth, glass surface. In celebration, I walked assuredly to the edge of the diving board, positioning for a swan dive. Bouncing off the board, I flew high into the air and kept ascending. I should've known it was just a dream when instead of hitting water, I zoomed into outer space and shared a glass of wine with Kathie Lee Gifford.

I descend the stairs with childlike anticipation and run outside to look at the pool. Disappointingly, this amateur maneuver did nothing to eradicate the floating green substance. If anything, it made it worse. Admitting defeat, I heave the skimmer into the pool and walk away.

There wasn't much I could do to clean up the cabana either. The exterior door was left open and the toilet seats were left up, inviting a family of frogs to move in. I may be many things, but a homewrecker I'm not. I apologize for entering their territory without an invitation as they cluster together, staring at me with frightened, bulbous eyes. Who am I to barge in unexpectedly? The cabana is of no use without a pool and the frogs clearly have more friends than I do. I proclaim that the cabana is theirs to keep.

The hillside infinity pool was designed to appear as if water was dropping off the edge of the property. Now, the floating globs accentuate my failures, a once-balanced life dropping off the edge of reason. I look over my shoulder one last time.

So. This is Armageddon.

I try to find the motivation to start cleaning, leaving behind footprints as I meander through the house on a settling of fine indoor soil. The dust bunnies are prolific, borne of an amalgam of dog hair, spider webs, and dirt; a whirling tangle of indoor suburban tumbleweeds that pirouette wobblingly across sprawling wood floors.

I think about vacuuming, but it's only a passing thought. Instead, I set down my makeshift cleaning supplies and climb the wide staircase to my office; an expansively apportioned retreat separated from the bedrooms and main living areas.

Settling at my desk gives me comfort even when I'm not writing. This desk was the one extravagant purchase I made when I sold my first book. Convincing myself that it was a great investment, I justified the price by telling myself that I'm only productive when surrounded by well-furnished appurtenances. This talisman first served as a reminder of where it all began. Now, it serves as an unhappy reminder of where it will end.

I once yelled at my housekeeper for not valuing its worth; for not using Q-tips and lemon oil to polish its deep carvings and crevices, and for not properly safeguarding the wood from the effects of central heat and sunlight. What kind of insensitive turd says things like that! *A woman focused on all the wrong things, that's who.*

I run my hands over the surface of this gorgeous desk, a mirror image of my life: neat and orderly on the outside and a scrambled mess of unfinished projects inside. My desk drawers are stuffed with magazine articles that I'd meant to submit, letters to the editor, garbled communiqués to political figures, ideas for newspaper and magazine columns, and fan mail I'd intended to answer personally, *someday*. There are also copies of nasty grams, which I somehow always took the time to send; impulsive missives dispensed freely with venomous intent. When I'm happy, I can be contentedly subdued, even pleasant. But when I'm mad, I make sure everyone knows it. I have a reputation for verbally assailing politicians, princesses, and anyone in between, and the content of these drawers represents the sum of my life.

I'm under the gun to produce something of substance to send to Linda and I'm terrified that this is the end of my career. Writing is all that I ever wanted to do, but I can't seem to find my muse. I give the computer the night off and take my own soured advice, reaching for pen and paper. When all else fails, troop onward and make a list!

Positioning the pen over a mostly blank legal pad, I stare mawkishly at my dry, wrinkled hands and appalling penmanship. My handwriting has become as sloppy as my life. And I could really use a manicure and some hydration! Excusing myself from my list-making task, I head for the master bath vanity on a quest for some soothing hand balm.

I've used up all the expensive collagen-enhanced lotions, cutting open tubes and bottles to eke out every precious drop. Thankfully, I've squirreled away a vast amount of those sad little hotel bottles of shampoo, conditioner, body wash, mouthwash, and lotions. Appreciatively, I won't have to purchase these items for some time because I am rich in freebies. I spend an unreasonable amount of time lining up bottles like toy soldiers readying for battle, choosing a pleasing fragrance from my private hotel collection. I thickly slather lotion onto parched hands. *Thank you, Crowne Plaza.*

Now that my hands look and feel better, I must work on my

penmanship. In my mind's eye, I picture a disgruntled fan submitting my signature for an expert handwriting analysis. The results, splayed across the cover of every trashy gossip magazine would also be the lead story on E! A skimpily dressed woman with a BMI of two and sharply chiseled features is interviewing the analyst, who sits staring blandly at the camera. He fingers a graying goatee while stating factually, "The results of these findings are simply staggering. It is my professional opinion that Angelarosa Morgan is a lonely, desperate woman who has spent a lifetime concealing her identity from the world. She is, in fact, a serial writer, murdering the English language and destroying lives, one word at a time."

Egad! If there's one thing that I'm truly proficient at, it's wasting time! I've lost three hours rehydrating tired hands and improving my penmanship. No wonder people loathe me. *I loathe me!*

I start a list.

1. Make money—NOW!

2. Ask Sharon to contribute cheap staged furnishings. Have a hunky crew deliver at night so neighbors won't get a good look at what awful faux taste I have. Will buy some time.

3. Start novel.

4. Finish novel.

5. Call Linda. Tell her that I'm writing a bestseller that will save both our careers.

6. *At least* clean the master toilet and bidet. They stink!

After writing my to-do list and completing exactly nothing, I rip the page off the pad, crumple it into a ball, and throw it away. I need a reviving walk to raise my heart rate, boost endorphins, and clear my mind. Snags is napping in the courtyard. He lifts his head to look up from bloodshot eyes as I tell him apologetically, "I'll be back for you." Something I say to a dog who never obeys a command and only comes running if there's something in it for him. In many ways, he reminds me of Robert, but with a conscience and better hygiene.

As I begin my walk, an eighteen-wheeler blocks the cul-de-sac, slowly backing into the driveway across the street. Certainly, no one is dull-witted enough to have purchased the notoriously refurbished slaughterhouse. Not only did someone buy this miscreation, it's a family with five small children, who are now spilling from an overflowing SUV. No matter the economic status, once that stick turns blue, expectant parents joyfully charge right out and buy a large rolling box with wheels and an entertainment system.

There's also a small ball of fluff that's chewing on a flexi-lead. It's so tiny that I can't tell what it is. Could be a cat, but it's most likely a dog. The parents probably stopped en route to buy the kids a puppy from a pet store, born in some stomach-churning puppy mill. I suspect it was a bribe for the kiddies to leave their friends behind in exchange for a dog and a life in the super-burbs.

With so many dogs needing homes, these people look like the shop-instead-of-adopt types. They think they're really getting something special by paying an excessive stipend for a designer dog that, they've been told, is hypoallergenic and doesn't shed. It probably doesn't shit either. I have no desire to know these people, but I decided on a name for their dog: Lunch. Because that's exactly what it will become if Snags gets ahold of it.

I shake off negative thoughts and try to focus on the quietness of a pleasant day, moving one foot in front of the other in long, slow strides. I usually stay on the sidewalks of Phase II and III of our subdivision. I haven't ventured down the older, established part of the development for some time, so I deviate from my usual route and head into Phase I. This is where the renegade country club settlers reside, many of whom are now in their seventies and eighties. They're the ones who could really use sidewalks, but the developer cut corners—quite literally, excluding them from the plans.

The homes on the far end of Phase I are nestled in a woody area of the subdivision. I refer to this area as Car Dealer Row, a trio of lush five-acre homesites accommodating equally sizable homes. The occupants are the three largest car dealers in the bi-state area, and fierce competitors as well. You'd think this would make for a not-so-neighborly situation, but it seems to work for them. Two of the owners are reclusive and antisocial. In fact, I've only seen them in passing and wouldn't be able to pick them out of a lineup.

On the other hand, everyone knows the most notable auto trader of the lot, the infamous Bob Beaverton and his pet squirrel, Nipper. These two bachelors are indisputably the most colorful occupants of Car Dealer Row; one with two legs, one with four, inhabiting a sprawling lionized brick fortress.

Mr. Beaverton doesn't feed the indigenous squirrels on his property as he believes it would make Nipper jealous. He's mentioned many times that "Nipper don't take too kindly to them low-class tree dwellin' varmints."

Walking by Bob's house always makes me happy because he's a non-conformist and doesn't care what people think. Smattered about his landscaping is an abundance of artsy squirrel-related oddities that only a curmudgeonly old rebel could fully appreciate—or get away with. In a very thick Southern drawl, Bob refers to his collection of gewgaws and gadgets as "objet d'art." This crap, as well as Nipper, is overlooked by the city and the HOA, as Bob is a celebrity of sorts. Everyone, it seems, buys cars from him.

I don't know how many Nippers Bob has shared his home with over the past forty years, but I do know this: trained squirrels sell cars! Bob Beaverton and Nipper are on every television channel at any given hour. The worst of these low-budget commercials are seen during the wee hours, sandwiched in time slots between kitchen knife infomercials and ancient reruns of *Leave It to Beaver*. Bob even capitalized on this strange opportunity, dressing up as a little freckle-faced boy and dubbing his two-minute commercial Leave It to *Beaverton*. Not to be outdone, Nipper played his brother, Wally.

Bob doesn't just sell cars. He sells cars to anyone. Bad credit? No credit? Incarcerated? Dead? No problem! *Just come on down and we'll sell y'all a VEE-hickle!* His numerous dealerships sell anything from brand spanking new luxury cars, to pre-owned certified, to barely drivable jalopies that probably won't even make it off the lot. There isn't anything that Beaverton Automotive can't sell, and nothing that he hasn't dressed poor Nipper up in to facilitate a transaction.

The other two neighbors who own dealerships can't compete with Beaverton Automotive. Bob is one of a kind and the only one who could pull off such a gimmick. I don't mind having to interact with Nipper because he has good teeth. However, with all the money that Bob is rolling in, you'd think he'd invest in a decent set of dentures. His is an oversized set of yellow chompers, appearing to be carved from oak around the same year that our state landed a star on Old Glory. Bob's dentures clack when he speaks as Nipper hangs dexterously onto his neck. But as much of a screwball as I believe Bob Beaverton to be, he would do anything for you and has a kind heart.

After unwinding with a long walk, I'm feeling clearheaded and rejuvenated. The feeling quickly passes when I round the corner and my street comes into view. I notice a blur of movement in the vicinity of my home and realize that the rookie neighbors have misplaced their young spawn. As I approach, the kids are climbing my gate and taunting Snags through the bars with a long stick. Ignoring them, I press entry codes on the gate and squeeze past them to let myself in. They take this as an open invitation to push past me, enter my private domain, and overrun my yard, screaming nothing intelligible at the top of their lungs.

My benevolent side wonders if the parents are overwhelmed and distracted by the stressful move-in process. However, the cynic in me takes over when I see their mother waving a friendly arm from afar with the expectation that I find her offspring as charming as she. That wave also signifies acknowledgment that she expects a stranger to watch her kids. I shake my head while mouthing into the air, "How presumptuous and wrong you are, Fertile Myrtle..."

I seize the stick and herd her ill-mannered children out the gate and back into the cul-de-sac where they dart in all directions. I must pay the new neighbor a visit, welcoming her to the hood. I'll ask how she likes living in a newly revamped crime scene, while also setting strict ground rules regarding her feral brood. I find the urban fad of raising free-range chickens marginally tolerable. But free-range children? Not so much.

Chapter Fourteen

I call Shar to wheedle more information from her on the Prescott Estate. It startles me when she answers on the first ring, "Sharon Bartelson here. Talk to me!"

I mischievously try to disguise my voice. "Shaaaron, dahling... How arrrrre youuu?!"

"What in the living hell is wrong with you, Angela?" she snaps in a harsh murmur. "I'm in the middle of a showing!"

"I just wanted to talk about the Prescott property."

"Prescott? What would you need to know about the Prescott Estate or any of my listings for that matter? Chat later!"

Click.

I need to talk to that woman about telephone etiquette. Also, about morals, scruples, manners, and all-purpose tact and diplomacy; subject matters that would be totally lost on Ms. Sharon Bartelson.

I decide that this is as good a time as any to call Randolph while I still have an ounce of courage left.

"Well, hello Ms. Bartelson. I was just thinking about you."

I fight the urge to blurt out my real name because this must be done delicately and in person.

"May I stop by later today? There's something we need to discuss..."

"How about dinner? Tonight?" he asks.

Oh, no. I can't do this in a public place. Then again, if we're in public, it may lessen the blow. The blow to my head!

"Dinner. Tonight? With *you*?"

"Yes, that was the general idea."

"Well, I'd love to but..."

"But you have other plans?"

I propose that I pick him up, using the excuse that I prefer driving and know the area well. He acquiesces, and I now have a dinner date with a man that I've done nothing but lie to from the inception. If I could afford to, I'd buy *him* dinner. Maybe we'll go somewhere cheap, but I doubt it. I hope he insists on paying because Lord knows, I haven't had a gastronomically pleasing meal in months. Maybe this will be my last meal before my impending, yet deserved, execution.

I'm standing in my empty closet, staring vacuously at my couture de jour. I've taken all my expensive evening wear and pricey outerwear to Peter Simon's upscale consignment shop, Pete & Repeat. Between consignment and pawnshops, I've been able to pay for the basics, but another property tax installment is coming due. I've taken all of Robert's suits, shirts, and ties to the men's consignment repository and don't see much else of value. I can't give in to the anxiety right now but promise my scared self that I'll spend tomorrow going over my ever-shrinking assets.

As I begin trying on my sparse clothing choices, Shar calls, asking why I'm acting so strange. She also demands to know why I'm meddling in her business affairs. I'm unusually demure and pretend I don't know what she's talking about. Even though I'm on the phone, I feel a certain vulnerability at my nakedness.

"Well, whatever you want to know about the Prescott Estate, know this: I plan on turning a quick profit by degrading its value and purchasing it myself. Sure, I could sell it and collect a substantial commission, or I can *really* fill the coffer! I'm going to meet with Mr. Prescott on Wednesday. My assistant is setting it up right now."

I can't speak. An inaugurated queasiness is welling deep in my gut. I hold my cell phone at arm's length and stare disbelievingly at the impertinence of this woman.

"Are you saying...?"

"I'm saying that I will systematically destroy the value of the estate in the mind of the owners with fake comps and stacks of official-looking charts and graphs meant to confuse. I'll produce phony EPA documentation stating that the water on their property is tainted with some chemical or another. I'll have their little empire condemned. Sellers want their attorneys to examine the fine print, but when they're told how much time *that* will take, they back down. Especially if they're looking for a quick sale.

And a quick sale they shall have! We lower the asking price and I purchase it myself through one of Bart's shell corporations. I can more than double my investment with a rapid turnaround. It isn't anything I haven't done before. They want to unload the property quickly and I want to profit from their predicament. It's a win-win!"

"You've never even seen the Prescott Estate! You've never even met these people!"

"Now, how would you know I've never been there?"

"You said you don't do country..."

"Oh yea, right. But I'm going to have to go out there at some point to fulfill my contractual obligation. You know, make it look good. You take your average sucker, add a moderate helping of foreigner to the mix and you have a delicious recipe called Bartelson Surprise. God, I love being me!

The nephew is his uncle's conservator and he's from one of those English-speaking countries. I don't remember which one—England, Scotland, Australia, *whatever!* Anyhoo, the nephew will be anxious to sell the place, dump the old guy at a nursing home, and get back to wherever he's from."

"But you said you were having your videographers make a movie trailer of the property."

"Oh, that. Just a ruse to let them think that I have some splashy marketing plan. My intent is not to actually post the listing. Just a carefully implanted stratagem to make the owners believe I'm giving it my all when presto, I produce a buyer. Me! Ha! Plus, my movie crew cleans up pretty well. If only you could see them in action! Guess who it is?"

Sharon never gives me a chance to speak and continues talking over me.

"It's Jay and Paulie from Bart's construction crew! Give 'em a shower, shave, leather jackets, and some camera equipment and they look the part. If they keep their mouths shut in the process, they can be downright believable. I don't know why I'm even telling you this. You couldn't possibly understand the complex inner workings of contractual tweaking."

Tweaking?

How could I have been this gullible? I'm an unknowing accomplice, who has just discovered the sickening verity of our long-standing relationship. I knew that Bartelson's business dealings were dodgy at best, but I never considered the extent of their deceptive practices. Their clients were nameless, faceless victims. Until now.

"Sharon, you're a poor excuse for a human being. You're a vile individual and I find you repulsive!"

"So now you're *Miss Goody Two-Shoes*? Are you a born-again virgin, as well? Why would you even care about these people? Gawd, Angela, get with the program! Dog eat dog! Survival of the fittest!"

"How many times have you done this, Sharon? How many times have you conned people to subsidize your insatiable greed? This obviously isn't just a random amoral fling!"

"Wow. You really are brainless! First of all, the vast majority of people are followers, and followers don't take chances. Second of all, they're sheep. They do whatever everyone else is doing. And third of all, they believe whatever crap they're fed."

The situation is bad enough, but when Shar begins committing grammatical homicide with her first, second, and third of all paradoxes, I want to muzzle her to keep her from talking.

"Do you really think you can get away with this? You think you can continue operating with impunity?"

"That sounds a lot like a threat, Angela. *Do not challenge me. You will not win.*"

I mentally stare Sharon down, willing her to spontaneously combust. That would solve many problems right now. My mind races for answers while battling my moral compass. This could be the break I've been looking for. I need cash and could extort money from Sharon by having her invest in my silence. This would be a quick fix, but it still wouldn't stop her from cheating the Prescotts out of millions.

Although the words are there on the tip of my tongue, I swallow them back. All I can think of is ad infinitum, *for all eternity*. I resist asking the devil incarnate for anything, knowing that she will unblinkingly drag me into the bowels of hell with her.

The dynamics have now changed. I need to be delicate when I break the news to Randolph that I'm a fraud. But there's a more dangerous fraudster lurking in the shadows. I consider the enormity of the situation. I can't postpone sharing this with Randolph, but I'll need to tell him everything. Before Sharon's admission, I was solely responsible for the lies. I imagined him throwing me out of his home and out of his life. Now, he'll see Sharon as the real imposter, knowing that I wasn't complicit in her iniquitous plan.

After showering, I choose a loud, multi-patterned blouse to distract from the news that must be delivered. My outfits are few, but it's not about the wrapping, but what's in the package. Maybe after I tell Randolph the truth, he'll look deeply into my eyes, pull me close, and plant a long, sensual kiss on my willing lips. Maybe he'll tell me that the day we met, the heavens opened up and the angels sang.

I do my hair, carefully apply makeup, and paint my nails. Ready much too early, I check to see if there's anything I've missed. Everything has been colored, trimmed, waxed, coiffed, shaved, plucked, and polished to a smooth finish. There's something about being clean that makes a person instantly feel better, even if that person is masquerading as a realtor.

I'll attempt to stay clean by avoiding Snags. That dog wants nothing to do with me unless I'm dressed up. Then he clings to me like static electricity, rubbing eye boogers and bagle stench on my clean clothes. While doing so, he'll invariably shed his entire coat. This too, is my fault. I've become an irresponsible caregiver. He's not had a bath or had his nails trimmed in a year; though for now, this early warning system is working well. Being able to hear his nails clattering noisily across the floor gives me time to skedaddle.

I've tried to bathe him and trim his nails myself. But he clawed and bit at me, baying and crying out as if he were the target of a hired assassin. When we were still bi-weekly clients of Pookie's Pampered Pets Mobile Grooming, he couldn't wait to climb into the state-of-the-art spa on wheels. Pookie's assistant would come to the door, leading Snags into the awaiting vehicle. As she slipped the diamanté lead around his neck, he held his head high, loyally marching forward with his guide. Before stepping into the van, he would pause, look over his shoulder, and smile back at me. I suspect that if he were able, his paw would have been raised, and a distinct middle finger would have pointed in my direction.

This same task would have caused bite and scratch wounds and taken days to complete. On the contrary, it took Pookie only two hours to transform Snags into a clean, well-groomed little man. Of course, that also included a back and shoulder massage with essential oils.

Depending on his mood, she used a different aromatherapy treatment each time, sending my dog into a calming state of being. She would also check his aura, making sure that his emotional, mental, and spiritual levels forming his field of energy were as they should be. The last time Snags was groomed, Pookie was mystified that his chi was off, telling me that I must do something about it immediately!

If Pookie could see Snags and his aura now, she'd report me to the ASPCA for animal cruelty. Besides being a stink factory and flea magnet, I'm sure his spiritual well-being is also a mess. After all, who in this highfalutin neighborhood would deliberately disregard their dog's chi?

Before departing for my date, I must find something mindless to ease this nervous tension. I haven't retrieved the mail in days—a pointless and depressing task if ever there was one. There's never anything encouraging in there, but today feels different.

Since going into seclusion, I've ceased interacting with others and it shows. I've been looking rough, skulking around in the dark, cloaking myself in the blackness of night. Today, instead of frittering away my time loitering in the shadows, I walk down the driveway with purpose using my best posture. For the first time in months, I'm feeling well put together and attractive and I want to be seen.

As good as I feel, my adopted persona briefly fades as I face the mailbox, an unfluctuating smokescreen. Look at it standing there, smugly basking in the sun with its burnished bronze coloring and baroque monogram. A red herring screaming, "I know all your secrets. Na-na-na-na-na-na!" I consider the insignia on the mailbox: M is for Morgan. M is for moron. M is for morose.

Don't stick your hand in there, I tell myself. It could be a trick! There may be a rattlesnake ready to strike. I'd collapse onto the sidewalk, retractable fangs still attached to my neck. People would dash over to help...

Pfft! Don't be ridiculous. They'd never help me!

What they would do is capture the moment; cell phones popping up, recording my last moments on earth. With dying breath, I think of only one thing to say, and exaggeratedly mime the words, *"I'm sorry, Randolph..."*

I open the mailbox door and jump back as it drops open. Slowly, I move forward, bending down to examine its insides. No serpents in here, at least none of the reptilian variety. Though, who knows? The contents could surprise me. There could be good news encased in this highly crafted repository. Perhaps there's a notice from my agent that she's sold a three-book deal on speculation, but she would have called for something that miraculous. Possibly a statement from a forgotten Swiss bank account or a letter from a wealthy, long-lost relative? Or the IRS notifying me that I've grossly overpaid and there's a windfall of money heading my way. But none of those things are in the mailbox, so I give the post a good swift kick. My foot aches, as the mailbox stands on solid ground, continuing to mock me.

As usual, there are only renewal notices for periodicals that I can't afford, past-due notices for bills that I can't pay, and stacks of catalogs from obscenely expensive stores that are no longer part of my world. There's also a large envelope from my attorney. With any luck, it's the final divorce decree concluding this ignominious mess.

I'm tired of wishing for a miracle, holding tightly onto something that's slowly slipping through my fingers. I'm tired of treading water, and I need someone to throw me a lifeline. To be thrown a lifejacket at this point would be a cosmic phenomenon; though I'm afraid that on the path I've taken, the only thing I may find myself enveloped in is a straightjacket.

Eyes closed, head tilted skyward with a glut of mail clutched tightly to my chest, I savor the warm sun radiating onto my appreciative face. Unfortunately, the tranquil moment is cut short. There appears one Ms. Posey Parker—*Nosey Parker* is more like it.

"Get out of the sun, Angela! You're simply inviting wrinkles!"

Posey saunters up the stone walkway, sans any encouragement on my part. I make a mental note to keep the gate always shut. I've never been on the nurturing end of our acquaintance, and no matter how curt I am with Posey, she still comes back for more. I'm dazed by her appearance, as Posey stands before me togged in flowing white.

"Ascending into heaven?" I ask presumptuously.

She ignores the comment, giving me the once-over hypercritical *girl look*.

It doesn't matter if you're twelve or 112, the *girl look* is the same head-to-toe scrutiny of your attire by the female persuasion. Her inspection of my outfit and disapproving expression speaks volumes.

"Posey, you're so transparent."

She blushes and begins lightly patting her cheeks. "Well, I did just have a chemical peel..."

"No, Posey. I said transparent, *not* translucent. Entirely different meaning. Look it up."

No matter the affront, it never slows Posey down.

"Oh Angela, I wish you'd come to the fashion show at the club last month. With your dark complexion, you could pull off the new exotic prints. As you must know, it's a sophisticated line of couture clothing. We have oodles of styles that would add panache and pop to your wardrobe, helping you look completely pulled together. A relevant and fashion-forward line that is positively au courant! I did invite you..."

"You're too kind, Posey. But I'm in a bit of a hurry and I have a dinner date."

"A date? With a man? I haven't seen Robert lately. Is he still traveling?"

If by traveling, she means bed hopping with young women who will eventually live to regret meeting him, then yes, Robert is still traveling.

"Robert's schedule is crazy these days. We hardly ever see each other."

Thankfully.

Posey can't seem to take her eyes off me. I must look incredible.

"Are you wearing *those* cropped slacks to dinner? With *those* heels? Are they from last year's trunk sale?" she asks incredulously.

"Oh, these? They fit like a glove, don't they? Costco. $14.99."

I turn quickly and walk away, while I surmise Posey Parker has passed out cold and swallowed her teeth. I fail to understand how anyone is crazy enough to pay hundreds of dollars for an article of clothing and ridicule others who don't do the same. If you ask me, I'm the smart one.

I sit on the stone entry steps and dig through mounds of mail. Opening the fat envelope from the firm of Johnson, Jacoby, and Jamison, I'm both relieved and sad. My divorce from Robert is final. Although I'm the one who filed for divorce, I've wasted the best years of my life on this unworthy man. I suppress an insistent melancholy as it attempts to strengthen its grasp. For the sake of sanity, and because I have no desire to ruin my carefully applied makeup, I shake it off and resolve not to shed another tear for what was lost.

Tonight, I'll celebrate what's been found. The new me. Even though the new me is a liar and a mere figment of my imagination, I'm going to roll with it. For just one evening away from my problems, I intend to relax, before the shit hits the fan.

Chapter Fifteen

I pick up Randolph while Wilson watches in the distance. Randolph appears to have stepped off the cover of *GQ* and even smells yummy. I wonder if he wakes up this way, all put together with not a hair out of place. I bet he doesn't snore or fart either.

Randolph solicitously compliments me on my outfit. I am observably underdressed, given that he's wearing an Armani suit and I, my wholesale warehouse apparel. Before getting into my car, he mercifully removes his tie. We are still far from being in fashion harmony, but I don't care. For a person who is close to being indigent, I look damn good.

Randolph gives me the restaurant address and I quickly type it into my navigation system. The location is an hour away. Still, I pray that I don't run into any familiar faces tonight, resulting in indiscreet questioning that would prematurely blow my cover.

I race through miles of switchbacks on the narrow two-lane road and finally peel onto the interstate. Randolph chuckles, "Well, look who has a lead foot! Someone must be hungry!"

"Oh, sorry. Guess I'm just nervous," I say, checking the mirrors as I slow down and set the cruise control to the speed limit.

"I have to ask you something if I'm not being too forward."

"Well, this sounds quite serious," says Randolph as he pivots in his seat to look at me.

I look straight ahead at the road stretched out before me. "Has anyone ever called you by any other name? For example, Randy?"

"Oh no, it's always been Randolph. My parents were insistent that I only use my given name. It's tradition, and besides, Randy sounds so common and unceremonious."

"Alrighty, then. Randolph, it is." And we drive into the night with one truthful insight between us.

The restaurant is on the top floor of a grand hotel, built generations ago when dining was a civilized event. One of a few remaining mainstays of American civility, this landmark draws in visitors from all over the world.

We walk across the grand lobby to rows of polished gold elevators, swans of attractive people gliding languorously about. I'm cognizant that some of the women are giving me the stink eye simply for being underprivileged. Sensing my discomfort, Randolph takes my arm as we step into a dedicated elevator, heading to the top floor. The attendant puts his key in, presses the lighted button, and we're off.

I can feel the heat emanating from a woman standing too close, her stare burning a hole through my head. Her wrists and fingers drip with diamonds and she's draped in fur, even though the temperature is very warm. I begin to think of the animals, slaughtered for the sake of this woman's vanity; how this used to be a living being, or *many* living beings. As well, the heady scent of her perfume has engulfed my senses, curdling my stomach and giving me an instant headache. I'm sure the animals she's wearing have died all over again.

When I can no longer hold my breath, I turn toward her, put my lips close to her ear, and speak softly, "You know, they have fabulous products these days to mitigate the stench of rotten crotch. You don't need to mask your odiferous problem with perfume."

The ding of a bell indicates that we've reached our destination as the doors swish open. Randolph touches the small of my back, courteously steering me out of the elevator. We both take in a deep breath of unpolluted air as he looks at me with sedate reassurance.

The restaurant is elegant and luckily, dimly lit. Randolph steps up, giving the maître d' his name. Without delay, we're ushered across the airy penthouse and promptly seated by floor-to-ceiling windows overlooking the shimmering city lights. I feel as though we're on the top of the world. The view is phenomenal and this night couldn't be more perfect.

The sommelier dutifully arrives at our table with an extensive wine list and recommendations that are always the most expensive. I'm a self-proclaimed oenophile and know what I like, but I insist that Randolph order for us. I see that this pleases him as he hands the wine list back and places our order with refined excellence.

Randolph would be appalled if he knew that I've been trolling the local grocery chains for free beer and wine samples. I'm not a big fan of beer but just look at my circumstances. *When in Rome!* I even stopped at a discount food store and tried lite beer during a tasting in aisle four. I was initially excited to try something new, but I will venture to say that lite beer may very well be like drinking urine; though right now, I would consume both pigswill and corn mash if it would give me added courage. If Randolph Prescott could see the real me, he would be sickened by his choice of a dinner partner. I'll at least wait until the end of the evening to tell him who I really am.

We have a lovely meal and share pleasant conversation over a vintage bottle of Château Margaux. My grandparents would have been pleased with the wine selection. They would've also been pleased that not only am I sitting down to eat, but I'm enjoying the hours-long European custom of making mealtime an event.

Conversation flowed as we took turns sharing sensitive information from our past. The initial topic centered on our upbringing, which was easy to discuss since it occurred before my lying phase. Randolph was reverently kind and attentive as we compared the typical my-childhood-was-worse-than-yours stories. He spoke of being an only child to disinterested parents who despised one another and scarcely tolerated him.

"They did send me to all the best boarding schools..." he recounted ardently.

Still, there was sorrow in his eyes.

I told of a storybook childhood that ended abruptly with my parents' passing. "You win," he said. Then with a reddened face, he immediately realized his gaffe and began stammering apologies.

I waved the comment away as if dismissing a servant. "No, no. You're right. I did win! I had parents who were deeply in love with each other and who adored me. I wish they'd been on this earth a little longer, but hey—it was great while they were here. No apology necessary, I promise."

Now that that was over with, on to the next subject that was thickly hovering above us.

"Love interest?" he queried.

"Newly divorced," I confess with satisfaction. "And you?"

"Confirmed bachelor. Don't want to travel down the same road as the torturously betrothed Mr. and Mrs. Prescott."

We agreed that neither of us is looking for romantic involvement, but rather a mutually affable relationship. It's too bad though. Perhaps there could have been something more in another time, another place. Randolph Prescott is a true gentleman who still believes in the good of humankind and freely displays the long-lost practice of chivalry. He's a gallant nobleman who merits a muscular white horse and a beautiful princess. He kissed my hand, for Christ's sake! The man deserves a parade!

I then suddenly decided to expose myself. Not in the physical sense, which admittedly would be much easier. I'm as surprised as anyone when the words come rolling off my tongue. "Randolph, I need to explain who I really am."

"Oh, Sharon, I feel as though I already know you, and we are the dearest of friends. By the way, your assistant called to set up a meeting for Wednesday afternoon. When I told her that I was having dinner with you this evening, she seemed quite confused. Strange girl. I finally just agreed to the appointment time."

"Randolph, please let me finish. There's something I really need to tell you."

"Let's not talk shop and save untold stories for another time, shall we?"

The waiter arrives on signal from Randolph, flaunting the sumptuous dessert tray with much fanfare. I quickly lose my nerve while staring at the decadent confections and salivate like Pavlov's dog.

"I'll have the lot!" I say greedily.

"Go ahead, Ms. Creosote," says Randolph. "Indulge!"

It was difficult to pick just one. I carefully choose the chocolate mousse, served in an elongated crystal flute with darkly shaved chocolate swirls and to-die-for raspberry drizzle.

"Two, please," says Randolph, mimicking my request.

It's been so long since I've had anything as satisfyingly sweet, and I'm savoring each bite. The flavors meld on my tongue, twirling pinwheels of pleasure. No one else in the room mattered. Just me and chocolate.

"It looks like you haven't had any in a while," observes Randolph with a sly grin.

I instantly blush, misinterpreting his statement. "Well, it has been a long time..." I say, licking the spoon.

Randolph produces a crisply pressed handkerchief and leans over, gently blotting chocolate from my mouth. Some things simply cannot be controlled. I surmise that I look much like a starving dog chasing the proverbial meat wagon.

I'm having such a marvelous time that I can't bear to ruin the evening. We share our innermost thoughts and feelings; things we most wanted from life that no amount of money could buy. Our hopes and dreams. How to solve the maladies of the world. What we would do if we were in command of a country or an army. We also talked about things our rebellious, impassioned selves would do if no one were watching. If we weren't afraid of being fools or breaking bones.

"I always fancied one of your American bucket lists," professed Randolph.

"You should *totally* do it!" I said.

"*Totally!*" he parodied in his most convincing Valley Girl impersonation.

Randolph and I have occupied this table for hours. At one point, I thought we might be ejected from the restaurant for uncontrollable fits of laughter. After all, we're anomalies surrounded by an atmospheric fug of puritans, all abstaining from fun.

Catching sight of our waiter, Randolph holds up his index finger, ostentatiously shouting, "Check pleeeeeeease!"

Even that made us howl.

If I tell Randolph that I've been posing as Sharon Bartelson, he'll hate me. If Sharon finds out, I'm dead. Any way you slice it, the situation will come to a head, either by my initiative or by fate. By the time Sharon meets with Randolph, and once they realize what I've done, there will be a quantifiable disturbance in the force.

The drive back to Hidden Acres is benevolently quiet. As we motor along in silence, the gentle cornering along backcountry roads cause our bodies to rhythmically lean left and right through each turn. An evening filled with friendly table talk and a delicious meal has left us pleasurably content, suppressing any desire for added conversation.

Meandering down the long private drive to Hidden Acres, I follow the gentle glow from the antiqued glass pathway lights to the main entrance. Turning off the ignition, I swivel in my seat to face Randolph.

"Would you like to come in for a nightcap?" he asks.

"Perhaps another time," I say, knowing there will not be another time, nor will there ever be an evening as special as this. Randolph unbuckles his seatbelt, leans over, and kisses me sweetly on the cheek. "You are lovely..." he says, with lips slightly upturned at the corners. A yearning wells up inside of me. It would be easy to surrender to visceral desire, but none of this is real. I shake myself out of a hypnotic state and hastily start my car. Randolph barely has time to exit the vehicle as I nervously thank him and drive away, leaving him standing in startled bewilderment.

Since I couldn't come clean with Randolph, I've made myself ill thinking about his meeting with Sharon. I tried to sleep, but that was futile. My eyes are dry and scratchy from staring at the ceiling and from contacts that I've worn far too long. My lenses are daily wear disposables, but I keep soaking and using them, eking out a little more wear each time. I have enough contacts and solution left to wear on special occasions, but I'll probably be blind by the end of the week. I'm damaging my eyes just to keep Randolph from seeing me in my glasses. They're the heavy, round black frames that were once popular, but have never fit the shape of my face. The thick lenses give me babyish anime eyes. I slip them on and look around the bare room, grateful that at least for now, I have my vision.

I hold my pillow out in front of my face. "*Don't I look fetching?*" I say to Eduardo.

Now I've done it. Fetching rhymes with retching, and I feel like I'm going to throw up. I don't have anything carbonated to quiet my stomach, so I lie still and wait for the unsettled feeling to pass.

It's too late to go back to sleep and too early to get up. I need to talk this out with someone. I could call Juan, but he *has* a life. Anyway, I've abused his good nature by bombarding him with a constant flow of my problems, and I'm sure he doesn't need a recap of the same tired story.

Perhaps a little food will help mitigate the knotted feeling in my stomach. I pull on my robe and head down to the kitchen. My purse and jacket are still on the counter where I left them. I remove the mints and fine teas from my jacket pockets, lifted from the restaurant when I excused myself to use the powder room last night.

Pirate's booty.

I spread my ill-gotten gains on the kitchen island and picked my breakfast selection. Oolong tea and crème de mint filled chocolates. I take my time sipping tea and nibbling on the small, buttery chocolate squares as I weigh my options.

The last supper.

With my blood sugar raised and hunger pangs temporarily satisfied, I decided that Linda may be my only hope. I'll call her and try an honest approach to my writing dilemma. I'll also see if she can help me disentangle this labyrinth of dishonesty that has me pushed into a corner with no clear escape.

I pause and try to remember what time zone Linda is in. Words, I know well, but simple math is all I'm equipped to handle. And even that leaves me stymied. I hold up my right hand, counting fingers, trying to figure out the time difference between here and the agency. If I knew any first graders, I'd ask them. They'd whip out their tablet or cell phone and within seconds, I'd not only have the time, but also the weather, and a full report on the commodities market.

As my agent, Linda and I have a long professional history and I respect her judgment as well as her counsel. She's not only my agent, she's my friend. A friend who I've been avoiding because I've accomplished zilch in the writing department. I've also reneged on our contractual agreement several times over, placing her in a difficult situation. Our past was intertwined with an undeviating reliability, until the threads, once connecting us, began to work loose and unravel. Now, I'm in fear of losing what matters most: writing. My professional life is competing with my personal life for the Disaster of the Year award!

I can reach Linda on her cell, but given the circumstances, I don't think she'd welcome a personal call from her least favorite author. Instead, I wait until the agency opens. Her assistant transfers me immediately as if expecting my call. Before Linda could speak, I set aside all hesitation and spilled my guts. Without a breath of interruption, she allows me to bare all regarding my circumstances, and the fact that things have mushroomed out of control.

"I hate my holier-than-thou neighborhood, the pretense, my ex-husband, my so-called best friend, and my life. I've been left with nothing. I can scarcely pay my bills and can barely take care of myself. I've told so many lies that I don't even know what's real anymore. My God, I'm even pretending to be a realtor!"

I blubber and snivel and whimper and cry. I expose the ugly side of myself and divulge the fact that I've been volunteering at the local food pantry for months with the intent of stealing provisions for myself and my dog.

"When I was down to only peanut butter and saltines, I divvied them up and created three meals a day, thinly spreading peanut butter on one cracker and placing another cracker on top. I put them in used plastic sandwich bags, labeling them for each day of the week. I stored them in the empty freezer, knowing I would never polish off a bunch of frozen peanut butter and crackers if they were out of sight. But I wish I'd purchased the chunky two-pack peanut butter instead of the creamy! The chunky would have taken longer to digest and I wouldn't have felt hungry so soon. When that ran out, I had no other choice but to steal...

I stock shelves at the food pantry and then handily stock an oversized Dolce & Gabbana tote bag with staples to sustain me for the week. I've pawned my jewelry, consigned my clothes, and sold most of my furniture. I traded personal items for household services until I had nothing expendable left. I gave the plumber a 70-inch flat screen to unclog the toilet in the master bedroom. All because I didn't know what a toilet plunger was for!

I go into public restrooms to steal toilet paper and fast-food restaurants for napkins and condiments. I've given up groceries, toiletries, recreation, television, and even the newspaper and periodicals just to pay for this house and keep up appearances. I've been eating pork and beans for shit's sake!"

The irony of this was not lost for I heard a muffled chuckle emanating from the receiver.

"Linda, I have no more stories to tell!" I confess tearfully.

When I finally finished purging my soul, there was only silence on the other end. I thought that I might have shocked Linda into speechlessness or worse—that she hung up on me.

"Linda? You there?"

"Oh, I'm here, Angela. I'm just taking it all in..."

I angrily wipe my tearful eyes with a sleeve.

"Well, are you shocked that your once celebrated author is a shameful woman who's lived life as if she were beyond reproach? Go ahead. Judge me. Tell me you're dissolving our agent/client agreement and severing any affiliation we once had. Go ahead. Tell me what I already know. That I'm a complete and total wash-up!"

"Are you finished with the pity party and self-flagellation? Do you want to hear what I think?" says Linda.

Here it comes. Another ally that I can mark off my list. Another person who I've lied to and disappointed. A woman who used to believe in me; an avid supporter whom I've left completely disillusioned.

"I think you've found your story, Angela. Tell it. Tell it like no one else can."

Chapter Sixteen

I swore I'd never go to another one of these, but here I am, in attendance at the Bryn Mawr HOA meeting. I tell myself that I'm attending for research purposes; delving into the lives of the self-absorbed to see what makes them tick.

I'll get the lowdown at the hoedown!

These people never fail to surprise me with their outspoken opinions. They browbeat neighbors, and homeowners prostrate themselves by kowtowing to the HOA's insupportable ultimatums.

As if I don't already have enough melodramatic storylines to build on!

Whatever happened to freethinkers? Have we become an extinct breed? I wonder if there's a coalition of humanity that's out counting the wild mavericks, trying to save us from complete annihilation. I brood over this while waiting in the vestibule, tucked behind a large potted Benjamin ficus.

I didn't attend the preliminary social hour, because frankly, I don't have the stomach for it. I call it the anesthetized hour, where they offer free cocktails. If you can call it free, as the charges are tacked onto our monthly dues. The brilliant move of using the word *free* placates the masses and keeps them pacified during the monotonous finger-pointing summit.

I suspect that in my absence, I've been the subject of their notorious jowl-slapping blather. How does that saying go? Be there or be talked about? I walk into the meeting and slip into a seat in the vacant front row just as Darcy's gavel hits the marble block. The Bryn Mawr HOA meeting has been officially called to order.

I'm sitting alone in an empty row with plenty of personal space. I stretch out my arms to the backs of the chairs on either side of me, demonstrating how comfortable it is to sit by oneself. For some reason, people must sit together in tightly formed groups, embracing mediocrity. Those same people are also found orbiting parking lots in search of a closer space, squeezing into a compact area with hardly enough room to open car doors. It makes me laugh when I park in a wide, unpopulated area. I exit my vehicle and walk briskly to my destination while the same individuals continue mechanically orbiting the lot.

Darcy goes into cheerleader mode. "The bi-annual Bryn Mawr Homeowners Association meeting is called to order. We have newcomers and introductions to make. Does everyone here have a street buddy?"

I raise my hand. "Pardon my ignorance, but what, pray tell, is a street buddy?"

Neighbors' heads simultaneously gyrate into whiplash mode, gawking at me for such an absurd question. Darcy pretends not to hear me and continues.

"Please go around the room and introduce yourself with your first and last names, your address, and number of years you've lived in Bryn Mawr. Also, a fun fact about your family. For the newbies, please let your street buddy introduce you.

I'll begin. My name is Darcy Danforth, 690 Bogey Court. I'm happily married to Richard and we have two marvelous children, Samantha and Richard III. We've lived here for ten years, nine of which I've been your association president. Fun fact: I sit on the Bryn Mawr Golf & Country Club Board as well as the Humane Society Board, the YMCA Board, the Bryn Mawr School Board, and the Delta Zeta Alumni Association Board. I'm also head cheer coach at the Bryn Mawr Academy and I've been secretary of the Bryn Mawr Ma Jong Club for, gosh...as long as I can remember!"

Darcy glances around the room, beaming, waiting for applause that never comes. She overdramatically clears her throat and continues with introductions of new neighbors and old, conveniently skipping over me and moving on to matters of the utmost importance. The first order of business is grass clippings. Evidently, this subject has been stuck in Darcy's craw for some time.

"I don't know about all of you," she drones, "but those people on Fair Oaks with the double lot? Their landscapers leave trimmings on the street and it drives me crazy! We need to uphold the grass-clipping guidelines. Suggestions?"

Everyone stares straight ahead.

What suggestions could there possibly be? They're grass clippings!

"Alrighty then, I'll have my virtual assistant send them a written warning." Darcy rolls her eyes upward as she ponders the intensity level of rebuke.

"They've already received a letter of caution," states Darcy in her most convincing tone. "Umm...I guess it's time to get tough. Let's go with a Level Two."

I become an instant enemy for mentioning the following problem that sadly, I've been addressing for the past fifteen years.

"What about the Cook residence on the south side of me? They have a lot full of waist-high weeds. They have the front mowed and do nothing to maintain the back or sides of the property. The garage doors and front doors have rotted through and they only do the bare minimum, never trimming hedges or cleaning up fallen leaves. I constantly have knee-deep mounds of debris blowing onto my property, yet no one says a word about the unkempt condition of their home."

Mrs. Cook jumps to her feet and screeches, "*We* have kids and *we* work!"

Apparently, that's code for fucking lazy, as no one bats an eye and Darcy moves on with her agenda.

"The next matter that we simply must address is basketball hoops. I realize there are families in the subdivision who think they need these contraptions, but it's against policy to have them in the front of the home or anywhere in plain view."

All the conformists look vapidly at their shoes, so again, I speak up and stand to address our fearless leader.

"I find it contradictory that you have a basketball hoop above your carriage house garage, Darcy."

"You can't *see* our basketball hoop *and* it's been grandfathered in."

"Does that mean that your grandfather once owned it? Because that would certainly explain why it looks like a splintered piece of crap."

"Angela, you're speaking out of turn and dominating the conversation! You need to be quiet as a mouse." Darcy holds up her hand deftly pressing fingertips together—the school teacher's universal sign language for *shush*. My drunken neighbors nod their heads in silent approval. There's no hope for these people.

Toward the end of the association meeting, it's customary to hold an open forum where anyone with concerns is allowed to speak. Those not agreeing with the HOA president are deemed an aggressor and snubbed; the unwritten rule brazenly apparent this evening. Although I'm sitting directly in front of her with my arm raised, Darcy pretends I'm not here, looking over and around me to see if there's anyone whose opinion matters.

Richard and Darcy Danforth are co-chairs of the leadership committee, the nominating committee, the architectural and landscape committees, and the head of the neighborhood commission on social justice. They're also co-conspirators of reprehensible behavior.

Someone needs to take these two down a notch. Someone needs to question their authority and dismantle their little empire. No qualified candidates come forth, so it looks like that someone is me.

After evaluating the comatose crowd, I determine that I'm surrounded by sheeple. Decisively, I stand as a lone wolf and approach the podium, an action that's caused an uneasy disturbance within the flock. They sit bleating their disapproval.

"Permission to speak, ma'am!" I shout, saluting smartly, startling Darcy from her command post.

"Angela, good grief! You need to take your seat. *Please!*"

"You mean, take my place?"

"I mean that we must have order! You must sit down!"

"Well, look here, Darleen Jean Grubwell. You don't mind if I use your given name, do you?"

Darcy appears stricken with a vernacular paralysis and is stammering spiritless undertones of drivel. I seize the opportunity to move Darcy aside and overtake the podium. I've declared her provisionally insane as I hijack the meeting, pounding the gavel to get everyone's attention. It seems that straying from protocol has awakened hecklers from the audience. Someone in the back yells, "Unconstitutional!" Another shouts, "Illegitimate!"

Even Herbert Fitch from 470 Fairway has climbed into the cuckoo's nest, chanting a litany of preordained tadut-ta-da's. These repetitive buzzwords are from Mr. Fitch's anger management class, used whenever he's feeling anxious or out of control. It appears that the tempo of this haunting repetition works. It's also what's kept him gainfully employed, after punching a coworker in the face during a contentious Intelligence Committee meeting.

Everyone in the room has joined in the pandemonium and Herbert is no exception. He's stepped up and enlisted in the crazy crusade.

"Tadut-ta-da, tadut-ta-da, tadut-ta-da, tadut-ta-da..."

Apparently, I'm the only participant operating in stone-cold sober mode. That, combined with my utter loathing for these people has equipped me with newfound bravery.

"I was always taught that one should begin with a compliment. Therefore, let me begin by saying that Darleen, you have really come a long way since your gangsta days back in the boondocks. Don't worry, Darcy. We all have a past. Some more shady than others, but a past just the same.

I was an investigative reporter during my college internship and dabbled in PI work as well. When people act like idiots, they draw attention to themselves. Naturally, my curious side wanted to find out just a wee bit more about you, and it wasn't hard to find. The surface dirt was interesting, but the info on the dark web? Well, that was riveting! And the movie. Yikes! That didn't leave a lot to the imagination...

What was it called again? *Darleen Does Davenport?*"

Redford Nester sits quietly in the back row with his arms folded, leering like the letch that he is. I gather that he's not only seen this flick, he probably owns it on everything from VHS to DVD to instant download. Red's pokerfaced expression verifies what I already suspected. But Richard Danforth is slumped forward holding his pale face in elfin hands, trying not to puke. I'll assume Darcy never mentioned her short stint as an adult film star to her husband.

Several more hecklers demand that I sit down, as I hold up my hands in transitory surrender.

"According to the bylaws, each homeowner is allowed to speak for five minutes on any subject, hence I will speak about your lives in 300 seconds," I tell them.

I look directly at Darcy and notice that one of her false eyelashes has slithered from its desired position and is now dangling precariously from the corner of her left eye. It's difficult to ignore a caterpillar-esque fragment protruding from one's eyeball. Impulsively, I point to the corner of my eye and blurt, "Darcy, you have a little somethin'some-thin' right there. I'm totally shocked, Darce! I thought a woman of your stature would be able to afford mink eyelash extensions, or at the very least, Latisse."

While everyone gasped and warbled their inarticulate babble, Darcy remained immersed in her own little world. As she fretfully twiddled with her eyelash, I kept the momentum going without taking my eyes off her.

"The first order of business is the way you bully your neighbors, Darcy. I'd like to know why you do that. Tell me, does it make you feel important, or special?

And while we're on the subject of special, what about the time you reported the couple next door to Child Protective Services because their Down syndrome son had wandered into your yard looking for a cookie? You told CPS they were negligent and inattentive parents. CPS began an unwarranted investigation that made this family's life a living hell. They were great neighbors. But like all great neighbors living in this col-ony of pompous rat bastards, they finally gave up and moved, as most normal people eventually do."

An intense stillness envelops the room as everyone stares at Madame President. Characteristically chatty, Darcy is now painfully groping for syntax that will mollify the spectators.

"You don't need to continue with personal attacks, Angela! This is an official HOA meeting and my private life is not up for discussion!"

"Oh, but it is, Darcy! You're our official representative and have made this an attack on humanity. So why don't you explain why you'd commit such a despicable act?"

A long pause ensues as we all wait. Eventually, Darcy stands, staring with one elaborately made-up eye framed by thick lashes. The other eye, messily streaked with blue eye shadow, exposes an area of unoccupied emptiness where luxuriant lashes once obediently adhered to her eyelid.

Blindly assuming that everyone feels the same way, she surveys the room for support and begins recklessly burping out her prejudiced beliefs.

"Retarded children shouldn't be living amongst normal people! *Okay!* Is that what you want to hear? They make me nervous and they need to be contained! They need to be around their own kind. I can't be expected to give out my homemade cookies to just anyone. What if the kid is gluten-intolerant or worse—allergic to nuts? The lawsuits alone would ruin me!"

I'm making a conscious effort to close my mouth, which is now gaping open.

"Good God, woman! What kind of intolerant bitch could even think that way, let alone utter those words out loud?" I yell back.

The altercation caused other homeowners to move their heads in sync as if they were spectators at Wimbledon. However, once Darcy began speaking, perpetual motion took over and she couldn't stop. Cell phones popped up and folks began recording her blinkered response.

"Gawd Angela! They shouldn't try to mainstream an abnormal child into society, especially into *our* neighborhood! Plus, I don't want a retard around my kids! Is that so wrong?"

"Well actually, it is wrong! Clearly, Down syndrome isn't catching. It's not a communicable disease. But you, madam, are a narrow-minded festering pustule, contaminating those around you with your archaically parochial views."

"What would this do to our property values, huh, Angela? Having kids like that running amok!"

I breathe deeply and exhale slowly.

"Darcy, you're demonstrably missing chromosomes and you're belittling a child with an extra one. You're the broken one here. You disgust me. You're damaged beyond salvation."

I begin to step down and realize that I've forgotten something. I return to the podium just long enough to conclude my polemic sermon.

"Since I was intentionally omitted from initial introductions, let me formally present myself," I say, scanning the room, smiling disingenuously at old neighbors and new.

"My name is Angelarosa Magdalena Morgan. I reside at 430 Golf View Court and I have lived in Bryn Mawr for, let's see...*too long*. Fun fact: I'm a novelist whose creative well has run dry. My infantile husband left me for a stripper and saddled me with an incalculable amount of debt. I'm on the verge of losing everything and I despise myself as much as I despise all of you."

With that, I drink the remainder of whoever's scotch and soda is parked in front of me, then quickly exit the meeting during a very pregnant pause. I turn briefly, knowing this will be the last time I'll ever set foot in this room. They're still quietly staring in my direction when I give a celebratory two thumbs up to the crowd.

"Hasta la vista, muthafuckas!"

Chapter Seventeen

After telling off Bryn Mawr's finest, I slept like a log. Now it's time for some heavy-duty soul-searching, right after I nuke a cup of water. I pocketed handfuls of gourmet instant coffee packets at the club refreshment kiosk last night. I didn't know that granulated coffee is considered gourmet, but I'll try to believe the claims on the packaging.

Before now, I never would have entertained the notion of drinking microwaved coffee. But in these bleak times, I seem destined to consume just about anything. I stir the contents into a cup of boiling water. After choosing a raw sugar packet from my arsenal of pilfered condiments, and stirring in a sinful amount of thick cream, I bring the cup up to my nose. It smells delightful.

Raking people over the coals took energy and intestinal fortitude, and I felt that I deserved a prize for my presentation. Upon exiting through the country club dining room, I walked off with an elegant crystal decanter filled with real cream. I placed it in a drink cup holder, and proudly, didn't spill a drop on the ride home. I also emptied a large bowl of fresh fruit into my tote bag. I don't think anyone saw me do it, but if they did, I can't imagine they'd care. After my castigating speech, I believe I could have walked out with a dining table strapped to my back, with no one batting an eye.

Leaning on the kitchen counter, I look out the large picture window over the sink. Appreciating each sip of coffee, I pretend that I'm drinking truth serum, something that will help reveal myself to the world. I compare my life to those that I told off last night and think about how I've treated people. I'm no better than anyone in that room! My bad behavior was thanks in part to my disreputable role model, but I can't blame everything on Sharon. Sharon walks over people to get where she wants to be. She has no respect for anyone and I find my association with her nauseating. But I have done the same, and now, I must own up to my actions.

I don't need to waste any more time creating a paper checklist. Instead, I make mental calculations, completing each task quickly by ticking them off in my head. *Let go of the crazy things first: Cease depositing the dummy newspaper at that unholy hour. This satisfies two objectives. Quit faking and get more sleep. Done.*

Next, I'll stop trying to blend in. I don't belong here. The only thing I like about this neighborhood is the confines of my personal space. I call an official halt to trying to impress anyone. This will make it easier when I execute my intended mission.

I've terminated my membership at the club, both verbally and in writing as decreed by their bylaws. Even though I'd barely maintained a social membership in the last year, it was for appearances only. Already, I feel better. No more mandatory meals in their overpriced dining room. No more listening to persons of highbrow descent belittle the wait staff who make barely enough to survive. These pugnacious two-ball bitches don't know what hardship is. What's worse, I've unintentionally become one of them by fraternizing with the in-crowd.

I've overheard many comments while partaking in various staged, yet overrated country club functions. "My arugula is a bit wilted; the asparagus is overcooked/undercooked/too green/not green enough..."

Shocking.

"I don't like the color of my meat..."

What the hell color would you like it to be?

"Excuuuuuuse me! I asked for another cappuccino over five minutes ago. Do you like working here, dear? Because if you don't..."

When did it become commonplace and acceptable to treat people like this? The real crime though, is that I never said a word. I never stood up for the underdog. I looked the other way, accepting that you treat people this way when you have money. And in my case, even when you don't. Well, no more! Sensing that an oral and written membership termination isn't sufficient, I drive the short distance to the restricted Bryn Mawr Country Club. I should be just in time for brunch.

As I drive up the twisting lane, golfers meander about the chemically saturated course. One budding enthusiast stands daringly close to the winding roadway, lining up a putt. I slow to a stop, ignore the sanctioned "quiet please" signs, put my window down, honk my horn, and heartily yell, "FOUR!"

I punch the accelerator, creating an impressive, smoking fishtail. As I speed away, I peer into my rearview mirror. There's an enraged duffer mouthing something indecorous, spiritedly brandishing his putter like a weapon. I smile, quite pleased with myself.

When I pull through the circular drive to the main entrance, a sprightly young man emerges to valet park my car. "Greetings, Mrs. Morgan!"

My name must not have made the revised exclusion list, so I jump out of my extravagant set of wheels, acting like I own the place. My car hasn't been washed in ages, and although I don't drive much anymore, the grill and windshield are slathered in a mass murder of varietal insects. The valet's smile fades and he appears traumatized.

"It's just a dirty car, for Christ's sake." Then I look down and realize that in my haste, I've forgotten to adequately dress for the occasion.

"Mindless me, wearing old sweats and no shoes." I shrug and point shamelessly to my face, stating the obvious. "No makeup either and I don't remember when I last brushed my hair or teeth. Fucking disgraceful, isn't it?"

The poor kid doesn't know what to do. It's probably his summer job and they didn't go over such a situation during training.

"No need to park it, I won't be long," I say with a wink, pressing my last crumpled five-dollar bill into his outstretched hand.

He manages a nervous smile and follows me inside, aware that he may be witness to something noteworthy. I traipse past the hostess and marshal inward as a hush falls over the dining room.

I see Darcy and her peeps at their usual corner table, smartly outfitted in country club attire. Darcy's bottle blonde hair is pulled back in a severe ponytail, held by a stylish cloisonné clip. Her eyes are protruding in globular surprise. Darcy looks none the worse for wear after having her lady-balls castrated at the meeting last night. I'm taken aback by her resilience.

Well, good for her!

On the way past her table, I hold my hand up, executing the four fingers to the palm cutesy wave. "Lookin' good, Darce!"

I see several patrons running. No doubt to retrieve the manager and security personnel, all of which are likely in the bar schmoozing with the regulars. Since I've already given notice to terminate my membership, besides bodily removal, I could also be arrested for trespassing.

Isn't spontaneity wonderful?

My first object of reprimand is Patience Tisdale. She's frozen in place, her fork hovering close to her mouth, suspended in mid-gorge. I assume that she's delighted to see me, so I take this as an invitation to join her and her feckless, pocket-sized husband, Scot.

These two remind me of the nursery rhyme about Jack Sprat who could eat no fat, and his wife could eat no lean. Mr. Scot Tisdale looks perpetually tormented. I contemplate the cause and deduce that it's because he's married to one of the most domineering gossipmongers that I've ever met. The man is in his sixties and has been struggling unsuccessfully to grow a mustache most of his adult life. I have more hair on my upper lip if I don't wax for a month! But the poor little guy is persistent, I'll give him that.

I pull up a seat and sit down heavily, taking a long drink of ice water.

"Howya doin' Scotty my boy! And you, Patience? You're looking simply ravishing, though I wouldn't go so low-cut at your age..."

I lean in to give some helpful advice. "The neck and décolleté area are a bit weathered and rucked. Y'know what I mean?" I give Patience an understanding wink, pinching the skin under my chin while moving it rapidly in a back-and-forth motion. "Gobble-gobble!"

I casually lean back, elbow slung over the arm of my chair. "Not feeling like talking this morning, Patience? No problem! I've got enough conversation in me for all of us."

Unless you count staring, there's little movement in the dining room. The wait staff and chefs are now lined up by the kitchen, expectantly waiting for history to be made. I shan't disappoint them.

"I've always wondered something, Scot. Why is there only one t in your name?"

"Well..." he says, while Patience glares, willing him to cease talking. "It's short for Ascot."

And there it is. Mine for the taking.

"Then may I call you Ass for short?"

Patience begins choking on something, which I precipitously conclude is her pride. Nonetheless, one can't take any chances where choking is concerned. I rush dependably to her side, pull her to her feet, and begin administering the Heimlich maneuver, even though I don't know what the hell I'm doing. Patience is slapping at me and protesting wildly. I finally let go as Mrs. Patience Tisdale, Queen Bee of Bryn Mawr, leans gracelessly on the table, slavering profusely.

Mr. Brown, the pudgy general manager, rushes to her side with a reddened face and a plethora of apologies. "Oh my God, Mrs. Tisdale!

Are you all right? What can I do? Do you wish for me to call you an ambulance?"

I push him aside. "I'll do it!"

Bending down, I look deeply into Mrs. Tisdale's bloated, alcoholic face.

"You're an ambulance. Besides that, Patience Tisdale, you're a rude, dictatorial, overreaching bitch. And that goes for many of you as well." I stand, pointing an accusatory finger around the room.

"You people treat the staff as your indentured servants. They bring your drinks and your food and put up with your bloviated dialogue and idiotic demands. You treat them like inferior human beings, put on this earth for the sole purpose of kissing your asses!"

For once, Patience Tisdale has nothing to say. The queen has been dethroned and her cloud of self-righteous anger erodes.

Bob Beaverton stands to leave as his lady friend holds onto his strong arm. I thought that I'd offended the one good guy in the room, causing his hasty departure. But on the way out, they stop briefly at the Tisdales' reserved table. Bob gives me a locker room atta-boy pat on the back.

"We got another engagement to git to, but good job shuttin' this one up, missy." Looking right at Patience, he adds, "'Cause she can usually talk the hind legs off a donkey!"

I love that man.

I look at the wait staff, hostesses, head chef, sous chefs, prep cooks, bartenders, wine steward, and even the manager, who've all stepped to the perimeter to listen. I continue to address the assembled congregants with a thought-provoking homily.

"Has anyone here ever thanked any of you for all that you do? Has anyone in this room ever said, 'You are appreciated'?"

They all stare at their shoes.

"Well, for what it's worth, I appreciate you. I think that you show a gratuitous amount of self-restraint, which thankfully, I have none of right now. I wouldn't blame any of you if you've ever spit in a drink, deposited a bug in the poached salmon, or rubbed your wee-wee on the silverware."

There are communal gags and groans from the dining patrons.

I stand, spreading my arms in a wide flourish. "Have any of you ever considered that the folks who you expect to subserviently fulfill your shallow whims are the same people who fall into bed exhausted at night? Or who leave here with barely enough time to get to their second jobs, or pick up their kids from daycare? These individuals work hard to take care of their families on what paltry pay they're allowed, while you sit back complaining that you're driving last year's Lexus."

I continue, giving a perceptive nod up to the club employees, all of which are now sporting wide smiles.

"Besides the industrious group of people before you, consider the young men and women who caddy for a collective bunch of drunks on the golf course; the people who park your cars, hang up your coats, retrieve your towels, and lifeguard at the pool so your unattended brats don't drown."

I take a deep, shuttering breath and let my shoulders slump.

"Well, I said what I came here to say. I'm tired, and I'm going home. If you want to arrest me, press charges, or give me a piece of your mind, you know where to find me. Until then, try to find some manners. Your behavior is atrocious."

I drive home, pull up into the porte cochére, and enter through the unlocked front door. I lean back and shut it with a gently pleasing click, sliding down to the floor where Snags takes the opportunity to lick my face, imparting his laudatory support.

The next matter on my abstract to-do list is introspection. I've treated people terribly, and not just since the divorce. I never understood how many people I'd hurt over the years until I began seeing myself through the eyes of others.

I resolve to continue my volunteer position at the food pantry during my regular Wednesday morning restocking duties. This time, I'm going to really stock shelves and not steal food for myself. I went to meet with the pantry director, Marjorie Fitzgibbons, and shamefacedly told her what I'd been doing. I also agree to reimburse them for everything I took. Instead of calling the police and being escorted from the building with instructions never to return, Mrs. Fitzgibbons looked into my eyes, patted my hand, and said, "You must have really been in need, dear..."

I broke down and cried at her generosity and compassion.

On my first day back restocking the food pantry shelves, I felt lighter with the knowledge that I finally owned up to my lies. Someday, when I can afford to, I'll present this place with an amazing gift equivalent to all the good that they do, and then some. How they manage to keep this place running is beyond me. Around the holidays, and in times of desperation, they send out an SOS to the community. Even with the local churches, Scouting for Food campaigns, Capital campaigns, and private donations, it's still not enough to fill the never-ending cavity of hunger.

The pantry is housed in a dingy warehouse that's quite austere and strictly utilitarian. A sad building, with its leaky roof and crumbling concrete floor. The only decoration is a wilted philodendron that like many of the clients, looks weakened and defeated. When I first began volunteering here, the entrance door was made of glass but has since been nailed over with a piece of weathered plywood. An elderly woman in a Crown Vic hit the gas instead of the brake, and well, we all know the rest of *that* story.

The structure design is Early American Quonset Hut, without interior walls. The storage area opens audaciously to the front counter, and like it or not, you can hear everything. The reception area is visible from my workspace, but I turn away from the throngs of people lining up to collect their provisions. I keep my head down, pretending not to see the many penurious faces picking up their monthly allotment; staying emotionally detached from the realities of those whose struggles are permanently etched into their daily lives. Sure, there are a few who play the system. I occasionally hear their echoing demands of entitlement reverberating through the warehouse; though the majority of those here are truly in need. They consist of single parents, the jobless, the working poor, the elderly, the infirm, college students far from home, and families who never thought they'd ever ask for help. There's also the enduring homeless, and people who have just fallen through societal cracks.

I'm aware of the blanketed populace who form the ranks of the needy, and ashamed that I don't want to see their faces. I'm a coward. I didn't swallow my pride and ask for help. In my arrogance, I chose instead to steal. I'm the lowest life form and I make a promise to God (if He listens to shoplifters), to never lose sight of that again. I hear "Amazing Grace" playing in my head and quietly sing along, for the first time paying close attention to the words.

"He saved a wretch...like me?" I guess I'm a wretch, or in modern-day terms, a good-for-nothing bitch.

"I once was lost, but now I'm found. Was blind, but now I see..."

There may be hope after all.

I'm engrossed in my restocking job, thinking about why people bequeath the pantry with thousands of cans of corn in every preserved state: whole kernel, creamed, salted, unsalted, spiced. And the beans! Good Lord! There are enough baked beans to cause a methane cloud of fissionable proportion. While wondering why I'm overthinking the generosity of others, I hear my name.

"You-hoo! Miss Morgan! Youuu-hooooo..."

I turn to see a short bubble of a woman as wide as she is tall, standing on her tippy-toes, waving animatedly in my direction. She's a bonafide ginger with enduring dimples, set deeply into a ruddy complexion. I stop what I'm doing and turn, waiting for her face to register or a name to pop into my head.

"Miss Morgan! Remember me?"

The truth is, I don't remember her. It's been a long time since anyone called out my name that wasn't from a collection agency or repo service. She doesn't look threatening, so I walk to the front counter to see what she wants.

"It's me, Dotty Dotson! Your biggest fan!"

I'm suddenly embarrassed. Not for the fact that she's prancing around me like an overexcited puppy. I'm embarrassed for myself because I now remember Dotty. She remained patiently in a long line during one of my local signings. She was unfazed by the wait and when it was her turn, she enthusiastically bounded forward to have her book signed.

"I'm your biggest fan, Miss Morgan!" she exclaimed breathlessly.

"How would you like the inscription to read?" I'd asked with rote undertones.

"I loved your book and read it in one night! I couldn't put it down! When is your next book due out? I can't wait to..."

I was becoming irritated and impatient that this woman was holding up the line. I needed to pee and she was precluding me from taking a much-needed break. I repeated the phrase, this time with more insolence, "What inscription would you like?!"

"Oh, my name is Dorothy Ann Dotson, but people call me Dotty or Dot for short. Dotty or Dot! I don't know...I'm so nervous!"

I was thinking, *don't tell me your whole life story. Just spit it out and hurry up!*

"Dot, then. Just sign it, To Dot."

So, I did. To •

What a piece of shit I was for doing this to an innocent person who was merely showing appreciation for my work. After all, wasn't that the purpose? To write for the enjoyment of others? To have them appreciate your work. That is the true payoff. Or at least it used to be.

"Of course, I remember you, Dotty! I'm so sorry for the way I..."

"Oh, Miss Morgan, I thought it was so funny the way you signed my book. I've shown it to everyone because not only are you the best writer on the planet, but you have a great sense of humor as well!"

"I don't deserve your kindness, Dotty."

I noticed that she was a bit disheveled and was anxiously fingering a loose button on her blouse.

"Are you working here at the pantry, Dot?"

"No ma'am," she said shyly. "I'm a client."

I speculated on what led her to this place. I wanted to ask Dorothy Ann Dotson about her situation, but we aren't allowed to discuss anything personal with the clients. There's an inherent need for privacy and although I've crossed a lot of lines, I'm not about to cross that one.

I needn't have worried about being forward, for Dotty is a naturally talkative person, proudly wearing her heart on her sleeve.

"I suppose you're wondering why I'm here... Well, Miss Morgan, I was going to college and had a great job with flexible hours. I had a boyfriend, an apartment, and even a cat named Whiskers. I also have a daughter with special needs. Her name is Delilah. She's my greatest joy! I lost my car and my job and had to quit school. Then my boyfriend left and took Whiskers with him. But we'll be okay, Delilah, and me. Everybody is faced with adversity and no one gets out of this life without it. I'll be fine. Really, I will!"

Dotty smiled widely with her whole being.

"You're so lucky, Miss Morgan! I really admire you. You entertain people with your writing and still find time to help others by volunteering. I hope I can be like you someday."

I'm mortified and deeply humbled. I hope I can be like Dotty Dotson someday.

Chapter Eighteen

I believe that running into Dotty was more than a coincidence. She's become my motivating force to do the right thing. But the longer this deception continues, the bigger the problem will become until the weight bears down and suffocates me. The pain this will cause is inescapable, but I can't delay the inevitable.

Driving to Hidden Acres with blinders on, I try to ignore the beauty and erase the fairy-tale adventures that have unfolded at this enchanted place. Randolph Prescott is a genuinely good person and I won't let Sharon destroy that. I militantly march up the steps to the mouth of the main entrance and firmly press the button that will cause the bottom to drop out of my fantasy world.

The wait is long. I hope that one of the staff answers the door, but Randolph told me that he likes to greet callers himself; though with a home this large, it could be eons before he makes it to the entrance. As I turn to walk away, the door opens, and there is Randolph, looking quite befuddled.

"Sharon, I wasn't expecting you until this afternoon."

"There's something that I need to tell you. Right now."

"Please, come in. You're scaring me. Are you in trouble? Are you in some sort of danger?"

Danger? Yes, you could say that.

"No. I don't want to come in. I prefer to stay out here."

Randolph places his arm around my waist in a caring manner, supportively ushering me to a garden bench. Before sitting down, I begin hyperventilating as the words tumble from my lips.

"My name is not Sharon. It's Angela..."

I finally came clean with Randolph, telling him everything. I convinced him to terminate our exclusive right to sell agreement, which really wasn't *our* agreement. I'd typed up simple contracts stating that they superseded all other documents, making the originals null and void. I forged Sharon's name on said documents and left a message with her assistant that she was to go to the Prescott property right away. This could take a while because Sharon does nothing immediately. And as she says, "I don't take directives from *anyone.*"

I've resigned to the fact that I'm guilty and will accept my punishment without resistance. After telling Randolph the whole story, I'd hoped we could find some common ground, having both been betrayed by Sharon Bartelson. But by the way he's shooting daggers with his eyes, I'd say that's a definite *no.* The thought of daggers makes me turn quickly, fearing that Randolph might end this conversation by handing Wilson a pitchfork to stab the living hell out of me. I don't feel the sharp pain of being impaled by a pronged object, so I try an alternate approach. Aligned empathy.

"I know you probably find me contemptuous and I wouldn't blame you if you brought legal charges against me as well," I sob.

Crying, it seems, does not affect Randolph as he continues to regard me with an expressionless gaze, his arms protectively crossed against his chest. I stand before him, disgraced, like a child facing a parent's reprimand. Digging a lint-laden tissue from the bottom of my worn handbag, I dab my teary eyes. He continues silently glowering as if contemplating my demise. I close my eyes and wait for the cacophonous tongue-lashing that never comes.

Although I've rehearsed this moment many times, I'd not considered the silent treatment. The silent treatment is far worse than yelling, and if this is intended to make me squirm, it's working. I deserve to suffer through the prelude to my impending sentence. However, if given the choice, I'd rather have the electric chair. Over and done.

Or, overdone.

After many agonizing minutes, Randolph finally speaks, over-enunciating through a clenched jaw. "Why did you do it, Angela? If that is even your real name! What could you possibly gain from deceiving me? And poor Wilson! He has become quite fond of you as well!"

"I didn't set out to deceive anyone. At first, I was desperate to find a story that would resurrect my inactive career. I saw a visual rendering of this idyllic estate that unearthed a spark of inspiration. I thought that one innocent visit couldn't hurt. Then, once we started talking, I became infatuated with the myriad of family stories. They were like a drug to me and I kept returning for more. I believed I could create a storyline from it, but eventually realized I was playing with the lives of real people. However, by then, I was in too deep and there was no easy way out. I'm so very sorry."

"You're sorry?" Randolph is understandably upset by my admission. Turning, he shakes his head in disbelief. As he whips back around, I reflexively back away.

"I trusted you! I told you personal things that I've never told anyone! All this deception so you could prostitute our lives to sell novels?"

Randolph swallowed back expletives while suppressing his anger. An oppressive silence lingered as the minutes ticked by. I'm thick-skinned and can stand being yelled at, but the quiet is crushing. I begin repeating my apologies.

"I've known Sharon Bartelson for longer than I can remember, and her ambitions can be considered ruinous at best. When I found out that she was planning to forge the appraisal, I looked deeper into her scheme. The plan was to have her husband's co-conspirators deem the land blighted, and then petition the county to rezone the property as commercial. They have overseas buyers who exist only on paper. The Bartelsons purchase the property for a fraction of the value, level the home and grounds, and build a massive conglomerate of subdivisions and commercial properties. There was also mention of a theme park and hotels... Still, my association with Sharon is no excuse for my execrable behavior. Again, I'm sorry! I know the words seem small and shallow, but it's all I have to offer."

At last, Randolph begins disgorging his verdict with a biting monologue. I stand before him accepting harsh condemnations and stern language about the importance of integrity. He didn't hold back or hesitate to state exactly what he thought of me, or my actions. This unpleasant, but necessary lecture continued for several hours. When he stops talking, and fitfully rubs his eyes, Randolph releases a heavy sigh, signaling that we have concluded this distasteful encounter. He pardoned some of my wrongdoings, contributing them to kismet.

"I'm not condoning what you did, Angela, but my Uncle Wilson could have lost a great deal and for that *one* thing, for warning us, I am thankful. That being said, I never want to set eyes on you or hear your piss-poor excuses ever again. And I hope that you have enough respect for our privacy that I never read about our personal lives in some rubbish novel."

"I promise," I whisper, knowing that I'll never again see Randolph Prescott. I hang my head, and with a heavy heart, try again to convey my feelings.

"I know you can't forgive me right now, but I hope one day you will. I wish we could be friends again. You're a good man with a good heart. I admire you and the way you care for Wilson. I truly like you, and that's the honest truth."

When Sharon pulls into the driveway and sees me leaning against my car talking to Randolph, her face contorts into a puzzled expression.

Her car is still running as the driver's door flings open. At the speed at which she exits her car, I think she might tear a ligament—or her body-hugging skirt.

"Angela, what the hell are you doing here?" she says in her usual abrasive manner.

I hold up the terminated contract that I forged, plus an outline of my intended manuscript highlighting her many transgressions.

"I'm in charge now, Shar. You'll be following my instructions. I'll provide you with copies, but if you'd like me to explain further, I will. Try to keep up!" I tell her, as I begin reading.

"Item number one: Conclusion of fraudulent practices.

Item two: Apologies all around. Wait. You'd never apologize. That's not your style. But knowing that you'll soon be begging for mercy in front of a jury may be apology enough."

"What is this, one of your sick jokes?" replies Sharon, in her panicky, penetrating voice. She looks at me, then back at Randolph who is staring straight ahead, indignantly mute, letting her hang herself.

"I have a binding contract as the exclusive listing agent on the Prescott Estate!" Sharon insists.

"Not anymore!" I say with verifiable sureness.

"*Back off*, Angela! This is none of your business. Who do you think you are, interfering with my clients? Mr. Prescott...please say something!"

"I believe Angela has said all that you need to hear."

"But I have other contracts riding on this sale! Contracts with developers and promises to fulfill! And just what the hell am I supposed to tell Robert?" says Sharon, as she forcefully flips a thick mass of blond curls from her face.

My mind is besieged with flashbacks.

"What does Robert have to do with any of this?" I ask, unsure if I even want to know.

"*What does Robert have to do with any of this?*" she says mockingly.

"Bobby was right. You really are clueless. All those years of teasing, calling me his *little buddy*. Use your imagination, Ang. We made quite the team, and I've already promised him the contents of this estate."

I'm paralyzed by this new development, as Sharon snatches the documents from my hand in her habitually hostile manner. She violently turns pages, randomly ripping at them, and pitching sheets of paper to the ground. Normally, she would never dream of uttering an expletive in front of a client but today is a game changer.

Randolph steps back. "Looks as if she's about to throw a wobbly!" he says.

Shar went from smiling to belligerent in a matter of seconds; spewing every hateful word and obscenity that she could think of. She promised to take me down with her, sharing my financial deficiencies and details of my failed marriage with the world. She also threatened to sue me for impersonating a realtor, which I don't think is really a thing.

Randolph reclined a safe distance from the commotion as Sharon lunged at me, shaking her fist, and taking an unpromising swing at my face.

"What the hell were you trying to accomplish, pretending you were *me*? There's only one Sharon Bartelson and I can't be duplicated! How dare you interfere with my plans. You, you, you...cunt nugget!"

When the tornadic Sharon Bartelson had finished her bombastic discharge, she exited just as quickly as she arrived, recklessly clipping an enormous oak tree during her exodus. The tree, as well as the Prescott domain, emerged from the melee unscathed. Randolph walked over offering a congratulatory handshake.

"I'm still very angry with you, but I'm glad you're not that. Whatever *that* was..."

Sharon Bartelson is hell-bent on ruining me and for the time being, she has the means to do it. As if I care. Driving home, my cell rings repeatedly until finally, I answer.

"Are you home yet, bitch? I'm coming over! We're having this out in person!"

"Go ahead, Sharon. Game on."

I have no intention of letting her into my home. I've battened down the hatches, locking doors and windows as there's a high probability that the Hun is on her way to invade the citadel. With shaking hands, I place a mug of water in the microwave for some chamomile tea. I need something to calm my nerves before World War III commences.

As I bring the hot cup of tea to my lips, there's a gentle knock at the kitchen door. I thought I'd locked the gate, but it can't be Sharon already. Anyway, she'd never knock. She'd have to make a grand entrance, like breaking down the door or shooting her way in. Just in case, I remove a long carving knife from a drawer.

Full of adrenaline from sparring with one unhinged Sharon Bartelson, I peek out cautiously through the double French doors, with the knife held securely behind my back.

It's Juan! I've forgotten to pay him this month and can't remember if I paid him last month either.

"Juan, come in! You know you don't need to knock."

"Well, I know you don't like the discordant chime that the doorbell plays."

"No, that's not it! You're family. You don't have to knock. You have a key. I'm afraid I've forgotten to pay you again, and I've treated you badly. You're like a brother to me; a brother with amazing gardening skills."

"That's not why I'm here. I just stopped by to do a welfare check. I've been calling and texting, but you haven't returned any of my messages. I see I've arrived just in time," he says, looking down at the knife still in my hand.

"I've never been so happy to see someone in my life! Get in here!" I say, grabbing him by the arm and reeling him into the kitchen.

"I'm sorry about this," I say, slipping the knife back into the drawer. "Things are in a state of turmoil and the situation is escalating."

"Are you okay? No offense, but you don't look well, Angela."

"I just had it out with Sharon. She's psychotic and probably on her way over to kill me."

"Well, I can stay to help. Or I can call the police. Or I can psychologically profile her for you, which in all honesty, I've already done."

"Well, as interesting as that sounds, I'll have to politely decline the offer."

"I wasn't kidding about profiling Sharon. I have a PhD in forensic psychology. I was an adjunct professor before we moved to Bryn Mawr and started our landscaping business."

"You never told me that! So, why in the world are you working here, doing—*this*?"

"*This* is what makes my heart sing. I enjoy working with my hands. Being outdoors. Working for people like you. Making the world beautiful. One blade of grass, one plant, one tree at a time," he says with even-tempered contentment.

"And don't worry about payment until you get back on your feet. I'm not poor by any means. I do this because I want to, not because I have to."

"Juan, you're a remarkable person who never ceases to amaze me. I've unknowingly been clinically assessed and treated at the same time. Kudos, my friend! Now back to business. I've already pawned most of my jewelry, and I'm just starting on my mother's and grandmother's. Things aren't looking up in the writing department either. I need to pay my property taxes on this monstrosity, but I can't afford to have you keep working here."

"Did I do something wrong?"

"Oh Juan, you did everything right! I wish I could continue to employ you, but I don't see my finances improving. I have no idea what I'll do without you! Probably kill everything, right before I lose the house."

"You know, I never stayed because I had to. I worked for you all these years because I like you. You paid me well and treated me fairly. You praised my work. You talked to me and asked about my life and my family as if you truly cared. You never talked down to me or spoke in amplified loutish tones, over-enunciating the simplest words."

I giggle. "Oh, I know who you're referring to—Mrs. Dirty Martini. She called you, 'That little brown man.'"

"Yes, she was incorrigible, but at least I never had to deal with your prick of a husband. That would have cost you double. I just want you to know that I would work for you any day. For free. And I feel that right now someone needs to protect you from a potentially dangerous situation."

"I'm going to be fine, I promise! Believe me, if I need help, you'll be the first person I call," I reply. "I'm going to miss you something awful!"

"I'm only a phone call away, so call or text, and I'll be here in a heartbeat."

I give Juan a tearful hug and send him on his way with the wages I owe him in the form of jewelry—what's left from my paternal grandmother's Tiffany collection. I want him to give them to his wife, Nina. He objects sharply.

"These are only things, Juan. They've become bargaining chips to buy more time, and for what? Anyway, I have no one to pass these down to. You and Nina are the closest thing I have to family."

I miss Juan already, and not just because the facade is over. He is, I now realize, my dearest friend. Starting to leave, he turns one last time.

"Hey Angela, do you remember that terraced garden that you'd always dreamed of building?"

"Oh Juan, of course I do. I was in love with the idea of honoring my family with a garden reminiscent of their homeland. Robert told me that it was a stupid idea and that I should leave well enough alone and let the landscapers do their thing. That it didn't mirror what the other neighbors had and our property would be completely out of place. It would have been a lovely addition to the hill by the side courtyard. Thank you for remembering," I sigh.

Chapter Nineteen

Sharon still hasn't arrived. She could blow in like a storm, or she could plan a surprise attack. Instead of sheltering in place, I decide that a bike ride is in order. If I must sell my car, I'll be pedaling around full-time, so I might as well get used to it. I'll leave the gate open and the alarm off. Sharon will do less damage if she can easily gain access. I shoo Snags into the laundry room and give him one last command before shutting the door—"Hide!"

Pulling my dusty bicycle from the empty garage, I leave my helmet and phone behind, pretending to be a kid again with no care in the world. After all, we never had helmets, cell phones, or pepper spray when I was young. We just hopped on our bikes and went, our adventures were only limited by how far we could pedal. Living by just one rule: Be home before dark.

I picture a much older me, letting my long chestnut hair go completely gray. I'll be known as the friendly old woman on the bike with fat tires that people see all over town. I'll have a little bell to ring, a basket on the front to carry my daily bouquet of fresh flowers, and a wide-brimmed straw hat with a kitschy plastic sunflower glued to the brim; an accessory to give people pause and have them wonder if I'm a little off my rocker.

I'll live in a tiny green clapboard house at the edge of town. It will have shutters and a storm door to protect the wreaths that will change with the seasons. I'll bake cookies to give to neighborhood kids. Not the miserly plain kind, but the gooey chocolatey concoctions that make kids go into orbit on cookie-induced sugar highs. They'll hang out with me on my pint-sized front porch and tell me about their day as I listen with interest, something their folks don't have time for.

I'm leisurely pedaling through the subdivision, my hair flowing behind me, when I see Shar. She's driving erratically with an outsized phablet plastered to her ear. People are so connected to technology yet have no idea how to use the hands-free Bluetooth feature in their vehicles. Or my favorite, those who place their cell phones on speakerphone, yet hold them in front of their faces while they drive and yack away.

Still not hands-free, morons!

Even as fast as Sharon is driving, I notice a certain disconnect about her as she roars something turgid and explicit into her phone. She doesn't even notice me. In fact, I don't think she'd notice if she'd plowed me down and had blood splattered all over her precious Mercedes. Twenty minutes later, she blows past me again on her way out. This time she realizes who she'd just passed and slams on her brakes, laying rubber on unblemished pavement. Throwing the car into reverse, she peels back without looking and partially lowers the driver's window.

After taking evasive action, I abandon my bicycle, walk up to her vehicle, and ask amiably, "What up Shar-Shar? You look nicely tarted-up today."

Sharon's face flushed so fast that I imagined someone opening the top of her head and pouring red Kool-Aid inside.

"I'll kill you, Angela! I'll annihilate any reputation you have left, and I will thoroughly destroy you!"

"Oh, is that all you've got?" I say while holding onto her half-open window with sweaty fingers splayed out like a five-year-old's. "Well, by all means, bring it!"

"Have you lost your mind? I'll lose my broker's license in the bi-state area. You'll ruin my career and my status in the community!" Shar screamed. "First, you pretend to be me. And now you're using my career as entertainment! What were you thinking, writing about our real estate dealings? And poor Bart! He can't be incarcerated! He's a frail little man who's claustrophobic and uses a CPAP machine! He'll be devastated when he finds out!"

"You mean he doesn't know?"

"I mean he's not here!"

"Well, as Shakespeare would say, 'Where for Bart thou?'"

"Oh, you've lost your goddamn mind! I'll have you know that Bart is on a mini vacay to one of those states that legalized marijuana and hallucinogenics. I don't remember which one...one of the 'C' states, I think. He's golfing with his investment club."

"Golfing with his fellow limp-dick buddies, you say?"

Sharon has always had the upper hand in our relationship. She's an overbearing tyrant and a greedy bitch. She once coerced me into attending the funeral of a wealthy stranger. The objective was one-upping her colleagues by obtaining the listings on the woman's many properties.

"You can never be too early to the party," she'd said.

I look unflinchingly at the great intimidator. Her self-confidence has eroded, leaving behind a very small, inconsequential individual. Shar was always at the wheel driving this noxious, inequitable relationship. She's never been a woman that I could depend on, and my association with her has changed the person that I once was.

My parents would be disappointed in me right now. I married an idiot. My closest friend is a manipulating slut. This isn't the daughter that they raised, and I've let them down. And now that my marriage is a thing of the past, I must purge this pernicious woman from my life as well.

My involvement with Sharon should have been limited to casual lunch dates, void of any intimate conversation or personal details. She was constantly babbling, "Wear this, not that. We will go here, not there. We will walk exactly one mile each day, touch this tree, and go back."

I was forever following Shar's lead, Shar's plan. Willingly, yet uneasily shadowing my tormentor. But here's the thing: best girlfriends shouldn't be fearful of one another. They're supposed to act devotedly and empathetically to shore each other up. Sharon will never shore up another person. She's incapable of being a friend because she only cares for herself. What I need is a give-and-take kind of girlfriend who will be supportive when I'm down, laugh with me, cry with me, and tell me when I have a three-inch long hair protruding from my chin.

I've fallen far from grace, but I'm prepared to drop to my knees, crawl, and beg for forgiveness. If it takes the rest of my life, I'll find a way back. I'll earn the respect of colleagues and win back the hearts of readers. I'll repair old relationships and forge new ones. Hopefully, I'll someday find that forever friend. And yes please, a man to love as well.

I'm finished with Sharon Bartelson and the rest of these heartless buttholes! I want out of this broken society. Now. I look down at Sharon as she sits death-gripping her leather steering wheel. "I feel sorry for you," I whisper generously.

Her eyes bulge in disbelief as she begins twitching and clicking her tongue to her teeth, a habit that I've always found bizarre and unnerving; a spasmodic reaction caused by losing control. Sharon Bartelson is unraveling before my eyes. For years, I've tolerated Sharon's many idiosyncrasies, her relentless fulminating, and unceasing bullying. Her hardened shell has cracked and fallen away, exposing a rotten, empty core. And as I look into her icy blue eyes, I see nothing but an artificial life and a hollow soul.

Sharon continues with the clucking, clicking, and precipitous twitching. At this, I begin to laugh, which only makes her involuntary symptoms increase in both severity and frequency. Besides having a circus quality to her actions, there's a certain soothing cadence to it.

I begin rocking from side to side, her frenzied vibrations and clatters simulating a metronome. Sharon looks like a chicken about to fly the coop. But chickens can't fly. They can only flee as far as the treetops to escape danger. Gone is her once unrestricted loquaciousness, as she searches for words that will hurt. Something that will shake me to my core. When the chicken finds her voice, she clucks, "We're not friends anymore!"

"Finally," I say. "The most factual statement you've ever uttered."

I remount my bicycle and ride home, grateful for being able to pedal up and down the rolling streets without walking my bike up and over anything more than a speed bump. I sense the gentle pull of muscles that haven't been used in a while and feel weirdly fulfilled over such a simple feat. The noiseless, pleasurable movement of going faster than walking, but slower than driving, is such a trouble-free way to travel. I must do this more often.

When I return home, there are files and papers strewn on an otherwise bare kitchen island. Sharon let herself in, all right. I check on Snags to make sure no harm came to him during her blind fit of rage. Thank goodness, he's safe, having taken refuge far under the laundry room counter, his head resting comfortably on outstretched paws. After enduring the ire of the high-heeled tempest, I coax him out, giving him reassuring pats.

While conducting a quick inspection of the rest of the house, I see the kitchen is as far as she got. However, in her haste, she left behind more listings that she expected me to fix. These stragglers are a hodgepodge from the stagnant listing collection, and no one, not even the famed Sharon Bartelson, knew how to showcase these duds!

I'd once read an article in the Mansion section of the *Wall Street Journal* about stagnant listing specialists. I learned a great deal from reading that exposé and never knew there were resources available. Sharon could've reached out for professional help, but that would mean letting an outsider in, thus jeopardizing her corrupt practices. The fact is, Sharon thinks of herself as an expert on all things real estate but doesn't want to invest in the time it takes to sell a more difficult property. Instead, she prefers low-hanging fruit that produces an easy sale, while depending on me to inflate what little merit each property possesses.

What's more, Sharon never understood technology and couldn't figure out how to scan or forward listings, even though the real estate world has their own elementary software, as well as technical training and assistance programs. And her personal assistant was of no help either. Amanda majored in texting and social media postings and isn't what I would consider tech-savvy. She was just as uninvolved in the technology process, leaving Shar to distribute her listings, photos, and acidic remarks in person.

I stare at the scattered files. An interesting dilemma indeed! I could pitch them into the garbage, or I could have some fun. For the enjoyment of others (and myself), I choose the latter. I elect to post them directly onto Sharon's web page under "Featured Listings." In case of an emergency, she gave me carte blanche, providing me with the passwords to her company's web-hosting and social media sites. Well, if ever there were an emergency, I believe this is it. Plus, if I'm to turn my life around, I'd best begin with honesty. After all, honesty is the best policy. I learned that in Grade School 101.

Pocket folders splashed with her agency's multihued logo wait to be opened. A lime green folder stands out from the others with a note clipped to its inside cover: "Here are a few of my time capsule listings. All the rage right now! C'est Magnifique! Cha-ching!"

"How utterly poignant, you mannerless, gluttonous, hedonistic bitch..." I whisper, returning to my office to finish what I've started. Here's a peach of a property: It's the highest peak in Castle Ridge Estates with a filtered lake view from a gently sloped lot. It's also called

a "peek-a-boo" view. We all know what this means. If there's a body of water named Jack Shit, then that is exactly what you'll be looking at.

Well, Shar, let's see if we can add to your professional platform...

800 Castle Ridge Drive

By way of an unmaintained dirt road, enjoy 360-degree views from the top of the world. Lap up the filtered lake views by climbing your ass to the rooftop. While there, you may delight in routine do-it-yourself maintenance, as you partake in the deliriously satisfying task of reinforcing the economically hammered shingles. The infamous Leaki-Leaki Brothers installed the original roofing on this blighted property, and it remained weatherproof for as long as it took them to pack up their tools and drive away.

If this doesn't make you want to write a check on the spot, you may be enticed by the charming trappings of this little prize:

1968 Squatting Bull Trail

Come home to the 1970s! Embrace the past by dwelling in the former summer home of the famed Madame Colette Chevalier, also known as the Macramé Maven. Who doesn't pine for retro avocado green appliances and turquoise decor from days gone by? Orange shag carpet, Formica countertops, and groovy happy face fixtures throughout. Madam's macramé creations and moth-eaten weavings cover every wall. Silverfish, spiders, and cockroaches are included. Lucky you! Sold as is and completely furnished.

44 Canyon Ridge Road

This obsolete hillside estate, suitably named Château Chèvre is precariously situated on an incline best suited for adventurous mountaineers. Spelunk onto your patio from the upper-level decking, because it's easier than traversing down miles of splintered stairways. Perfect for mountain goats and off-road vehicle enthusiasts! Off the grid means off the radar, and out of range. No cell service, mail delivery, Internet, or garbage pickup. This overpriced, overrated, turnkey property can be yours for only $1.5 million. Goats not included.

120 W. Main Street, Bryn Mawr Historic District

If future plans include downsizing, take a peek at this darling historic bungalow on an adorable lot. Depression-era home situated on a barren postage stamp lot. Original electrical system (fire). Original plumbing (lead). Original flooring (asbestos). Original design (small). All bedrooms are non-conforming, which means there are no closets. During the Depression, you didn't need closets because you didn't have anything to put in them.

Bring your offers! You'll have to bring offers because for the eight years this has been on the market, there haven't been any. Expansion potential!

The last listing is abominable. I'm acquainted with the woman who owns this horrific paragon of stockpiled knickknacks. She's the clichéd Queen of Indecision and vacillates between wanting to sell her home and never wanting anyone else to have it. Suzie Huffington chops and changes the descriptive verbiage, placing it on and off the market while driving realtors and prospective buyers mad.

Every real estate company in the bi-state area has listed this abysmal abode, and Sharon may have been her last hope for a sale. Suzie's asking price fluctuates as she overvalues her overfilled estate. Her home, bursting at the seams, contains every item offered by the Home Shopping Network. These tawdry collections have taken over what could have been a lovely home; though one may never know what lies underneath the muddled mess of chaos and confusion.

On the rare occasion when someone makes an offer, she quibbles on the price until people lose interest altogether; though one young couple must have had the vision of saints. They were full of imagination and could tell that under all the junk, the home was solidly built. They optimistically planned for a complete renovation and made a generous cash offer. There were no contingencies, and the only condition of the sale included Suzie's dog, Gigi. They fell in love with poor unloved Gigi, more so than the house itself. This, everyone believed, was a reasonable and fair request.

Everyone, except Suzie.

Suzie became incensed, insisting that no one would ever have her home or her dog. She tore up the offer and fired her realtor. When enough time had passed, she hired another to represent her. And so, the cycle continued...

I've heard that people often use whatever means necessary to complete a real estate transaction—even haggling over living things. Sharon once told me that she's had buyers who included the seller's family pet on the contract as a stipulation of sale.

"It happens," she said glibly. "Big deal. Get another one and get over it. It's just an animal."

You'd have to be morally bankrupt to use the family pet as a negotiating tool. Even Suzie Huffington, who can't see that she has a problem, can still distinguish right from wrong. Then again, despite being overfed, Gigi, who is starved for attention and in desperate need of grooming, may benefit from a rehoming agreement.

If Suzie is serious about selling her home, she could have asked for help. It's probably too late to suggest that she read Margareta Magnusson's self-help book, *The Gentle Art of Swedish Death Cleaning*. The old gal needs to embrace the concept of döstädning, or decluttering, before she dies, so as not to be a burden on her family. Or her realtor. Or civilization.

If anyone can help with Suzie's pigpen, it's the Swedes! But I'm sure she'd be offended by the insinuation that her home is anything less than perfect. I fear that it's too late for reform, so we'll skip the book suggestion and proceed straight to an episode of *Hoarders*. In the face of future stardom, I take a crack at Suzie-Q's listing and let loose with a variety of clarifying verbiage.

> *Crummy Contemporary located at 70 Posh Commons*
>
> *Showcase everything you've ever owned, as you pork-stuff this once-elegant habitat to the brim with novelties and souvenirs.*
>
> *But wait! That's already been done for you!*
>
> *Abundant windows, covered in heavily faded, tattered curtains, effectively block out any natural light. Perfect for vampires, as well as those without smell, sight, or taste.*
>
> *Forty years of chain smoking have allowed nicotine to comingle with an unyielding covering of dust, offering a protective coating to the dated period furniture and hordes of bric-a-brac. If you delight in living amongst a foul, unorganized heap of refuse, look no further! In fact, it would be impossible to look further, because you*

can't safely navigate through the clutter. Make an offer.
I dare you.

When the only guideline is to dish out the harsh sting of reality, the words spill onto the page. I finish my assignment and check the folders to make sure I haven't missed anything. I may be cunning, but I'm also reliable and thorough. Satisfied that I've completed Sharon's listings as promised, I scan and backup files to a dedicated flash drive.

After organizing and stacking all hard copies, I lock them in the safe with the others. The listing agreements, as well as Sharon's many hand-scrawled dispatches, are telling. They include sharing details of clients' personal and financial information with a third party; making crass comments about the homeowners; recording private conversations; breaking confidentiality agreements; devaluing property with the intent to purchase; and playing lender roulette. All admissible evidence, I presume.

Though not a crime per se, I include a postcard sent from Aruba last year. Another testament to Sharon's character, or lack thereof. She still hasn't grasped the concept that everyone whose hand touches a post-card will read whatever is written. Common sense aside, she bragged about how much fun she was having lounging at the beach, drowning herself in alcohol, compliments of a banner year in the housing market.

She also broadcasted that before departing for her trip, she attended a broker's open house hosted by one of her many rivals, Honey Merriweather-Ford. Sharon's hatred for Ms. Merriweather-Ford is widely known in the real estate circle, so it came as no surprise that Shar pulled a remorseless stunt. One that obviously made her very proud.

"The home is vacant, so I left the bitch a little 'present' in the private upstairs commode. In the honey pot! Get it? Don't usually eat Indian before flying—gives me tummy trouble. But it came in handy for the open house. LOL!"

Unbelievable.

There's one last thing I need to do. Saving the best for last, I decide to go nuclear. The brilliance of this little tour de force will generate a materialistic mushroom cloud resulting in total obliteration of the Bartelson Dynasty. My objective is to create a sense of urgency with garrulous prose and propaganda, attracting buyers from around the globe. By considerately assisting in promoting their property, Bart and Shar will be able to jump-start the liquidation process.

You're welcome.

PUBLIC AUCTION:
668 Vineland Avenue, Bryn Mawr

Quick possession. Owners desperate to relocate.

Don't miss this rare opportunity to live like a pair of smooth-talking impostors. A two-faced whore and an eminent money-laundering aficionado currently occupy this hidey-hole. The X-rated realtor, Sharon Bartelson, and her husband, the clammy-handed, slime ball developer, Bartholomew Bartelson, are the current occupants.

Classic stone Normandy Tudor on Bryn Mawr's prestigious West side. Architecturally significant and replete with amenities, this stunning 12,000-square-foot mansion is the epitome of unparalleled elegance. Arched doorways abound, which lead to rooms boasting richly carved wood moldings, paneled French doors, and stagey magnificence.

No expense was spared on the kitchen as the piggish owners went hog wild with every imaginable appurtenance known to the culinary world. Unfortunately, the only thing cooked here were the books.

Warm your cold heart by one of many fireplaces as you count stacks of cash. Decorative staircases, artful European stained glass, and a titanic-size sunken living room are just a sampling of the many highlights.

A local art student routinely forged the signature of an acclaimed artist as he sloppily painted murals throughout the estate. The fledgling portraitist also captured the homeowner in all her glory while she humped his lump for services rendered.

Sharon does go on about how she charitably supports the arts!

After a long day of pillaging and plundering, survey the peasants below from an extensive array of towering, wrought iron balconies. The swanky pool, spa, and cabana are adorned with opulent imported Carrera marble.

Simply too much licentiously acquired paraphernalia to mention!

This ritzy residence can be yours. And should be yours. After all, it was purchased and extensively renovated by screwing others out of their hard-earned cash.

All furnishings included.

The resonant aftershock of the Bartelson demolition plan should be epic. This should also keep them off my back for a while. They'll be busy fighting off news crews hungrily circling their decayed lives, reporting on the scandalous morsels of these two charlatans. It will give the authorities, as well as private citizens, time to file charges as well. The National Association of Realtors and MLS will also have a field day levying fines, terminating her privileges, and taking other disciplinary measures when they learn of Sharon's divided loyalties, breach of fiduciary duties, and deceptive practices.

I continue lobbing verbal grenades into the wee hours, then adroitly post them online for the world to see. I add everything to the MLS and Sharon's social media pages, because why not employ a blanketed media blitz? Shar always said that exposure is the name of the game. You can't stop a freight train and this one has left the station with an unstoppable velocity.

I also don't see any reason to withhold her many indiscretions. To show her clients *who* represents them, I substitute her professional online photo with a pose more plausible to her everyday life. A selfie that was taken just last month, texted with the caption: "Bitch just wants to have fun!" It depicts one drunken Sharon Bartelson at the casino martini bar, holding her drink high into the air as someone (not Bart) nibbles a cornucopia of olives from her cleavage. It is mean, but I can't resist the opportunity to show her many swindled clients a more realistic view of their realtor.

Chapter Twenty

I was having so much fun that I lost track of time. The sun is just peeking up over the reddened horizon. How does that saying go? Red sky at
night, sailor's delight. Red sky at morning, Angela take warning? Ha!
Who cares! I'm invigorated by the cleansing tide that's come in, washing away the lies. I take Snags out for a quick potty and plop him down
in front of a bland bowl of kibbles.

"This will hold you over for a bit," I tell him.

He stares up at me as if to say, "Kibbles, again? Are we poor?"

Even after being up all night, I'm not tired. Racing upstairs for
an abbreviated shower of tepid water leaves me feeling revitalized. I
squeeze the toothpaste tube. When nothing comes out, I cut open the
end and fish around inside with my toothbrush, hoping for a few more
brushings. *Beggars can't be choosers!*

When the conventional toothpaste runs out, I have a box of baking
soda that's spent years in the back of the fridge soaking up odors. It
tastes nothing like toothpaste, but it works. I learned this helpful hint
on the Internet, though they did suggest using a fresh box. As I no longer have medical or dental insurance, this gritty substance will also serve
to replace the duties of my dental hygienist, Cassidy. If Cassidy could see
my teeth now, she'd strap me to the dental chair and whip out a bench
grinder and icepick from her personal cache of torture tools. She'd then
give me a lecture about oral hygiene, indignant with the news that I've

been flossing with thread from a sewing kit.

Wearing the sweats that I slept in would be easier and comfier than getting dressed, but I need to make an effort. I still have a roof over my head, clothing to wear, and the ability to be clean. I need to break away from this pity party, where I've been a card-carrying member of shame and disappointment for too long.

The emphasis needs to shift to what I still have, not what I've lost. The old glass half-full thing. I'm not living on the street and my walk-in closet is undeniably larger than most people's living areas. This is something that went unnoticed when it was overflowing with clothing, shoes, accessories, and designer handbags for every day of the year. Now, my outfits are few and I could fit everything into one suitcase.

I've kept three pairs of jeans—two denim, one white, and a pair of cropped slacks. In addition to a black suit that will never go out of style, a sundress, four turtlenecks, and three timeless blouses that will go with anything. For colder weather, I have my mother's old parka, my dad's college jersey, a leather jacket, and a tweed jacket that another volunteer hung up at the food pantry and never reclaimed.

I also have an assortment of T-shirts that I took from the bargain box at the pantry thrift shop. One that says VOLUNTEER in huge block print letters, a pink knock-off with a misspelled Helo Kity above a cat caricature, and my favorite, a faded black long-sleeve with white lettering that says, "Instant Asshole, Just Add Alcohol."

I've kept a small number of shoes for different situations. A pair of tennis shoes for walking, running, or loafing around. One wildly expensive pair of black heels. A pair of brown and black high boots for their versatility. One pair of everyday knock-around shoes, and some mismatched flip-flops. There's also a pair of silk slippers flecked with rhinestones that match my robe. They were outrageously priced and are for show and *not* comfort.

After carefully dressing in a pair of dark washed jeans, black cashmere turtleneck, and leather jacket, I put on makeup and style my hair. I remove several necklaces and earrings from the barren jewelry safe to be used as currency exchange. When my cash flow began diminishing, my wedding ring was the first to go. I parked behind a dumpster in the rear of a local pawnshop and slipped in a side door to avoid being recognized. I remember the way the clerk looked at me when I dropped the massive diamond ring onto the glass counter.

"Oh yeah, it's real," I told him after noting the stunned look on his face.

"You sure you want to hock this?" he said, looking down at the deep indentation on my abandoned ring finger.

After dealing with many pawnshops over the past several years, I've become familiar with the bartering procedures of each. I've learned what might be expected payment for certain trinkets and that compensation can fluctuate as often as the commodities market. Today, I'm sure I'll be able to score enough cash for a tank of gas, a cheap motel room, and meals for several days.

I've been penny pinching to pay bills, and though I can't afford to go anywhere, I don't want to be here when Sharon realizes what I've done. I root through the file cabinet for instructional manuals so I can change the codes on the gate and house. I also set the alarm, just in case she decides to climb the fence and pop in.

From the back of the kitchen pantry, I pull out the automatic pet feeder and waterer for my slow-moving hound. Patting Snags on the head, I tell him to be a good boy as I head out the door, bound for quiet adventure. I point to the doggie door reminding him to use this if he needs to go potty, but I can tell by the droopy-eyed stare that he'll end up relieving himself wherever he chooses.

The day is fresh and the possibilities are endless. I opt for a change of scenery and point my car into unfamiliar territory. I'm on a quest to find a mom-and-pop restaurant, the equivalent of running to one's parents for comfort, no matter how old you are. After driving for several hours, I come across a little place in the middle of nowhere called Chuckwagon Café. I've driven far enough away from the customary chain restaurants, for there appears to be only locals and truckers partaking in their morning meal. My navigation system shows my vehicle in the middle of a green screen; the location comprised of unnamed roads and a dollop of periwinkle blue that appears to be a lake.

As I pull into the gravel lot, people stare at me through the murky restaurant windows. There's obviously not much happening in this small town. I'm an interloper, and even though my car is in desperate need of a wash and wax, it sticks out like a diamond in a coalfield.

A waitress with kind eyes and harsh expression seats me in a small booth, the burgundy Naugahyde bench held together by a plethora of peeling duct tape. She hands me a thickly laminated menu and stares unapologetically. I must be grossly overdressed for this place.

"You in town for the Hinkley wake, hon?" she questions.

"Um, no. Should I be?"

"Coffee?"

"Please."

"Decaf or regular?"

"Regular, if it's strong."

"What other kind is there?"

When the waitress returns with a pot of coffee, I note the name on her yellowed nametag: Margie. She's the type that has a lifetime of hard-scrabble stories to tell, but keeps them tucked neatly away from people, especially curious strangers. She's also the type of hard-edged soul that has just enough kindness, you could pour your heart out to her.

"What do you have that's low-cal?" I ask.

"Nuthin," says Margie, looking down with a scowl.

"Good. Then I'll have Carl's Breakfast Special, eggs over-easy, ham, biscuits and gravy, and a side of grits."

"Now that's more like it!" says Margie enthusiastically, while raising her painted-on brows. With creaking knees, she implements an inexperienced curtsey. "Excellent choice, madam!" she says, and we both burst into laughter.

"By the way Margie, how's the meatloaf?"

"Good Lord, woman! You have one o' them eatin' disorders, or somethin'?"

"No, not another order. I've just had an awful craving lately for meatloaf and mashed potatoes. I wonder if I should come back for some comfort food."

Margie looks like a hitchhiker, pointing her thumb upward to the kitchen behind her. "Well, Carl here makes a mean meatloaf, but if you come back for the Tuesday Special, his wife, Doris, is doin' the cookin' and hers puts Carl's to shame."

I smile, considering how I may have discovered a place so special, I'll never tell another soul about it. No one knows me here and I don't have to worry about how much things cost, watching my figure, or what's dripping down my chin. This is something that I haven't engaged in for years—nourishing the soul. To hell with my cholesterol! And my weight! And my arteries! Sometimes you must take risks with things that are more life sustaining than others.

There've been times I've gone to restaurants to mingle with strangers, sitting among the masses for inspiration. But my hearing isn't what it used to be. And just when the conversation becomes interesting, those around me begin to mumble. I want to stand at my invisible lectern and implore other patrons to speak up when they talk. And would it kill you to enunciate?!

Margie returns with my order and the smell is heavenly. I've been writing furiously in my notebook and toss it into my purse with abandon. Eyeing the notebook protruding from my bag, Margie asks, "You tryin' to find yourself?"

I grab the saltshaker and position it over my eggs, undaunted by how many toddlers have licked the top. "I'm trying to find real people," I say.

"Well, you've come to the right place. This is 'bout as real as it gets."

I really needed this spur-of-the-moment trip. I feel more comfortable in this small town than I've ever felt in my neighborhood. Even though I'm a visitor, people are approachable and talk to me without it feeling like a forced conversation.

I spend the day exploring the town, then take a drive through pastoral farmlands. I book a room next to the Chuckwagon Café in a small motel that looks more like a strip mall than a roadhouse. I feel like a desperado taking cover in a dingy hideaway, plunked right in the middle of Anytown, USA. If anyone asks what I'm doing here, I'll tell them the truth: *I'm runnin' from the law.*

I inspect the room. Clean and quiet. Good. My only requirements. I lock the door and attach the too-small chain that we all know does nothing to protect you from intruders. Even though people seem trustworthy here, I look through the peephole, confirming that my car is still where I parked it. Parting the light-blocking curtains, I'm curious to see what kind of view comes with a forty-dollar a night room.

Headlights from the busy interstate create a continuous stream of light bursts, sending Morse code to the well-lit sign in front of the Chuckwagon Café—Open 24 hours! Not a lot of movement in the town itself, but the tavern across the street is bustling with activity. I hear rhythmic chords of an acoustic guitar and a throaty soloist singing a heart-wrenching country song. Interestingly, there's a wide variety of transportation in the parking lot. The expected cars, trucks, and motorcycles, but also a row of hitching posts for a trio of horses. There's a John Deere combine and a lone riding lawnmower, which just goes to show you, when you need a drink, *you need a drink!*

Oh yeah, this will do just fine. I unzip my case, power up my laptop, and begin pounding on the keyboard. *Joan of Arc, preparing for the Hundred Years' War.* Even with the unfamiliar sounds in this unfamiliar place, I was able to compartmentalize my thoughts and focus solely on the structure of the manuscript. I wrote for hours, then fell into a deep sleep on the surprisingly comfortable bed.

Before dawn, the rumbling sound of semis idling together awakened me. I felt a sense of unity and decided that I, too, should be hitting the open road. Right after a long, hot shower and a stop at the Chuckwagon Café for sticky buns and coffee.

Returning home, I am wholly satiated. I tiptoe through the house looking for Snags, though I'm not sure why. He's almost deaf and assuredly suffering from some form of doggie dementia; an enduringly surprised look on his face, as if he's seeing me for the first time.

Just as I suspected, Snags has scarfed everything from the automatic feeder and even chewed off the little door in search of the last morsel. I take him outside and try throwing a stick for him to fetch. He runs briefly, staring in the wrong direction as the stick hits him in the head. "I don't blame you," I tell him. "Fetching is overrated."

I sit on the ground and give Snags belly rubs, an act that's triggered a comical gyration of his back legs, putting a smile on his grizzled little face.

Electing to withdraw from the world until I have a completed first draft, I turn off my cell and unplug phones. I turn off the fax machine in my office, wondering why I've even kept such an antiquated device. When I'd tried to pawn it, the guy just shook his head. "Lady, welcome to 1982. Nobody uses these anymore."

Walking purposefully to the end of the driveway, I tape a hand-printed sign to the outside of the gate. PLEASE, DO NOT DISTURB! THIS MEANS YOU!

I take the scholarly advice of Ray Bradbury, who I'm sure was referring to me when he said; *"You must stay drunk on writing so reality cannot destroy you."*

Since I have no alcohol in the house, writing will be the only thing I'm tanked-up on. I know exactly what Ray meant by this. I must retreat to the fictional world that I know, because if I dwell on reality, it'll drive me insane.

I worked night and day. The words flowed as quickly as the repetitiveness of standard novelist instruction: write what you know. I must have looked like a mad scientist, passionately typing, cloistered in a dark, desolate lab. The words emerged fast and furious, dancing fingers barely keeping up with my thoughts. It was not only a story; it was *my story*. It was retribution and reverence and righteousness all rolled together. Although greatly embellished fiction, I took many liberties and delivered justice freely and impulsively. For the first time, the progression energized me, and I was on a high that I never wanted to end.

I gave up many things during the process, exchanging cleanliness for librettos and sustenance for character development. For once in my life, I found personal clarity and meaning. Each time I peeled back layers from inconsequential people with their superficial priorities and posturing power cravings, genuineness and benevolence moved closer to the forefront. Closer to my reach. I once shared the same shallow ambitions with these small-minded people. But as I write, I feel priorities begin to shift into place, like great earthen plates collapsing and settling into new positions.

Every few days, I turn on my cell to see if anyone important is trying to reach me. Just countless messages from Sharon, who I now refer to as Shar-Shar, just to demean our once solid association. Plus, it makes me snicker every time I say it, even though I'm the only one seated in the audience. I can ignore Shar-Shar indefinitely, because frankly my dear Scarlett, I really don't give a damn! If she knew how I used her histrionics as the baseline for fictional conversation, she'd come unglued all over again.

I've never felt so assured with a first draft, but it needs to be right. I spend my days editing for grammatical errors, continuity, flow, and repeated words. I spend my nights rereading and revising, never tiring. Around the fourth or fifth revision, I read aloud, finding things I may have otherwise missed. Tonight, I carry Snags up to the bedroom, set him down next to me on the mattress, and begin reading.

"Bedtime story," I tell him.

As I read, Snags looks empowered. His ears perk up whenever he hears his name, as well as other familiar words: food, treats, bone, and outside. I may be suffering from severe sleep deprivation, but it looks like he's smiling.

During the past few years, writing became a struggle. Characters, with their interwoven personalities seemed uninteresting and cut from the same cloth. The unvarying storylines lacked depth, and I felt as though I was squeezing out a variety of hackneyed words just to populate the pages. I used to write with great deliberation and a million revisions, exhaustively nitpicking its nucleus or mulling over alternative endings. I fretted over place and plot and it was often painful to wrap things up, never feeling it was good enough.

Conversely, this story has spilled onto the pages with ease. The characters talked and I listened. I pinned back my ears and transcribed their story as it was narrated to me. My characters didn't need a break, so neither did I. I heard them in my head, urging me to keep typing and imagined them saying, "Keep going! No breaks for you! Whatta you think we are, union?"

Feeling that the manuscript has been polished enough for others to lay eyes on, I transfer the document to a dedicated zip folder and email it to Linda. The irrevocable act of hitting *Send* leaves me feeling empty. So much time is invested in giving birth to and raising characters that one must be certain they're developed enough to interact with others. Sending a novel into the world must be how a parent feels sending a child to school for the first time. They put them on a large yellow bus, watching with a gentle twinge of regret as the bus pulls from the curb, getting smaller in the distance. A time of great joy and great sadness.

Besides a sense of loss, I feel liberated by inscribing details of what good can come from erasing the bad. Like gold mined from rivers, flecks of treasure are sluiced from the silt, while the sediment washes away with the current. The lies and pretense, having been transferred to the written word, feels like the weight of deception has been lifted from my shoulders. What's left is the promise of a second chance, and a future filled with purpose.

I take off my cheaters and rub the bridge of my nose, feeling the dent left by ninety-nine cent eyeglasses. Closing my laptop, I exhale a sigh of relief.

The laying down of arms, accepting whatever is to come.

I look over at my gently used dog with his faultless imperfections, snoring like an old man in a church pew. I'm sure that listening to my hours-long discourse helped send him into this deep, narrative-induced slumber.

Snags was a throwaway, a disposable dog. I often wonder what he did to be cast aside, unwanted, and unloved. People want perfect in an imperfect world. They want immediate gratification and dogs that come instantly trained. They want to interact with them on their terms and then neatly put them away like a toy, locking them in crates for hours on end. Snags is one of the lucky ones. He's a survivor. I'll be a survivor, too.

Chapter Twenty-One

It is said that waiting to hear word on a manuscript is the hardest part. Not for me. While waiting, I busy myself with other projects. There are always new manuscripts to be started, and articles, ideas, research, and marketing strategies to plan. The hardest part is wondering if someone else will find my characters compelling. If they'll care for them as much as I do. You want to know that others will like your kids and want to be around them. These characters may not be real, but they're real to me.

I hear Doris Day in my head singing, "Que Sera Sera, whatever will be, will be..."

Thanks, Doris. You're right! Whatever happens, happens. It's out of my hands now.

My phone vibrates in my jeans pocket, which is the most action I've felt down there in a while. It's Linda, responding to the draft I'd sent earlier in the week.

"Hey, Linda. How are you?"

"Angela, dear, you're sounding much better than the last time we spoke. What's changed?"

"I have."

"Good!" said Linda approvingly. "I hope you've changed back to the woman I used to know. I've missed her."

"Enough of the oversentimental schmaltz, Linda. I know you read it or you wouldn't be calling. What did you think of the manuscript?"

"I've sent it to the editors for some polishing."

"Okay... But what did you think of it?"

"You haven't cared what I've thought for a long time, so why ask now?"

"Linda, you're killing me!"

"All right, all right. I couldn't put it down. I loved it! I'm planning on shopping it to several publishing houses and may even put it out to auction. I think we may have another bestseller on our hands. Everyone is fascinated with the upper crust. Nobody likes them, but people are voyeurs and have no problem peeping in the windows for a glimpse into their lives.

It's raw and honest. And who on the face of this earth doesn't loathe their homeowners association? You'll become a hero to some and an enemy to others. Even though your storyline is fictional, keep in mind that your neighbors are paranoid as well as vain, and they might think it's about them."

"You mean Carly Simon vain? Remember that song?"

"Stay on track Angela," says Linda, making a supreme effort to be the adult in the conversation.

"You know as well as I do that the wheels turn slowly in the publishing world, even for established authors," said Linda in her practiced, steady tone. "I shall do my best to fast-track, if possible. Remember, you've been AWOL for some time and you're going to have to rebuild trust as well as your professional platform."

"You don't think it's too much, do you? It doesn't read like a tell-all from one of those weekly tabloids?" I ask.

"There's no substitute for the authenticity of life experience. And by today's standards, I think it sounds a lot like the six o'clock news.

Looking forward, my suggestion is this: Leave town for a while. And when you finally have your publicist book events, don't make any appearances close to home, or even be home until the initial shockwave wears off. Start another manuscript during your sojourn and keep up the momentum. You're on a roll!"

"Well, bugging out is a splendid idea, but that's going to take money, and I'm still operating with a negative cash flow. And royalties trickling in from past sales won't take me very far."

"I get it. In many ways, you're starting over. You're restructuring your life and career. Let me handle the details. I can't make any promises, but I'll try to negotiate a decent advance from the publisher. And I would never do this for anyone else, but if you need a short-term personal loan, I can help. And if you ever tell anyone, I'll deny it. Right before I murder you in your sleep."

"Linda, has anyone ever told you what a kind woman you are? I think I'll go to the Upper Northwest. I hear it's beautiful and I've always wanted to explore that part of the country. Want to come along?"

"Do they have malls, concrete, and room service in the mountains? Be real, Angela. Also, be smart and safe. I care about you. You're like the older sister I never had—or wanted."

"I'm deeply touched, Linda Cooper, best agent in the world. We'll chat soon, sis!"

"You're really laying it on thick. You bet we'll chat soon. And don't ignore my calls anymore. It's unprofessional and impolite. You used to complain about people like that, remember?"

I plan my departure. Linda and I devise a communication strategy. I agree to call her at noon MDT every Monday. I don't know how reliable Internet service will be so we agree that phone calls make more sense.

Years ago, while in Europe on a book signing tour, I found out just how unreliable communication can be. I was in Sicily for a week. Cell service was sporadic and the Internet was a rare commodity. I stayed in a luxurious hotel in Palermo and had spent an evening composing and answering emails—dozens of communiqués sat in my outbox, waiting to be sent. At 9 a.m., along with a mob of other hotel guests, I packed into an elevator bound for the basement. From 9:15 to 9:45, there was Internet connectivity, and we set up our laptops and plugged in. There were many people just trying to communicate with the outside world that I had to look at the calendar to make sure it wasn't 1944, and we weren't refugees taking shelter underground in war-torn Europe.

So many people were connecting at once that it caused the intermittent system to slow or crash. Expletives flew in many languages, all with the same frustration. Before I knew it, our half-hour allotment was over. Everyone packed up, slamming laptops shut, zipping up cases, kicking into the air, and making hand gestures. Clearly, being pissed off is a universal language we could all understand. There was nothing left to do but trudge back down to the basement the next day and try again.

I followed Linda's plan, keeping my nose to the grindstone and my face out of sight. This added a certain intrigue to the upcoming release, as people were obsessed with finding out what the novel was about. My publicist sent out teasers, touting the book. The social media blitz included a mysterious profile of a woman's face. In the ad, a black-and-white photograph showed only a dark mane of hair, one eye, and a simple, but succinct message: "A new twist on an old subject; an established author with a fresh voice moves out of the shadows."

This skillful maneuver temporarily piqued interest in the literary world. However, people have short attention spans. You can only get so much mileage out of a teaser before you need to deliver the goods, or interest will be lost altogether. Readers left bookless will turn on you faster than a squirrel at an empty bird feeder. As a result, I can no longer compete with authors who regurgitate a book a year. I've already lost much of my audience to other, more dependable authors who can churn out timely novels, feeding the voracious reading habits of their fans. I'm sure there were some who saw my name and thought, *Angela who? Is she still alive, or are they publishing her posthumously?*

Scheduling an in-person meeting with my agent sounded like a good idea at the time. Seeing Linda and the old gang would be fun, I'd told myself. A meeting sounds important and exciting until the time comes to do it. I want to stay in bed, burrowing under the covers, but I'm already committed. At least there's the potential of a return to prosperity, and something to focus on besides loneliness and debt.

The early morning flight, combined with the stress of long security lines and outrageous traffic has reminded me that I'm no longer used to traveling. I stand groggily in line at a trendy coffee cart, paying eight dollars for a cup of coffee that I instantly spill down my shirt. I don't know why I bothered getting a coffee this early in the morning when dexterity is nonexistent.

In my previous life, I never had to wait in busy terminals, heaving with people hurriedly moving in every direction. I belonged to the air line's club, where private bathrooms were gloriously clean, hand towels were flawlessly stacked, and an array of deeply scented lotions and fresh flowers were always on display. The airline's club was a sanctuary where you could recede from the noise, filth, and frustration of riding a tide of people sprinting to their gates. If you had long layovers, you could take a shower and redo your hair and makeup. It was a palliative area where club employees caringly greet you by name and ask where you're headed and when you'll return; a place where you feel important, welcome, and glad to be away from spaces where there are too few seats for too many people.

I make my way to the gate at the end of the crowded terminal. It's a miracle that I've arrived in one piece after being shoved through a groundswell of bobbing heads and cumbersome luggage knocking into my legs. There's nowhere to sit and the gate lice have already begun swarming, forming irregular lines. Everyone wants to be first, which I don't understand. Who in their right mind would want to spend additional time packed into a smaller place than where they started?

Even though I'm receiving automated texts, I check the e-ticket on my phone many times, ensuring that I'm at the right gate. I also keep looking at my boarding group number, wondering if I'm reading it wrong, wondering if I could be anything but last.

There's a reason that passengers are skeptical. Airlines have been known to secretly change gates and not tell anyone. I think they enjoy seeing just how fast a person can run. I imagine airport security sitting in a secure location among glowing screens, as someone leans forward with a stopwatch, taking bets on whether a person will make it to their gate before the door slams shut.

The gate agents are feverishly helping passengers with special needs and those who just think they're special. They constantly remind people to check bags that will not fit in overhead bins but passengers pretend not to hear; knowing they will take a chance, and try to force extremely large cases into spaces already filled to capacity. In doing so, they'll hold up the entire plane and not care that the rest of us followed the rules. We'll wait and watch those who are disinclined to follow the tenets of air travel as they try to change the law of physics. Finally, a perturbed flight attendant will pry the bags from reluctant fingers, sending them off to the belly of the plane.

Everyone has a sense of entitlement as they cram their possessions into overhead bins, putting other passengers at risk of being crushed during turbulence. Why they'll spend fifty dollars in the airport bar on drinks but won't spend thirty dollars to check a bag is anyone's guess. Everyone is important and can't be expected to wait for their bags to spit out onto a squeaking carousel.

In my glory days of public engagements and book signings, I was airline royalty, racking up frequent flier miles with a second address in first or business class. Now, I'm a nobody, shoehorned into coach with the rest of the herd. I sit with my knees bent clumsily into my chest, dreaming of warm nuts and cold champagne.

Some people are nervous fliers, but I'm not. Especially when I was seated in my own little airline apartment with all the gadgets and luxuries one could want, including reclining seats that extend into a bed, where I slept soundly on overseas flights, waking up rested and refreshed.

Today, I'm traveling with only a small carry-on and fond memories. I glance across the aisle of our cramped quarters to an elderly woman clutching a handbag in her lap, staring straight ahead. She's old enough to remember how elegant flying used to be—when traveling was an event. The good old days when passengers dressed for the occasion and were well-mannered.

I wonder if she's thinking about that now. I wonder if she's trying to detach herself from the coarse language, drunken conversations, screaming children, and the gentleman next to her, too large for his seat, his form spilling into her personal space. Does she wonder why she bothered to get dressed this morning while others look and smell as if they just crawled out of bed? The woman looks over at me with a dispirited smile. The poor lady probably just wants to reach her destination without being trampled to death.

Besides arranging airfare, Linda's assistant also offered to book me a hotel room. I graciously declined, explaining that I have someone to get back to—even though that someone has four legs, an overbite, and drools. I also didn't care to explain how people repulse me, and how I've lost the ability to hold my tongue. During my last book tour, an incident in a hotel dining room warranted lambasting a fellow guest. I'm sorry if you hate your life and you've completely given up, but could you not wear your natty pajamas to breakfast? It's bad enough to stand in an elegant buffet line with others' greasy, uncombed bed heads, butt cracks, tramp stamps, back hair, and braless, drooping breasts. And if tactless, sloppy appearances are not enough to stomach, it turns out, it can be worse.

Standing in the buffet line, I held out my plate as the server carved a thick slice of prime rib. Looking up, I saw a guy sauntering in wearing tattered pajama bottoms and a muscle shirt, his hair standing on end and his chin smattered with stubble. That alone caused a bile-rising disturbance. But what put me over the edge is when my eyes wandered down to his bare, yeast-encrusted feet, and thick, yellow toenails, that were so long they were clacking on the floor. People quit eating and stared. But, no one spoke up. So, I did.

"Hey, you! Foot Fungus!" I shouted, "Put some shoes on!"

Even though I declined the offer of a hotel room, I'm grateful that the agency sent a cab to pick me up. Renting a car in the city would prove disastrous. Cars, motorcycles, buses, pedestrians, and cyclists, moving together through this crazy metropolitan maze—just thinking about plotting a course through the congestion of a big city makes my head spin.

Having rented a vehicle in London once, I don't want to repeat history. The city swarmed with uninterrupted streams of traffic, and I shall never drive there again! In addition to sitting on the wrong side of the car, driving on the wrong side of the road, and shifting with my left hand, there were roundabouts at every intersection. If these weren't confusing enough, someone from traffic management had the brilliant idea of adding traffic lights inside the roundabouts.

Admittedly, my coordination skills are nil, but I tried my best to blend and harmonize with the flow of traffic. I was piloting an under-powered car so small it appeared to have driven right out of a cereal box. Despite being at a disadvantage, I bravely drove my clown car into the flow of a three-ring circus. However, as much as I tried, I couldn't keep track of whose turn it was. So, I closed my eyes and went—accidents be damned! My screams were the only noise drowning out the infuriated drivers who honked wildly as I cut them off, or yelled in frustration, "Bloody fool!"

Yet I continued driving in circles while the GPS on my phone prattled on, telling me to take the third exit in the roundabout, then enter the next roundabout and take the fourth exit, then enter the next roundabout and take the first exit...Becoming discouraged, nervous, and dizzy, I could no longer tell where I was or where I was going. I finally pulled over, called the rental agency, and told them to pick up their stupid car.

Even though I'm familiar with the rules of the road here in the States, I don't care to drive in large cities for the lost factor and the stress factor. Streets are frequently under construction or closed due to high-rise projects. There are broken water mains, or ladder trucks racing to put out fires. Mobs of people protest something-or-another regularly, and accidents block the thoroughfares, necessitating an alternate route. Thanks, but no thanks! I'll let the cab driver have an aneurysm over the honking, gesturing, and yelling. Let someone else take control while I look around, watching the crowds ebb and flow from the safety of the backseat.

The hour-long ride between the airport and the agency consists of creeping along congested streets or sitting in stopped traffic. It makes me think that we're traveling a great distance, but for all I know, it may only be a few blocks.

As much as I dislike the endless grid of gray monolithic buildings, I find comfort in the modest old brownstones where the agency is located. These grand old structures have endured the test of time thanks to regular refurbishments over the decades. Still, there's a distressed tiredness about them, akin to having too much plastic surgery. The outer layer is cosmetically saved while contesting the inner age with a jaundiced eye. Efforts have been made to modernize the interiors with updated lighting and new paint in pleasing pastel hues. Despite that, a faint musty odor remains, a stark reminder of the building's true age.

While I really should take the stairs, the antique birdcage elevator was added at great expense, so I feel obligated to use it. The tremulous elevator rattles tiredly to the third floor and shudders to a stop. Sliding open the scissored door, the rusted hinges obstinately groan in opposition. Down the hall to the left, stands the commanding presence of the agency's heavy, wood-paneled door. It takes muscle to open the door with the ornate brass lever tarnished to a green patina. I'd forgotten how much work is entailed just to get into this office! I grit my teeth and push, reminding myself to start working out a bit more. Or just start working out. Say, lifting something heavier than a fork to build upper body strength.

As I check in at the reception desk, I'm nearly knocked to the floor by adoring fans. Licked to death by the resident dogs makes me feel welcome, unlike the receptionist who is coolly staring in my direction while chewing and popping her gum. She tells me to take a seat as the dogs fall in around my ankles, following me to an outdated floral sofa in the waiting area. I turn my attention back to the dogs, who have more personality and a higher level of communicative skills than the receptionist. They're spinning in circles, jumping on my lap, or flipping onto their backs, submissively waiting their turn to be petted. While they are well trained, I encourage their rambunctious behavior with high-pitched, "Good dogs!"

The receptionist, annoyed by my unconstrained adoration of the dogs, announces that Linda will see me now. The girl is new, or perhaps a temp. She doesn't have a clue who I am, and that's fine. She doesn't need to know me, but she could manage a smile, or just attempt to be nice. On the way past her desk, I tried a lighthearted approach.

"Having a bad day?"

"Huh?" she says.

"Somebody kick your cat this morning?"

The young woman grimaces and hisses, "I don't have a cat."

"Huh. You don't say."

I'll have to ask Linda why Miss Congeniality has been given a job with any human contact. I wonder if this is an internship. A staff member's relative? Or, court-ordered work detail. Couldn't she just collect trash on the side of the road like everyone else?

The dogs trail closely behind me as I make my way toward Linda's office. Too cute to ignore, I bend down and pet them again. While playing with dogs should be the crux of my visit, it's not. As I'm fawning over them, the surly receptionist bluntly reminds me that Linda is waiting. While gathering my things, she gives me directions to Linda's office as I march past her.

"No need. I know the way."

I feel like I'm taking the long walk to the principal's office after getting booted from class for smarting off. I knock on Linda's door and when no one answers, I guardedly enter her office. There could be a bucket of water over the door with a trip wire, or worse. I instead see Linda's familiar face as she crosses her spacious office, the floor covered in colorful Asian rugs. Her hair is much shorter than I remember and cut into a bob. She walks toward me with something in her hand, her stylish auburn hair bouncing above her shoulders. I wonder if we're going to rumble, we're on Linda's home turf after all. I'm relieved when she stops, handing over an indispensable lint roller.

"I knew you'd be on the floor with the dogs," she says, looking at the intermingling of fur sticking to my clothes.

Linda and I are back on solid ground, our working relationship has improved exponentially. We're not yet sharing the tongue-in-cheek jousting that we once enjoyed, but with time, we'll get there. I never wanted to be one of those precious authors that have a reputation for being difficult; the ones that agents and editors grumble about behind closed doors—the Darth Vader of novelists that send people bolting into cubicles to avoid personal interaction. I also never wanted to be an unreliable flake, but here I am.

"Have a seat, Angela," says Linda somberly, as if I'm hawking wares door to door and she can't be bothered to listen to my unscripted spiel. Linda and I haven't seen each other in years, not counting FaceTime or Zoom. A face-to-face meeting is much different from hiding behind a phone or computer screen a thousand miles away. For starters, no one looks the same on a screen as they do in real life. Faces appear cartoonish and contorted as if someone combined your driver's license photo with your passport photo and overlaid it with a chalk doodle. I can't concentrate on what the person is saying because I'm always wondering if they really look like that, or if it's just the sad reality of virtual communication. Some people lean far back in their chairs while talking, or sit too close to the screen, making them appear like a caricature, their huge balloon head is proportionately floating above an undersized body. The distorted images, combined with the sound delay detract from the conversation.

This personal appearance has served up a huge slice of humble pie. "Linda, I can't tell you how sorry I am. Truly. I never meant to..."

Linda remains impassive and does not respond to my servile apologies. I've given her plenty of reasons to doubt my sincerity. She sits at her desk with folded hands under her chin, considering words that must seem insufficient. With a distrusting look, she peers over her bifocals during an excruciating silence. I believe she's enjoying my uneasiness with the conversation.

"Can you ever accept my apology? Please say something..."

I tuck my hands under my thighs and lean back, expecting chastisement. Linda waits until I begin fidgeting in my seat. Satisfied that she's made me reasonably uncomfortable, she pushes a lock of hair behind her ear, leans in, and looks me square in the eye.

"No apology necessary, my little Golden Goose!" she says, and we both crack up laughing.

In contrast to avoiding Linda, I made up for lost time, scooting forward to the edge of my seat, peppering her with uninhibited ideas, thoughts spilling from my lips like hot, molten lava.

"Let's talk about movie options. Can you put me in touch with that Kendra Whatshername? That film agent you know. Also, merchandising. I've outlined a related business plan tying in merchandise with the novel, with a proposal to add an e-commerce link to my web page. Oh, and I'd like to meet with Brad as well."

Brad oversees global rights. I've never taken a hands-on marketing approach, as I usually complacently park myself in the background and let others do everything for me. I've also never been interested in turning my novels into screenplays. But I'm interested now.

"I want somebody funny to play the protagonist. Sandra Bullock is a scream! Or perhaps Patricia Heaton with her easygoing, deadpan humor. They're both hilarious. I want a woman who will hold her head high and her middle finger higher. In fact, that's my new motto! If I had children, I would pass this slogan on to them."

"Whoa, whoa, whoa Nellie! Pull back the reins!" says Linda, barely able to get a word in. "You're getting way ahead of yourself. First, you're in a lethargic, unproductive stupor, and now you're dashing to the finish line without running the race."

After I dialed back the frenetic chatter, we got down to business. As we concluded a productive meeting, Linda stated, "Partners we have been and partners we shall be."

"Who said that?" I ask.

"I did," she said. "Just now."

Chapter Twenty-Two

It's early September and the leaves are prematurely changing to blazing hues of yellow, orange, and red. The temperature drops more each week, and a threadlike covering of hoarfrost obscures the grass. We're in for an early, harsh winter. This I learned not from listening to weather radio, but from an incredibly wise man. Juan taught me to observe animals as they prepare for winter, methodically gathering and storing food, not waiting for others to provide for them but depending only on themselves for survival.

"Animals give a more precise forecast than any toothy weather person," said Juan. "They survive by hunting, gathering, and planning. Their very existence depends on timing and accuracy. The animal world takes care of themselves, and many times, of each other. They're not out randomly murdering their own species but only kill to sustain life. We could all take a lesson from them."

I'm glad that I'm bugging out, even for a short time. The idea of another winter alone makes me want to burrow deeper into my sprawling habitat and hibernate. A thought that's neither practical nor healthy for us lowly humans. It would be wonderful to watch old movies, snuggling into oversized sofa cushions with a thickly crocheted blanket, and bowl of hot buttered popcorn. If only I had a movie. Or something to watch it on. Or a sofa. Or popcorn! I also didn't consider how I'd heat this ice castle during the winter months. Perhaps I would emulate a countess from medieval times. Like Joan de Valence, coiffed in layers of heavy garments, constantly changing locales to stay warm.

This has been a life-altering experience and I've learned to live with less. My closet used to be packed with clothes, half of which still had the tags on. I had too much of everything and didn't even realize it. Since I'll be traveling light, I've already finished packing. I set my small valise and toiletry case next to Snags' large rolling duffle bag and bed, proving he has more possessions than his keeper.

I've taken Linda up on her offer of a short-term loan. I'm clean and healthy, and I'm slowly paying off my debts. I'm on my way to a working sabbatical in the mountains, with nothing more than my laptop, some clothes, and my trusty hound dog. Just like the Beverly Hillbillies—in reverse.

Things are finally turning around, so why do I feel like the lone extant? I walk through darkened rooms, calling my name over and over. It makes me feel as though someone is looking for me, or that I have company—company in the Grand Canyon perhaps, as my echoing voice ricochets off bare walls and floors; the hollow, resonating clatter of a mad woman. I lean against the wall, sinking down to the cold, exposed floor. I imagine this is how they'll find my lifeless body, my ample rear end frozen to the floor in a pool of buttsicle. The ticking sound of the enormous wall clock has intensified, though when I look at its placement two stories up, I see that time no longer advances. It no longer serves its purpose, but there's just enough battery for the hands to pulsate in place and just enough sound to absorb the silence.

I begin to think about how much we're preoccupied with time. How much we have and how much we wish we had. I've carefully planned this trip, but I won't depart until tomorrow. Anything can happen, like the dedicated employee who works for forty years at the same job and dies the day after they retire. Where's the fairness in that? If I'm going to die of loneliness in an unheated home, I should probably put on some makeup and pluck my eyebrows. I imagine a ruggedly handsome first responder bending down to zip up the body bag, then writing the time and cause of death: Fugly woman dies of hypothermia at approximately ten p.m.

I'm veiled in a continual loop of dejection and self-doubt, and it's no wonder. I've alienated every living soul who's mattered and pissed off casual acquaintances as well. I didn't mind morphing into a middle-aged recluse. Rather, I enjoy isolation. Now, lonesomeness has come to call, tapping me on the shoulder. I don't want to turn around to face it, but if I continue playing into the depression, it will eat me alive.

Eat. That's the answer!

I suddenly have an epiphany that sends my heart swelling with expectant possibilities. I hoist myself up and run to the kitchen on my stocking feet, coming to a sliding stop in front of the cookbooks. I start pulling untouched books off the shelf, blowing dust from the tops of their long-neglected splines. I thumb through the pages with wonderment. There's a beautifully staged photo of a turkey, cooked to perfection, a garland of rosemary encircling the platter. Lightly browned stuffing protrudes from the cavity, and an idea surges forth with a fervent desire. Cooking a large meal for others.

My tummy is growling and is trying to tell me something. If stomachs could talk, mine would stand at attention (sphincter down, of course) and salute smartly with my esophagus. It would then state rather perceptively, "You can do this. You can give thanks. You can cook for those you care for. You're an accomplished woman capable of following simple instructions. If nothing else, cook for me, your beloved gut. I'm starved!"

Okay, belly-o-mine, you're on! I'll make a Thanksgiving feast, the likes of which will amaze even you. To fulfill this sudden longing for company, the strategic planning starts now. I vow to follow all directions to a tee. I'll need recipes, a menu, shopping lists, and naturally, a guest list. I will write down all the people I'd like to invite, reading each name aloud. And here it comes. The apprehension. Unavoidably, I begin to worry, and the worry plays into dread. I massage my temples in a circular motion. *Think, think, think.* What if no one comes? What if they all have a better offer? What if it's just me and Snaggletooth and a ton of food?

Suddenly, I see myself as the wicked witch, shunned by the kingdom. I hunch over, looking into my crystal ball. My knobby fingers cup the magical orb, and I see an extended dining table opulently set with service for twenty. A misty haze temporarily shrouds the vision. Squinting, I concentrate harder and make out two figures ceremoniously seated at opposite ends of the elongated table. Heads of the household, each holding up a champagne flute in a ritualistic toast. Then the two faces come into focus. Me and Snags. If I didn't anticipate the pain of it, I would slap myself across the face right now. Hard.

I concluded my guest list, which is surprisingly long. I also squelch my overactive imagination, stop obsessing, and commence preparations for the best Thanksgiving feast ever. It's too early to send out invitations; though if I don't do it before I leave, I'll nix the idea with a variety of excuses and it will never happen.

From a mostly empty drawer, I remove a box of linen stationery with my name and address embossed stylishly across envelope flaps. I believe it's important for one to have tasteful stationery, impressive handwriting, and impeccable manners. I can't afford custom invitations and won't lower myself to sending the tacky electronic kind. A handwritten note is personal and shows that a supreme effort was made. I begin with the guests of honor:

Ms. Angelarosa Magdalena Morgan
requests the pleasure of your company for the occasion
of Thanksgiving Dinner

Miss Dorothy Ann Dotson and Miss Delilah Jean Dotson
Thursday, November Twenty-first, One o'clock
The Morgan Residence
Four-Thirty Golf View Court, Bryn Mawr

My hand starts to cramp as I finish addressing and stamping each for the post. I have addresses for everyone, except Dotty, having no idea where she's living. I make hers out c/o The Bryn Mawr Community Food Pantry with an added underlined notation: Personal!

Mailing a letter has become an expensive indulgence, but if there's something I still have lots of it's stamps. Not long ago, when I had limitless credit and disposable income, I always said "Yes, please" when asked at the checkout counter if I needed stamps. Now, I have enough Forever Stamps for what just might be forever.

I splay the envelopes in front of me like a skilled Las Vegas card dealer, pleased to have invited such an eclectic group. I arrange and rearrange a simulated seating chart, worried that my guests might not have anything in common. I also worry that I'm the only one with no life. My guests surely must have other plans, never considering spending their holiday with a liar and a cheat. Regardless of my past, I walk down the driveway and mail the invitations with divine optimism. The outcome will either be a path to redemption or violent confrontation.

With Linda's help and a handsome advance from the publisher, I was able to catch up on my bills and trade my luxury car for a durable, pre-enjoyed SUV. It's roomy enough to sleep in, which is exactly what I'd be doing had this novel been rejected. If I couldn't make the next tax installment, I'd be in the critical stages of losing my home; something that I held onto tightly while dangling perilously close to the edge of ruin.

Benjamin Franklin said, "In this world nothing can be said to be certain, except death and taxes." Well, Benny my boy, in my situation, death might be easier to accept than the inequitableness of property assessment. There's never any doubt what's in the large, perfectly square envelope. The property tax bill comes with an attention-getting mnemonic stamped across the front: Last property tax installment to be paid by January 1st. Properties are considered delinquent if not paid within thirty days, at which time a tax lien is attached and property will be sold.

And they're not fooling around. For now, my property taxes have been satisfied, but not without uncompromising penalties and interest. Nevertheless, there's no alternative when it comes to paying taxes. It's as if a thug has come up behind you, holding a razor-sharp switchblade to your neck, and says, "Give me your money or I'll take your house!"

The choice is clear. Besides steep property taxes, I believe that my income taxes have been unfairly levied. But what am I going to do? Beyond small sums from royalties, my income these past few years could be considered petty cash. Like every other schmuck, I bemoan the fact that taxes are unreasonably high, then compliantly pay until the next bill comes along. Each time I pay an installment, I feel that I've cued back into a winding chain of taxpayers, heads down, submissively awaiting instructions from the regime, as we communally slog to the sweatshop to work.

Work. Pay taxes. Repeat.

When it came to money management, I could declare ignorance. I just wasn't paying attention, indiscriminately letting others manage financial details for me. However, after the way I've conducted myself, I have no room to criticize the federal and local governments over strong-arm tactics. If anyone had owed me money in these desperate times, you bet your britches I'd be meeting them in a dark alley to collect!

My accountant, Mr. Grigsby, is a gem. He still charges the same fees since I hired him and has never asked for more, even when he knew the coffers were full. As my life began spiraling, I couldn't pay him for money management because I didn't have any money to manage. Now, I've gone back to him with my head hanging in shame as if I'd just chewed up the cushions on the couch. But instead of masticated cushions, there lies the entrails of something much more serious: a financial mess.

Mr. Grigsby never asked what happened. He never derided me for making bad decisions or gossiped behind my back. He just calmly picked up the files from my overdrawn, insolvent life, and cobbled together a plan to satisfy my creditors and put me on a path to solid financial ground. I intend to compensate him for the work he does, and not just what he charges me. When I'm able, I'll begin paying Mr. Grigsby what he deserves, plus a little more to pad his retirement fund. It's the humble, faceless people in society, those who do not demand or complain that are the true heroes. They're the ones most deserving.

Going out to the lower grounds, I walk the fence line, stopping to look back at the house at the top of the hill. I study its architecture, the fine structural design and details. Pondering the difference between a house and a home, I decide that what I'm living in is lodging and nothing more. If I lose this house, then so be it. It's time to think about downsizing anyway. Over the years, this house served to shelter and segregate, to keep people out and keep me in seclusion. The walls have been marinated in angst-ridden tempers, bold-faced lies, and negligible arguments. Just thinking about the past makes my cheeks redden with embarrassment. Even though the memories were mostly unhappy, I now have an opportunity to make new memories. To find my nirvana and not wait for joy to come knocking; to open the door and let providence come marching in.

Before leaving the area, there's one more thing I need to do. It's Tuesday evening, and I make the familiar drive to the Bryn Mawr Library. The short five miles don't give me ample time to think about what I'll say. Nor is it enough time to consider retreating with my tail between my legs. It's now or never, and I exit my vehicle with great trepidation. This is how others must have felt when they saw me coming: pure unadulterated terror. Angela Morgan, conceited creator of the Bryn Mawr Writer's Association. If truth be told, there was a time when I enjoyed tormenting others. I used my status as a published author as a form of manipulation. I was the founder, moderator, and self-appointed authority on the written word. Being in control of others meant that I couldn't lose control of myself. Moreover, the incessant persecution of my peers gave me a sense of power. There! In the time it took to walk from the parking lot to the imposing set of double doors, I've given myself a thorough psychological examination.

The library is closed to the public and the monthly meeting has already begun. The automatic doors open with a swoosh as I enter the restricted area, where hushed tones reverberate from the conference room. Pausing at the open doorway, I sneak a look inside while my heart begins beating wildly. There is devout determination chiseled on familiar faces and the expressive eagerness of new arrivals, taking detailed notes on the writing life.

Leaning over to get a better look, my heel snags a piece of carpet on the threshold, and as I pull back, my leg bangs into the door. I'm rubbing a painful knee while my bare foot probes around for my shoe, which is still stuck in the carpet. My attempt at noiselessly entering the room without detection fails miserably, as heads turn, and a hush falls over the group. Margaret Foster is the first to speak.

"Well, now! It seems that we have a famed author in our midst this evening..."

Unknowing of my sordid past, new members swivel in their chairs, clapping enthusiastically. When they realize that Margaret and many others do not share their enthusiasm, the clapping slowly tapers off and expressions turn to confusion.

"What are you doing here, Angela?" inquires Margaret sternly with arms crossed defensively across her chest.

"Don't worry, Margaret. I'm not staying. I owe all of you an apology and that is the sum of my presence. I'm truly sorry for everything."

"You're sorry? Do you honestly think you can waltz in here unannounced after what you did? It's been over five years, Angela, and we've all moved on. Sorry means nothing."

Patsy Millard stands to voice her opinion. "Let her speak Margaret. I, for one, am interested in hearing what she has to say for herself. Let her do the groveling for once."

"Thank you, Patsy," I say, clearing my throat, not advancing from my protected position in the doorway.

"When I started this group, I was a newly published author. I was excited and determined to share my passion with others. I thought it would be wonderful to have everyone do readings, critique each other's work-in-progress, and support one another during the enervating publication process."

"Thanks for the backstory," said Margaret. "If this is going to be one of those long, drawn-out stories about life's regrets, nobody here has that kind of time. It's only a two-hour meeting."

"Oh my god," says Patsy. "Are you dying?"

"No, Patsy, I'm not dying. Though right now, I don't think anyone would miss me if I disappeared from this earth. I'm here because I had to hit bottom to realize what a jerk I was. I acted like a prima donna, insisting that my writing was more important than anyone else's. I became the kind of person that I've always detested—an egocentric, overbearing, insufferable bitch."

Heads nod in affirmation of agreement.

"I should have been here to cheer you on during successes and shore you up during rejections. I did nothing to help any of you and I'm more disappointed in myself than you'll ever know. I broke the very rule that we initiated from the beginning. That no one person is better than another. Please forgive me…"

After an awkward pause, I say, "Well, I don't want to further disrupt your meeting, so I'll be on my way."

No one responded, though I could hear everyone talking at once after I'd left the room. It will be up to each person to either reconcile or hold me in contempt, damning me to literary hell for perpetuity.

Chapter Twenty-Three

For my working retreat, I've rented an old, but cozy log cabin over-looking a lake in the Upper Northwest. It's secluded yet not desolate enough for a setting in a horror flick. If I hear a chainsaw running it's because someone needs firewood, and for no other reason. I feel lulled by the creaking wood floors, heavy uneven beams, and river rock fireplace, whose flue emits a faint whistle when the wind blows. When I first stepped inside, I felt the tender pull of belonging. I expected a petite granny with a salt-and-pepper bun to toddle up, offering a plate of freshly baked cookies and a warm embrace.

The cabin came fully furnished with hand-me-downs from every era, stirring a predestined awakening. To enhance the hominess, some-one took great care in smattering lace doilies about. Some may find this enriches the Granny Chic ambiance. I do not. I scoop them up and carefully stack them in a drawer, where they'll live out of sight for the remainder of my stay.

When I was thirteen, my maternal grandmother passed away. After the funeral, my parents began the obligatory task of packing up her belongings. I was instructed to help. We wrapped up my grandmother's personal effects and the usual household items.

There was also carnival glass, Depression glass, and what seemed like millions of vases in every size, shape, and color. We packed up china, silver, stemware, everyday dishes, and glassware. Then my mother handed me a tattered box, rubber-banded together with a yellowed hand-scrawled note tucked inside: "For Angela. An angel for my angel." She told me to put it away and open it later. It's still one of my most cherished possessions.

I'd always wondered why my grandmother preferred to live in a small corner room overlooking the gardens when her house was so large. At the time, I chalked it up to not having the energy to schlep from one end to the other. Now, I understand that everything she needed, and all that was necessary for living was in that small space. A well-worn floral chintz chair strategically placed by a large leaded glass window served as her reading nook. A simple lamp with a cream-colored silk shade sat on a side table next to a black-and-white photo of my grandfather, a proud young man standing tall in his woolen military uniform.

Although Nonna's home was neat as a pin, we found drawers stuffed with a disconcerting number of "I might need these someday" or "What if there's a shortage?" items. There were empty toilet paper rolls holding short, tightly wound extension cords. There were safety pins and paper clips of every size sorted into glass containers. There were also enough twist ties that, if placed end-to-end, would go around the world several times. Nonna was wealthy but not wasteful. She made use of things long before the recycling craze existed. And just when you thought something was too worn, she'd quickly repurpose the item, finding another use for it.

Besides the familiar soupy smell of old person, and the repellant tinge of mothballs and Bengay, there were the endearing scents of perfumed powders, department store lotions, and bars of soap that permeated Nonna's home. These are the things kept inside of us for safekeeping, returning when a trace of fragrance sparks something stored deep in our memories.

Nonno passed away long ago, but I once heard Nonna tell my mother that sometimes in the night, she felt his presence and could smell his aftershave. I stood behind Nonna, looking at my mother while spinning my index fingers in circles close to my ears, signaling that she was nuts.

I pick up a new bar of soap from the cabin's tiny bathroom and press it into my face. I feel foolish and disrespectful for making fun of Nonna all those years ago. I believe that she did smell Nonno's after-shave. Mostly because I can feel her here with me right now. *I believe you,* I say belatedly, taking another whiff of soap.

These days, people have abandoned bars of soap for convenient liquid soap dispensers. We must constantly wash and sanitize with antimicrobial this or antibacterial that. We're no longer satisfied with a clean fresh scent. We must stock up on bottles of liquid elixirs in every color and every scent from every corner of the world. But right now, what I truly long for is one of Nonna's soap dishes with a simple bar of soap. What I wouldn't give to walk back in time to her pink-tiled bathroom, breathing deeply into a bar of Camay or Dove or even Ivory. Ivory—the soap that you'll never lose in the bathwater because it was always happily bobbing along, floating on top. It didn't have an attractive scent, but boy, was it dependable.

If I could be in Nonna's bathroom one more time, I'd retrace my steps from the past, skipping straight to her white pedestal sink. I'd open the mirrored medicine cabinet above, quieting the squeaks with nimble fingers; a detective, searching for clues into her private life. I loved inspecting the Mercurochrome that I was not allowed to touch, but did anyway, opening and staring at the thin glass applicator with the rounded end. It was thrilling to know that spilling one tiny drop would ruin my clothes or anything else it touched, giving way to my snooping, and causing my parents to think of a just punishment.

I always checked her medicine cabinet when I was visiting to see if she'd added anything new. But she never did. There were the usual reliable items: an oral thermometer, a bottle of peroxide and one of rubbing alcohol, calamine lotion, and an almost empty bottle of Hexol. There was toothpaste, denture cream, all-purpose tar salve, and a tin of Band-Aids.

I found solace in opening the Band-Aids, inspecting the different shapes and sizes, neatly indexed from small to large. I was relieved to find the one giant bandage still in the back because that meant that no one had been seriously injured. Having bandages on hand served a purpose, but I'd always wondered why those little round ones were even included in the assortment. Everyone it seems, our home included, had a surplus of tiny round Band-Aids. They were the ones that we had the most of because they were never used, having been transferred over when a new tin was opened. They're too small for even the tiniest child and wouldn't stick to the plastic limbs of a doll. But it was satisfying knowing that they were there.

That's the way I felt about Nonna. I might not see her for weeks, but I knew she was there, just in case I needed her. She always knew what to say and helped me through many childhood dilemmas. Now, there's no one. When I could really use someone to talk to, or a bandage to patch over my sorry life, I'm out of those as well.

I like to think that I knew Nonna well, but when we began sorting her belongings, one element of her home confused me. Though they had always been there, under lamps and knickknacks, draped over arms of chairs and backs of sofas, protecting everything from furniture to candelabras to vases, were the doilies. I never knew how many she had until we had to pack them up.

My mother brought along stacks of tissue paper, insisting that I properly wrap and roll each one, carefully packing them for storage. I packed boxes and boxes of doilies in every conceivable size, shape, and weight; some so ethereal they appeared made with fine, white thread. It was a boring task that about shook my eyeballs out of their sockets. After a while, I was tired of looking at them. I wanted to throw them out the window or stomp on them. I eventually took a large round blue and cream-colored doily and threw it across the room like a Frisbee—just to see if it would fly. Regrettably, it did not, so I kept at the wearisome chore and concluded that doilies served no rational function. And I never, ever, *ever* wanted to see one again.

On the way home that day, I was not concerned with the fact that my mother had just buried her mother, or what feelings may have stirred after having to go through my grandmother's belongings. There was an urgent question that needed to be answered, and it couldn't wait. I asked my mother what purpose doilies serve, and not being satisfied with her vague answer, I stubbornly asked again. "But what are they *for?*"

Little did I know, nine years later, I would have to make decisions about my own parents' belongings. And then my grandparents' and great-grandparents' belongings as well. Things they couldn't bear to part with, for the memories or the guilt, one will never know. I spent most of a year going through each item, each drawer, each cabinet, each file, and each paper. Then I saw them—boxes and boxes of those fucking doilies stacked high in the corner of my parents' basement.

When you've repeatedly moved things from one place to another, opening the same boxes with surprise and disgust, they quickly lose their sentimental value. I loved Nonna dearly, but I did not love her doilies. I could think of nothing else than ways to get rid of them. I wanted to douse the boxes in gasoline and light them on fire. Better yet, have them dropped from a military transport over an insurgent's encampment in a faraway country. They'd stand numbly looking at the skies as doilies rained down on them. *That would teach the bastards.*

I inspect the small kitchen and take inventory of my little rented cabin. I open and close cabinets and drawers, examining the contents. The cabinet shelves are made from cedar and when I open the doors, a rich, woodsy smell is released. *Another pleasant surprise.* There's a mishmash of utensils and enough spices to make me want to spend my days trying new recipes and doing nothing but cooking and eating. There's a sundry of jelly jar glassware, white melamine service for four, a stockpot, assorted frying pans, all made of seasoned cast iron—none of that non-stick nonsense! It's a fact that food just tastes better when cooked in cast iron pans. It also tastes better when cooked outside on an open campfire. But I do have my limits. I don't want to be responsible for burning down an entire forest while frying an egg.

There's one bedroom, one bathroom, and a room combining the kitchen and living area. I use my bed pillow (yes, only one!) to sleep on at night and to bolster my back while I write. Making my bed is also less stressful. Pull up a sheet, blanket, and a simple down comforter. No need to spend twenty minutes stressing over the placement of color co ordinated pillows piled high on the bed. I have just the right amount of everything here. I don't see why a person would need more than this.

In the small common area, there sits one worn leather couch positioned in front of the fireplace. Beyond that, a large picture window looks down at the lake below. I ease onto the couch and tuck my feet underneath me, taking in the view. Breathtaking. I'd expect nothing less. I lean back on an embroidered pillow that says, "If You're Lucky Enough to Live by the Lake, Then You're Lucky Enough." I wholeheartedly agree with this reflective statement.

Folded neatly over the back of the couch is a faded, but delicately hand-stitched quilt that's probably covered hundreds of laps. I pull it down and cover my legs, countering the light chill in the room. Looking closely at the fabric squares, I imagine the many hands that played a part in creating something so special and yet so useful—how they used fabric left over from favorite sewing projects or scraps of a child's clothing or beloved blanket; how when they finished, the women stood back to look at their creation, unknowing what an impact this quilt would have on future generations.

In front of the fireplace is a thickly braided blue and white rug, peppered with specks of burn marks from stray embers. There's a floor lamp cleverly made from the trunk of a tree and a smaller desk lamp of the same material. My eyes drift upward to check the ceiling. Good. None of those annoying spotlights shining down on you like an FBI interrogation room.

I look over my shoulder at my new office. It's only steps away from the couch, consisting of a tiny corner desk, and a tiny wooden chair under a tiny corner window. The window looks out to the mountainside at the back of the property where low-lying scrubs cling to moss-covered ground, crowded out by old-growth forest. Chipmunks occasionally scamper by, busily on their way to do this or that. Watching rodents gather groceries from nature's supermarket leaves me charged and ready to work.

I settle in and open my laptop which takes up a good portion of the desk. I don't need an expensive hand-carved desk the size of an aircraft carrier to be creative, nor an ergonomically designed chair to wrap my rear in comfort while writing. This is just what the doctor ordered, and I'm appreciative of this dedicated workspace and picturesque slice of heaven.

Next to the desk is an antique oak bookcase with three long shelves. I unpack the books that I've brought with me: reference books and favorite paperbacks with dog-eared pages, worn out from many late-night reads. I never embraced the concept of borrowing books from the library. Once they were in my possession, I didn't want to give them back because I had never finished reading them. As a result, I became a fugitive of many public libraries. When I was a child, I spent my entire allowance on books. I was either reading or read to—a solid investment in my future. So, I bring along my favorites wherever I go, reading them again and again.

Alfred Nobel once said, "A recluse without books and ink is already in life a dead man."

Or a dead woman! Good ol' astute Al. He hit the nail on the head!

One of my regular haunts is a used bookstore in the historic district of Bryn Mawr, placidly eclipsed by surrounding businesses. It's all but swallowed up by the larger establishments. Yet somehow, it continues to survive among gentrified neighbors of hip gastro pubs, marijuana dispensaries, and glitzy specialty shops with eye-catching storefronts and ultramodern accoutrements all offering free Wi-Fi.

Bosley's Books is a bit seedy and has a fusty odor of dormancy, awakened when the front door opens. The proprietor, Ned Bosley, is a wealth of information for book lovers of all genres. When researching, I've often consulted Ned when all other resources have failed. He has many out-of-print books, rare books, and banned books that survived provincial book burnings of the past. The resident cat has been at the shop since the day Ned retired from his first job and embarked on the second half of his life, opening these doors almost twenty years ago. Cindy was a foundling kitten mewing to come in and she's not set foot outside since.

After my act of contrition in front of the Bryn Mawr Writer's Association, I paid a visit to the bookstore. As aged as Ned and his shop cat are thought to be, I didn't want to miss an opportunity, because each visit could be the last. Despite the off-putting smell of the place, I like going there because Ned is one of the good guys. But also, because he maintains an overflowing box of free or exchange books that he cannot sell; those with missing or damaged covers, or those with first-print typos. You may give a book, get a book, or both. It's on the honor system and no one is watching, no high-tech cameras recording your every move. On the free box hangs an ordinary handmade sign with a profound declaration: "Take only what you need."

Ned is a loner, and that's something that I'm an expert on. Besides pleasant greetings and talk of weather, Ned is not much of a conversationalist. I make it a point to talk books or pay attention to his cat when I'm there; to get him engaged in dialogue with something he cherishes. During our conversations, Ned uses phrases such as "sticky wicket" or "slippery slope," and whimsical words such as "dillydally" or "poppycock." Some may consider this corny. I do not. Ned is a dear, sweet man who is, in my book, one class act. I hate that people are mean to him, calling him a variety of unkind names. I can see why both Ned and Cindy don't venture outside these walls; for here, they are shielded from an inconsiderate world. Everyone has value, and everyone has a story. We shouldn't be so intolerant of people unlike ourselves.

Even though I know how Cindy Lou Who Cares got her name, I always ask for the gratification of hearing the version from a gifted storyteller. Hiking my purse strap higher on my shoulder, I prepare for what promises to be a long story. Ned has likely told the story a hundred times, but he never tires of telling it and I never tire of hearing it. I appreciate knowing Ned starts a story the same every time, with the same even tone, "Well, you see, it's like this..."

Cindy Lou Who Cares spends most of her time sleeping and looks mummified. She seems to have lived well past her expected nine lives, as she moves stiffly about the store, stubby legs barely able to hold up her heavy frame. Cindy quit grooming herself long ago and it's questionable whether she's ever been brushed. With long, thickly matted fur, her once lustrous coat has faded to a muted tone of black, sprinkled with an alarming case of dandruff. If I didn't know better, I'd swear she just ambled through a light snowfall, but it's sixty degrees outside!

Ned and Cindy live in a studio apartment above the shop, and I envisage what his life must be like. Rising each day to put the coffee on, perhaps in a percolator. I decided that he would prefer the old-school method of brewing to those plastic premeasured coffee pods. That form of coffee is great when you're in a hurry, which most people are these days. But Ned has no reason to hurry. Besides, on days when you need a little extra help waking up, you simply add an extra heap of grounds to the infusion.

Ned dresses with great care in the same slacks and collared shirt draped neatly over a chair from the night before. He combs his gray hair and beard with equal attention and brushes the same teeth that he came into the world with. After a cup of black coffee, he feeds Cindy and fixes himself a bowl of oatmeal, stirring in just a little milk, sugar, and a dash of cinnamon, the same way his mother made it. After breakfast, Ned heads downstairs to flip the closed sign back to open. Then, unlocking the door, he begins the disciplined wait for customers. On days when business is slow, and it usually is, Ned reads and reads and reads, for what else is one to do?

Upon reversal of his morning routine, Ned trudges up the narrow wooden stairs at night, carrying the dead weight of an unconcerned feline. He'll open a nondescript can of something for himself, and a can of cat food for Cindy that smells just as bad going in as it does coming out. Over time, he'll lose the ability to tell the two cans of rations apart, and they will sit staring dazedly at one another, uncomplainingly eating each other's meal. *Take only what you need.*

Beginning to look at the world from a different perspective, I step back to view the wide angle of a much bigger picture. Had I continued living with prestige, opportunity, luck, and power, I wouldn't have been able to see through the unconscious strata of having too much. As I begin the long way back from the ashes of deficiency, I'm grateful for this wake-up call. We spend our lives amassing treasures, stuffing our homes with furnishings that enslave us. We spend a lifetime cleaning, protecting, and saving things for later—furniture that we keep people from sitting on; floors that are too nice to walk on; and museum-quality rooms that are cordoned off from everyone, especially children. What we've created are exhibition halls instead of homes!

When I was a young girl, I wasn't drawn to other children. But there was one girl in my neighborhood who I thought we could become friends. It would seem she thought the same about me. Diane Weber was also an only. She was my age and went to my school but rarely spoke to me around others. Privately, she begged her mother to have me over and every so often, her mother relented. I recall going to her house to play on several occasions, but I never felt welcome there. It was clear that her mother didn't like me, though I'm not sure why.

The Weber home was sterilized and smelled like bleach and lemon furniture polish. There were no pets because pets meant hair, dander, filth, and disarray. Evidently, children also fell into the same undesirable category. Diane's mother wore crisp unmovable dresses, whose fabric was as rigid as she. She wore a single strand of pearls and I always wondered if they were a little too tight, because she spoke as if she were being strangled.

Diane's father was never directly present during my visits. He was a shadowy apparition that I'd occasionally see moving through their house in my peripheral, unknowing if he was real or make-believe. Once, I saw Mr. Weber imprisoned in a smallish den as we passed through the stingy hallway to Diane's bedroom, not a photo or painting in sight. He sat stiffly in a forest green recliner with his stretched-out pair of legs covered in perfectly creased khakis, and his feet snugly slippered and crossed at the ankles. Mr. Weber, a featureless man holding up a newspaper, thinly shrouding him from the world.

The Weber home was too quiet. I felt like someone *was* watching when Diane and I retreated to her room to play board games or talk. And someone was watching.

"Leave the door open, girls!" Mrs. Weber would say with ruthless conviction. I don't know what she thought we would do, but I suppose it would've been more difficult for her to hear what we were saying if the door was shut. Marian Weber also followed us around the house with her constant reminders, "Now girls, look, but *don't touch*."

I don't recall her ever calling Diane or me by our names. It was always, girls this, or girls that. Did she use the singular when I wasn't there, calling Diane, girl? Like Timmy and the ever-obedient Lassie, "Come, girl. Sit, girl. Stay, girl." One time, Diane parroted her mother's ceaseless reminder, "Don't sit on the furniture, Angela. My mother will know if the fabric has been disturbed." I'm positive that the fabric was not the only thing in that house that was disturbed. What a suffocating environment for a child to grow up in!

Years later, I flew back to where my life began, to a different time when my parents were still here and everyone was happily going about the daily business of living. Out of curiosity, I attended my first and last high school reunion—the twentieth, having no reason to go back before or since. Diane never returned after college and never looked back, and I understand why. Still, I was curious. After the reunion, I paid a brief visit to old Mrs. Weber. I wanted to see what she was up to after all these years, and if she'd changed.

"Remember me?" I said when she opened the door. Though I knew she wouldn't have reason to invite me in, I could see past her to the same furniture, covered in the same plastic that had lost its appeal and attraction, just like the lady of the house. Marian Weber looked me up and down. With the same judgmental tone, and the same pearl noose wound tightly around her sagging neckline said, "Oh, I remember you, all right."

I don't want to awaken one day to find that I've turned into a Marian Weber. I don't need a huge home with a pretentious address, a flashy car, or even a paved road to be happy. I only require the essentials: fresh air to breathe, clean water to drink, food for nourishment, and an income to support myself. Yet one must also nourish the soul, a truth my mother so wisely imparted. Children really should listen to their mothers, at least the sane ones. Honestly, it would save everyone a lot of grief.

Less is definitely more, and I believe that one day I could become a minimalist. But for now, I still require the fundamentals to facilitate my writing life: electricity, cell service, and a reliable internet connection. Also, praise the Lord and hallelujah for indoor plumbing! Although tempting, living entirely off the grid isn't an option.

I'd looked at dozens of rentals online but waited until I arrived to find a place that felt right. I was shown short-term rentals that ran the gamut. There were overdone cabins with all the creature comforts, close to conveniences, but miles out of my price range. There were rustic charmers with lovely outhouses, "only fifty feet from the main home," the handout would say. I don't want to be holed up in an outhouse waiting for bears to go away. And I don't care to go from a sitting position to a sixty-mile-per-hour sprint, praying that I make it back to the cabin before getting mauled.

Each time my realtor showed me furnished cabins for rent, I felt like an intruder, prowling through someone else's property, pawing through their personal effects. I thought of Goldilocks as she snuck into the Bears' home to catch some Z's. How she thought nothing of checking the thread count on the bedding, finally settling into the one bed that suited her neurotic desires. That behavior was acceptable back in the day, but not now. By today's standards, Goldie would be charged with voyeurism, trespassing, and home invasion. But like the storybook, I found that one home was too big, one home was too small, and one home was just right. And that's precisely where I've landed—just right.

I love watching the black bears. While they're comical and their motives mostly food-driven, I have a lot of respect for them and give them a wide berth. On the recommendation of my realtor, I always keep bear spray with me. She also offered this helpful advice, "You can't befriend them and you can't outrun them. Oh, and Angela, it doesn't work on grizzlies. Try rolling into a ball to play dead."

Play dead?

On longer hikes through dense forests, I've seen warnings for grizzlies. Signs illustrating the silhouette of a mammoth creature sporting a hump (them), bearing down on a small human stick figure (me). While I was delighted watching the black bear, moose, deer, elk, marmots, chipmunks, wild turkeys, and the perfection of nature's bounty, I would unquestionably shit my knickers if I encountered a grizzly.

Early morning walks around the cabin are more energizing than any cup of coffee. Before bed, sitting on the deck in the crisp night air is a good way to cap off the day, giving way to restful sleep—more soothing and infinitely more natural than pharmaceuticals! This place has allowed me to find a sense of worth. To be present and relish each moment. To rediscover the healing power of nature.

When I rise each day and look out the windows, I can scarcely contain my emotions. I want to cry for the beauty of it all. The invincible mountaintops girdled by low-hanging clouds, and the snow-capped peaks with summits stretching far into the horizon. The crowning glory is the serene lake, her widely spread arms beckoning wildlife to drink from her clear waters.

I'm in awe of the birds of prey. Gliding overhead, the ethereal Osprey and mighty Bald Eagles stealthily glide on air currents, scanning the water below. Abruptly diving into the water, they emerge with the catch of the day. Sure, they occasionally cheat, poaching in private waters to resourcefully feed their young. I find it amusing to think that somewhere a homeowner stands scratching his head, wondering how the ornamental koi went missing from the pond.

The scavengers are equally as interesting. Vultures and crows create an in-flight mosh pit, circling over a cache of newly discovered carrion. They're nature's cleanup crew, tidying up, picking clean the bones of the dead. Letting nothing go to waste. Instead of watching my old neighbors partake in the daily activity of pretentiousness, I watch my new neighbors modestly go about the circadian task of survival.

The longer I'm here, the less I think of what I've left behind, and the more I understand the difference between a want and a need. Who cares about stuff when you can have all this? This is true adornment! I imagine a reality-based show called "Extreme Home Decorator: Mother Nature Edition." The lead decorator would go by the name Mo Nat, instructing the viewers on down-to-earth interior design. "Open a window to frame the outdoors. Bring rocks, pine cones, and leaves inside, touching them every time you walk by. Remember that simplicity sometimes replaces all the riches in the world."

Snaggletooth seems to love it here as well, and it didn't take him long to become acclimated. He's too old to chase small woodland creatures, and too slow to run from the larger ones. Still, his olfactory senses are just as sharp as a younger dog's. His nose fixed resolutely on the ground, he sniffs in a zigzag pattern, picking up one scent after another. His little stump wiggles as he processes the pungent tang of wild animal smorgasbord. Snags has also taken a liking to fox scat and owl pellets, and I've been unable to stop him from eating them.

"Don't lick me," I remind him. "Ever!"

During daily walks with Snags, I've learned to follow his lead, and take my time, paying attention to my surroundings. Stop and listen. Breathe deeply and smell. Bend down and look. It's amazing what you'll see when you're not plowing over things, hurrying through life.

I've also developed a fondness for the smallest creatures, and delight in watching snails and slugs move slowly, yet determinedly toward rotted foliage. Where I'm from, people poison snails or stomp on them, believing that they eat their prized plantings. They do not. What they mostly eat is organic matter, an essential element of nature's compost. One day, I sat on a fallen log, staring at them for two hours as they gathered around a dead plant and shared a meal. It was a regular snail hootenanny! I shall be careful never to step on one again.

Chapter Twenty-Four

My fingers can't keep up with my thoughts. I have so many ideas that I've begun several manuscripts at once. I'm not writing anything as caustic as the one about to be released. While that novel was cathartic, it's time to embrace less mordant subject matter. I'm enjoying the writing life again and can't imagine doing anything else.

Writing was never just a job to me, but it was not something that I could openly talk about to others. It's a closeted profession that's not taken seriously. Many believe that to work, one must climb into a car and sit for hours in bumper-to-bumper traffic with a cup of high-test coffee. Not so. Some of us never get out of our robes, brush our hair, or commute any farther than to a home office or kitchen table.

What really drives me crazy are the folks who delight in making small talk, fumbling around for something insightful to say. Yet what they come up with is always the same blasé question: "So...what do you do?" Whoever utters this question, be it a seatmate on an airplane, or someone in line at the grocery store, it makes me cringe. If I say that I'm a writer or author, they look upon me with suspicion and then fall silent. Others assess me using a stale archive of polygraph-worthy questions that don't warrant answers, such as, "Have you ever written anything I would have read?" "Do you have a real job as well?" "What are you working on right now?" "What is the title of your book? Would I like it?"

And not knowing the genre or my writing style, one of my top picks for absurdity is this question: "Where can I find your latest novel? Because I will go out and buy it right now!" As if I'm begging someone to read my work, standing on a street corner holding a cardboard sign and tin cup. I always think of a great comeback after the fact. Something cleverly delivered with smooth timing. I'd hold up my phone, my grocery list displayed on the screen. "See? I wrote this," I'd say proudly. "It's a good read. You really should get yourself a copy!"

Thoughtless comments aside, writing is that surreal experience where you become someone else, whose dreamlike state writes things that you never recall writing, about places you never recall being. Even though this is a solitary profession, what I do miss is the camaraderie of a critique group. Those are the people who get me, and whom understand that writing is a process.

I once suggested coauthoring a book with a non-writer friend. She had so many great ideas and was funny! But she didn't understand the process and was impatient, treating it like a book report due the following week. She reminded me of a small child in the backseat yammering away, "Are we there yet? Are we there yet? Are we there yet?" I knew the first day that I'd made a terrible mistake, and there wasn't a thing I could do but let it play out to its bitter conclusion.

On days when I edit and re-write, I'm always surprised, as if reading pages for the first time. Writing is a magical place where you give birth to characters, raise them, and nurture them as your own. You become endeared to them. Those unique characters with their flawed personalities and complicated lives. You go to sleep worrying about them and rise in the morning thinking about them. Finally, when you feel they're ready to go out on their own, you launch them into the world through problematic plotlines and hope they weather the storm. But if they don't, you kill them off, quickly mourn them, and move on to characters who have the tenacity to survive.

I'm grateful for an unobstructed view and close connection to these fictitious beings. I feel them channeling through me, a vessel through the written word. I can bring them to life, or I can annihilate them. But mostly, I just listen to them speak because they always have a lot to say. This makes my job easy. Except at three a.m. when they're clamoring for attention. On these occasions, I want to tell them to shut up and let me sleep!

I could spend the rest of my life here, but that's not realistic. This small cabin is fine for a quick getaway, but I'd like to have a tangible goal to work toward. Something permanent. Something to come back to. A special place to share with others.

I met a realtor as genuine as Sharon is fake. She too, had been a refugee seeking a better life. Kim is eager to help others find their sanctuary as well. She thought I should look at properties while I'm here to get a feel for the area. She didn't ask for a pre-approval letter. She didn't question my motives or my financial abilities. Refreshingly, she's not driven by greed.

"When the time is right," she said, "and when you're financially able, we'll find something that matches your criteria and budget. It won't happen overnight, but I'm willing to stick with you for the long haul."

I like this woman. I like her a lot.

Kim and I toured many mountain retreats nestled among tall pines; close to town, but rural enough to enjoy visits from wildlife and unaffected people. What's more, the smell of pine reminds me that I don't miss the acrid pong of lawn chemicals, over-chlorinated drinking water, or being fogged to death by mosquito trucks. I had numerous questions for my realtor, but the first thing I asked was this: "Do people here saturate the soil with chemicals?"

Her expression spoke volumes, and it was one of pure revulsion.

"Why would we do that? It would poison our waterways and kill the animals. It would poison *us*! It would destroy the ecosystem. Plus, most of us don't even have lawns," she stated obligingly.

I also asked about homeowner associations.

"For or against?" she said.

"Against," I replied through a reflexive smile. "What do *you* think of them, Kim? Off the record, of course."

She looked into the distance, thoughtfully ruminating over the question.

"In my opinion, homeowner associations have served their purpose well. They've kept neighborhoods neat and tidy. They've kept their communities safe and respectable. Yet they've also created division where there once was union. Neighborhoods were formerly places where people talked to one another and worked out problems on their own. They met in yards for friendly chats over common fencing. They gathered at clotheslines to be nearer to kindred spirits, helping one another with life's conundrums. Before clotheslines were outlawed! And before associations had to lawyer up just to have a conversation."

"Good answer," I said. "And very diplomatic. Sold!"

I intend to pursue this and not overthink it, as was indicative of the old Angela. *Throw caution to the wind*, I tell myself. *Go out on a limb! Live in the moment!* Or a variety of other idioms meant to inspire.

The dream of this place and the promise of a different life is what keeps me going. I go to bed exhausted but wake up with something to look forward to. With my upcoming travel schedule, I can't move right away. But I can visit this place often and reenergize with warmhearted people, while respectfully learning more about the natural world.

I consider what it might be like to gather here in the winter months with snow covering the landscape. When I was a kid, and severe winter storms rolled through my hometown, I hoped for a power outage. Losing power meant that initially, my parents yelled expletives out of frustration while scrambling for flashlights. There was inaudible muttering, wishing that whatever was in the freezer would stay frozen; though if it did not, we knew we would be eating a mishmash of long-forgotten, thawed foodstuffs for at least a week. When everyone accepted that we'd be in the dark for some time, we yielded to our fate and turned it into a good time. That's when the firewood, candles, marshmallows, and board games would come out.

At first, we prayed that the lights would come back on. Then we prayed that they wouldn't. For when they did, the closeness would be extinguished just like the candles and the warm, crackling fire. Once the power came back on, each would return to their mundane tasks and unchanging routines borne from electricity, sending us zipping back to the television or radio, washing machine or oven, turning on every switch, every light in the house to ensure that they work.

As I prepare to leave the mountains, it feels as though all the switches have been turned back on, the light of reality blinding me. Leaving behind this bucolic place to return to enemy territory feels like walking into fire. Even though it's time to go, leaving here has proven more difficult than I imagined. While I load my vehicle for the long trek home, I begin to cry. I don't want to go, but my short-term lease is up. There have already been several light snowfalls, and my little cabin is not accessible year-round. Besides, I need to make money to be able to feed the dream of returning here, though I've already started thinking of this as home.

I haven't thought about my old home since the day I drove away. Instead, this beautiful place has given me time to think about people and nature instead of things. Upon realizing that I'd fallen in love with this place, I texted Juan that I may not be coming back.

"You have to come back! We received your Thanksgiving invitation!" said Juan during a brief texting session, complete with emoticons.

Thankfully, Juan agreed to maintain the yard and keep an eye on the house in my absence. He has plenty of other landscaping jobs, but mine is the only one he's retained in the neighborhood. He said he refuses to work for a bunch of egomaniacal dickwads, but he would always be there for me.

Juan has my keys and codes as I trust him explicitly. The house still requires upkeep, and I couldn't just leave it to deteriorate. A family of raccoons might move in while I'm away and everyone knows what raccoons are capable of. They may be cute and furry and live in hollowed-out trees, but allow them to move into a house and they become unlawful tenants. Living up to their name, the masked bandits will chew through walls and have wild parties at all hours. And just *try* to evict them!

Before I left, Juan and I agreed that it would be a good idea to drain and cover the swamp. The swimming pool would be one less thing to worry about as the city threatens to sue me for harboring mosquito larvae. Ironically, our local government shows concern about itinerant blood-sucking pests. The HOA was also on my back, doing what they do best—warning of legal action if the pool was not properly maintained. Juan and his crew brought over equipment and pumped the gelatinous water into the street and down storm drains. This generated more letters from the authorities. But they got exactly what they'd asked for. Where did they think the water would go? Down the toilet?

Besides regular communication with my agent, editor, and publicist, and an occasional text to Juan, I haven't had contact with anyone. And I'd like to keep it that way. I'd also like to thank whoever developed the call-blocking feature on our cell phones. I've had enough of Sharon's tirades and having already mined her voicemails for research purposes, I blocked her calls. Sharon can no longer reach me and wouldn't dare wander out of the small radius of her safe zone, even though that zone is rapidly crumbling. Her world is also about to get much smaller. Federal prison should be quite the experience for someone so arrogant. Let her try telling some of the hardened internees what to do. Let's see how well that flies.

While my days were spent writing and revising, my evenings were spent planning the upcoming Thanksgiving feast. It's the only incentive drawing me back. While returning home is unavoidable, seeing those who truly matter to me will be wonderful. Getting away has been a purgative experience and I feel spiritually empowered, thanks to the quieting influence of Mother Earth.

I call Juan to let him know of my arrival date. "I'd like to start maintaining my own property, and I'll need to buy a few things when I get back," I tell him matter-of-factly. "A lawnmower for starters," I said. "And one of those pronged things for leaves..."

"You mean a rake?" replied Juan with a hint of sarcasm in his voice.

For whatever time I have left in the suburban compound of Bryn Mawr, I want the satisfaction of caring for my own things. I've also taken an active interest in promoting my books. In the past, I sat on the sidelines, exerting the least possible effort while others took the reins for me. Now, I'm happily seated in the front row. To embolden others, I've created Hoity-Toi-Tees. The shirts feature cheeky quotes from my books, as well as vulgarities we'd all like to utter out loud, yet don't dare. We offer boxy styles for men but also figure-flattering tees for women. They should appeal to anyone from eighteen to 118 who's grown weary of those with a pompous attitude. I'm sure others feel as I do. I just want to see how many of us are in this loosely organized club.

I also want to take time to talk to people. To get to know them. To look attentively into their eyes and listen to what they're saying. I'll answer emails and keep bloggers current and engaged. I'll be communicative and agreeable, instead of rushing people through an assembly line. It's amazing what we can learn from others if we simply shut our pie holes! Loyal bibliophiles take time out of their busy lives to reach out. The very least I can do is give them a reception worthy of their patronage.

I love planning long drives as I find cross-country travel to be an American rite of passage. There are stops to make, snacks to buy, and sightseeing to be done. Think of all that's missed if you fly over quaint locales, hurrying to your destination. Instead of hours, it takes days to travel over highways and backroads, meeting people, seeing history. It's an experience you won't find at 30,000 feet. It's also interesting that people are bad mannered when flying, but slightly better behaved when on the ground.

I've always traveled alone, though on one occasion Robert acquiesced to a road trip. While we had many vehicles to choose from, he insisted on taking his Jag convertible, with limited space for luggage or souvenirs. Or us. When I'd rolled my eyes, he said, "It's either this or the vette."

Impractical selections, indeed!

Robert would never dream of taking the road less traveled for fear of spoiling the spotless condition of his car, or his Ferragamo loafers. I wanted to take my time and enjoy the journey. To stop at roadside fruit stands and eat a freshly picked peach for the pleasure of warm, sweetened juices running down my chin. However, Robert was disgusted by my need to explore small towns and made fun of rural folk, calling them slow-witted hicks. He hated that I wanted to take it easy, to see where a back road would take us; to stop for an ice cream or grab a package of Twizzlers and soda at an out-of-the-way truck stop. He became angry when my bladder could not outlast his, which necessitated stopping at each rest area. When I'd spot a sign that said, "Next rest area 150 miles," it greatly increased the urgency and that's all I could think about.

"Holy shit! You need to go *again*? Stop drinking! Then you won't have to pee so often!" he said.

Robert rushed through the trip and received two speeding tickets, which was also my fault. "If we didn't have to stop for your fricking ice cream, I wouldn't have had to make up time!"

Traveling alone is much easier. I'm not encumbered by someone dictating where and when I will stop, or for how long. I can take my time. I can sing at the top of my lungs to a nostalgic song that makes me feel decades younger. I can have a good cry. Uninhabited stretches of highway leave you alone with your thoughts, making you shed tears for all of life's disappointments. A private cry with no one asking, "What's wrong?"

If I see a weird billboard in the middle of nowhere advertising a two-headed cow, I'll pull off the highway. If there's an ad for a foot-high pie, I'll pop into the secluded café for a slice. If up and over a hill, an enormous iron cross juts up out of nowhere, I'll stop at the base of it and pray.

My four-legged family member accompanied me on a road trip only one other time—on a book tour. Against my better judgment, I insisted on driving to several destinations with Snags in tow. I thought it would be fun to have a dog along for people to pet. I was one of those assholes who bought an official-looking emotional support certificate and vest online for $59.95 that guaranteed his entrance anywhere. The vest had his name emblazoned on one side with the title of the book on the other. I thought it was genius. It was not.

Despite careful planning, Snags became anxious and farted during every event. When people bent down to pet him, he farted. When he was curled up by my feet in his portable doggie bed, he farted. This was not your run-of-the-mill passing of gas. This was a constant stream of flatulence hanging thickly in the air, which made one's eyes water and caused people to retch.

When I spotted the venue staff giving Snags treats, I bounded from a seated position, tackling anyone contributing to his cataclysmic gastral difficulties. I wondered if some thought it was me, assuming I'd brought the dog along to mask my own odious problem. I'm sure the bloggers were busy during that tour, and social media followers were abuzz with vaporous debate. Another good reason not to read reviews. And a good reason to board Snags whenever I travel.

Nevertheless, preparing for a trip is exciting, as you're all keyed up and ready for adventure! Clothes are clean and neatly packed. Unopened packages of toiletries wait to be used for the first time. I love those cute little tissue dispensers placed in one's handbag specifically for travel, and the sample-sized hand sanitizers that make you feel like you're saving humanity from an outbreak of plague.

The return trip is a different story. Dirty clothes, slam dunked into a who-gives-a-shit pile, are crammed into suitcases, and thrown behind the back seat where they will most certainly ferment like kimchi. The drive will be protracted and toilsome, the miles ticking by like the slow plodding of a mule through the dustbowl.

Clearly, Snags knows we're leaving. So as not to be forgotten, he's parked himself by the driver's door of my loaded vehicle. Using my upper body strength, I lift the corpulent little bugger onto the seat and we're on our way.

Chapter Twenty-Five

As the distance toward home lessens, my shoulders tense up and I tighten my grip on the steering wheel as if I'm trying to strangle someone. Perspiring like a spigot steadily releasing water, I try to remember if I applied deodorant. I raise an arm and I'm instantly repulsed. If I do have deodorant on, the antiperspirant feature that the commercials rave about isn't working. I feel like marching up to the store's returns counter with a half-used stick of deodorant. I'd show them my stained blouse, pointing to the leeching bands of underarm sweat while demanding my money back.

Even though the air is cool and crisp outside, I'm roasting. Snags is in the back panting, though I can't tell if he's too warm or just anxious. I turn up the air conditioner and selfishly turn all the vents on myself. I'd love to put the windows down but learned that lesson the hard way. Even an old, cadaverous dog with atrophied muscles can still pole-vault out an open window if he smells food. I once lost him in an intersection of fast-food chains. The only way I knew he'd gone out the window was the constant honking and pointing of other drivers who'd witnessed his daring escape. I stopped my car in the middle of traffic and scooped Snags up from the pavement, still intact and still seeking whatever food source stirred his insatiable desire.

When I cross into my home state, I feel an uncomfortable bristling, alerting me to turn around. I brush off intuition and refuse to answer its call, pressing onward, returning to the marginalized life that I escaped. As I drive past the sign, "Welcome to the Community of Bryn Mawr," I open the sunroof to raise my middle finger as a show of dissent. At least I opened the sunroof this time. One time I did not, and the urgent care doctor pushed for an answer as to how this happened and kept directing me to tell him if I was being abused. To outlast his flagrant disregard for my pain, I simply sat and stared, waiting for him to finish grilling me. Yet he took this as a sign of depression and ticked off questions from a mandatory patient checklist. Growing tired of his assiduous interrogatives, I pulled my hand away and with my middle finger, already broken and immobile, held it up in his face. "This is how I broke it!"

It doesn't take long to remember the many reasons that I hate living here. Traffic is a nightmare and people are rude and entitled, running red lights, and driving as if they're the only ones on the road. Having been removed from this atmosphere long enough to become acclimated to a kinder way of life, I'm now a true convert to the whole nature versus nurture philosophy. I've been living in ebullient remission, following one basic principle: Be nice. Now that I'm back, it's only a matter of time until the malignant anger returns.

Pulling into the subdivision, I stop in front of the weighty black granite sign, "Bryn Mawr Country Club Estates." I'd never considered the large pineapple icon engraved on the signage; a sign that looks more like a tombstone than a subdivision logo. Pineapples are a symbol of welcome and this place is as far from welcoming as one can get.

I need to use the bathroom and would like to get home. Instead, I make a U-turn, driving to the flower shop down the street for a spontaneous purchase. The woman who owns the tiny, but expensive shop recognizes me. She's polite but impartial, offering up a blithe hello. She remains apolitical, dispassionate, and neutral—like Switzerland—for inserting her opinion on any subject would result in the sudden death of her business.

Despite the unfortunate name of her floral shop, Babs' Bloomin' Bloomers is highly profitable, rewarded by the benefit of location, location, location! Her establishment is cleverly positioned across the street from the distinctive Bryn Mawr Cemetery, the resting place of many well-to-do people.

Parallel to the main thoroughfare, the Bryn Mawr Cemetery stretches on for a mile; a reminder that we'll all eventually change our address to this final destination. Families of importance vie for positions of high visibility, shrewdly placing gargantuan statues and monuments streetside. This signifies wealth, supremacy, and the fact that their grief is greater than anyone else's. I consider it both sad and comical that the deceased continue to be uppity, even in the afterlife.

Babs has substantially profited from her grieving clientele, cornering the funeral market as the go-to gal. Her shop is also known for custom combinations of flowers and Belgian chocolates, and one-stop shopping for cheating spouses and forgotten anniversaries. And in this community, business is booming! I choose a large, preassembled arrangement and ask Babs to add a black bow and balloon. She doesn't ask who the flowers are for, and I don't offer any information. I pay with cash, and I'm quickly on my way.

Snags sniffs at the unwieldy arrangement as I force it into the backseat of the SUV. The ride home is short, and for once, I don't care what he's chewing on back there. One frigid winter morning, shortly after adopting Snags, he begged to go with me on a quick trip to the grocery store. I submitted to his relentless whining, lifting him into the backseat, and setting him on his Sherpa blanket. I ran in for milk and eggs. I couldn't have been gone for more than fifteen minutes, when, upon returning, I found all my shoulder belts chewed in half. Who knew one second-hand dog could do that much damage? And who knew that that day, milk and eggs would cost me $1,700?

I park in front of the subdivision sign. There's no one in sight.

Other mourners must be sequestered inside their homes as the measured march of the death knell resumes. A tombstone signifies death, and I feel remorse, as I've never adequately paid my respects. Placing the overgenerous arrangement at the base of the pineapple sign, I fold my hands in prayer, as the attached Sponge Bob foil balloon dances in the breeze.

I thought I'd miss home, but turning onto my street, it's not the happy feeling of repatriation. It's returning to a domain that's familiar and nothing more. I have a feeling that I'll be cold-shouldered, which may finally make living here easier. Perhaps no one will talk to me or bother me with their myopic squabbles, fearful of what, or who I might write about.

Good. Privacy. My only regret is not having thought of it sooner.

When I arrive, Juan's truck is parked in the driveway. I'm confused to see both Juan and his beautiful wife Nina sitting on the open tailgate, smiling brightly. Although I didn't expect to see them so soon, I'm ecstatic that they're here. Snags runs up and starts licking Juan's hand. I give Juan a quick hug, blow a kiss to Nina, and dart past them toward the house. "Be right back!"

After my scramble to the bathroom, Snags takes his cue after being cooped up for hours. He tries lifting a leg on Juan's truck tire, but it turns out to be more of a squat, as Nina smiles woefully at his old-man attempt to mark his territory. Snags subsequently lumbers over to her and begs for ear rubs, which she gives uncomplainingly.

I notice Juan is holding an overflowing basket of garden tools and a rake with a bright red bow. "Here Angela, this is for you!"

I'm surprised and bemused by the gift. "For me? Yard tools? I love them! How do they work?"

Nina jumps forward, kisses me on both cheeks, and hands me a book called *The Art of Canning*. "For your new life," she says.

I look at her quizzically, knowing absolutely nothing about canning.

"I'm scared, but thank you, Nina!" I say, flipping through the colorful pages with astonishment.

Juan takes me by the arm. "That's just part of it. We have something else for you Angela, and it can't wait!"

Juan tells me to close my eyes as he and Nina lead me further up the hill to the south side of the house. As I open my eyes, it's impossible to miss. An exquisitely terraced garden with raised beds planted with a bounteous expanse of poppies, sunflowers, lavender, and vibrant perennials spilling over stone walls. There's also an abundant section teeming with edibles: rosemary, thyme, basil, arugula, peppers, artichokes, garlic, and every imaginable kind of tomato!

I look at Juan and Nina, then the garden, then back to Juan, searching his face for an explanation. I'm overwhelmed by their generosity and I'm tearing up, struggling to find the right words.

"The gift of a fresh start," he says.

I survey the expert construction, lovingly crafted from busy hands. The beauty of the heavy stone steps, highly structured rock formations, and bountiful flowers make me think of the motherland. My emotions are jumbled together, while my mind tallies up tens of thousands of dollars' worth of labor and materials. Nina runs their nursery business and oversees the landscaping crews. I can tell by this impeccable project that she was the architect, and Juan, the gifted engineer. They're both busy people and besides the cost, I can't imagine the labor-intensive investment of time and love that went into this project.

Stammering incoherent protests, I burst into tears. "I can't afford any of this right now!"

"It's from us to you. To welcome new friends and new opportunities."

"Juan, I don't know what to say! I can't accept this... Nina, it's too much!" I tell them while bawling like a baby.

"If we didn't think it would be nurtured and loved, we wouldn't have done it. Plus, this will help with your cooking. And you're going to owe us a meal. Or two!" he says, winking at Nina.

"Oh my gosh... This is amazing! This is the most thoughtful thing anyone has ever done for me."

"It's all natural too. No chemicals."

Juan hates that my neighbors are unable to think for themselves and mimic whatever they see others doing.

"It doesn't take a chemist to understand that lawn chemicals and pesticides are harmful," says Juan.

"These idiot neighbors of yours stampede to the nearest Whole Foods to buy the healthiest organic fruit, vegetables, and grain; yet they slather the earth in poison, killing the good nutrients in the soil. The runoff ends up in the waterways and our drinking water. They can't understand why their pets die of cancer and their children are stricken with unexplained illnesses. And have you seen a frog lately? I wonder why!"

I needn't wonder for long as Juan continues.

"Well, I'll tell you why! Because the man in the official uniform who spreads this insidious shit, tells them it's safe, and they lap it up without question. People might not use it if they knew the truth—and that might affect the bottom line. That's the true meaning of green! Sorry, Angela. I didn't mean to get on my soapbox..."

"There's nothing to be sorry about," I say. "When you're right, you're right!"

"You're going to want to harvest everything before the first frost. That's where I come in," says Nina. "Once you get settled in, let me know when you're ready for a lesson."

I feel like a kid running downstairs on Christmas morning. I look down at the canning book, still in my hands. "I'm *so* ready for this."

We continue catching up on everything that's happened while I've been gone. I ask about their kids, two of which are in a study abroad program in Barcelona. Their eldest son just completed his internship in criminology, and they couldn't be prouder. Nina fills me in on the details while whipping out her phone faster than a ninja with a shooting star. We look at photos of their attractive, intellectual progenies and reminisce about how fast they've grown up.

"By the way, I loved your manuscript!" says Nina, her hazel eyes twinkling with delight. She holds up the draft copy that I'd mailed to her. "Sign it for me, will you, Angela?"

I conscripted Nina as my trusted beta reader. She gives me an honest critique, is a great first editor, and is completely discreet. I hop up and situate myself between them on the tailgate, our feet swinging like grade-schoolers on a playground. We're laughing and talking up a storm when an uninvited guest attempts to sidle up to the party.

Judith Johansson is coming up my driveway, pushing a pram with her twin granddaughters impounded inside. Judith is part of a new movement spawned by naughty nannies and high-priced au pairs. She's one of many grandmothers residing subtly in the background with adult children, helping to care for their grandkids. I call them Granny Nannies, and boy, do they think they're special.

As Judith waddles up my driveway, she waves a flabby bingo arm in my direction. "Well, look who's back! I hear you have a new story in the works..."

Judith stops in her tracks when she sees the terraced hillside.

"What in heaven's name is *that*? Did you get approval from the architectural committee for this project? And are those tomatoes? You know tomatoes aren't allowed where anyone can see!"

"Seriously, Judith?" I hold my hands out in front of me as I simulate typing into the air.

"I'll tell the BMHOA!" warns Judith.

"Well, la-di-fucking-da! I'm also going to start canning. I may even open a fruit and vegetable stand at the end of my driveway. How do you like them apples!"

Judith's sanctimonious expression dissolved into her double chins as I waved her away in dismissal, turning my attention back to Juan and Nina. Judith is aghast that someone stood up to her, and turned on her heels, squealing the wheels of the pram in retreat.

"C'mon my little ladies! Glam-ma will take you away from this horrid woman!"

"Who was *that*?" asks Nina.

"That, my dear Nina, is something that used to refer to herself as 'Barbie Grandma.' She's delusional. There's only so much that plastic surgery can do to support that misconception!"

"Barbie?" says Juan. "More like a churlish, toffee-nosed figurine called Boorish Barbie, or her cousin, the ever-popular thickset version, Bumpy Frump. And did she just refer to Bryn Mawr as BM? Does she realize that also stands for bowel movement?"

"Hmmm. Fitting..." I say.

"We're all going straight to hell!" says Nina, giggling, gesticulating the sign of the cross.

I resonate with the feeling. "Save me a seat!"

The following week, Mrs. Lasley pulls into the driveway, struggling to remove several large receptacles from her mail truck. I run to help her and she has a huge smile on her face.

"I heard what you did at the country club. And what you said to Mrs. Johansson was priceless! You're my new idol, Mrs. M. You've inspired me!"

If there's anyone who knows every tidbit of information on my neighbors, it's Mrs. Lasley. I don't even question how. She has magical powers, and I'm just glad we're on the same team.

Mrs. Lasley has me sign for a certified letter, then hands me the remaining parcels. She stops short of her delivery truck and looks back at me, flashing her endorsement by spinning in a circle with a gratifying one-finger wave to the neighborhood.

"I've always wanted to do that!" she yells, looking around, blushing. "Oh, my goodness. I hope no one saw me!" As she starts her truck, she adds, "It's nice to know that people can be real. Thanks for making my day, Angela!"

I used to dread opening the mail. There was frequently a missive from the Bryn Mawr HOA containing some official notice or another. There was never a stamp on the envelope, and it was hand-delivered to my mailbox by a board member or street captain in the dead of night. Evidently, dwelling in the inner sanctum of country club life means that paying for postage is optional. This time, they not only paid for postage, they went all out with a certified letter.

I'm being fined for failure to submit plans to the architectural committee for what they call "an unauthorized suburban vegetable farm." The charges include keeping and raising livestock, specifically a Nubian goat. As evidence, they've inserted an out-of-focus photo taken from the rear of my house. I'm perplexed, as my property is privacy fenced and backs up to woods with no access from the rear. I look closely at the blurry photo. I haven't laughed this hard in ages! The goat in question is none other than my ancient, arthritic beagle/basset hound, standing on a rock outcropping. They've really outdone themselves this time!

This warning is mildly entertaining. And the HOA's poorly written circulars are more like *The Weekly Squealer*, stool pigeons busily tattling on their neighbors. Now, lucidness has come to perch on my shoulder, whispering in my ear: *Don't let small people ruin your day.*

Well, two can play this game! I'm not able to afford professional monitoring of my surveillance system. But I did have the wherewithal to invest in convictable high-definition security cameras with 4 TB backup storage. And they're *always* recording. I plunk down with a large bowl of popcorn (extra butter and salt) and begin to play footage from the cameras in the back of the house. The investment of time was well worth the effort. Cameras four and five caught the culprit in all his glory: the senior Richard Danforth, climbing over my back fence.

I save the captured surveillance footage to my laptop, adding music, descriptive captions, and a title to this little production: "Creeping with Dick! Bryn Mawr HOA board member and head of the architectural snub-committee. In his spare time, he likes long walks through the woods, peeking in his neighbor's windows, and chasing livestock with his pants around his ankles."

As soon as I posted it online, the video went viral. Like his porn star wife, the Danforth patriarch is now a celebrity. When I last checked, it had been viewed over a hundred thousand times. Posting a neighbor-shaming video online is like throwing flesh into the Amazon River, where shoals of red-bellied piranha converge on the carcass, devouring it in minutes.

Soon after, the HOA threw out threats as freely as candy at a parade. There would be a lien placed on my home. I'd be sued for defamation of character and libel. There was also the matter of illegally posting a person's image online. Blah, blah, blah... Richard Danforth was trespassing and the videos were recorded by private security cameras on private property. I told the neighbors that I'm considering entering this little dick flick at the Cannes Film Festival. And they believed me!

Because I live in this subdivision, I'm legally bound to this club of snobs by mandated covenants that are as passé as hoop skirts. Their lives are of inconsequential value, but there's still the matter of trespassing on private property. To add to his humiliation, I insinuated that the little pecker was probably looking in my windows and taking photos of me as well.

All correspondence abruptly stopped after that and a For Sale sign went up at the Danforth Homestead. I've also heard that Darcy and Richard are splitting, citing irreconcilable differences. I find the news distressing. Even though both whack-a-doodles are completely off the rails, they're still compatible, proving that there's someone for everyone. I wonder if this will ever be a normal neighborhood or will other nuts move here and take their place. The Danforths were at the helm during the HOA Reign of Terror. Now, they're all but a bad memory.

As the confetti flies, my mind begins partying, waiting for my body to catch up. Freddie Mercury has settled into my psyche, channeling through me with his wide-ranging octaves and flamboyant cavorting. I unreservedly begin singing "Another One Bites the Dust" at the top of my lungs while jazzily skipping through the courtyard. And I don't care who sees me. *Look who's super-freaky now!*

Chapter Twenty-Six

The week leading up to Thanksgiving is a blur of fanatical cleaning. I feel buoyed by gratitude, my feet springing down the basement stairs, where I unearth extra dining chairs and check them for damage. Upholstered furniture can die a slow death if left unused, but they look to be in decent shape since their demotion to storage.

I see something crammed in a corner and stop to examine a stack of flat items wrapped in protective canvas covers. Standing with my hands firmly planted on my hips, I try to remember what they are without having to unwrap them. They must be the table pads that I'd had custom-made for the dining table. I stick my hand under the canvas draping to confirm, running my fingers over the smooth suede underside. I decide to leave them where they are, choosing instead to dine dangerously without protection.

One by one, I carry table leaves upstairs, building up strength to lift larger items. I feel like a leaf-cutter ant, carrying things twenty times heavier than their exoskeletal body weight, diligently working for the good of the colony. As each cumbrously upholstered chair is lugged up the stairs, I hear my imaginary coach shouting, *"Lift with your knees! Move it, Morgan! Move it, move it, move it!"*

I position the chairs around the table, then rearrange the dining room, the only space filled with furnishings. I oil the parched wood so that the finish will blend with the unused leaves. I'll let it sit overnight before giving it one final wiping with a dedicated lint-free cloth. I move on to clean candelabras and wall sconces and replace burned-out light bulbs. I throw open tapestry drapes and open blinds, uncovering a wall of dirty windows. There's no way I can wash all the windows in the house, but I can tackle the main floor. I shall complete the task without complaint. If I have windows to wash, that means I still have a home, and I shall clean them with a happy heart!

Juan loaned me a ladder and a commercial-grade pressure washer, so I've been washing stonework, walkways, and anything else in my path. He showed me how to use the equipment and it made me feel powerful—a force to be reckoned with! He explained what psi meant, that it's not just the twenty-third letter of the Greek alphabet. Juan then cautioned me about washing certain surfaces. I found the experience liberating, especially while blasting jets of pressurized water onto every immobile object. Like a junkie high on housework, I began looking for things to clean. However, I should have followed Juan's instructions and not used it on painted surfaces. Even so, I couldn't seem to stop barbarically hosing down everything; pillars and posts now stripped bare of their color.

When I finished, I was soaking wet and covered in peppered flakes of dirt, mold, and paint. But it was one of the most rewarding things I've ever done, and the exhilarating feeling of deep cleaning gave me a better understanding of the value of hard work. I climbed up and down the ladder with my bucket of vinegar water and squeegee. The dining room windows glistened, giving the room an effervescent afterglow.

I later shop at many specialty grocers and agonize over the details. I remind myself that this isn't about perfection, but it's hard to dial back expectations. This is my one good chance and I don't want to blow it. During my errands, I'm ambushed by several neighbors eager to chat about the teaser trailer of my novel. One woman had the audacity to question the subject matter and took issue with one point in particular, "No one goes hungry in *our* neighborhood, Angela! That's a real stretch—even for you."

I opened my mouth to explain but decided that it would be lost on this dyed-in-the-wool devotee of stupidity. No one knows what others are going through and everyone is going through something. Even in this cosseted little commune.

As I shuttle bags of groceries inside, I notice a stream of cars driving past my house to rubberneck. There really isn't anything that can be seen from the street, but I can see them. Add a few floats and giant balloons and we'd have a regular Thanksgiving Day parade! I used to be anxious about people peering into my private life, but I'm no longer bothered by these sycophantic boobs. I've purged the toxic, malodorous resentment from my life and moved on. No need to put on airs or other such nonsense. I'm free!

After putting everything away, I check grocery shopping off my list and move on to setting the table. When I was still part of the privileged crowd, I'd assumed that everyone had multiple china patterns, crystal out the wazoo, and cutlery choices for every occasion and every day of the week. I was out of touch with the real world. I kept the important things that sparked fond family remembrances. But the rest of my prized chattels were vended from my traveling bazaar.

I was the carny shouting hyped-up sales pitches from a virtual booth. I advertised many items on Craigslist and Marketplace and sold expensive place settings from the trunk of my car. The first thing I sold was my Royal Crown Derby collection to a middle-aged woman wearing a vest decorated with cat mosaics. She was trying to repress her excitement, but I could tell by her nervous talk that she knew she'd scored the bargain of the century. I made numerous trips to meet up with strangers in commuter lots and police stations. Some knew the value of the items. Others just wanted something for nothing. One guy even went so far as to challenge me. "You tryin' to rip me off, lady?" he said, flicking a spent cigarette butt to the ground. Even though I needed cold hard cash, there were certain things that I just couldn't let go of. I refused to sell Nonna's Haviland or her silver place settings. There were just too many memories.

I trudge up to the attic to retrieve her dishes, carrying dusty boxes down to the kitchen. Removing the round lid from a storage container, I unwrap the first plate, my heart fluttering with anticipation. As I unpack dinner plates, the smooth weight in my hands lends a certain importance, like something wonderful is about to happen. Next are the salad plates, bread and butter plates, tea and coffee cups, saucers, soup plates, a teapot, cream and sugar bowls, covered dishes, and platters. I carefully stack the fragile dishware on granite countertops, fearful of chipping or breakage. Now I understand why young people no longer want to use fine china—it really is a pain in the ass! Even so, the immaculate condition of this set astounds me, given its age and use. Mindful of this, I wash and dry each piece with great care, taking time to reflect on special dinners with my family.

Opening the large mahogany chest, a sentimental niff is liberated, stirring deep-rooted memories of family celebrations. The silverware lies swaddled in a burgundy velvet lining. I take time to feel the weight of each piece in my hand: the pierced tablespoons, cold meat forks, spreaders, ladles, cocktail forks, butter knives, and every type of server imaginable. Like life itself, even that which you'd thought to protect can become tarnished with time.

I look around for cleaning supplies and locate a box in the butler's pantry. There's an unopened jar of silver polish, a neatly folded pair of rubber gloves, and an old toothbrush. I go on a cleaning and polishing frenzy with the creamy silver polish and clean, but holey athletic socks.

I never appreciated my housekeeper or the tasks that she did without question. She came in early and left late, even though she had her own home and family to care for. I never recognized the value of her efforts until I had to do the work myself. If she were still speaking to me, I would call and tell her just that. But we didn't part on the best of terms, and I didn't give her much notice and no severance pay. I did, however, write her a shining letter of recommendation.

"What I should do with this?" she said. "Cook it and feed it to my family?"

After spending the afternoon buffing silver to a gleam, I hold up a large serving spoon and look at my misshapen reflection. I consider the person in the spoon. There is a tuft of hair, and eyes staring back that are enlarged and deformed. The lips are a thin narrow line collapsing into my jawline. When I speak, the lips move, but in warped, twisted movements that make me wonder who exactly this is.

"Is that you?" I ask.

Yeah, it's me. Who else would be talking to a spoon?

I perform a quick inventory of the wet bar, dry bar, and cabinets. No alcohol and just a handful of mixers. I pull out my phone and add LIQUOR STORE! to my list. I'd also forgotten to clean this space. The shelves are covered in dust and like the rest of the house, filled with cobwebs. It looks like an abandoned saloon in a spaghetti western, sans the card tables and dartboard. I imagine a cowboy confidently strolling in after riding the range.

"Howdy ma'am. I'll have me a double shot of whiskey."

"Sorry partner, we're fresh out," I'd say, hiding behind the bar, quivering.

"Whatta ya mean you ain't got no whiskey, you lily-livered coward!"

I used to have enough Baccarat glassware to stock Bloomingdale's wedding registry, but it's all been sold, so I'll just have to improvise. I wonder if red Solo cups would be in poor taste because I still don't have the funds to resuscitate the bar.

All things considered, I'm fortunate to have any heirlooms left. Without an income, these family treasures were slated to go on the auction block by year's end. I hope the place settings coalesce, conspiring to bring a new generation of people together. Imagining the easy exchange between old friends and the joy of new acquaintances gives me confidence. In my addled mind, this will be a wonderful Thanksgiving, but it's anybody's guess how it will turn out.

I wish I could talk to ghosts and ask their opinions. I concoct an image of famous nineteenth-century authors gathered around my table. If it were possible, I would like to dine with Wharton, Cather, Emerson, Thoreau, Stowe, Twain, James, Alcott, and Melville. And, just to spice things up a bit, Poe.

Oh, how the wine and stories would flow!

I'd also like to invite two other literary geniuses. Two men born centuries apart, linked forever by a rodent: Robert Burns and John Steinbeck. They could place bets on the outcome of this slapdash celebration.

The best laid plans of mice and men...

Setting the table, I hold a dinner plate in my hands and remember. I can almost smell the pleasant aroma of Nonna's cooking and hear murmurs of chitchat from my small family unit. Nonna's china educes memories that have been tucked away in the back of my mind, and I'm instantly comforted. As an only child, whose parents were also onlies, there was never a need for an additional children's table at get-togethers. Even when my parents' friends had their children present, my family would have thought it preposterous to separate children from adults. They said that the child's table was created for the children of heathens; those who never bothered to teach their offspring mannerly conduct.

I surmise that a present-day child's table might emanate all the comportments of *Ruffian's Feast*. I chuckle at the thought of Snags inviting his mannerless canine counterparts to a beastly no-holds-barred banquet. A mutinous uprising atop the table while fighting over the turkey carcass.

Astonishingly, a good number of my invitees have responded with a resounding, yes! They've all offered to bring food and assist with preparations. I cordially refuse the offers, requesting instead that they each just bring themselves, though wine is always welcome. This is a mission that I'd like to complete on my own. I want to cook for my friends and show appreciation to everyone who stood by me, even when their loyalty was undeserved.

I also invited the entire wait staff from the country club, but most are working the overstated Thanksgiving banquet in the grand ballroom. The headwaiter replied with a phone call, "Miss Morgan, I speak for everyone when I say that we are touched by your gracious invitation. It's truly an unprecedented gesture, and although many of us must work that day, we are deeply affected by your offer."

The few club employees who didn't have family obligations after work promised to come by afterward for pie and coffee. I hope they do. I'd like to wait on them for a change. After shopping, prepping, and cooking, I have a greater appreciation for restaurant personnel, and anyone else with the demanding task of preparing meals and serving others. I'm already tired, but in a good way, feeling true accomplishment.

While I was married to Robert, we hosted many dinner parties. They were dreary, catered spectacles. I loved to cook, but Robert was adamant that I looked and acted the part of a socialite, a role that I found contemptible. Robert looked down on women who didn't use servants, and when I think back, he looked down on women in general. He also believed that I should be ever-present to dote on our guests, pretending to like the boors that he called friends and associates.

Though decades past the '50s, the outcome of any social event still reflects entirely on the woman, and I played into that outdated philosophy. I wanted everything to be exactly right, trying to make a favorable impression. I was companionable and accommodating and could be relied upon to host an enjoyable party. I laughed at jokes that weren't funny and nodded agreeably as moneyed loudmouths grumbled about frivolous matters. They were stuffy people who sucked the air right out of a room, and I couldn't wait for them to leave. I'd think of reasons to excuse myself from their company—a debilitating headache, decision-making issues with the help, or poking my eyes out with a sharp stick.

Good thing I'll never have to see Robert or entertain his fellow con artists again. I wouldn't stand for their repetitious bragging about what they have or who they know. The new me is no longer accepting of the high and mighty, and I'd gladly tell them off with a choral of explicit obscenities.

I set my laptop on the kitchen counter and surf the web for centerpiece ideas. I'm learning that there's a lot one can do to spruce up a table on a budget. After finding concise instructions complete with photos of each step, I returned to Costco for the second time today. Not having any decorative vases, I head to the produce section, choosing three medium-sized pumpkins from a cardboard bin. The price is right, and I notice that theirs are not burdened with lumps of dirt like the ones at the grocery store chains. Our local grocers must take the whole farm-to-table thing literally, never bothering to wash the pumpkins before putting them on display.

Fresh flowers are conveniently located on the way to checkout as a reminder to not forget the flowers, fool. I chose three fall arrangements filled with lilies, gerberas, eucalyptus, tangerine roses, and bright sunflowers. I'm glad to see that they don't include those hideous dried lotus pods. I'd have to throw them away because I don't believe floral arrangements should sound like maracas! I paid at the same checkout aisle from my first trip this morning. The clerk recognizes me and lightheartedly asks if I'll be back.

"Probably," I tell her.

Setting up a floral arranging production line on the kitchen counter, I read the online directions. This will be messy. It's advised to take precautions, protecting clothing and work surfaces. I don't have paper towels and try to think of something that would adequately cover the area. Then I remember the newspaper still sitting in the corner of the foyer. I removed it from its plastic wrapper one last time.

Goodbye, old friend...

I take my time hollowing out each pumpkin, my bare hands beginning to itch from the stringy guts. Not having any floral foam, I go outside and begin to look around for other options. I settled on environmentally friendly landscaping stones that will later be set free after stabilizing the flower stems. I populate the pumpkins with the arranged flowers and sugar water, then place the pudgy arrangements on plastic charger plates. I set them in the center two-thirds of the table, using the tried-and-true technique of eyeballing for symmetry. *Accolades to Ms. Stewart for the idea and online instructions!*

I tried out each seat around the table, pretending to have a conversation with the person seated across from me. I take into consideration the height of the arrangements and perform a smell test, careful that they won't overpower my guests. When Robert used to drag me to those awful booze and schmooze parties, I'd have to peer around congested floral arrangements, trying to converse with other guests. It was ridiculous and exhausting. By the end of the evening, my head throbbed from contorting my neck through thickly festooned floral trimmings. I envisioned clearing the table of the irritating showpieces with efficient swings from a baseball bat. The other guests would have been grateful for my actions, while the hosts stood by, uncomfortably stunned by such an uncouth deed.

"There now, isn't that better?" I'd say, smoothing my evening gown as I settled back into my assigned seat.

I set the table and closed the doors as an added deterrent from my nosy, pot-bellied roommate with a keen sense of smell. I push open the double pocket doors and reenter the staged dining room, acting surprised. It's exactly how I left it—at least the last ten times I checked.

Do I need to consult Emily Post on the etiquette of entertaining, or could I simply straighten and fiddle, remembering what I was taught? Just to be sure, I retrieve a newer abridged version written by Elizabeth L. Post, no doubt kinfolk to Emily. I love reading the condensed answers to entertaining quagmires, such as the topic, "Service Without Servants." What is one to do? That could bring a bead of sweat to any homemaker's furrowed brow!

Checking the place settings, I add a few finishing touches, placing folded napkins on plates with placards on top. I stand back, taking in a panoramic view of the table. It may not be textbook perfect, but it is lovely if I do say so myself!

I then complete the prep work, putting together hors d'oeuvres and kid-friendly nibbles. I stuffed the turkey, readied the side dishes, and baked the pies last night. I used old family recipes but wanted to start new traditions as well. A taste of home that would make my guests remember this day. My passion for cooking and the need to have something for everyone resulted in an excessive amount of food. I hope they're hungry because too many leftovers could cause me to go on a three-day turkey bender.

My hairdresser, Preston, and his spouse, Quentin, are the first to arrive, along with their Cavalier King Charles Spaniel, androgynously named Pat. I didn't know whether Pat was a boy or a girl until Snags started humping her. It's been so long since he's mingled with his own species, he's overly excited. Already, I'm apologizing for the old coot.

Quentin is a real estate attorney and has shown an inordinate amount of interest in my novel. He's also elated at the comeuppance some of his least favorite people have received, including two smarmy lawyers from his firm. Even though this is a fictitious story, it strangely parallels cases that he's recently been assigned. Quentin has given me an interesting take on realtors and is a knowledgeable source for legal jargon as well. I've never asked for specifics regarding his high-profile cases, but he's often helped translate the confusing legalese associated with real estate law. He's a true professional and would never compromise his integrity by discussing confidential information.

Mr. P has forgiven me for abandoning him for the cheaper version of a stylist and shoddier version of a friend: Sharon. "Good Lord, girl," he said, "Had you spilled the juicy particulars, I would have done you— no charge!"

Quentin shoots him a look.

Preston blushes and gasps, "Gawd! Nasty McNasterson. That's not what I meant!"

I love Preston and Quentin, the way they lovingly banter with just the right balance of sweet and salty. I don't know how many times I've heard Preston pronounce, "Now mind your P's and Q's!" As cliché as it is, it always brings a smile to my face.

Juan and Nina typically spend Thanksgiving with their three grown children. But with all of them scattered about the world, they opted to fly everyone home for Christmas break instead. Upon their arrival, they both stuck their noses high into the air.

"My, aren't you two turning into quite the pair of elitists!"

Nina dismisses my impulsive comment. "Something smells heavenly," she says.

Juan compliments me on my attire, which is one of my outfits that didn't sell at the consignment shop. One of several that I impudently went back to retrieve.

"Oh, this old thing? This little number was previously worn by a complete and total bitch."

"I don't have a clue who you're referring to, Angela," says Juan.

With her unassuming nature, Nina winks in solidarity.

"I harvested the vegetables and dried the herbs! I ground my own sage and made stuffing from scratch. I shouldn't tell you this, but the turkey dropped on the floor when I was massaging it with olive oil. I looked like an oleaginous mud wrestler trying to pick it up before my opponent, Mr. Snaggletooth Potlicker, seized it as his own. The good news is, it cleaned up nicely and I haven't burned it—yet!"

Linda Cooper and her new beau, William, have flown in for the long holiday weekend. Linda isn't much for physical contact, but I hug her anyway for the thrill of seeing her stiffen up like a cardboard cutout.

"I'm glad you were able to get away, Linda. It's great to see you! And you must be William," I say with a friendly outstretched hand. William bypasses my hand and goes in for the kill.

"Call me Bill!" he shouts, pulling me into an uncomfortable bear hug.

Linda rolls her eyes and groans, "He's Canadian."

I offer to have them stay here, but Linda says, "Angela, I read your book. Where exactly would we sleep? Rolled up in that chilled plastic burrito that you call an air bed? Thanks, but no thanks! We have a suite at the Hilton, but I'm not telling you the room number. You'll do something stupid like send up champagne and scented condoms or show up wearing an "I Fart on the First Date" T-shirt."

She knows me so well.

"Mix and mingle, you two lovebirds! And help yourselves to the bar. It's finally been restocked."

"The bar yes, the glassware, no," adds Quentin. "This is the first invitation that we've received that says BYOG."

Several people from my old writing group are in attendance as well. Margaret, Patsy, Rondell, and Clark arrived at the door in a tightly formed clique, more curious than anything to see if I'd reformed. I'd invited everyone from the group, even those I didn't know, but at least these four made the effort. I've given them every reason to be reluctant, and they're smart for sending the hardiest of the fold.

When my writerly friends first walked in, they collectively gaped at the soaring ceilings and scanned unadorned walls, their eyes settling on bare spaces where furniture used to be. The ever-shy Margaret pipes up, "Well Angela, this is some place you have here, though a little more sparsely decorated than I'd imagined..."

"My sentiments exactly," said the thickly bespectacled Clark, cautiously chiming in with his two cents.

"Here," says Rondell, "we pitched in and bought you this."

He hands me a bottle of blackberry Mad Dog 20/20 in a rumpled paper bag. They all look at me for a reaction and I erupt into laughter. Together, they push past me and head to the bar as Margaret states unflappably, "She's baaaack!"

My home has come to life again. Inviting conversations comingle with the sound of the crackling fire, clinking glasses, and occasional barking. The dogs are doing zoomies around the house. Pat is doing most of the zooming while Snags eagerly tries to keep up. The air is filled with many scents, particularly turkey potpourri, the neutralizing waft of tryptophan lulling my guests into a docile splendor. This is one of life's perfect moments. It's that rare place in time that, if we're lucky, we recognize that it's happening and stop to appreciate it. Watching this day unfold feels as if I've been handed a delicate keepsake, with one simple rule: Take good care of this.

We're going to eat soon, but two guests have not yet arrived. I was beginning to wonder if Randall and Wilson had second thoughts, when the doorbell rang, sending Snags scurrying to the entrance for the umpteenth time.

"You came!" I said, kissing each on the cheek.

"I haven't been to a real family dinner in over fifty years," said Wilson shakily, tears welling up in his tired eyes.

"I don't know how real it will be or how good, but we're all together, and that's what matters!" I say, my face stuck in a perpetual smile. Standing between these fine gentlemen, I hook my arms through theirs, leading them into the dining room. Leaning over, I whisper to Randolph, "I never knew Wilson could speak!"

"This is all he's talked about for weeks. Having dinner as a family. I haven't seen him this happy in years."

"I'm standing right here. I can hear you, you know! Thanks to these newfangled contraptions," says Wilson, pointing at his ears.

I search for delicate wording. "So, you're not...?"

"Not what, *barmy*?" growled the weathered buccaneer.

I take in a sharp breath. I'm beginning to feel that I crossed a line when Wilson's face softens. "Na, just deef. Deef as a herring, I was!"

"Obviously, the old chap could have afforded the best audiologists, but he chose instead to live in silence," said Randolph.

"Oh, Wilson," I said, "I'm afraid I've misjudged you."

Wilson turns to face me and with all the candor that comes from a man in his twilight years, says, "Don't feel sorry for me, love. People just didn't have nothin' to say that I wanted to hear!"

He receives double hugs for this candid admission.

"Contrary to rumors that we may be warming canned meat over a fire pit, this is the dining room." A necessary proclamation, giving my guests added reassurance.

"Even so, tis nothin' wrong with tinned meat!" adds Wilson.

"It's quite lovely, Angela," says Randolph, squeezing my hand.

I give a quick introduction all around and excuse myself. I'm running between the kitchen and dining room, shuttling serving platters to the awaiting table. Dotty insists on helping me, and at this point, I no longer protest. Six-year-old Delilah is the center of attention as my guests dote on her. Wilson is teaching her jokes and she's giggling wildly while bouncing on his knee.

"Look at me little poppet!" says Wilson proudly. Delilah, grinning from ear to ear, shrieks with excitement.

Margie and her husband, Vernon, hover closely, eagerly awaiting their turn to shower Delilah with attention. Margie and Vernon, whose simple aspiration in life was to become parents and grandparents one day. Sadly, that didn't happen. But now, Delilah is drawing in grandparents like moths to the light. My heart expands with the notion that it's never too late and anything is possible.

Vernon has been coming over to help fix items in need of repair. He admitted that retirement is not all it's cracked up to be and doesn't mind the drive. "It feels good to have a purpose again. To be needed," he said.

I've acted as his eager assistant, and he, my patient instructor, never criticizing or treating me like some dumb woman. He occasionally gives me grief, calling me "Magoo" whenever I do something inept, yet somehow managing to land on my feet.

"Oh, Magoo," says Vernon, "you've done it again..."

On days when Margie isn't working at the diner, she accompanies him. She's been teaching me to bake pies and desserts, which has never been my strong suit. In fact, it would be fair to say that I'm a pie-making failure. After all, bakeries were created for people like me who can cook but fall short when it comes to baking.

Margie proved that her surefire teaching methods worked. She convinced me to try it her way, because the secret, she says, is in the crust. The first baking session produced lip-smacking strawberry rhubarb pies with buttery crusts that held together perfectly until it melted in your mouth. She came over last weekend to help me do a trial run with the pumpkin pies as well, guaranteeing that my guests wouldn't choke on my dry crust. She brought along her mother's food-stained recipe, reminding me, "I don't share this with just any ol' so-and-so."

She was right. The secret *is* in the crust. Her mother's pumpkin pie recipe is heaven on a plate. And according to Margie, my crust was "dry as a popcorn fart."

At her urging, I also tried my hand at fall crafts. The result of my crafting ability was somewhere between slipshod and crap. I'd attempted to make a wreath, but in the process burned my hands and her wooden folding table with a hot glue gun. Trying to mitigate flying threads of hot glue proved maddening as well. During the battle to contain the sticky airborne mess, it ended up stuck to my hair, fingernails, and clothes.

Margie looked down at my creation and shook her head. "Well, this is the saddest lookin' wreath I ever laid eyes on. How can one person cause this much destruction?" she said with confusion. "Well, at least you're pretty and you can write. You got those things goin' for you."

Margie good-naturedly tried to help salvage the wreath, by deconstructing and trimming, tidying up, and having me start over. I gave it my all, but some of us should just stay away from artsy endeavors.

Margie held the wreath at arm's length, surveying the damage. With great contemplation followed by a heavy sigh, she made an executive decision. "Get the trash can," she said.

Preston came over during one of my domestic lessons and stopped in mid-sentence when he saw newspaper-covered surfaces strewn with glue sticks, artificial flowers, and foam bases. He covered his eyes with his hands. "I can't watch," he said.

Parting his fingers just enough to peek through, he added, "Listen, Miss Martha, if you start sewing your own clothes, we'll have to stage an intervention."

Delilah and Snags have also developed a bond, which surprises me since he's never taken an interest in children. Inexplicably, he comes running every time Delilah calls his name with her inflection, "Sags!"

It is, we all agree, a more fitting epithet.

Thanksgiving dinner is ready, the moment for which we've all been waiting. I place a variety of plastic relish trays on the table, made to look like cut crystal. They should have been served as starters, but who cares about stiff regulations and serving sequences? Plus, there's something about having to wait for a large meal that makes it taste even better.

My guests are surely tired of standing around and appear ready to gnaw off their arms. I vociferously summon everyone to the dining room with the eloquence of a farmer calling hogs to the trough. They all filter in, taking their seats. I've honored Wilson and Dotty by seating them at the head and foot of the table, indicating that each holds a special place in my home and heart. I couldn't bring myself to cover up the intricacies of my dining set, foregoing the table pads and formal linen tablecloth. To protect the wood surface, I'm using books as makeshift trivets! It proves to be functional and adds a surprising touch of whimsy.

I'm not the only one who appreciates fine furniture. Wilson is running his hands across the table and down along the edges. I even catch him peeking at the underside, mumbling something to himself. Though just when I'm about to dismiss Wilson's many eccentricities, he catches my eye and smiles.

"You're aware of what you have here, eh?" says Wilson with an upward nod and wink. "You don't see this every day. No sir. Exquisite Boulle marquetry work. European made. Inlay work is superb, very intricate. Arabesques and motifs hand cut from satinwood. No siree, you don't see this every day."

"Wilson, you're the only person I've met who knows how special this set truly is! I couldn't bear to part with it. For the flawless rarity, and significance of how many souls have gathered around this table sharing a meal. I hope to continue the tradition."

Not to be outclassed, Margie holds up a dinner plate. "Look," she says, turning it over to show everyone the inscription—Haviland & Co. Limoges. "This here's the real deal! No Theo, Charlie, or Johann for our Angie!"

The rest of my guests find their names on the handmade turkey placards that do not match the elegance of the place settings. Last weekend, Delilah and I spent a good amount of time making these with colored paper, crayons, and scissors. I've never been prouder of such an achievement! We laid on our bellies on the floor with color crayons fanned out before us. I've always loved the smell of crayons and apparently, so does Delilah. We picked them up, sniffing each one. Then, she put a blue crayon under my nose. "Smells like blue!" she said. *And it did!*

Everyone settles into their assigned seats, looking around the table. Delilah is beaming as each person holds up and inspects his or her card, showering her with praise that she rightly deserves.

Ned Bosley and Mrs. Barkley are seated together and discover that they have much in common. He, the well-read owner of Bosley's Books, and she, a retired curator from the Library of Congress. They are engrossed in quiet conversation and I'm not sure they know that anyone else is at the table.

Randolph stands at the long sideboard and expertly uncorks a variety of vintage wines that he brought, allowing them to breathe. I watch as he picks up a jeroboam and swaddles it in a Santa Claus tea towel. He holds the bottle at arm's length while inspecting the label, nodding his approval.

Everything seems to have fallen into place, so I retreat to the kitchen to check for forgotten items. There's always a side dish left in the refrigerator or oven, discovered after the meal. Or the next day. Naturally, it's the one that took the longest to prepare or the one that required multiple trips to procure rare ingredients. I checked the subzero, ovens, warming drawers, and microwave. Miraculously, I'd even remembered to bake the rolls!

I'm internally celebrating this small miracle when I see her. Dotty is standing at the kitchen sink staring trancelike out the window. She holds very still as water trickles over her hands and splatters indistinctly into the stainless sink below.

It's the most generic of terms, but I ask anyway. "Are you okay?"

"You never appreciate turning on a faucet and having water come out until you no longer have that convenience. Let alone warm water. This feels so good," says Dotty without turning around.

I suddenly feel quite insignificant, for my pettiness over the most trivial things. For thinking I'd lost everything when many people were suffering real, unimaginable hardships. People like Dotty, who wonder where they'll be living, if they'll be able to make the bills each month, if they'll be too hot in the sweltering summer heat or too cold to make it through the winter. How they will feed and clothe their children, or God forbid, someone becomes ill. How they rise each morning, trying to find motivation to put one foot in front of the other. How their needs may be more, yet their means, less.

"May I ask a personal question, Dotty?"

"Ask away, Miss Morgan…" she says distractedly, carefully drying her hands on a dishtowel.

"Please, for the last time, drop the formalities and call me Angela!"

"Okay, Miss Mor…I mean, Angela," she says, slowly pivoting around in her practical, scuffed loafers. Her socks have lost their elasticity and lie bunched around her ankles in compliant abandonment.

"What I'd like to know, is, do you have family somewhere?"

"Oh, that," she says haltingly. "Yes, I have a family, but they want nothing to do with us. They disowned me when I became pregnant with Delilah. I sent my parents a picture when she was born, thinking they would soften and change their minds. Maybe fall into the natural role of grandparents and love her as much as I do."

"So, what happened?"

"My parents sent a brief note saying that Delilah was not normal because I sinned. That God was punishing me with a disabled child. That I should never contact them again."

"I'm so sorry, Dotty. That will forever be their loss," I say, gritting my teeth.

Margie pokes her head in the doorway. "You two in here havin' a private party? Cause the rest of us fools out here are 'bout to starve to death! And the food ain't gettin' any warmer!"

We both giggle. "Be right there, Margie!"

I turned to face Dotty, taking her hands in mine, and looking directly into her bright blue eyes said, "There's one more thing. I would like you and Delilah to live with me. I have plenty of room and I'm not taking no for an answer."

"But I have no job and can't even afford rent or child care right now! I never even finished college."

"I didn't say anything about rent. And from what you've told me, you're only a few credits shy of a communications degree, right?"

"Well, yes, but..."

"But nothing. You're officially my new assistant. We'll set up an office for you here, so you'll never be far from Delilah. There are great schools in the area, but you may want to go the private route. You'll be able to afford it. I'll see to that. You can finish your degree and continue your education if you so choose. Plus, I'll need someone to take care of that mangy mutt of mine when I'm traveling. Now, let's go eat!"

We walk into the dining room and Dotty is a blubbering mess.

"Why in the Sam Hill have y'all turned on the waterworks, Dot?" says Margie. "You ain't even tasted her cookin' yet!"

Delilah climbs down from Vernon's lap and runs to her mother's outstretched arms. "Mommy! You crying!"

"Tears of joy, baby girl. Tears of joy..."

Chapter Twenty-Seven

After dinner, we sat around the table chatting for hours. I never wanted this day to end, but one by one, my guests left. Hugs all around, arms waving goodbye, and voices trailing into the night. The Prescott men were the last to arrive and the last to leave. They elected to have an angry Uber driver take them to the airport instead of the customary limo. "Uncle Wilson's idea," says Randolph. "He wants to try something different, though I hope there's no whiff of sick or smoke inside their automobile."

The three of us stand solemnly in the portico, saying our long good-byes while the driver honks impatiently. We turn toward each other, ignoring him.

"Group hug!" exclaims Randolph as we squeeze together in a communal embrace.

"I can't believe you're leaving already! I wish you could've stayed through the holidays. I'm going to miss you two terribly..." I say lachrymosely.

"You won't have a chance to miss us. I've leased a pied-à-terre downtown so I may conduct business here," says Randolph. "And we're not selling the estate. These two British expats are going to London for the holiday, then embarking on a bit of adventure through Cornwall. Nothing mad, just a quiet excursion through the countryside."

"May even visit a few pubs—get in a row or two for old time's sake!"

adds Wilson excitedly.

"You'll be back? This is the best news!" I say, nimbly jumping up and down.

"That's not the only news," says Randolph. "Wilson is converting the equestrian center to a year-round therapy center for special needs children. We didn't want to say anything until plans were firmly in place, but we've already been approved by the planning and zoning commission."

"Yup," says Wilson, "Going to name the facility after my late wife and daughter. I think they would have liked that. It'll bring the place back to life."

"Construction shall begin after the first of the year," explains Randolph. "While Wilson and I are both quite excited, let's not spoil this perfect day with talk of business. Let's talk about you for a moment, my dear Angelarosa."

Uh, oh. Being called by one's given name can only mean something serious.

"By the time we return from holiday, I hope to hear that you've begun dating again," states Randolph in his most articulately sobering accent. "You know, new year, new beginnings, and all that rubbish. I think you've finally gotten the whole caring for others thing down pat. Time to start caring for yourself."

My heart sinks and my shoulders slump forward in mournful disappointment. I kept pushing my feelings down to avoid getting hurt again, but here it is, rearing its ugly head. The ache of unrequited love. I hadn't realized how much I cared for this man, or how these words would send a wounding pain into my soft center. I began to sob.

Randolph lightly touches my shoulder. "Angela, you told me when we first met that you never wanted to be in a relationship again. And that you don't date."

"That's true. I did say that. But..."

"But I think you need to open yourself up to the possibility of love. You may be missing out on something quite spectacular. Put yourself out there, as they say. Take a chance."

I must look like a total mess. Some women look gorgeous, even elegant when they cry. I think of old romantic black-and-white movies, the heroine standing heartbroken, alone. The camera pans in, an intimate close-up reveals two single glistening tears streaming down slightly flushed porcelain cheeks. I always shed sympathy tears for the women in these classic films. And when I was a young girl, I believed that's what heartbreak looked like.

It's not!

No one could feel empathetic toward me, a woman so maudlin and grief-stricken. Plus, I'm an ugly crier, complete with a snot-encrusted nose and bulging red amphibian eyes. I stand wilting like a wounded flower in the hot sun, disfigured by heartache.

The Uber driver then begins honking his horn again, which is ridiculously tinny for a car that size. A muffled *meep-meep! meep-meep-meep!*

Exasperated, Wilson turns to the man and yells, "My dear chap, must you further emasculate yourself by beeping your impotent little horn? Bugger off!"

We all chuckle after being momentarily distracted. Turning back to our private circle of seriousness, Randolph says, "Angela dear, please don't make things so complicated. You tend to miss the obvious by thinking the worst. Somehow, you've convinced yourself that you are undeserving and unlovable. If you would stop your persistent weeping and listen, I'm trying to inquire if upon my return, will you do me the honor of going out with me?"

Chapter Twenty-Eight

Over the long holiday weekend, Vernon and Margie took Dotty and Delilah out to a local tree farm, with instructions that young Delilah was to pick out the biggest Christmas tree she could find.

"You tryin' to kill me, Angela?" said Vern. "I'm the one who's got to haul it to your place and set it up! And I ain't no spring chicken, you know!"

Margie, Dotty, Delilah, and I stand shoulder-to-shoulder, a cohesive unit of strength. "Don't worry, Vern. What stands before you are four very capable, very strong women who can handle anything. We've got this!"

The comedy routine that followed was parallel to Laurel and Hardy hoisting a piano up winding stairways. Nevertheless, we managed to position the Christmas tree by the staircase in the high-ceilinged foyer. With prudent forethought, Vernon reinforced the store-bought tree stand, placing it in an oversized livestock tub. And Margie fashioned a tree skirt to hide the functional, but unsightly container that we'd sloppily filled with water.

We then took Delilah on a shopping spree, letting her choose new ornaments. My stock of holiday decor had been hawked, except for an angel tree topper, the lone survivor from Nonna's voyage from the old country. Dotty and I may not have any memories hanging on this tree, but by golly, Delilah's holiday memories begin today! Margie and

Vernon contributed as well, giving Delilah some treasured family ornaments. "Why wait till we're dead?" said Margie. "Let's pass 'em down to
little cutie-pie now."

Vernon lifted Delilah high over his head to hang ornaments, which
took quite some time. She was so excited, naming and kissing each one
before hanging them on the branches. With Margie's help, we also tried
stringing popcorn, working tirelessly for hours, until we realized that
Snags was at the other end, eating our creation, string and all.

"You ever considered gettin' a cat?" asked Margie, peering down
incredulously at Snags, his distended belly touching the floor.

Dotty and Delilah oversaw decorating the lower portion of the
Christmas tree, while Vernon, Margie, and I took the top three-quar-
ters, running up and down the stairs like insects. We rotated the tree
many times, winding uneven strings of tangled lights around and
around. It may have been an unconventional method of tree trimming,
but it worked!

Hacked off by the whole process, Vernon sat down heavily on the
stairs and proclaimed, "When it's time to take down this giant sequoia
of yours, it ain't goin' out the same way it came in. I'm bringin' over my
chainsaw!"

Weeks before Christmas, news broke of the Bartelson scandal. Both
state and federal authorities are now involved. By hook or by crook, the
Bartelsons were able to make their cash-only bond. The shocking com-
mentaries also tarnished the reputation of Bryn Mawr, and of course,
I was to blame for upsetting the apple cart. What Sharon and Bart had
been doing was illegal and immoral, ruining many lives in the process.
Most closed their eyes to the unpleasantness, taking no interest in the
Bartelsons' felonious practices unless it involved them directly.

Though the Bryn Mawr real estate scandal was front and center,
it was briefly upstaged by another newsworthy report. I turned on the
evening news to see one bedraggled Phyllis Mallet being led away in

handcuffs. Seems the feds frown on someone other than the doctor treating patients and dispensing controlled substances.

The news anchor stated in a sensationalistic tone, "Breaking news! Phyllis Davinia Mallet, of the upscale community of Bryn Mawr, was arrested at her husband's psychiatry office after accusations of fraudulent practices surfaced. Her husband, Dr. Paul David Mallet, a prominent local psychiatrist, had become physically and mentally incapacitated after a long illness. Phyllis Mallet, wife and caretaker of the doctor, allegedly continued to virtually treat her husband's patients. Posing as Dr. P.D. Mallet, she purportedly bilked insurance companies out of millions!"

If the allegations are true, Phyllis, with her imaginative, yet short-lived con game, will be going away for a long time. Conceivably, she and Sharon could become cellmates in the ever-inclusive membership in Club Fed. Though who am I to pass judgment? If it weren't for the power of forgiveness, I might have traveled down the same path.

Chapter Twenty-Nine

I've decided to stay in Bryn Mawr, at least as my home base. I split my time between here and the Upper Northwest, having grown an affinity for mountain living.

Finding my one true love was an unexpected surprise. I never imagined that I could feel this way, or that out of the ashes of despair, love would grow. Randolph stirs a flame of desire that burns intensely within me; a passion that's only increased with time. Although we come from different worlds, we are deeply and madly in love. And we make each other laugh, proving that a sense of humor is an important prerequisite for a life partner.

My home and business are in good hands with Dotty exuberantly managing both. Speaking engagements and signings are booked for months, and my e-commerce shop, which began as a joke, is more profitable than I'd ever imagined. I've also begun teaching a writing class at the community college. There can never be too many authors in this world, and although writing is my passion, reading is a close second. I'd hate to think of all the wonderful stories that may be lost, simply because someone wasn't encouraged and mentored along the journey.

I have my favorite authors as well, voraciously devouring everything they write. On occasion, I've written letters imploring them to write another book. I'm sure I sound like a desperate groupie, reaching out with the sole satisfaction of touching a famous person. I can't stand being bookless, so they need to hurry up and write something new!

I've been reinstated as a member of the Bryn Mawr Writer's Association. But I'm no longer in the driver's seat, as I've been emancipated from my inclination to be a control freak. In my newly unfettered state, I've found an overwhelming passion to help other authors succeed.

To be happy in this life, it's imperative to give back. My first Pay it Forward campaign consists of visiting private homes, nursing homes, and senior communities to record the life stories of the elderly and specifically, veterans. Acting strictly as an instrument to document their lives, I gift them the only copy. I'd never betray such an intimate trust by sharing a story that's not mine to tell.

There's much that I wish I'd known about my own family. History that my parents would have shared when I was old enough to appreciate them. I know how my grandparents came to the United States for a better life after my father was born; that they were royalty in their homeland; fleeing religious and political persecution with only the clothes on their backs and seed money to begin anew.

I'd learned how many on the journey had died in the hull of a bucking steamship on the way to freedom. That they arrived here as nobodies, undergoing incessant questioning and xenophobic rants. How they endured humiliating delousing chambers and segregation by ethnicity and sex; separated for months in locked isolation units awaiting naturalization papers. Being fed unfamiliar food in an unfamiliar land, the sudden change in diet made many extremely ill. Women and children were placed in one building, men in another, with no contact and no idea if their loved ones were dead or alive. How they left their home and their native tongues behind, becoming fractured families, compelled to adapt and fit into a foreign land.

A new life. A new beginning. Renewed hope.

They rebuilt the family empire and realized the American dream without complaint or hollow chants of entitlement. They suffered to keep future generations from enduring what they went through. Nonno used to gently hold my face in his hands and tell me with his halting accent, "Angelarosa, ask for what you want. Work hard for what you need. Do not demand. And never, never, *never* give up."

I wish I knew more about my parents, grandparents, and the ancestors that went before them. They probably thought there was plenty of time to tell those stories. But there isn't always time, is there.

I was shocked by the number of seniors who signed up for my services and deeply affected by their urgency to leave a written legacy to their families. But I found that one person, one day a week, was not enough time to complete this goal. So, I put out a plea to my writers' group and then to the community. I was overwhelmed by the response with offers of help. Everyone, young or old, good or bad, has a story to tell. It would be unfortunate if those stories were never told.

Delilah has blossomed in her new school and has become quite the accomplished equestrian, spending every spare moment at Wilson's facility. In celebration of her riding abilities, Wilson presented Delilah with her very own horse, a dapple mare that she named Sprinkles. When asked about the name, Delilah said knowingly, "Sprinkles means happy." *A spot-on observation!*

Years ago, destiny formed an alliance of unlikely friends, and a tradition had begun. I wonder if divine intervention sent Margie and Vernon to me, taking over where my parents left off. And my friends are the aunts, uncles, siblings, children, and grandchildren I never had. Perhaps I needed to live a solitary life to be able to accept others and open my heart to love.

While we stay in close contact, celebrating life's joys and grieving its sorrows, our yearly excursion to the cabin is the highlight, a perpetual date that's never broken. Margie and Dotty made everyone quirky holiday sweatshirts, complete with caricatures of our group holding hands around a giant turkey. We wear them with pride and laugh at how ridiculous we look. But most importantly, we give thanks for a jubilant, grace-filled life, and the serendipitous moment in time that brought us all together.

At the beginning of our lives, we're delivered into families. Although sometimes, families are created by chance. Ingrained in our genetic makeup is a fundamental need to be around those who know us intimately; a need so strong, that it instinctively leads us on a migratory route home.

Epilogue

Angela stands in the arched doorway looking toward the darkened street. A gentle breeze lifts an undulating veil of fog that previously obscured her view. She can see clearly now as she gathers her new family into her outstretched arms. And with a full and happy heart, she couldn't feel any more loved, or any less alone.

About the Author

ANNE MARIE ROSADO has worked as a humor columnist, freelance writer, business owner, heavy equipment operator, and first responder. She proudly holds the coveted title of shortest real estate career in history.

Anne resides in Montana with her husband and four Belgian Malinois. When not writing, Anne can be found training her dogs in Scentwork and tracking or out looking for the next best adventure.

annemarierosado.com

www.ingramcontent.com/pod-product-compliance
Lightning Source LLC
Chambersburg PA
CBHW071241300726
48975CB00002B/512